HEART
OF
DIAMONDS

HEART
OF
DIAMONDS

A novel of scandal, love and death in the Congo

DAVE DONELSON

LARGO, USA

HEART OF DIAMONDS
Copyright © 2008 by Dave Donelson.

All Rights Reserved. Published and printed in the United States of America by Kunati
Inc. (USA) and simultaneously printed and published in Canada by Kunati Inc. (Canada)
No part of this book may be reproduced, copied or used in any form
or manner whatsoever without written permission,
except in the case of brief quotations in reviews and critical articles.

For information, contact Kunati Inc., Book Publishers in both USA and Canada.
In USA: 6901 Bryan Dairy Road, Suite 150, Largo, FL 33777 USA
In Canada: 75 First Street, Suite 128, Orangeville, ON L9W 5B6 CANADA,
or e-mail to info@kunati.com.

FIRST EDITION

Designed by Kam Wai Yu
Persona Corp. | www.personaco.com

ISBN-13: 978-1-60164-157-1   EAN 9781601641571
FIC000000 FICTION/General

Published by Kunati Inc. (USA) and Kunati Inc. (Canada).
Provocative. Bold. Controversial.™

http://www.kunati.com

TM—Kunati and Kunati Trailer are trademarks
owned by Kunati Inc. Persona is a trademark owned by Persona Corp.
All other trademarks are the property of their respective owners.

Library of Congress Cataloging-in-Publication Data

Donelson, Dave.
 Heart of diamonds : a novel of scandal, love, and death in the Congo /
Dave Donelson. -- 1st ed.
   p. cm.
 Summary: "A political, romantic thriller set in the war-torn Democratic
Republic of Congo in which an American reporter uncovers a deadly
diamond-smuggling scheme that reaches all the way to the White
House"--Provided by publisher.
 ISBN 978-1-60164-157-1 (alk. paper)
1. Journalists--Fiction. 2. Diamond smuggling--Fiction. 3. Congo
(Democratic Republic)--Fiction. I. Title.
 PS3604.O545H43 2008
 813'.6--dc22

                    2008025236

Author's Note

"Whether we fall by ambition, blood, or lust,
like diamonds we are cut with our own dust."
—John Webster

The events and characters in *Heart of Diamonds* are all fictional, but unfortunately they are not entirely figments of my overwrought imagination. Ruthless, evil murderers still haunt the Democratic Republic of the Congo and many other countries in Africa. They may wear a cloak of patriotism, tribal self-realization, religious fervor, or some other propaganda, but they are actually driven by one thing—unadulterated greed. While the rhetoric rolls on, so does the genocide. The only thing that doesn't change is the total indifference of the so-called developed nations of the world.

In the 1960s, millions died across the African continent as the whips and lashes of colonialism were replaced by the automatic weapon fire of "self-government" by strong-arm dictators. In the 70s and 80s, civil wars claimed millions more while creatures like Idi Amin, Milton Obote, Hissene Habre, Mengistu Haile Mariam, and Mobutu Sese Seko murdered their own countrymen and pillaged their countries' treasuries. In 1994, the world was horrified by 900,000 hacked and bludgeoned bodies in Rwanda.

More than five million people have been killed in the Congo since 1988 according to the International Rescue Committee. There is no end in sight. Today, rival warlords and gangsters rape and pillage the country while the world pauses briefly to wring its hands and sniffle before turning back to its TV dinners.

Some of the death and destruction in the latter half of the twentieth century was the direct result of rebellion against the affront to humanity that was apartheid as well as against other vestiges of the colonial era. Today's killers, though, are after what men have always lusted after in Africa—gold, copper, timber, ivory, cobalt—and the new riches, coltan, uranium, and oil. And diamonds, always diamonds.

—Dave Donelson

Acknowledgements

No one completes a book like *Heart of Diamonds* without significant help. I was aided along this journey by numerous individuals and several groups, some of them unwittingly. In the latter category are the wonderful residents of Siankaba, a tiny village on the Zambezi River in Zambia, who welcomed my wife and me into their homes and cheerfully showed us their way of life.

I'd also like to thank the Westchester Library System and its thirty-eight member libraries, whose collections gave me a world of background information on everything from the Congo's history and politics to its flora and fauna.

Several supportive readers helped shape *Heart of Diamonds* as well. Harvey Karp and Marv Tobin offered valued (and taken) advice on early drafts. Connie Zuckerman, a cheerful and well-read friend, offered ways to make the final version better. Matt Sullivan, friend and eagle-eyed editor, made several suggestions about the final draft. I also owe a debt of gratitude to the genius of the team at Kunati Books, Derek Armstrong, James McKinnon and Kam Wai Yu.

My wife, Nora, deserves my heartfelt thanks for faithfully reading and critiquing every single word of every single draft, not to mention going to Africa with me to keep me out of trouble.

Chapter 1

Mai-Munene

Dr. Jaime Talon sliced into the boy's cheek where the corrupted flesh festered just below the eye. When he pierced the skin with the lancet, a thin, clear fluid dribbled from the incision. He applied a little pressure with the flat of the blade and was rewarded with a gush of viscous brown pus. The boy flinched each time the knife touched his face, but that was his only reaction. Jaime guessed he was no more than fourteen. He placed a gauze pad over the weeping incision and told the boy to hold it there while the wound drained. With antibiotics and constant attention, the infection could be kept out of the eye, he thought. The antibiotics would come from the clinic's nearly empty medicine locker; Jaime didn't know who would attend to the dressing when the boy returned to the Lunda Libre guerillas who held him in the mopane forest of the Congo highlands.

"What is your name?" Jaime asked.

"Christophe," the boy answered. His voice was high and tight with tension. He cleared his throat quietly, as though he were afraid to disturb Jaime's concentration. Jaime put the lancet down and smiled gently, hoping to calm the boy's fears.

"Would you like to stay here for a few days?" he asked. The boy shook his head slowly and looked down. "What if I give you food?

Enough to take some back for the others?" Christophe shrugged but shook his head again, glancing furtively at the armed figure waiting for him near the trail at the edge of the forest. Even from a distance, Jaime could see the man's eyes constantly shifting from the boy to the road and back to the trail leading into the forest.

"You must stay at least for tonight so the wound can drain. I will speak to him. Stay here and do not remove the pad." Jaime locked his meager tray of surgical instruments inside a cabinet to remove temptation, then walked purposefully across the clearing to the gunman, keeping his hands out of his pockets and in full sight. He stopped a few feet away when the rebel shifted his weight from one foot to the other and casually pointed his rifle at Jaime's stomach.

"The boy will stay with me tonight," he declared firmly, trying to forestall any argument.

"No, *dakta bandia,*" the man replied with a sneer.

Jaime ignored the insult. He had been called much worse than a sham doctor by many people, including his ex-wife, whom he deeply offended when he walked away from his career in New York to come to Africa.

"If you take him away now, he will become blind. He won't be of much use to you then, will he?" Jaime demanded boldly. The man shrugged as if he didn't care, but looked Jaime in the face to see if he was lying. Jaime pressed the slight advantage. "If you let him stay, I will give you some food to take back. You can stay with him in the breezeway and I will give you the supplies in the morning. Okay?" The rebel pondered the offer.

"I want 'cillin," the man said.

"Ampicillin? Do you have bloody shits?" Jaime asked, then thought to himself, of course you have bloody shits. You all have them.

"I want 'cillin," the man demanded again. He thrust his chin upward with defiance. He gave a slight nod toward the boy, offering his grudging cooperation, then shifted his automatic rifle from one hand to the other to remind Jaime he had the means to enforce the bargain.

"Okay, fine. He stays here and I'll give you some ampicillin." The deal closed, Jaime turned abruptly and walked back to the boy waiting on the veranda. The ampicillin won't work on the shigellosis bacterium that's causing all the dysentery in the area, he thought, but it's all I've got and it's all they'll take anyway because they think it cures everything. Jaime had learned long ago that the psychology of practicing medicine in the Congo was as important as the mechanics of it. Most of his patients regarded him as just another *nganga*, a witch doctor; his salves and ointments and pills and potions just another form of the traditional healer's herbs and feathers and powders ground from their ancestors' bones. Sometimes he wasn't sure they were so wrong.

Jaime took the pus-soaked gauze away from the boy's face and told him to sit still while he deadened the skin with an injection of chloroprocaine and sewed a small drain into the wound to keep it open for the night. The boy didn't move while Jaime stitched just below his eye. He dusted the skin with antiseptic and taped clean gauze over it. Then he handed the boy two antibiotic capsules. He would give him another dose in the morning along with enough capsules to complete the course of medication on his own after he left.

"This ampicillin won't do much for your friend's bloody shits, but it should clear this mess up," he said. "Come with me." He took the boy into the breezeway between the two low buildings of the clinic and pointed to a bench near the back.

"You stay here tonight. If I had an empty bed, you could stay in the ward, but I don't. Your buddy can stay with you if he wants. I need to check on you later and give you some more medicine. Understand?" The boy nodded and sat on the bench made from rough planks resting across empty wooden crates. Jaime could surmise a great deal of the boy's story without having to ask. The infected mess on his face came from a brand burned into it by his captors, the Lunda Libre. The scabrous mark kept him from running away because it matched those worn by soldiers in the rebel army. If he were caught alone by rival insurgents or by the government authorities, he'd be immediately arrested or worse.

"Where are you from?" Jaime asked.

"Bumba."

"Then you are Chokwe?"

"Yes."

"What happened when you were taken from your village?"

The boy didn't answer. He looked at the ground between his feet.

"It's okay," Jaime said soothingly. "Was anyone hurt?"

Christophe sucked in a sharp breath and stiffened his small body against his memories. "Everyone was hurt," he said. He glanced quickly at Jaime to see if he had said too much, then looked back down at the ground. He still hurt inside from the things that had been done to him, as well as the things he had seen.

"What happened?" Jaime asked gently. He wasn't curious about the tale; he had heard more than enough of them already. But telling it might incise the wound festering in the boy's heart.

Once he started, Christophe talked softly but rapidly, as if he wanted to get the story over with. "The Lunda Libre came in the morning. It was so early no one had gone to the fields. We tried to run to the forest to hide, but there were too many of them and they shot us and chopped us and beat us with clubs. The noise and the smoke, it was horrible.

"I ran with *ma mere* and the baby, but she fell. Her feet tangled in her *pagne* and I couldn't pull her up. The soldiers grabbed me and held my arms. I tried to fight them but they made me look at her anyway. I could not stop them.

"One soldier yanked the baby from *ma mere* and threw him on the ground. When the baby cried, the big soldier kicked him like a football and he flew threw the air and bounced on the ground on the other side of the road and then he lay still." His voice became more agitated. "The other soldiers laughed. It was a big joke." He lifted his head, staring at something in the distance Jaime couldn't see.

"One man pulled *ma mere's pagne* over her head. Another big soldier stomped on her until she stopped struggling. Then they all violated her, taking turns. One soldier kicked her between her legs before he stuck his thing into her. I tried to fight the soldiers holding me and yelled at them to stop hurting *ma mere* but they would not and one hit me in the stomach with his gun and I got sick on the ground. *Ma mere* screamed. Then the big solider cut off her *sein* with his machete and then he violated her with the blade and then she died in the dirt. I could not help her because they held me too hard." His head drooped. He took a deep, shuddering breath before he looked up.

"*C'est très triste,*" Jaime said solemnly. Christophe went on as if he had not heard him, as if he could not stop telling the story now, his voice falling lower and lower until it became little more than a husky whisper. Jaime could barely hear him.

"Then they dragged me to the other end of the village. There were two of us. Eduard and me. They took us to a man from my village tied up in the road. It was Maurice Lumbanga. He was on his knees and they told us to kill him. Eduard would not do it, so they smashed his head with a club. The big soldier gave me a machete so heavy I had to hold it with both hands. He made me cut Maurice Lumbanga with it.

"They shouted and pointed to Eduard and waved their weapons at me until I raised the blade and swung it at Maurice Lumbanga's head. His skin split and I saw his white bone. He fell over but he did not die. He cried out to me but my ears would not hear him.

"I chopped again and again. The machete was too heavy. I hit his shoulder and a piece of his flesh flew off. I hit his head again but he would not die. The soldiers kept yelling louder and louder. When I swung the blade, they laughed and cheered. Then the big soldier took the machete away from me. He put his pistol in my hand and held my wrist to aim it. 'Be a warrior' he shouted at me. So I shot Maurice Lumbanga in the face and his head blew up and his blood ran into the ground. Maurice Lumbanga gave me a whistle one time, but they made me kill him."

Christophe stopped talking and sat motionless on the bench, his head bent so low Jaime couldn't see his eyes. The breezeway was hot; the late afternoon sun baked the tin roof and no air moved through to cool it. In the stillness, Jaime could hear the distant grind of the machinery at the mine and the soft panting of the boy.

"Rest here. It is over now," Jaime said, although he knew that it was never truly over in the Congo. He gentled the boy with a light hand on his shoulder. "We will see what happens tomorrow." He left Christophe sitting quietly in the breezeway and walked back into his simple office. The rebel had disappeared into the brush, but he would be back because the thugs always come back sooner or later. They inhabit every landscape, scurrying about beneath the surface of civilization in some places but rampaging right over it in others, like swarming cockroaches. Like here. Jaime had faced them before, even in America, forced to choose whether to fight them or to endure them many times before he escaped from the rough streets of Chicago to go to college. The right choice always seems clear to someone who doesn't have to live with the consequences of the decision: villains must be defeated. But it is never as easy as that. What about the victims? Are you supposed to leave them dying by the side of the road while you pursue their tormenters to get retribution in some kind of self-aggrandizing crusade? The real choice, the one that rips your guts, is between cleaning the blood off the wounds of the victims or abandoning them to their pain while you march off righteously to gun down their tormentors.

Jaime fought the boiling urge to go looking for Christophe's guard. In his youth, he would have waded in and pounded the smirk off the man's face. Instead, he closed his eyes and forced himself to take three deep breaths to clear his mind.

When the edge left his anger, he went to the medicine locker for a bottle of ampicillin to ransom Christophe's time at the clinic. The supplies were lower than usual. He thought about emptying the capsules and refilling them with sugar so he could save the real antibiotics for those patients who deserved them, but he couldn't bring himself to do that. Even though the ampicillin wouldn't cure the shigellosis that plagued nearly everybody in the region, it would help them ward off secondary infections and allow their bodies to better cope with the bacterium that caused the violent diarrhea. Jaime was a doctor who lived by his oath; he couldn't bring himself to do the wrong thing even in the right cause. He couldn't ignore a plea for help—even one that came wrapped in extortion.

Jaime's medicine locker, like the one that held sterile dressings and all the other supplies, was nearly empty. It was never completely full, but the relief aid meant to funnel through Moshe Messime's government had slowed to a trickle as more and more of it was diverted to the place where all the other resources in the country went, to the foreign bank accounts that would support the dictator's opulent lifestyle after he fled the country at the end of his regime, whenever that might be. Jaime's pleas for help had drawn impassive shrugs from the bureaucrats at the Ministry of Health the last time he was there. Their own rich lives were crimped by the lack of aid funds they normally skimmed with impunity, so they had little sympathy for him. When the crooks have only each other to steal from, times are desperate. The medicine cabinet was bare. He needed a new source of support and he needed it soon.

Quick footsteps crunched in the breezeway. Jaime looked up just as the rebel gunman burst into the office and pinned him to the chair with the muzzle of his rifle. The rebel snatched the ampicillin from the desk and ran back out without a word. Jaime rushed to the door and saw the man dragging Christophe across the road toward the forest. "Wait!" he shouted after them. A low rumble mounted steadily in the distance. Christophe looked desperately over his shoulder. As he disappeared into the forest, his eyes flashed briefly with gratitude.

The rumble became three trucks full of soldiers that roared past the clinic on the single road through Mai-Munene to the diamond mine by the river. The village was little more than a scattering of one- and two-room mud-and-wattle houses stretched along the side of the road opposite the fenced-off mine compound. A few of the huts had tin roofs, but most had thatch, which was considerably cheaper. The houses didn't sit in neat, ordered rows like bucolic, picture-postcard English cottages, but rather in organic clusters separated by small garden plots and struggling corn fields. Across from the clinic was a village square of sorts, an empty place around a cluster of raffia palms where a handful of merchants set up a market every week.

Soldiers constantly came and went, but this was more than the usual squad or two in a truck guarding the river. Curious, and unable to follow Christophe, Jaime followed them. As he walked rapidly up the dirt road, villagers peeked out cautiously to see what kind of threat the trucks full of soldiers presented. Since the mine had opened near the end of the colonial era, the village had been assaulted by everyone from so-called freedom fighters to invading armies from Angola, as well as local tribal gangs eager to profit from the rich diamond deposits in the river bed. Living under near-constant threat of bloody destruction had made the people of Mai-Munene both resilient and careful. A few of them, seeing no immediate danger, joined Jaime and followed the trucks up the dusty road.

Jaime reached the mine gate just a minute after Pieter Jakobsen arrived. Pieter, his assistant, had been making a house call on a pregnant villager to administer some pre-natal vitamins in person so the mother-to-be couldn't sell them to someone else, which was a temptation when he gave her more than a day's supply at a time.

"What's up?" Jaime asked as he joined Pieter at the gate.

"Don't know. An F.I.C. convoy full of regular army goofs just pulled in. Doesn't look violent, but there's something going on."

The two men walked into the mine compound and were waved past the pole barrier by the guards. A handful of Fédération Indépendante du Congo soldiers milled around the trucks, displaying their guns before the women in the small crowd like peacocks fanning their tail feathers. A captain with fierce tribal tattoos across his cheeks eyed Jaime and Pieter intensely. A tall white man, muscular but going to fat, stood beside one of the trucks talking to Joao de Santos, the mine manager. As Jaime and Pieter worked their way through the small crowd, de Santos waved them over.

"Dr. Talon, this is the most Reverend Thomas Alben, who represents the new owners of the mine," de Santos announced grandly, displaying the obsequious talent that had ensured his job under several successive governments. "Reverend Alben, Dr. Talon is the proprietor of the clinic at Mai-Munene. Pieter Jakobsen is his assistant."

"Call me Brother Tom," the heavy man said as he offered Jaime a sweaty handshake. Road dust caked the creases of his wrist.

"You own the mine now?" Jaime asked.

"No, not hardly," Alben chuckled. "I'm just a lowly missionary from the Church of the Angels. Our pastor, Gary Peterson, made an investment in the mine at the invitation of President Messime. That opened the doors for us, and I'm here to establish a mission for the church. I'm a miner of souls, if you will, not a miner of sparkly stones." Alben smiled beatifically throughout his little speech. Jaime groaned inwardly at the forced metaphor.

"I'm surprised anyone would make such a risky investment," Jaime said. "This mine must be a target in the sights of every warlord on the continent."

"Things will be a little more stable in the future," Alben smiled. "We have very strong support."

"From whom?" Jaime asked.

"We're Americans, you know," Alben answered opaquely.

Before Jaime could ask another question, de Santos came to Alben's rescue. "Brother Tom is going to reopen the school," he told Jaime. Then he turned to the missionary, who had removed his hat and was mopping his head with a large white handkerchief. "Would you like to see the building now?" he asked. Alben carefully smoothed his thin sandy hair over his head and replaced his wide-brimmed hat before he answered.

"What I'd like better would be a glass of something cold to drink and a place to sit down out of the sun," he answered.

"Of course! You can tour the village after you have washed off the dust of the road," said de Santos. "Come into the office and rest for a moment."

"Good. I don't know what ever possessed me to make this trip in August. If you'll excuse us, Dr. Talon?" the missionary said.

"Of course," Jaime nodded.

"What the bloody hell is that all about?" Pieter asked when de Santos and Alben had gone inside the low concrete-block mine office and the onlookers straggled back to the village. Jaime and Pieter followed them.

"It's hard to tell. Messime gave the mine to a preacher in Atlanta? There's a snake in that woodpile someplace," Jaime said.

"I smell CIA, don't you?" Pieter said.

"Maybe. But Alben doesn't look like a spook. He's too out of shape. I'm curious about what he meant about 'strong support.' That sounds ominous."

"The Second Coming, do you suppose?" said Pieter.

"I'm sure Brother Tom would be the first to know," agreed Jaime.

A few of the villagers waved casually to them as they walked by. The excitement over for the time being, most people settled back into the shade of their houses to wait for the heat of the day to pass. Children played in the dirt while their mothers sat in the doorways watching the two white men stroll by.

"This might be a good thing, you know," Pieter offered.

"How so?"

"Well, my da always said there's money flying loose whenever something gets bought or sold, so a bright fellow can grab some if he stays nearby and keeps his eyes open."

Jaime chuckled at the vision of the gangly Pieter jumping around in a vortex of dollar bills, snatching at them as they swirled around his head. "Your da may be right," he said. "But preachers are better known for raking money in than for giving it out, especially the ones who own diamond mines."

"Might be worth a try, though," Pieter insisted. "His money's as green as the next man's." Pieter was a South African Jaime had met during the Ebola outbreak at Kikwit. He was tall and angular, earning him the nickname marabou *dakta* from the children in the village because his long legs and nearly white blonde hair greatly resembled a marabou stork. Pieter went into his quarters at the end of the clinic when they got there. "See you in a bit," he said.

As he walked on toward the dispensary, Jaime peered across the road into the forest where Christophe had vanished. He wondered if he would ever see the boy again. The odds of the wound flaring up to destroy the boy's eye were still not in his favor, and Jaime thought about going after him, but he knew he'd never find the constantly-moving rebels in the maze of narrow foot paths and animal trails in the bush.

An old woman from the village, Kafutshi, waited for him in the breezeway. "*Bonjour, dakta*," she said in a gravelly voice. "My granddaughter pricked her thumb. She cannot help me make my *nkisi*. Can you heal her?" The old woman dragged a young girl in a ragged yellow dress from behind her and thrust the girl's hand toward Jaime. The girl hid her face with her free hand, but otherwise let the old woman manhandle her as she would. Her thumb was wrapped in a bit of dirty cloth.

"What is your name?" Jaime asked as he unwound the rag. The girl giggled but didn't say anything.

"She is Celestine," Kafutshi answered for her. "She is a good girl, although her head is empty. Her mother brings her from Mpala. She tends to her little brothers and helps me make the *nkisi*." Jaime had seen the little rag dolls Kafutshi and the other women made from scraps of clothing that had been worn beyond wearing; very little went to waste in the village. At one time, similar figures were made to hold charms to invoke various spirits. Today, for the most part, they were simply craft goods made to earn a few pennies from passing traders. The people still believed in the spirits, but the dolls were a source of cash; they were a practical folk who needed income.

The girl's thumb had reddened around a small puncture wound. Jaime was happy to see there were no lines of infection shooting toward the wrist and the pus was clear. He applied a topical antiseptic and wrapped it in a sterile bandage. "Keep this clean, but do not get it wet. Okay?" he said. The girl dropped her other hand from her face and nodded shyly. Her dark eyes shined up at him. Kafutshi handled Jaime a cloth doll.

"I have no money to pay you, but you can sell this *nkisi* when the trader comes," the old woman said. Jaime thanked her and smiled at the little figure with its hemp hair and crudely sewn eyes.

"This *nkisi* looks like someone who needs a job," he said to Celestine. "I think I will keep her here to guard my instruments." Celestine giggled as he propped the cloth doll up on a shelf next to a cabinet.

Kafutshi cackled, "I think your head is as empty as this girl's, *dakta.*"

The next day, Joao de Santos brought Alben around to the clinic on his tour of the tired village. They were accompanied by a squad of soldiers led by the scowling captain with the tribal scars, who looked like he was casing the village for a robbery as much as guarding it against rebel attack.

"Looking for a place to build a cathedral?" Jaime asked as he greeted them in the breezeway. The short, swarthy mine manager and the tall, corpulent missionary filled the small space, blocking the late afternoon breeze that was just beginning to rise. The soldiers milled around on the other side of the road.

"No, nothing like that," Alben answered. "Joao was just telling me what fine work you do, Dr. Talon, and I wanted to see your facility for myself." He looked around, taking in the two sparsely furnished rooms on either side of the breezeway with a quick glance.

"This is it, what there is of it," Jaime said. He gestured to his left. "This is the ward—all three beds' worth. And this is the dispensary." He pointed to his right. "That cabinet is where we would store supplies if we had any. I sleep in the next room, at this end of the building. Pieter's room is on the other side of the ward." Alben looked into the ward where a man wiped his bedridden father's face with a damp cloth and two other villagers lay quietly staring at the ceiling. Jaime expected Alben to go in to offer them some Christian comfort, but instead the missionary turned away and stepped into the dispensary. He surveyed the room, then picked up the *nkisi*, turning it over curiously in his thick hand. His damp fingers left a stain on the doll's breast.

"I've seen voodoo dolls like these in New Orleans. Do you practice a little juju on the side, doctor?" he asked with a smirk.

"I'm thinking about it," Jaime answered. "If I don't get money for medications pretty soon, juju may be all I have to work with. Actually, dolls like these used to be religious totems. Now the village women make them to sell to the traders, who probably mark them up a thousand percent and sell them in the tourist markets."

"Interesting. How many of them do you think they turn out?" When Jaime shrugged, Alben changed the subject. "Who funds your clinic now?" he asked, very businesslike. For a minister, the man was highly interested in cash flows and balance sheets. Jaime explained that the clinic had been founded by Methodist missionaries who fled during the genocidal violence that swept the country before Messime came to power. Jaime re-opened it using World Health Organization money after the Ebola outbreak in Kikwit, where he had been sent as part of a team to fight the horrendous plague. Now, though, less and less WHO money made its way through the sticky fingers at the capitol in Kinshasa, so he needed to find a new source of funding. Alben only half listened as he inspected the doll closely.

"Do you think your church would give us some financial support?" Jaime asked.

Alben tore his eyes off the doll and looked at Jaime. "Maybe," he answered offhandedly. "Are you a Christian man?"

The question surprised Jaime. "Not exactly," he answered honestly.

"But you're not a Jew, are you? Talon doesn't sound like a Jewish name."

"No. I'm pretty neutral about the whole God thing," Jaime said, trying to cut off any proselytizing. He was beginning to stiffen under the inquiry. Jaime had little patience for the personal questions, unrelated to treating patients, that potential donors and grant administrators always asked. It was as if they needed to own a little bit of you before they would let you see any of their money. That was one reason Jaime hadn't fit well into the world of institutional medicine in New York.

"A man of science. That puts you above the fray, of course," Alben smiled condescendingly. "Well, that's a strike against you, but you never know. I wouldn't count on it, though. The Church of the Angels is spread pretty thin right now expanding our mission in the Congo and elsewhere."

"But there's enough money to buy diamond mines?" Jaime asked pointedly.

"Those financial arrangements are rather complex, quite beyond your ken, I'm sure," Alben snapped. His rebuff made Jaime bristle, but before he could pursue the subject, Alben put the doll on Jaime's desk and took a step toward the door. He turned back with his hand on the doorframe and smiled with his mouth, his eyes cold. "I hope we haven't gotten off on the wrong foot, Dr. Talon. Mai-Munene is a small place and it would be in our best interests to get along."

"Sure, why not?" Jaime said, trying to keep the sarcasm out of his voice as Alben walked out the door. He picked up the doll and put it back on the shelf. The corn husks inside rustled in his fingers as if the doll were whispering, relieved to be out of the missionary's sweaty grip.

Chapter 2
New York

Valerie Grey looked across the café table at David and wasn't sure she liked him very much right at that point in time. She loved him—at least she thought she did—but right then she was royally steamed at all television news executives as a group. Since David was the only representative of that loathsome species present at the moment, he was catching the brunt of her fury. It wasn't rational, she knew; he wasn't involved in the events of the morning, nor was he anything like most of the Ivy League–anointed bean counters who masqueraded as television journalists in the managerial suite at the MBS network. But David was near at hand, so she took it out on him. She felt entitled to a little irrational rage since the over-promoted accountant who served as the president of the news division had just pissed on her career.

That was bad enough, but something else really fueled Valerie's anger. As mad as she was at the stuffed shirts in the managerial suite, she was absolutely furious with herself for the way she had been blindsided by the decision and even more so by her own totally ineffectual response. As Carter Wilson, the news division president, delivered the disappointing news in his nasally Greenwich voice that morning, Valerie's brain had simply gone numb. She listened, she heard what he said, she even understood it; she just couldn't respond. She sat there like a lump on the other side of his massive desk, her usually ready wit immobilized by the unexpected blow. The mental impotence frustrated her while it happened; later, after the meeting, it infuriated her. Afterward, her head teemed with sharply barbed comebacks—but where were the cutting responses when she needed them?

The numbness enveloped her for some time after she left Wilson's office. Valerie walked like a zombie to the elevator outside his suite and stared unseeingly at her distorted image on the brushed chrome wall as she rode down to her floor. If anyone was in the elevator with her, she didn't notice. As she walked through the newsroom, she didn't return the greetings from the staff, leaving them exchanging wondering glances in her wake. She went to her office, closed the door and sat down at her desk. The message light on her phone flashed insistently, so she automatically punched the button. David's voice came through the speaker. "I'll meet you for lunch at the Rock Center Café," he said.

That's when Valerie's brain blared back to life like a radio left on during a power failure. She couldn't turn it off now, and the longer it played, the angrier she became. For the rest of the morning, Wilson's speech resounded over and over in her mind along with the razor-sharp replies she should have—but hadn't—delivered at the time. I've had to make one of the toughest decisions of my career, he began, as if she should feel sorry for him. Did he really think his "anguish" could compare to hers when she found out her career was at a dead end? He assured her his decision wasn't based on her reporting as an international correspondent, which was clearly excellent. Gee, thanks for the compliment, but I'd rather have the promotion, she wanted to say. He droned on. Her skills in front of the camera were superior, too, of course, and she was certainly a highly regarded and well-appreciated member of the team, blah, blah, blah. If I'm so highly regarded, Valerie imagined herself saying, why are you sticking a knife in my heart? But she didn't say that, at least not then. The latest market research was the deciding factor, Wilson said. Good old market research, Valerie wanted to add now. It's the perfect fall guy: you get paid to make the decision, but you blame it on market research. She heard these words in her head now, but none of them came out of her mouth while Wilson blathered on.

At the end, the news division president struck a soul-crushing blow. Valerie had been passed over for the evening news anchor job in favor of Preston Henry, toothful host of the network's money machine, the morning show. After Wilson delivered the decision, he sat there, imperturbable. Even now, Valerie had no sharp, witty response for that final twist of the knife. She had one for everything else, but not for that. What's wrong with me, she fumed.

As a reporter, Valerie Grey was ferocious. She never hesitated to ask a confrontational question, grinding away at the hard shell of official obfuscation until she found the truth. She was driven to be the best, unafraid, unflappable, almost righteous in her quest for real answers. Valerie was respected as a pro's pro in the snarky, claw-your-way circle of top journalists. In her heart of hearts, though, Valerie knew that her professional drive was the flipside of her personal insecurity. Her drive compensated for a well-suppressed belief that she didn't deserve success. Deep inside, Valerie was an insignificant little girl, and unless she kept up a fierce front, someone, someday, was going to find out and send her back to Scranton where she belonged. That was why her impotence in the face of Wilson's decision so infuriated her: it confirmed that deeply repressed self-image.

The ice skaters swirling in the bright sunlight at Rockefeller Center brought Valerie back to the present. She watched them glide silently by as she let some of her anger subside. After a few more seconds of blackly wondering where her life was going, she turned back to the table. She was still mad, but not as much at David now. It wasn't fair to turn him into collateral damage.

"So what do you think I should do about losing the promotion?" she asked. She picked vaguely at the saffron risotto crab cake in front of her. She should have ordered a salad, but with Wilson's words and her unsaid responses ringing in her ears as she examined the lunch menu, Valerie had ordered the rich, creamy risotto in a flurry of rebellion. Now, her stomach roiled by unspoken vitriol, she had no interest in it.

"You shouldn't make any decisions in this frame of mind," David answered. He was an experienced journalist himself, as well as a sharply analytic manager—an unusual amalgam. The combination gave David an exceptional ability to take a cloud of rumors and circumstances and distill them into facts pertinent to a decision. "Wait a while. You still have two years left on your contract, don't you? There will be other anchor slots open between now and then. In fact, the timing could be good. I hear Kensington's talking about retiring from ABC after the election. You'll have a good shot."

"Fat chance," Valerie said disgustedly. "The market research dweebs will be completely in charge of all the network news divisions by then."

David sighed in exasperation. "The suits in marketing have always meddled in television news, you know that. They're like cockroaches whispering in the king's ear. What matters is that you're still the best reporter in the business." He pointed his fork toward her. "What's more, your contract will be up for renewal then, and you'll be in position to jump networks and take Kensington's job, which you aren't now. That will give you some serious leverage in the negotiations."

Valerie's brown eyes flashed a warning, the green flecks in the irises dancing with anger. Her eyes were one of her strongest features, but they sometimes got her in trouble by revealing her true feelings at inopportune times. "What makes you think ABC will want a journalist instead of a cover girl two years from now? Troglodytes run that joint just like they do MBS," she snapped.

"Not all of us troglodytes prefer cover girls," David protested. His career as a journalist had led him into the second tier of management suites at MBS, with a good chance that he'd be in the top rank before he retired.

Valerie realized she had taken out her frustration on the innocent David—again. "I know," she apologized. "I'm sorry I lumped you in with the rest of the assholes." Then the anger bubbled back to the surface and she gave a very un-ladylike snort of dismissal. "But with all due respect to Barbara Walters, Connie Chung, and Katie Couric, I just find it ironic that the only time a network hires a female anchor is when it's in last place."

"That's nonsense and you know it," David snapped. "Gender has nothing to do with this decision—or those. All of those women are respected broadcasters. Just like you."

David was right, as usual. Valerie had fought her share of battles against stereotyping early in her career, but she hadn't been faced with it lately, at least as far as she knew. When she first started looking for a job in broadcasting, her looks got her more than one offer to be a weather reporter, a position she characterized as the "barometer bimbo." She turned them all down and sent audition tapes to stations around the country until she landed a reporter's job at a tiny television station in Elmira, New York. The news director who hired her made it a point to send her to cover lost puppy stories and the grand openings of local dress shops, but it was hard to tell if the assignments were due to her sex or just because she was a rookie. She eventually got the chance to prove her mettle on more serious stories and, when a newer novice reporter joined the staff, Valerie was relieved of the rookie assignments. It didn't matter now; those days were behind her.

David gave up. He polished off the remains of the chop on his plate and sat back to look at Valerie, something he never grew tired of doing. Sun splashing from the skating rink brought out natural russet highlights in the dark hair framing her high, graceful cheekbones. Valerie's mouth always reminded him of Julia Roberts'—a little too wide for her otherwise classic features—but her teeth were perfect and she had a spectacular smile. David was several years older than Valerie, but the difference didn't bother her as much as it did him. "We need a break. Why don't we go to Cape Charles for the weekend?" he suggested. "Let's get away for a couple of days and I promise we'll find things to do besides talk about network politics."

A skater whipped around into an easy spin right next to their table and the effortless perfection of the figure finally broke Valerie's foul mood. She knew she was acting like a petulant child. It was her turn to sigh. "That sounds like a good idea. I obviously need some time away. And no work—I promise if you promise."

David smiled broadly. "I promise."

The tension in Valerie's shoulders drained away as she relaxed just thinking about a whole weekend without deadlines and office politics. David and Valerie met when he was a senior producer for MBS News and she was a fledgling reporter for the network's station in New York, where she had jumped eagerly after her stint in Elmira. Not long after she got to the city, she got a last-minute assignment to fill in for a network correspondent with whom David was working. One thing led to another as the planets aligned very nicely for them. By the time their relationship blossomed into something serious, she had moved to the network news division with a gold star next to her name, and David was offered a high-profile job overseeing the network's news bureau in the nation's capital—a probable precursor to running the entire news division. His promotion eliminated their problem with the company's fraternization rules since she no longer worked with him directly. Their long-distance romance wasn't difficult since shuttle flights between New York and Washington ran every hour and they had apartments in both places where they alternated weekends as often as their schedules allowed.

"I've got to go back to DC today," David added. "Will you be all right tonight?"

"Yes, I'm fine," Valerie answered. She wasn't, but there was no point whining about it now. At least she could look forward to the weekend in Cape Charles.

By the time Valerie got back to the office after lunch, unofficial word of Preston Henry's promotion had circulated throughout the building. More than one well-meaning co-worker offered their condolences as she walked through the newsroom, making Valerie want to shout back, "I just lost a promotion, I don't have cancer!" But she didn't. There was a memo on her desk from Carter Wilson calling a mid-afternoon staff meeting; Valerie assumed it would be the official announcement that Preston Henry was to be anointed. She would go, of course, and put on her best corporate face, but she didn't have to enjoy it. Valerie had just wadded up the memo and tossed it into her wastebasket when Nancy Justine tapped on her doorframe and stepped into the office. Her frizzy brown curls shook as she angrily shook a copy of the memo in the air.

"Is this what I think it is?" she demanded.

Valerie nodded. "Sorry I didn't get a chance to tell you in person," she said.

"Fuck that," Nancy said, waving away Valerie's apology. "What's wrong with these people? How can they not give you this job? You earned it! And Pressed-Puss Henry, for God's sake! That son of a bitch is a blow-dried talking head! If he didn't have a teleprompter, he couldn't tell you what day it is. I bet he's out there right now signing autographs for the interns."

"Whoa, girl!" Valerie laughed. Nancy almost always cheered her up, especially when she expressed opinions Valerie couldn't voice. Nancy and Valerie had been a team since Valerie moved to her first correspondent's job in the network news division not long after she had been drafted to help David. They couldn't have looked less alike; Valerie was tall and graceful, Nancy short and in nervous perpetual motion. The camera loved Valerie's classic features; it cringed at Nancy's incipient smirk. Valerie knew the hardened producer had sized her up the first time she worked with her and liked the grit she saw in the younger, more photogenic version of herself. From then on, she made it her business to give Valerie every edge to get ahead in the cutthroat world of television journalism. As one of the best news dogs in the trade, she did what a truly great producer does: make good things happen for her boss. She researched stories to sort out the facts from the rumors, she cut red tape wherever it got in the way, and she played her overstuffed Blackberry like a concert pianist, enabling Valerie to reach people who didn't want to be reached. She was Valerie's right hand, arm and shoulder, and Valerie valued her even more than her real limb. Most of all, she valued her as a friend.

"So what are we going to do?" Nancy asked.

"We are going to go to the meeting and wish Preston the best of luck in his new position," Valerie answered with mock primness.

"No, really. What are we going to do? We can't let him get away with this. Let me load his makeup with cayenne pepper. He'll never know what hit him."

Valerie laughed again. "No, we're going to act like adults for a change."

"Aw, boss, you never let me have any fun." Nancy stopped to look again at the memo in her hand. "Seriously, are you going to look for another job?"

Valerie grew somber. "No, the timing's not right for that. Besides, you win some, you lose some, you know?"

"Yeah, but you deserve better."

"Thanks, kiddo," Valerie smiled.

Nancy smiled back and looked closely at Valerie. She grew thoughtful. "What you need is a good story to work on—preferably one far, far away where the suits can't bother you."

Valerie liked that idea. "You're right," she said. "Any place in particular?"

Nancy thought for a minute, her mind rifling through the headlines and weighing the possibilities. "Russia's interesting these days. They can't decide whether to be a capitalist dictatorship or a democracy for the gangsters." She shook her head. "Nah, too many phones. We need someplace remote. Antarctica, maybe?" She shivered and shook her head again. "It's almost winter there now, way too cold."

The more Nancy talked, the more she brightened up Valerie's day. Valerie laughed. Then she remembered a story about an artillery attack on Kinshasa she'd seen on CNN that morning. "Things are heating up in the Congo," she offered. "It's been a while since we've been there.

Maybe it's about time for us to do a follow-up."

"You're right," Nancy said. "There's some meat on that bone too."

"Yes. From what I gather, Messime's government is under attack from all over—inside and outside," Valerie continued. "There's plenty of news there. I think I can sell it to Wilson."

"Good! I'll start packing."

Valerie laughed again. "Wait until after Preston's announcement."

"Oh yeah, I almost forgot," Nancy said. "I'll see you at the meeting. I've got to go get my cayenne."

Carter Wilson was easily sold on the idea of Valerie's disappearing into the Congo for a few weeks. Having her away from the newsroom would put a damper on the gossip columnists who were already trying to make a story out of the rivalry between Valerie and Preston Henry. Despite Valerie's perfectly professional denials, the rumormongers would cast a pall over the network's promotion campaign for the new anchorman. The tabloid reporters wouldn't follow her to Africa. The Congo was legitimate news too, and Valerie was the obvious person to cover it since she'd been there when Moshe Messime first came to power. He gave her the green light to leave right away.

As Valerie was telling Nancy to pack for the Congo, she remembered her weekend with David. He'll understand, she told herself as she dialed his number. It wouldn't be the first time they'd had to change plans to accommodate an assignment. "Hi," she said when he picked up the phone. "We're going to have to make Cape Charles another weekend. I'm leaving for the Congo Friday."

"Damn!" he said. Valerie thought she heard something more than simple disappointment in his voice.

"I'm sorry, David, but it's a good story. I need to go before Carter changes his mind."

"I know, but there was something I wanted to talk to you about this weekend."

"What?" Valerie asked.

"Never mind. It will wait," he said.

"What? Tell me! Is something wrong?"

"No, no. Nothing like that." David's voice changed. "You go and work well," he said. "When are you coming back?"

"I'm not sure, but I don't think it will be more than a couple of weeks. It's not in the budget and you know how Carter is."

"Yes I do. We can talk when you come home."

Her mind off the Congo for a moment, Valerie thought she knew what David wanted to talk about. He was right; now was not the time.

David said, "Be safe, okay?"

Chapter 3

Kinshasa

Of all the injuries he treated, Jaime hated machete wounds most of all. He was offended by the purposeful brutality it took to inflict them. The ten-year-old girl he was treating had been snatched from her mother's arms by a marauder in a gang sent to terrorize her village. She had wriggled in the brute's grip while he stretched her skinny arm upward until her toes barely touched the ground. Then he swung his machete around with his other hand, aiming for her outstretched arm just above the elbow. Machetes don't make neat, clean slashes. The wide, flat knives are not surgical instruments, they are cheap, heavy blades made dull by chopping brush. Their cutting edges aren't honed sharp—they are jagged, dented by woody stems and unseen stones. Machetes aren't wielded with the swift, efficient chop of the butcher's cleaver, either. Leg of lamb is a passive target; machete victims see it coming so they try to run, they dodge and flinch, they twist away. This girl squirmed as her assailant swung the machete around his body in an awkward blow. The dull blade cut the flesh but chunked weakly into the bone of her arm. The man wrenched it free, took slow aim, and struck harder. This time the bone gave and the girl fell to the ground, leaving her severed arm dangling from his grip. He threw it disdainfully at the keening mother. Just then, someone called out a command and he ran away. The mother twisted her scarf into a tourniquet around the girl's arm to stop the gushing blood. She found an old man in the village who carried the little girl to Mai-Munene on an ancient bicycle.

When Jaime saw her, the girl was in shock but still alive. He cleaned up the wound, closed off the blood vessels, pulled out the bone fragments left by the dull machete, and sewed a flap of living skin over the stump. He didn't have any other antibiotic, so he dosed her with gentamicin. The antibiotic checked the incipient infection in the arm, but it has a flaw; it isn't effective against E-coli. The girl's mother fed her some thin, tepid soup the next day. Within hours, the bacteria ravaged her weakened system as her helpless body spouted fluids faster than Jaime could replace them. She died within hours.

Pieter found Jaime slumped face down over his desk in the dispensary, his face hidden in the crook of his arm. Pieter touched his shoulder. "You best get to bed, Jaime," he said.

Jaime raised his head slowly as if he were coming out of a drunken stupor. "She did not have to die," he said.

"It's not your fault," Pieter said.

"I know. I've lost patients before." His voice rose. "But this girl did not have to die, damn it!"

"No, she didn't, but you can't kill an elephant with a slingshot," Pieter said. "She needed medicines we simply don't have."

Jaime sat up and straightened his shoulders. "Then I've got to get them."

Both official and unofficial baggage handlers work the scene in Kinshasa N'Djili International Airport. The official porters, who secure their jobs by kicking back a third of their tips to the airport manager, wear aquamarine shirts and black pants that match the pictures on the posters reminding passengers that regulations prohibit hiring anyone other than them anywhere on airport property. They spend most of their day lounging against the wall around the luggage carousel or smoking cigarettes and chatting with the taxi drivers lined up at the curb outside the terminal. When passengers are directed to the arrival area by the soldiers guarding the facility, the official porters rouse themselves to greet them, then hover possessively by their sides while the luggage finds its way from the plane to the terminal. As soon as a passenger points out his bag, his legal porter motions officiously to one of the scruffy boys milling around in the background. These unofficial handlers do the actual work of lifting and carrying the bags, while the official ones collect fees from the passengers and guide them to the proper line for customs inspection. The passengers assume the boys lugging the heavy baggage get their fair share of the tips, but they don't know for sure. Most passengers, intent on getting through customs and getting on with their business in the Congo, couldn't care less anyway.

Valerie, though, didn't let the posted rules stop her from rewarding the boy who grabbed her small bag off the carousel. She remembered the routine from her last trip to Kinshasa, when she covered the bloody coup that put Moshe Messime in power. This time, while Nancy distracted the uniformed porter by intentionally miscounting the money to pay him, Valerie edged closer to the boy with their bags and slipped him three dollar bills behind her back. She didn't look at him, but she heard a whispered "*merci*" from behind her. She hoped he would be able to hide the money before the official porter saw it.

Bobby Blaine, the seasoned MBS videographer who came with them, drove their rented minivan the twenty kilometers from N'Djili into Kinshasa, giving Valerie a chance to look at the countryside to see how it had changed since she was there four years before. Despite the grim state of the economy, signs for consumer products like Claire cosmetics and Coca-Cola lined the highway. Two competing beer brands seemed to own every other billboard all the way into Kinshasa. Brilliant yellow signs read *Primus Vous Souhaite Bon Voyage* while Skol, the leading brand as Valerie remembered it, screamed its slogan on fire-engine red signs with black and white letters. *Tindika Lokito*, they read, Lingala for Send the Thunder. The slogan was particularly appropriate in a place where automatic rifles sell on the street for less than the price of a six-pack of beer.

The rough four-lane highway was full of vehicles: Mercedes four-by-fours and six-bys trundled along with goods from the interior, Volkswagen taxis carried businessmen from the airport, more than a few troop carriers and other military vehicles moved purposefully in both directions. There were more minivans than anything else, though, most of them Toyota models like theirs. Every one of them was packed with passengers who paid a few cents for a ride after flagging down the van from the side of the road. Even the rear compartments were full of passengers who sat backward with their legs hanging out the rear windows. If another vehicle followed too closely, the legs withdrew quickly back inside like a centipede retreating into its carapace.

Considering that four years had passed and non-stop armed conflict still raged across much of the nation, Valerie was surprised to see that the countryside didn't look much different from the days right after the coup. The road had crumbled and burnt, and blasted buildings lined the way, but people lived their lives as if things were normal, which, for the Congo, perhaps they were. Pedestrians ambled along the shoulder of the highway, stopping at small booths where vendors sold a little of this and a little of that, but always only a little of whatever they offered, since a little was all anyone could afford. Children kicked ragged balls across dusty makeshift playgrounds. Mothers carried babies slung in their *pagnes* while casually balancing baskets and bundles on their heads. Maybe the Congo was like an alcoholic, she thought, always partly inebriated so that sobriety looked like an unnatural state. For the Congo, war was whiskey, and there was always some of it circulating through its bloodstream.

The next day, Valerie began her assignment by interviewing Moshe Messime, president of the Democratic Republic of the Congo and self-proclaimed leader of sub-Saharan Africa. She met with him at the presidential palace on the outskirts of the capital, one of two lavish residences Messime's predecessor had constructed in a completely incongruous Oriental style. The other palace, farther from the city to the east, had been bombed into gilded rubble during the coup that brought Messime to power.

Valerie and Messime sat in comfortable rattan chairs on the veranda overlooking a long, manicured lawn where peacocks strutted and guinea hens pecked in the grass. It was early in the morning, before the heat of the day began to rise, and the veranda was cool. Perhaps that was why Messime, trying to look more American than usual, wore a three-piece suit whose vest would otherwise be grossly inappropriate for the tropical climate. Messime's single concession to his African heritage was a leopard-skin fez he wore at all times. Valerie found the headwear ironic; the style had been introduced to the continent by Arab slavers. If Messime knew, he apparently didn't care.

Valerie had first met Messime when he elected himself president four years earlier. His predecessor, Ingaway Seto, committed suicide in his prison cell by shooting himself three times—once in the back of his own head. Messime had thrown Seto in jail and moved into the presidential palace after violently stamping out the opposition in a series of genocidal rampages by F.I.C., the Fédération Indépendante du Congo, his base of support and now the country's regular army. When she interviewed him after he first came to power, Valerie found Messime dangerous and dynamic, coldly calculating, fairly sophisticated in his grasp of world affairs. He professed concern—perhaps heartfelt— about how his regime would be viewed by the developed countries of the world. On camera, he appealed for recognition by the United States and promised repeatedly that his country would be a stalwart partner in the fight against Godless communism. Once he got rolling, though, he didn't stop after making a rational plea for world respect. The Congo, he proclaimed, would be the anchor state for a Pan-Equatorial African Union allied with America. Moshe Messime would be the self-appointed messiah of the subcontinent.

During that first interview, Valerie listened patiently to his pipe dreams, then asked several penetrating questions in a way that not only didn't offend him but actually made him like her more. He was a raw man, possessed by the virility of power. He knew that a pretty young woman like Valerie couldn't help but be overwhelmed by his manliness. Valerie had encountered many men and even a few women just like him in other capitals around the world, including Washington. Pursuing, grasping, exercising power kept them in a constant state of arousal. Valerie knew how to use her charms to play into their delusions and get answers to her questions.

Messime hadn't changed much over the years, Valerie observed now; he was still vulnerable to her direct, sensuous manner. She began today's interview by asking him about the threats to his country.

"Let me begin in the south with the Angolans," he said. "They are international criminals. They claim to act in the interests of African peace, but all they truly want are our diamonds. The Angolan tyrant, Kenda Sanko, needs them to buy arms so he can make war against his own people."

"What about reports that there are Congolese people supporting the Angolan forces?" Valerie asked.

"You refer to the Lunda Libre, a gang of thieves that pretends to be freedom fighters." Messime's lip curled and Valerie thought for a moment he was going to spit in disgust. "The Fédération Indépendante du Congo is the only army of freedom in the Congo. The Lunda Libre is in league with the Angolan invaders. They have done horrible, horrible things to the people of the Kasai River valley. Atrocities that have been well-documented by the international community."

"Mr. President," Valerie said, "What about the reports of rape and looting attributed to the F.I.C.?"

"Lies. Lies! They are all lies promulgated by my enemies. F.I.C. liberated the people of the Congo from the evil regime of Ingaway Seto. It is an army of patriots dedicated to keeping our people free from tyranny. They move bravely to crush the Lunda Libre and repel the Angolan hyenas even as we speak."

He paused and lowered his voice until he sounded like a banker lecturing a home owner who was late with her mortgage payment. "Remember, Miss Grey, Lunda Libre is not a popular uprising as they are often portrayed by the media. They are gangsters allied with the forces of evil from outside the Congo." His voice rose again to a pontificating pitch. "They are evildoers who would destroy us and steal our vast natural resources."

Valerie interrupted the rising tide of rhetoric with another question. "What about the Republic of the Congo? What is the status of the dispute with your neighbor to the north?"

"Pascal Mondojo is in league with the Angolans as well. They try to squeeze us from two sides. As the world knows, Miss Grey, Mondojo was put into office two years ago not by the popular vote of his people but by the Angolan army. They marched into Pointe Noire from Cabinda just before the election and all the other candidates withdrew to save their country from destruction by Kenda Seko. They made a disgraceful mockery of the cause of democracy in Africa."

Valerie hoped her eyes didn't betray her thoughts about Messime's own fealty to the democratic process. "The Angolans withdrew, didn't they?" she said, careful to keep her inflection neutral.

"Yes, but Mondojo remains their puppet. At every opportunity, he harasses us along the border on the river in a vain effort to tie up our forces so we cannot use them against the Angolans in the south. Last month, as I am sure you recall, he even had the audacity to shell Kinshasa! It was a single artillery shell, laughable in its futility, but many innocent lives were lost."

"Will you retaliate?" Valerie asked.

"I do not think it wise to discuss our military plans with your viewers, Miss Grey," Messime said.

Valerie sensed Messime was about to end the interview but she had more ground to cover so she pressed on. "What are you going to do about Nord Kivu and the other provinces to the east? Have you abandoned them to the Hutus and the Lord's Resistance Army?"

"It is absolutely intolerable that the internal conflicts of Rwanda and Uganda have spilled across the sovereign borders of the Democratic

Republic of the Congo. Uganda is using pursuit of the LRA as an excuse to illegally occupy Ituri Province. The Tutsis of Rwanda have done the same in Nord Kivu. They supposedly crossed our border in pursuit of the Hutus, but remain on our land even after the end of the civil war in their own country." Messime looked ostentatiously at the jeweled Rolex on his left wrist. "I am afraid I must bring our most pleasant conversation to an end, Miss Grey. The affairs of state demand my full attention."

"Just one more question, please," Valerie said with her most disarming smile. She didn't wait for him to grant permission. "With armed enemies pressing you from all sides and rebel armies on the rise everywhere, how will your government survive?"

Messime's fleshy jaw tightened and his eyes blazed. Looking into his face, Valerie could believe the stories she'd heard of him roasting and eating the testicles of vanquished foes in the early days of his terrifying rise to power. His thick fingers gripped the arms of his chair so hard the rattan crackled.

"I am the Great Father of my country," he said forcefully, each word distinct and hard. "My people will not let me fail. Nor will the governments of the first world, Miss Grey. Not only does the United States of America know I am its best hope to create a free and democratic Pan-Equatorial African Union, but your country has business interests in the Congo to protect as well." Valerie didn't think there was very much American investment in the Congo, but she didn't get a chance to ask the question. Messime stood up and the interview was over.

⁓⊙ ⊙⁓

At the Reuters Satellite Communications Center, Valerie and

Nancy edited the Messime video, added the standup she had recorded outside the presidential palace, then sent the package via satellite to New York. With the time difference, it arrived well before the evening news. Afterwards, they headed for Bandal, a borough between the Cité, the tarpaper slums that surround Kinshasa, and Gombe, the upper-crust section of the city where the old colonialists built their bungalows behind high cement walls topped with broken glass. A thin line of rusting railroad tracks separated Bandal from Gombe, but the two places were so different the track might as well have been the Atlantic Ocean. One of the Reuters engineers had told Bobby about a neighborhood restaurant, Mama Colonel, just on the other side of the tracks. It served exactly four dishes: grilled chicken, grilled fish, fried potatoes, and fried plantains, all cooked to perfection and served on paper plates at tables covered with plastic sheets under a red and white striped awning. The three Americans settled in to one of the tables near the street. They were separated from the traffic by a low concrete-block wall plastered with posters for rock bands and beer and cigarettes.

Across the street was a nameless bar where an energetic dancing crowd overflowed onto the sidewalk. A joyous band with strident brass blared blues from a platform under a tin roof. Dusty strings of Christmas tree bulbs lit the space, leaving plenty of dark corners where couples leaned across small tables to whisper beery-breathed to each other in the shadows. The mob of dancers was large and happy, filled with raucous students celebrating their last day of studies at L'École Secondaire de Bandalungwa. For most of them, it would be the end of their formal education; for two or three very lucky ones, freshman slots waited at the national university. Tonight, though, they danced. In Kinshasa, people dance—some to express their joy at being alive, some to forget, others simply because it feels good while they're doing it. The raw rhythms called to Valerie from across the street. She swayed happily along with the throbbing beat while she washed down the delectable chicken with sips of Primus. It was great fun just watching the dancing crowd, although she hadn't ruled out joining in after she finished eating.

"Wouldn't it be wonderful to be that young again?" she asked cheerfully between bites.

"I was never that young," Nancy answered with a wry smile.

"I was," Bobby said, "and it wasn't that long ago—in spite of what you might think." The videographer took off his ever-present NY Yankees cap and brushed thinning hair back from a decidedly receding hairline. "This is way premature."

Valerie's thoughts turned to David as she watched the dancers. He loved most music but complained about how loudly pop music always had to be played. You knew it was too loud, he said, when the bass made your sternum vibrate. He couldn't understand why music had to hurt you to be considered good. He also wouldn't dance, even though Valerie loved to. It was one of those minor irritations that rub between two people but never quite get smoothed over no matter how hard they try. It wasn't all that important in the grand scheme of things, but compromise on this point with David wasn't going to happen.

Valerie was delighted by the free, unself-conscious movements of the kids across the street. A few couples concentrated on each other and a dozen or so girls organized into a complicated line dance, but most of the dancers gamboled on their own, sweat running down their joyous faces, eyes focused on nothing or closed in surrender to the insistent beat. The band ended their set with a sudden crescendo. The crowd clapped and whistled for more before it settled down to catch its collective breath in the sudden silence. One boy, oblivious, danced on in the middle of the street to a beat only he could hear. Valerie laughed. As she reached for her beer, a low whistle arose in the distance then turned into a scream from the sky.

"Down!" Valerie shouted. She dove under the table and pulled Nancy with her behind the concrete wall just as the shell exploded. The white burst rolled into an angry flare that left blue rings behind her eyelids. The blast threw pulverized flesh and shrill whistling shrapnel over her head. In an instant, the air was drawn back into a roaring ball of flame. Concrete chunks and fingers and plastic shards and pink wetness rained down from the sky. The world was burnt and ripped; crushed in a roar. Valerie snapped back to coherence. The shock wave had passed above her, then sucked back into the vacuum created by the explosion. White and orange and blue dots danced in her eyes. Her head rang. She knew there was screaming and crashing but she couldn't hear it. Her chest ached like it had been struck by a fist. The awning frame, stripped of its striped canvas, teetered and collapsed onto the wall where she crouched.

Where was Nancy? She sensed her scrunched against the wall beside her. Okay! Bobby? Where was Bobby? She didn't see his blue jeans or well-worn photographer's vest anywhere.

Valerie pushed upward with her back against the collapsed awning frame. It moved, scraping against the concrete, silent in her ringing head. Bobby crawled toward her through the jumble of upended tables and chairs. She strained harder against the tubing until it gave way with a clatter. She couldn't tell if she heard the noise or just felt it. Nancy was beside her, shouting something. Bobby stood, blood streaming down his face. He leaned his broad shoulders into the remnants of the collapsed frame and tried to pull her away from the street. Nancy shoved her in the same direction, shouting.

Her eyes burned. The flashing dots faded. She squinted through gray smoke and dust suspended in the air so thick it looked like a wall. She couldn't see the other side of the street where the shell exploded. It must have been a direct hit on the bar. Valerie tried to climb over the top of the wall but Nancy and Bobby pushed her in the other direction. "Help them!" she tried to shout, but the smoke ripped her throat as soon as she opened her mouth. Nancy shouted something too, but Valerie couldn't understand her. She finally shook them off and scrambled over the wall.

The smoke lifted slowly from the ground. Twisted bodies of dancers lay where they had been scattered by the blast. An arm waved delicately in the middle of the street. Valerie ran to it and found a girl pinned beneath a boy in a muscle shirt, a boy whose tall, lithe body was headless. Bobby helped her roll the dead boy off the struggling girl. Nancy tried to check the girl for injuries, but she pushed them all off and staggered away, sobbing. Valerie realized her ears must be recovering because she heard the girl's cries. They were muffled, but she heard them. She also heard—or felt, she wasn't sure—the heavy thuds of explosions in other parts of the city. They came singly, spaced like lugubrious beats on a bass drum. With Nancy and Bobby, Valerie did what little she could to help the injured survivors, mostly offering comfort and sympathy, as the police arrived and ambulances took the wounded away.

Chapter 4

Brazzaville

The ferry from Kinshasa to Brazzaville was operating as usual the next morning despite radio reports that the mortar attack the night before had come from the Republic of the Congo capital across the river.

"Messime obviously isn't going to let a few dead teenagers get in the way of holy commerce," Nancy said as they boarded.

The ferry was packed, mostly with people who had business to conduct on the other side of the Congo River, which separated the capitals of the Democratic Republic of the Congo and the Republic of the Congo, two nations carved from blood-soaked colonies of Belgium and France.

It was a short crossing, less than thirty minutes once they finally got underway, but Valerie felt cooped up sitting in the van so she stood at the rail and watched Kinshasa recede into the morning haze rising off the water.

Another day, another disaster, she thought grimly. The authorities speculated that the shell that struck the bar in Kinshasa the night before was one of several fired from an 81mm mortar somewhere in Brazzaville. If Gombe had been the intended target, it was on the outer reaches of the weapon's range, which made an inaccurate strike more likely. She suspected the shell had been intended for the rich homes in the district, meant to destroy one of the colonial-era mansions hidden behind its ten-foot wall topped with broken bottles and razor wire. If it had been on target, it might have caught a high-ranked F.I.C. officer at home with his family, or obliterated one of Messime's bureaucrats. But she didn't know for sure and probably wasn't going to find out, so she dismissed the speculation. She never got an official count of the casualties last night, but there must have been more than a hundred killed and wounded. Valerie wondered if the boy who had kept dancing after the music stopped had survived the blast. Somehow she didn't think so. What higher purpose was served by blowing up a crowd of dancing kids? Valerie knew those kinds of questions led nowhere, but it was impossible to stop asking them. It was just one more random act of war, which is how she characterized it in the initial report they filed with the network after the attack.

Once in Brazzaville, Valerie spent the first part of the day trying to get an interview with Pascal Mondojo, president of the Republic of the Congo. His office flaks shoved her off to the minister of defense, who flatly denied that the attack had come from any of his forces. "It is widely know that Moshe Messime stages such events to foster sympathy in the West," was his only comment. Valerie talked to a few other functionaries and added some man-in-the-street comments, but she was far from satisfied by the quality of the story. She wrapped it up anyway with a standup at The Beach, the docks in Brazzaville, with the Congo River in the background and Kinshasa in the distance. They would add it to the footage Bobby had taken as the officials loaded bodies into trucks at the scene the night before.

By the time they were finished, the ferry was no longer running. Nancy tried to hire a private motorboat, but no one wanted to venture out onto the river because F.I.C. helicopters had been swooping up and down the channel all afternoon. Word on the dock was that retaliation was coming. None of the boat owners wanted to find out if the rumors were true.

Stranded on the ROC side of the river, they finally found rooms at the Hotel Protea on the edge of the city. They checked in, went to their rooms to wash up, then met for dinner. Sitting in the well-appointed hotel restaurant, Valerie felt vaguely disoriented by the swift changes in her surroundings. They had driven from the hustling crowd at the docks on the river—no different in mindset and attitude from the commerce-driven denizens jostling along the sidewalks of Wall Street—to the bombed-out city blocks of Brazzaville, remnants of the most recent civil war and already tentatively rebuilding: a lean-to here, a tin-roofed shanty there rising among the rubble. At the edge of the city were the silent suffering slums, a Cité just like Kinshasa's, packed with refugees from the countryside and the abjectly poor who lived there always. They ended the day at the glittering Hotel Protea, with duvet-covered king-size beds, mini-bars, in-suite Jacuzzis, not to mention two swimming pools, a high-tech fitness center, golf, tennis and satellite TV. They could have been in Miami Beach as easily as the heart of Africa. Valerie had traveled the world reporting everywhere from the steps of marble palaces to the stoops of plywood hovels; the bitter contrast had never been so stark as it was in Brazzaville.

She tried to focus on the menu, but Nancy nudged her elbow and nodded at the man sitting at the next table. He was dressed for the bush, although his khakis were clean. His attire would have been unremarkable had he not been sitting in a four-star restaurant with white linen napkins and candles on the table. He was a roughly good-looking man, tall and tanned, but what drew Valerie's eye first was his hair, which looked like he had cut it himself, impatiently, while standing before his hotel room mirror just before dinner. She looked back at Nancy inquisitively, glad for the distraction. Nancy raised her eyebrows as she jerked her head discreetly in his direction again. Valerie looked back just in time to see him slip a dinner roll into a bag on the seat beside him. From the bulge in the bag, Valerie guessed this wasn't the first. The bread basket on his table was empty. Just as she noticed the basket, he asked a passing waiter to refill it. Nancy coughed to cover a snicker and the man glanced their way. His eyes casually met Valerie's for a moment just before the waiter stepped between them with his bread.

Valerie wondered idly what he was doing here. The hotel was adjacent to the sprawling campus of the World Health Organization regional headquarters for Africa. Visiting dignitaries, not to mention medical industry reps and UN bureaucrats, couldn't be expected to stay anyplace less plush. The other forty-odd tables in the restaurant were filled by men in pressed khakis that had never seen a thorn bush. A few wore fine English wool or Italian silk suits, white shirts stiff with starch, and club ties neatly knotted. The bread thief, as Valerie labeled him to herself, stood out in that crowd with his well-worn khakis and recently-cleaned boots.

When the waiter stepped away, the man nodded politely in her direction. She acknowledged his greeting with a neutral smile.

"So, where to now, boss?" Nancy interrupted the exchange of glances. "I assume you don't want to spend the rest of the week here interviewing bureaucrats." Valerie's attention snapped back to business. She knew Carter Wilson had agreed to her trip to the Congo mostly as a consolation prize for not giving her the anchor job. He'd specified that it wasn't an open-ended assignment, though; a couple of weeks on the ground was all the budget would allow.

"I think we better check out the Angolan border," she said. "The eastern provinces have been a mess as long as anybody can remember, so that's no news. We couldn't do more than scratch the surface there in the few days we've got left anyway."

"If we're leaving the capital, we better find someplace we can reach by plane," Nancy said. "I don't think we have time to drive across country."

"Excuse me," interrupted the bread thief. "I couldn't help overhearing. Where are to trying to get to? Perhaps I can help."

His voice was authoritative without being commanding. Valerie was surprised at his American accent; most English-speakers she encountered in Africa were British or from one of the former colonies. She also noticed his bread basket was empty again. There were a few more lumps in his bag.

"Do you know where the fighting is in the south?" Valerie asked.

"Are you trying to avoid it or find it?" the man replied.

"Find it, preferably. I'm a reporter. Valerie Grey with MBS TV News. This is Nancy Justine and Bobby Blaine. And you are …?"

"Jaime Talon," the man answered.

"Do you know the region?" Valerie asked.

Jaime nodded and shrugged. "Pretty well," he said. "If it's fighting you're after, you might find it south and east of Tshikapa. There's an airfield there too. There's no scheduled service, but you can charter a plane easily enough."

"Thanks for the advice," Valerie said. "What can you tell us about the fighting? Is it the Angolans or the Lunda Libre?"

"All of the above," Jaime said. "Everybody is fighting over the mines like they always have. Copper and manganese in Shaba farther south. Diamonds where I am."

"Diamonds? You own a diamond mine?" Nancy interjected.

"Not hardly. I just work at a clinic near the mine at Mai-Munene."

"Is there fighting where you are?" Valerie asked. She thought he might have fled the region.

"No. Not yet, but there will be. We heard Xotha himself is operating in the region. He's the head of the Lunda Libre."

"He's somewhere around Mai-Munene?" Valerie asked, deciding right then to go after an interview with the guerilla leader. If they overstayed Wilson's budget, he'd just have to get over it.

"I don't know how close," Jaime answered. "Besides, it's just a rumor. We have seen a few more refugees in the clinic, but it's hard to tell who they were running from. The countryside is full of freelance gangs too."

"I would think the diamond mine would be a target," Valerie said.

"Right now, the mine is protected by the government. Or divine intervention." Jaime smiled at a private joke.

Valerie smiled. "What makes you say that?"

"An American preacher took over the mine last year," Jaime explained. "My assistant, Pieter, says God must be on his side—especially since he can afford a diamond mine."

There was a long tradition of American churches with missions in the Congo, Valerie knew, but this was the first one she'd heard of that was making money at it. She asked, "Who is it?"

"Some guy named Gary Peterson. Know anything about him?"

"Sure," Valerie said. "He's a big televangelist in Atlanta. He's also the president's personal spiritual advisor or something like that. But I had no idea he owned a diamond mine."

Nancy added, "That didn't show up in my research. He must be one of the few Americans with any investments in the Congo."

"I wouldn't be surprised," Jaime said. "The country is not exactly a money magnet these days."

"What can you tell me about his mine?" Valerie asked. There might be an interesting feature story in Mai-Munene, she thought. A minister who owned a diamond mine would make a unique subject.

"I don't know much. I try to have as little to do with them as possible," Jaime said. "It's an alluvial mine, which means they find the stones in the old riverbed. It's pretty successful, from what I understand. That's why everybody and his brother has tried to get their hands on it. Since independence, it bounced from the Congolese, to the Angolans, and even the Namibians before Messime got it back a couple of years ago. Late last year, he sold it to the American preacher Gary Peterson. He sent a guy, supposedly a missionary, to run it. We thought he'd build schools and other things the community needs, but all he did was give the village women jobs making dolls."

Just then, the waiter brought his check. Jaime carefully counted out a pile of Congolese francs onto the table. "I hate to go," he said as he stood, "but I have a meeting in the morning. Say, are you going to eat those rolls?" He nodded toward the basket on their table.

"No, I don't think so," Valerie said. "Would you like them?" She looked at Nancy and Bobby for confirmation. Nancy suppressed a grin.

"Thanks," Jaime said. He unself-consciously emptied the basket into his bag. "Have a good evening."

As soon as he was gone, Nancy let out the laugh she'd been holding. "He walked out of here with enough bread to open a bake shop!" she exclaimed. Valerie looked thoughtfully after him.

Valerie had a restless night despite the soothing soak she took in her room's whirlpool tub. She tossed most of the night in the luxurious bed, flitting between sleep and wakefulness. At home in New York when she had nights like these, Valerie would sometimes get dressed and go out to roam the sidewalks of the West Side around her apartment, checking out the darkened shop windows, observing the traffic, but mostly watching the people. There were always people on the streets, even at three or four in the morning, and she liked to speculate about their lives, make up little biographies for them in her imagination. The stories weren't something she would ever share with anyone else, even David, but Valerie entertained herself with them. The lives her characters led were remarkably mundane. They all had everyday jobs, happy marriages, sweet, obedient children, happy-go-lucky dogs and frisky kittens. They were always on the street in the early hours on innocuous missions like buying cough syrup for little Susie or celebrating one of life's achievements like a wedding anniversary or passing the Bar exam. Some of them were dedicated public servants going to work to make the trains run on time or hard-striving immigrant nannies on their way to make breakfast for some wealthy, over-scheduled family. It was a fantasy world of Valerie's devising, with no vagrants or drunks or hookers, no gang-bangers, no sneak thieves, no cheating husbands crawling home after a night of guilty copulation. The imaginary stories were a nice counterpoint to the grim ones about the real world Valerie reported most days.

It was nearly dawn when she finally gave up trying to sleep in Brazzaville. She threw off the covers, slipped into her clothes and went downstairs to the hotel lobby. The drowsing bell captain asked if she needed a taxi. When she told him she was just going outside for some air, he asked her to stay within the walls of the hotel grounds. "Sometimes there are undesirables outside the gates on the road," he warned.

Valerie walked around the hotel pool, past the tennis courts, and looked at the golf course with no interest in its perfectly manicured landscape. There was no one else outside on the hotel grounds, not surprising since the sun hadn't yet come up. The sky was growing lighter with a pale peach glow in the east, but it would be several minutes before the sun came above the horizon. She felt the heat rising. It would be another steamy day. Without realizing it, she had wandered back around toward the front of the hotel. She couldn't see the entrance, but she heard someone exchange familiar greetings with the bell captain, then walk briskly up the drive toward the front gate. She followed, making a game of keeping in the shadows to avoid detection as long as she could. As Valerie closed the distance and the sky brightened, she realized she was following Jaime Talon. He was carrying something, but Valerie couldn't make out what it was.

At the main entrance to the hotel grounds, Jaime waved casually to a uniformed guard, who nodded and opened the pedestrian gate. He turned right and disappeared on the other side of the bougainvillea-covered concrete wall that separated the hotel grounds from the road. Valerie gave up her cover and trotted to the gate so she wouldn't lose him. When she got to the road, she saw Jaime stroll toward a knot of merchants setting up on the roadside. Some of them spread blankets to display their wares on the ground. Others stocked simple folding tables with cheap trinkets and Chinese-made souvenirs they hoped to hawk to the hotel visitors as their cars stopped at the iron-gated entrance of the hotel. Jaime paused at each vendor, reached into the bag he carried, and handed them something. When she got nearer, Valerie realized he was passing out the bread and rolls he had collected from the restaurant the night before, a regular Robin Hood of baked goods. The characterization made her smile. She caught up to Jaime just as he handed the last roll from the bag to a woman kneeling next to a small cloth displaying beaded and braided cords twisted into colorful bracelets. "I wish I'd thought of that," Valerie said.

"Oh, it's you! Good morning," he said. "I hate to see it go to waste. The hotel staff can't take it or they're accused of stealing."

"I guess that makes sense," she said.

"It does in Africa." They turned and walked back toward the hotel. "Do you always get up before dawn?" Jaime asked.

"No, I couldn't sleep. I got up to see if the world was a better place today. I think you've just given me hope." He didn't say anything; Valerie realized she had embarrassed him. "What are you doing in Brazzaville besides raiding the hotel bakery?" she asked.

"It's no vacation. I'm here begging funds for the clinic."

"It doesn't sound like you enjoy it," Valerie observed.

"I hate it. But somebody's got to do it."

"Why Brazzaville?" Valerie asked.

"It's WHO headquarters for all of Africa," he explained.

"Any luck?"

"Not a dime so far," Jaime answered bitterly. "You would think the World Health Organization would offer a solution to my problem. After all, that's where our funding comes from! But all I get is the old bureaucratic run-around. 'Your budget is part of the aid given to the DRC,' they tell me. 'I know that,' I say. I explain that most of the money doesn't get to us. 'Someone in Kinshasa pockets it,' I tell them. 'If you can prove that,' they say, 'we will stop the funds.' But how will that help? If they cut off the funding completely, I'll never get anything, nor will any of the other clinics and hospitals and other institutions in the country that depend on WHO funding. 'Why not just give it to me directly?' I ask. 'We can't do that or we'd be violating the national sovereignty of the Congo' is the answer. I'm damned if I do and damned if I don't."

"Do you get any private funds? Foundations, grants, that sort of thing?" Valerie said.

"Not now. Going after them is my next step," Jaime said.

"What about Peterson, the mine owner. Doesn't his church support clinics like yours?"

"You'd think so, wouldn't you?" Jaime answered. "I thought we'd get some help from Peterson when the so-called missionary running the mine flew to Atlanta a few weeks after he'd first come to Mai-Munene, but he just came back a bigger asshole than before he left. He walked around with a secret smile—you'd think he swiped a winning lottery ticket from a little old lady. When I asked him again for money, he told me he didn't represent the Bank of God. I took that as a *no*."

Valerie and Jaime had reached the hotel entrance.

"So what do you do now?" she asked.

"I have a few more stones to overturn here and in Kinshasa. If I don't find any money under them, I'll go after grant money in the States."

"You don't sound very enthused about that," Valerie observed.

"It's the games they make you play," Jaime said. "Here, you know where you stand most of the time. The explanations aren't rational, but the horse-trading is straightforward. Give me a bribe, I'll give you what you want. There are hassles, but at least you know what they're about. There, you never know whose tender sensibilities are at stake or which hidden agenda you're part of. The bureaucrats in the States aren't angling for bribes; they're looking for a piece of your hide. Some people are very good at dealing with it. I never was."

Valerie wanted to hear more about Jaime Talon's successes and failures, but Nancy was waiting for her on the hotel steps. She gave Valerie an inquisitive look.

"Pardon me for interrupting," she said, just a hint of bemusement in her voice. "But we've got a pilot waiting for us at Brazzaville airport.

"Where are you going?" Jaime asked. Valerie sensed he didn't want to end their conversation right then either.

"Tshikapa," Valerie answered. "If we get to Mai-Munene, will you be there?"

"I hope so," Jaime said. Valerie liked his answer.

Chapter 5

Mai-Munene

As soon as Valerie landed in Tshikapa, she put out feelers about Lunda Libre and Commander Xotha. She and Nancy talked to the town's taxi drivers, the fishermen along the riverbank, the vendors in the market, and even to idlers hanging around the crumbling municipal building. A few people acknowledged that there was fighting in the hills around Tshikapa, but none admitted knowing who was involved, much less where the rebel forces were actually located. Their naturally open, helpful attitude disappeared when Valerie asked about Xotha, which surprised her. Most insurgent groups—at least the ones with political agendas—are eager to gain access to the airwaves so their claims of injustice and diatribes about moral superiority can be heard by the ignorant masses. By making discreet inquiries and putting out the word that you want to interview them, a reporter can usually make contact fairly easily. When the movement is about piracy, though, there is little to be gained by media exposure. The Mafia has lawyers, but it doesn't have a press office.

The answers Valerie got to her questions around town were useless. When people have been treated as ignorant children for generations, evasion becomes second nature. Commander Xotha? Me no understand. Or worse, a blank, stubborn stare, lips tight, a furtive look around to see if anyone is listening. Valerie couldn't tell if the evasion was due to fear of Xotha or a willingness to protect him. Either way, something was going on, but no one was willing to talk about it with a white woman from America, even one with an open, winning smile and a respectful attitude. After several fruitless days, Valerie felt like she was swimming in molasses. Under pressure from New York to either file a story worth airing or come home, Valerie gave up trying to make contact with the Lunda Libre and decided to go to Mai-Munene. The American televangelist and his diamond mine would at least make an offbeat feature.

Nancy hired a driver, Mr. Sami, whose ancient pickup truck had no glass in the windows but was festively painted with lime green and white circles over the original sun-faded finish. The rusty truck bed was loaded with a remarkable variety of merchandise, everything from motor oil to penny candy, that Mr. Sami explained was inventory for the roadside store he operated with his brother. As he and Bobby moved cartons to make room for the Americans' duffel bags and equipment cases, more passengers showed up. Mr. Sami ignored the truck's protesting springs and left the tailgate down so two women, a handful of children, and an old man with a leaf-wrapped bundle tucked under his arm could fit in the back. The old man's bundle seeped blood, making a dark stain on his white shirt, but he gripped it tightly as if the contents were precious. Bobby rode in back too, perched on his camera case, while Nancy and Valerie sat on the spring-busted seat next to Mr. Sami. With no glass in the windshield, the front seat was only marginally more comfortable than the back of the truck.

The pavement ended as soon as they drove off the rusting bridge over the Kasai. Mr. Sami slowed his overloaded truck to a crawl out of consideration for his passengers and for the sake of the pickup's tired suspension. The washboard road wound up into the hills beyond the river, then back down to parallel it on the other side. The route was less susceptible to flooding that way, although the many streams it crossed probably made it impassable during the rainy season anyway. After twenty bone-rattling minutes, one of the passengers rapped on the truck bed and Mr. Sami stopped near a dry streambed. The two women climbed down and walked up the path made by the stream, each balancing a large bundle on her head. The children tagged obediently along. One of the women waved.

"Thank you and good day!" Mr. Sami called after them.

A few miles further, the old man signaled for Mr. Sami to stop. Valerie couldn't see any path or other sign of a village where he got out. The old man stood with his bloody bundle, watching the truck and its passengers until it was out of sight, his face expressionless.

"What was he carrying?" Valerie asked.

"He is a *nganga*. It could be a specimen for his magic." Mr. Sami smiled mischievously. "Or a piece of bush meat for his dinner."

He drove on. Not long after he left the old man by the side of the road, he rounded a bend and slowed. He pointed to a concrete block building with a tin roof a hundred yards ahead. "My store," he said proudly. The small, low building was freshly whitewashed and had large green circles like giant lime Lifesavers all over it, matching his truck. Valerie smiled at the name lettered above the door: Happy Store – Good People. Several mud-and-wattle huts, all neatly painted or whitewashed, were scattered under a huge mahogany tree on the opposite side of the road. Laundry decorated a line behind one. Most had small gardens surrounded by reed and thorn-bush fences. Mr. Sami got out of the truck and said apologetically, "I will unload my merchandise, then take you to Mai-Munene."

Valerie stepped out of the truck and stretched. Nancy got out pressing her hand against the small of her back. "I'll never complain about a New York cab again," she groaned as she straightened up. She wiped a hand across her face, licked her dusty lips, and spat into the road. "At least they have windshields," she said.

"Is that your home?" Valerie asked Mr. Sami. She pointed to the huts on the other side of the road.

"Yes. Also my brother's and my mother's," he said. Bobby passed him a box from the back of the truck. Before he carried it into the store, he said, "I would be honored to introduce you to my family, but everyone is working in the fields now."

"I would like that," Valerie said. "Perhaps when we return."

What hard-working people, Valerie thought. They may move slowly, but they are never not purposeful. Once away from Kinshasa, she had seen no lay-abouts, no knots of unemployed, vacant-eyed men, no klatches of chattering, idle women. Even in Tshikapa everyone was occupied with something. The unemployment rate was atrociously high, but everyone was busily engaged in looking out for themselves and their families, putting food in the pot, scrounging for something to sell in the market, scraping together a few coins. When not to work is to starve, there is no sense of entitlement. The only people in the Congo with the attitude that the world owes them something are the bureaucrats and the army.

After another long, dusty, teeth-rattling drive, they got to Mai-Munene. The village was nothing like the Pennsylvania coal-mining towns of Valerie's youth. There were no neat rows of weathered houses, just a haphazard array of mud-and-wattle huts along paths that meandered away from the road between stubbly fields and roughly-fenced gardens and livestock pens which took the place of white picket fences and marigold-lined flowerbeds. The yards around the huts were enclosed by bundles of tall grass and reeds bound together into flimsy, shoulder-high walls that turned them into simple rooms without roofs, extensions of the single dark rooms under the thatch of the hut itself. Just as at the homes of working people everywhere, laundry flapped on lines and children played in the dirt with stones and sticks and whatever detritus of adult life they could find. The village had one other thing in common with the mining towns of Pennsylvania: a layer of gritty dust lay over everything regardless of how frequently it was wiped away. A tall, slender woman sweeping her hard-packed yard with a palm-frond broom paused to wave as they drove past. Two little boys, twins, waved too; the pink palms of their hands flashed in the sun.

Mr. Sami slowed at the entrance to the mine compound, but Valerie told him she wanted to go to the clinic first. He drove on. The clinic was at the other end of the village, closer to the river, next to an open space around some raffia palms that looked like it must be the village square.

At the clinic, a tall, light-haired man sat outside on a stool angled over a board game of some sort opposite a grizzled, ageless man with one leg. Where the man's other leg should be, a stump ended just above the knee, jutting out bare and puckered from the hem of his shorts. A crutch made from a tree branch padded with cloth lay at his side. The one-legged man stuck the crutch under his arm as he hopped up to see who was in the old pickup. The tall, light-haired man stood up too. As his lanky frame unfolded from the stool, it looked like his body had too many elbows and knees. Standing together, the two men, one long-legged and white with a crest of white-blond hair, the other one-legged and dark with big, watchful eyes, looked like two species of water fowl standing side-by-side in the shallows waiting to see what the current had washed their way.

Mr. Sami stopped the truck and announced, "I am pleased to bring you to your destination." He turned off the engine and hopped out to shake hands with the two men like the cheerful salesman that he was. Bemused, Valerie wouldn't have been surprised to see him pass out some brochures. The tall light-haired man, welcomed them to Mai-Munene and told them he was Pieter Jakobsen.

Valerie explained that they were there to do a story about the mine. "We met Jaime Talon in Brazzaville," she added. "I was hoping to see him while we're here."

"Jaime's on his way home from Kinshasa," Pieter said. "He's driving our old jeep, so it's hard to tell when he'll get here. Is he expecting you?"

The hint of suspicion in his voice and his question gave Valerie a little moment of uncertainty. She was surprised at how let down she felt at the news that Jaime wasn't there. What was she really doing here?

"He told us we might find the Lunda Libre operating around Tshikapa," she said. "We've been there for the last few days but we didn't have any luck making contact." She decided she better get down to business. "He also told us the mine here belongs to an American, so I thought we'd check it out."

"Ah, yes. The diamond mine. It is indeed operated by the Church of the Holy Moneychangers or something like that," Pieter said.

Valerie laughed. "That's an interesting way to put it," she said. "I guess they're not your favorite profit-making religious institution."

"I don't know anything about them," Pieter said. "Except they run this mine like a concentration camp." He looked closely at Valerie.

"Sorry if they're your friends. No offense."

"They're not friends of mine," Valerie assured him. "I'm here to find out how an American church ended up with a diamond mine in the Congo. It's not the norm, not by a long shot. From your description, it sounds like there may be more to the story. Are the workers mistreated?"

She could tell Pieter was weighing his response, probably still not sure if he could trust her or not.

"Worse than I've ever seen anywhere," he finally answered. "Why don't you come in out of the bloody sun? I'll tell you about it. It's a little cooler in the shade."

As they followed Pieter into the breezeway, Valerie noticed the board game the two men had been playing when they drove up. The board had two rows of carved depressions and a larger one at each end. There were green seeds, like peas, in several of the cups and white beans in others. "What are you playing?" she asked the one-legged man.

"It is mancala," the man said. "Would you like to play?"

"Sometime. But you would have to teach me," Valerie said. She held out her hand. "I'm Valerie Grey. What is your name?"

"I am Joseph Karim," the man said, taking her hand as if he were afraid it might break.

"Just don't bet with the one-legged bastard," Pieter said with a smile. "He's taken a small fortune off me today." The man grinned and Valerie laughed.

"I'll keep that in mind," she said. Pieter didn't seem as defensive as he had a few minutes before. In the breezeway was a bench made from rough planks resting on wooden crates and a table with benches on either side of it. It was considerably cooler in the shade. Valerie and Nancy sat at the table with Pieter. "So what can you tell me about the way the church runs the mine?"

"I haven't seen anything like it since I was a boy. I grew up in South Africa, on a farm on the Vaal River north of Kimberly. Even DeBeers didn't treat its workers the way Alben does."

"Who is Alben?" Nancy asked.

"Thomas Alben. 'Brother Tom' he calls himself. He's the bastard they sent over here from America to run the mine. He's supposed to be a missionary, but I've never seen him crack the Good Book."

Nancy unobtrusively made a note.

"What does he do to the miners?" Valerie asked.

"I've not seen the abuse with my own eyes," Pieter said, "but the men are kept in barracks and fed once a day. They pay them next to nothing. The place is full of soldiers, but I don't know if they're there to protect the mine or keep the miners in line. He's put two chain link fences around the whole place with bare ground in between so nobody can pass any stones to someone outside. If a man gets hurt and can't work, they just throw him out. That's how Joseph got here. His foot was mangled by a piece of machinery. It wasn't too bad, but it got infected. When they found out he couldn't walk on it, they literally dragged him outside the mine gates and left him there. One of the villagers brought him here and we took the leg off. If he'd received proper treatment in the first place, his foot would have healed."

Valerie turned to Joseph. "What will you do now?" she asked.

"I will go home," he said.

"You don't live in Mai-Munene?" she asked.

"I am from Luiza. My daughter is there."

"We've sent word," Pieter explained. "He's waiting for her to come get him."

Valerie knew the sad history of the Congo under King Leopold of

Belgium; the hippopotamus-hide whips, the hands chopped off for not working hard enough, the sepia-tinted photographs of men shuffling through the jungle in chains beneath the haughty eyes of their pith-helmeted overlords. Valerie hoped Bobby wouldn't be shooting scenes like that in living digital color and sending them back to New York via satellite.

"I can't wait to ask Alben a few pointed questions," Valerie said. "But first, can we help Joseph in some way? Mr. Sami, could you drive Joseph to Luiza? I would pay you."

"I am sorry, but my truck would not survive such a journey. Luiza is too far," Mr. Sami said.

"I think my daughter will come on the river," Joseph said.

Pieter added. "To come by road, she'd have to loop all the way round back through Tshikapa. There's no such thing as public transport, so she'd have to walk most of the way. Hopefully, she can hire a mokoro. That's a canoe. It's well over a hundred kilometers on the river. Maybe twice that by road. And there are more bad guys on the roads too. The river is safer."

Mr. Sami interrupted apologetically. "I am afraid I must be going, madame. It is getting late and the lights on my truck are not illuminating. Do you wish to return to Tshikapa? You can spend the night with my family and I can take you in the morning if you wish."

Before Valerie could answer, Pieter jumped in. "You can stay here tonight," he offered. With a nod to Bobby, he added, "You can bunk with me if you don't mind a bit of a snore. And you ladies can use Jaime's room. He'll be back tomorrow, though, so we'll have to rearrange the accommodations if you stay any longer."

"I thought you said you didn't know when he would get back," Valerie said.

"Sorry, love. You caught me. That was a fib," Pieter said sheepishly. "We're all a little more careful of what we say and who we say it to these days. Between the rebels and the gangs and the army—not to mention the missionary and his mine—you don't know who you can trust."

Valerie smiled. "I understand," she said.

"Jaime stopped at the refugee camp in Bukedi on his way back from Kinshasa," Pieter added. "They radioed and said he was going to help them out for a couple of days. He'll be here tomorrow."

That sealed the decision for Valerie. "Thank you for your kind offer, Mr. Sami. We will stay here."

Chapter 6

Mai-Munene

The next morning, Valerie organized her notes while Nancy set up the satellite phone to call New York so she could let MBS know where they were and what they were working on. After she disconnected, Nancy said, "The evening news producer wasn't thrilled with the story of the minister and the diamond mine, but he said to send the package as soon as we can get it put together if that's the best we could do. I told him to stuff it up his ass, since that was obviously the only thing he knew how to do."

Valerie shook her head but grinned as her irreverent friend continued. "Then he told me Carter Wilson wants us to come home as soon as we file the story since there doesn't seem to be much hard news in the Congo at the moment. You don't want to know what I told him then. You're too nice a girl."

Nancy's eyes lit up with devilish sparkle as she added, "David Powell left a message for you, too"

"What was it?" Valerie asked.

"He said, 'I'm ready for Cape Charles, are you?'" A knowing grin spread across Nancy's face. "What is that supposed to be? Some kind of secret code? Let me guess … it means, 'I want to jump your bones on the Eastern Shore.'"

Valerie scowled at her.

Nancy threw her arms up in mock defense. "Hey, boss, sorry. I didn't mean it!"

Valerie's scowl disappeared. "No, I'm sorry," she apologized. "I know you were kidding. It just touched a nerve. Thanks for the message." The nerve Nancy touched was the one already inflamed by Valerie's guilt for not having thought about David for the last several days. David and Valerie were close. She liked to imagine his intelligent eyes watching her, his understanding visage encouraging her as she reviewed her questions before an interview or pondered which line of inquiry would produce the most enlightening quotes. After an on-camera appearance, she often mentally checked with him to see how she'd done. Valerie counted having David in her life among her blessings. Good thoughts or bad, happy or sad, Valerie had always considered David's constant presence in her mind as a sign of love. On much of this trip, though, David had been far from her thoughts for some reason. Now she felt guilty.

Nancy didn't let her dwell on it. "Apology accepted," she said. "Are we going to pay a little visit to the missionary of the mines this morning?"

When an American television crew showed up demanding entrance to the mine compound, Thomas Alben thought the guard at the gate had lost his mind. "What do you mean there are American television reporters here?" he shouted into the telephone that connected the gatehouse to his office. "Who are they? What do they want?" He stood with the phone to his ear and looked out the small window in the low concrete block building. He could see three people on the road on the other side of the pole barrier blocking the entrance. One of them did, indeed, have a television camera with the MBS-TV logo on his shoulder pointed into the compound. As Alben watched, the camera swung around until it seemed to be aimed directly into his window. He instinctively stepped back out of sight. "Don't let them in!" he ordered. He slammed the handset into its cradle and stormed into the next room.

Joao de Santos looked up from a mine production report he was puzzling over. It fell from his hands when he saw Alben's face. "Is something wrong?" he asked.

"There are people at the gate. Get rid of them," Alben ordered.

"Who are they?" de Santos asked.

"They say they're reporters," Alben answered distractedly while looking back toward the door as if they were following him. Then he exploded. "What difference does it make! I said get rid of them!"

"Yes sir!" De Santos jumped from his seat and rushed out of the office.

Alben went back to his window to watch de Santos scuttle toward the gate. Now was not the time for reporters, American or otherwise, to be snooping around. Production at the mine was finally beginning to respond to Alben's "management methods" but the results weren't anything he or his boss wanted spread across the pages of the *Wall Street Journal*. They particularly didn't need publicity about the mine—positive or negative—while delicate meetings were under way in the White House. With rebel forces moving closer every day and Messime's army proving less and less capable of protecting the mine, those negotiations had to come to a fruitful conclusion soon. Alben watched de Santos stiffen his back as he approached the gate.

Valerie waited patiently as the man unlocked an inner gate and walked up to them. He didn't open the outer gate. A soldier from the guardhouse stood behind him with his automatic rifle at the ready.

"May I help you?" the man demanded officiously through the fence wire.

"I'm Valerie Grey with MBS News," she said. "Are you Thomas Alben?"

"No. I am Joao de Santos. I am the mine manager. Reporters are not allowed on this property. You must leave now." Message delivered, he turned to walk away.

"We're not going anywhere," Nancy said. "You better ask Brother Tom if he wants the congregation in Atlanta to hear about his slave camp."

The mine manager turned back with a scowl. "What do you mean?" he said.

"She means I'm going to report that workers are mistreated here," Valerie bluffed. "We have pictures of abused miners and reports of forced labor. If I can't visit the mine and see otherwise, that's what I'll report on American television."

"Wait here," de Santos said. He went into the guardhouse and picked up the intercom.

"You scared him silly," Nancy said.

Valerie shook her head. "I don't think it's me he's afraid of."

While de Santos was inside, an F.I.C. truck came through the village and pulled to a stop at the gate. A barrel-chested Congolese officer stepped down from the front seat. He barked an order and a squad of men jumped from the back and surrounded Valerie and her crew. The officer was a giant of a man with fierce tribal scars across his forehead and cheeks. A large carton was tucked securely under his arm.

Apparently, he didn't want to leave it in the truck while he got out to deal with the visitors. It looked like it was wrapped for mailing, but Valerie couldn't tell.

"What is going on here?" the officer demanded.

"We are reporters from America," Valerie answered. "Who are you?"

"You have no business here," he said. "Leave before I have you shot." He made the threat as calmly as if he were telling her it was closing time at the library. Valerie didn't doubt for a second that he would carry out his threat, but her sense of the situation told her they were still several steps away from gunfire. She played for time, careful not to challenge him by directly refusing his order.

"We're here to see Thomas Alben," she said. The officer didn't respond. "Bobby, are you getting this?" Valerie asked coolly without breaking eye contact with the captain.

"You bet," the videographer answered. He made a slight adjustment to the camera perched on his shoulder. When the F.I.C. captain turned to glare at Bobby, Valerie saw the label on the carton under his arm. It had an address in Alexandria, Virginia. She whispered to Nancy, who calmly flipped open her ever-present notebook and jotted it down for future reference.

"You are not authorized. Leave now." He nodded sharply to the soldiers surrounding the three Americans. The safeties on the automatic weapons clicked, most of them just once, meaning they were on full automatic. One of the soldiers put his rifle to his shoulder, aiming it at Valerie's face.

"Captain Yoweri!" a jovial voice called just then from the other side of the fence inside the compound. "That is no way to treat a famous television reporter from America!"

Valerie turned to see a tall, corpulent man waiting for a soldier to open the gates. He was nearly as big as the F.I.C. captain but not as well-conditioned physically. He didn't have tribal tattoos, either, but he didn't need them; his eyes were menacing enough on their own. The cold, piggy orbs gave the Jesus-loves-me smile on his face a feral twist. Valerie wondered how far she would be able to push him before he started biting back.

"Are you Thomas Alben?" Valerie asked levelly, her voice betraying no sign that an AK-47 was aimed at her head.

"Yes, I am. The Reverend Thomas Alben. But you can call me Brother Tom," he added with a deprecating nod. "And you, of course, are the beautiful and famous Valerie Grey. I have often admired you on television." He motioned for the soldiers to lower their rifles. "Your men can stand down, Captain. I'm sure Miss Grey and her friends pose no threat to us."

Yoweri didn't change expression. He jerked his head toward the truck and the soldiers climbed back in. The truck pulled through the gates, but Yoweri stayed behind. He held onto the package, too, Valerie noticed.

"Would you like to come in?" Alben asked. "I hate to see a pretty girl like you left standing in the road." They walked into a smaller fenced area that functioned somewhat like an airlock inside the main fence. The tall gates were topped with razor wire as were the two chain-link fences that stretched around the compound. Valerie felt like she was stepping into a prison.

"It looks like you run a pretty secure facility here, Reverend," Valerie said.

"These are dangerous times in the Congo, Miss Grey," Alben said. "By the way, just to set the record straight, I don't run the mine. The manager is Mr. de Santos here. I am just a simple missionary from the

Church of the Holy Angels. That said, what can I do for you?"

"We're here to do a story about why a church in Atlanta owns a diamond mine in the Congo," Valerie said. "Could you tell me how that came about?"

"The best person to answer that question is our Pastor, Gary Peterson," Alben said. "But I believe President Messime offered him the opportunity to invest in the mine as a gesture of his appreciation for the Holy Angels Crusade Reverend Peterson brought to the Congo. The Crusade brought thousands of our Congolese brothers and sisters to Christ. It also demonstrated to the world that the Congo isn't some dark hellhole populated by cannibals. The mine was not a gift, by the way. The church invested heavily in it in hopes that its profits will fund our relief work in Africa and elsewhere."

"What kind of relief work?" Valerie asked.

"Schools, hospitals, churches, that sort of thing," Alben answered vaguely.

"I didn't see anything like that when we drove through here yesterday," she pointed out.

Alben paused to weigh his words. "These things take time, Miss Grey. The mine is just now beginning to be productive. You will see more as the cash flow improves. Would you like to tour the facility?" he asked, changing the subject. "It's actually quite interesting."

"I'm sure it is," Valerie answered.

"If you'll excuse me for just a moment, I have some business with Captain Yoweri," Alben said. He stepped out of earshot with the officer. A moment later he returned to the news crew while Yoweri walked toward the mine office.

"Say, what's the captain got in the box? The crown jewels?" Nancy asked.

Alben glared at her sharply for a moment, then chuckled mirthlessly. "Those are dolls," he said. "They were made by our village women. It's one of the betterment programs we started in an abandoned building. I'm quite proud of it."

"That sounds interesting," Valerie said. "Perhaps we can visit it later."

"Ahhhh, yes, perhaps," Alben said.

Valerie noticed his reluctance. Behind her, Nancy whispered, "Why would you ship dolls to the Washington suburbs?"

Alben insisted on driving them the short distance from the headquarters to the mine. "This is the main deposit," he said when they arrived. He pointed to a shallow pit in the earth the size of three football fields placed end to end. Black smoke poured from an old earthmover gouging up loads of the dry red dirt and dropping it into a waiting dump truck. As they watched, another truck drove slowly down a narrow ramp into the pit. It was difficult to make out a lot of details from the distance because a thick cloud of dust mixed with oily smoke from the equipment filled the air. "This is an alluvial mine, which means the diamonds are found in kimberlite gravel that was washed here by an ancient river rather than in pipes that are pushed up from the ground by volcanic action like you'll find in the big mines in South Africa. What you are looking at is the old river bed. The Kasai's channel now is beyond that rise." He pointed in the direction the second truck had come from. "The processing plant is over there too."

Alben drove them up the dusty road to a row of concrete block buildings connected by an enclosed conveyor belt. When Valerie got out of the jeep, she felt the ground vibrating under her feet. The noise outside the buildings was deafening; she cringed when she imagined how loud it was inside. A dump truck backed up a ramp to the end building. It emptied its load onto a platform where a gang of men waited with rakes and shovels. As they pushed the gravel back and forth on the platform, most of it fell through to the conveyor running beneath them, which carried it into the building. Valerie noticed that about half of the men didn't have shoes or even the rubber sandals made from old tires worn by many Congolese. Instead, their feet were heavily wrapped with cloth, she assumed to keep the grid of the platform from cutting into their feet, although it would provide no prtection at all against a wayward rock tumbling out of the dump truck. All of their faces were wrapped with cloth from the eyes down to help keep the dust out of their lungs.

Alben continued his explanation, shouting over the racket. "We scrape up the gravel and run it through the machine you see there—called a grizzly—to screen off large rocks. Inside, the gravel is fed into another machine, a dense media separator, which further segregates the gravel from the diamond-bearing rock. In the next building, the magnetic material is removed and the concentrate is classified into three sizes. Finally, it goes to the last building where it is fed through the Flowsort. That's a very sophisticated X-ray machine for recovering diamonds. We have to process about a ton of gravel to find four carats of diamonds. Put another way, it takes nearly three tons of gravel to produce diamonds that weigh about as much as a dime."

"For a minister, you know a lot about mining technology," Valerie shouted back.

"Just because I am a man of God doesn't make me ignorant of the ways of industry and commerce, Miss Grey."

Bobby touched Valerie's arm and pointed past the buildings to a treeless ridge where Nancy stood waving to attract her attention. She had slipped off to explore while Alben was expounding.

"What's over there?" Valerie asked.

"Just another deposit in the river bed," Alben said. "There's really nothing to see." But Valerie and Bobby were already on their way.

An entirely different vista lay over the ridge, which marked the high-water channel of the Kasai River. The river glinted beneath the sun in the narrow channel it followed during the dry season. Between the river and the ridge, hundreds of men worked in a trench dug into the gray mud of the ground water that lay deep below the dry topsoil of the riverbed. Every man in the trench was coated with mud. The trench walls were higher than their heads in most places. Some stood thigh-deep in the slurry at the bottom, filling sieve-like buckets with the ooze, letting the water drain off, then handing the heavy containers up the line like a bucket brigade. A dump truck waited at the end of the line on firmer ground on top of the ridge. One by one, the dripping buckets were emptied into it and handed back down. Overseers stood under umbrellas all along the line, one in every ten men or so watching, Valerie supposed, for any miner who might spot a gem in the muck and slip it into his pocket. It was a scene from a hundred years ago, contrasting darkly with the highly mechanized operation she had just seen.

"If you have to move three tons of gravel to find a dime, this looks like a very inefficient way to do it. What's going on here?" Valerie asked as Alben joined them on the ridge.

"We have to work this deposit by hand," Alben said. "The ground won't support heavy equipment."

"Or is it just cheaper to use manual labor?" Valerie said. "This looks like the way you run a mine when you have very little regard for human life."

"Just the opposite, Miss Grey," he answered brusquely. "We're giving hundreds of men jobs that wouldn't exist if the entire operation were mechanized."

The trench looked unstable to Valerie; there were a few piles of rubble sticking above the surface water at the bottom where a section of the side wall had fallen in. "Wouldn't there be a tremendous loss of life if those trench walls collapsed?" Valerie asked. She found herself on the edge of outrage at Alben's blatant rationalizations.

"Perhaps," Alben answered. "But we take precautions."

"What kinds of precautions?"

"We have an early warning system further up the river so they can evacuate in case a flood threatens. Also lifelines. We provide them for every man."

Valerie thought the early warning system sounded like something Alben had just made up on the spot, but she couldn't disprove it. The lifelines, though, were obviously a figment of his imagination. "I don't see any lifelines on anybody," she pointed out.

"The men won't wear them," Alben answered quickly. "We can't force them, you know. Regulations. The Congolese are very touchy about how the workers are treated. It's a holdover from the colonial era. You can't make them do anything."

"That sounds like a convenient excuse," Valerie said. "What do the regulations say about locking them into a labor camp?"

"Miss Gray! I'm offended. As I explained earlier, conditions force us to maintain tight security for the good of the entire operation. If these men were allowed to come and go at will, we'd never be able to keep subversive elements out. Next thing you know, there would be armed rebels inside the compound." Alben noticed Bobby panning his camera across the grim landscape. "Let's move along," he said.

Valerie took another long look at the men grubbing in the muck like mudworms, eating ever deeper through the slime. She marveled at the amount of dirty, dangerous toil they did in quest of a minute chip of carbon to grace the earlobe of a debutante in some cold, dry land far away. As she watched, one of the men lost his footing as he tried to hand his heavy bucket to another man perched on the lip of the trench. The second man reached to grab the bucket, missed, and toppled over the edge onto him. They rolled in a tangle of arms and legs into the mire at the bottom, the bucket tumbling with them. An overseer shouted angrily as they struggled to their feet, waist deep and sputtering as they choked on the thick ooze. In a moment, they had resumed their places in the relentless line.

"You see, no harm done," Alben said.

Valerie said, "I'd like to see where they live."

The barracks were long, low buildings that, from the outside, looked like the living quarters on every army base Valerie had ever seen except for the thatch roofs that covered them. Inside, though, they were different. Rows of rough wooden beds lined both walls, their thin, stained mattresses leaving just enough space between them for a man to stand to take off his filthy clothes at the end of the day. The narrow aisle down the middle was cluttered with discarded rags, odd, worn-out sandals cut from old tires, and the general rubbish left by the men who slept there. The only light came from the door at one end and a window at the other. Bobby got some footage near the door, but the rest of the building didn't have enough light for his camera, even in the middle of the day. The air was close and dank with the odor of disconsolate bachelors who toil in the mud from sunrise to sunset every day, an earthy, sweaty stench tinged with urine long soaked into the hard-packed dirt floor. It mingled with the sour smell of the rotting thatch above their heads.

"Is this the best you can do?" Valerie asked once they were outside again.

"The barracks are no different from the mud huts these men call home," Alben said dismissively. "This isn't New York, Miss Grey, it's Africa."

"What about sanitary facilities?" Nancy asked.

"The latrines are on the other side of the hill. Come with me so you can see where the men are fed," Alben said. He led them between buildings to an open yard. Along the far side of the small clearing was an open-sided pole shelter, also with a thatch roof, where a kitchen crew was cleaning up, scrubbing huge pots and utensils in vats of soapy water. "We give them two hot meals, one morning and one evening, every day." Anticipating a question, he added, "We feed them the same things their little wives and mothers would feed them at home. *Nsima*—that's cornmeal porridge—or *fou-fou*, which is made from cassava tubers. Also greens, chicken or fish, a typical native diet."

Valerie looked back at the barracks they had just passed. Heavy iron rings were set into the mud walls on either side of the windows. The walls around the rings were scuffed and blotched with dark stains, the ground beneath them muddy as if someone had poured water on them just a few minutes before. When she looked down the row of barracks buildings, she saw identical rings on each one. Some were dry beneath; it looked like the walls themselves were wet around some of the others. Valerie walked over to the nearest one and lifted the heavy ring away from the wall. It was large enough to fit her fist through the center, the iron as thick as her thumb. She noticed it was worn smooth, not pitted and crusted with rust like everything else in the Congo. "What are these for?" she asked.

Alben shook his head as if the sight saddened him. "Those are left over from the bad old days," he said, "when less humane managers used to flog their miners. Or worse. As you can see, they are in full view of the mess. That is so the other men could learn a lesson while they ate."

"They don't look very old to me," Valerie said. "And why is the ground wet? It looks like they were just washed."

Alben blinked in the sun. "Oh, that's from when we sprinkle the yard to keep down the dust."

Valerie didn't buy that explanation. She made sure Bobby shot some close-ups.

"Let me show you our little doll-makers," Alben said. He seemed anxious to change the subject.

The doll workshop was outside the mine compound in a two-room building that Alben explained he found abandoned when he got there. The outer room was more of a covered patio, with half-height walls under a tin roof. A handful of soldiers lounged on benches under the roof. Valerie noticed several others standing near the grated windows of the other room, which was fully enclosed. The soldiers jumped up alertly when Alben's jeep rolled into view.

Inside, a group of women sat in a rough circle on the hard-packed dirt floor sewing by hand in the light from the windows. Small piles of worn cloth lay next to each woman. A table with a container of plastic pellets, a funnel, and a large shallow bowl stood at one end of the room in front of a blackboard with a list of names with marks next to them. Valerie assumed the marks tallied each woman's production. A soldier sat behind the table like a bored schoolteacher in a camo cloth uniform. A small row of completed dolls was lined up beside him. Another soldier stood behind him against the wall with a clipboard in his hand.

The women were chatting quietly but stopped when Alben and Valerie came into the room.

"Good morning, ladies," Alben puffed officiously. "This is a television reporter from America. She's going to make you famous."

Valerie gave him an annoyed look and knelt among the women as Bobby pulled his camera from its case. "My name is Valerie Grey," she said. "Thank you for allowing us to film you. We want to know about your work. How long have you been making these dolls?"

The women exchanged shy glances until one, who looked to be the oldest, spoke up. "We always made *minkisi*. They are from the old time."

"I am Valerie. What is your name?" Valerie asked.

"I am Kafutshi," the old woman answered.

"You call your dolls '*minkisi*,'" Valerie said. "What does that mean?"

"'*Minkisi*' is the word for many dolls. '*Nkisi*' is one. *Nkisi* is a spirit vessel. In the old time they held powers for the *nganga*. Sometimes they held earth from the graves of our ancestors. The *nkisi* could be used to heal. Others could be used to talk to the dead. Some are carved from wood. Others are made from gourds or horns. These are made from cloth."

Valerie was intrigued. She picked up a partly-sewn doll. "Does this one have powers?" she asked.

Kafutshi looked at the *nkisi* seriously. "Oh no. The power of the *nkisi* comes from what is within it. The *nganga* puts powerful relics inside. These are like the ones we made for the children to play with. Or for the traders. Now we make them only for Brother Tom."

"Why did you switch?" Valerie asked.

"Brother Tom pays more," Kafutshi answered with a worldly grin. The other women nodded.

"What does he do with them?" Valerie asked.

"We ship them to Atlanta," Alben jumped in. "You'll find them in the gift shop at the Church of the Angels. The profits go toward our African relief programs."

A small alarm sounded in Valerie's head. If the dolls were sent to Atlanta, why was the captain's box addressed to a Washington suburb?

"Really?" she said, trying to hide her interest by sounding bored.

"Oh, yes. I send them to Reverend Peterson directly. He takes a personal interest. He actually keeps one on his desk. He sees the dolls as a symbol of God's bounty."

"I'm sure," Valerie said. She turned back to Kafutshi. "Would you show me how you made this *nkisi?*"

Kafutshi held up a scrap of faded but clean cloth. "We cut the cloth to the proper shape, then sew them together very, very tightly so nothing can leak out. Up to here." She showed Valerie an open seam in the back. "Then we take them to the soldier. He puts the special pellets for America inside. In the very old days, the *nganga* would put bones from our ancestors in them. It was good to keep it with you at all times so you could be near them. For the traders, we stuffed the *nkisi* with corn husks and dried grass, but now we use the special pellets from Brother Tom."

Kafutshi pulled a line of stitches tight, then took her nearly completed *nkisi* to the soldier at the table. Valerie followed while Bobby framed a shot of the table with the blackboard behind it. When the camera turned to him, the soldier jumped up and preened. Kafutshi handed him the *nkisi* and pointed to the container of pellets.

"What do you mean, 'special pellets'?" Valerie asked.

"We have to use inert materials to pass the agricultural products inspection at customs in the States," Alben interrupted again. He had moved closer when Kafutshi went to the table.

"I see," Valerie said.

Kafutshi held the *nkisi* over the large shallow bowl while the soldier carefully poured pellets through a funnel into its back. When it was full, a few overflowed into the bowl. He poured them back into the container. "Then we sew up the hole," Kafutshi said as she took several quick stitches while holding the doll over the bowl under the watchful eye of the soldier. Finally, Kafutshi wrapped a small scrap of blue and orange-patterned cloth around the figure over the seam, covering it from the chest to the feet like a *pagne*, the traditional dress worn by both men and women. Then she took another swatch of the same material and wrapped it around the head, fashioning a complex scarf. When she finished, she held it up for Valerie.

The *nkisi* was more than just a rag doll. It held one arm down along its body, the other outstretched to the side as if it were pointing to something in the distance. The body was wrapped with the *pagne*, but the feet dangled loosely from beneath it, ready to walk or run or dance. A sliver of red corduroy was turned up at the ends to make smiling lips. Small scraps of black felt were tack-stitched to white circles for eyes, which looked heavenward as if the *nkisi* were laughing at some celestial joke. Valerie took it in her hand. She felt the special pellets moving beneath the cloth like live things. They weren't soft like she expected. She was charmed by the mirthful expression on the doll's face.

"May I buy this one?" Valerie asked.

"No, sorry," Alben said quickly. He took it from her abruptly and handed it to the soldier. "We need that one for a rush shipment. Perhaps you can get one from the next batch."

Before Valerie could protest, the soldiers in the next room started shouting. Three children burst through the door. A sobbing girl in a ragged yellow dress dragged twin boys across the room, chased by two soldiers from outside. The children fell into Kafutshi's arms.

"Celestine!" Kafutshi exclaimed. "What happened? Where is your mother?"

"We were walking with mama when they came," the girl began breathlessly.

Chapter 7

Mpala

"Who came?" Kafutshi demanded.

"The men in the big truck," Celestine answered. "When they came on the road we ran to the forest, but ... but ..." Her eyes took on a vacant stare. Kafutshi shook her gently.

"Start from the beginning," the old grandmother urged. "Where were you?" Celestine focused on Kafutshi's face. Valerie could see her struggle with memories she could only want to forget. With a shudder, the girl went on.

"We were walking to your village to make *minkisi*. Mama said she didn't want to, but she was afraid."

"Afraid of what?" Kafutshi prodded.

"She said the Lunda Libre would come where we live and take the boys some day. Maybe me too, she said." The words started tumbling faster and faster. "They killed papa and now our field is no good and we have no money for school or food or ..."

"Stop, girl," Kafutshi interrupted. "That was before. What happened today?" Celestine focused again, frowning with the effort.

"We were walking on the road with the boys. Juvenal was a slow poke, so I pulled him along. Mama held Kenda's hand because he is a slowpoke too. Then we saw dust from the truck coming the other way.

"'Quick,' Mama said, 'Run for the trees!' She yanked Juvenal away from me and pushed me toward the trees. I ran and ran, just like Mama said. She ran behind me carrying the boys, but I ran faster. The truck came off the road after us. I jumped over the grass and dodged the thorn bushes but I tripped. The truck drove right at me, but Mama got there first. She fell on me with the boys and tried to cover us all up but the men jumped out of the truck and ran all around us yelling with their machetes and their guns and one man pulled his thing out of his pants, but Mama covered up my eyes with her hand.

"I heard one man order the others to put the boys and me in the truck. 'For later' he said. They pulled Mama away and carried us to the truck. I heard them dragging Mama to the trees. She cried for me, but I couldn't help her."

She stopped suddenly to cock her head as if she heard her mother's cry. The room was silent. Celestine looked back into her grandmother's eyes, sobbed once, and collapsed against her chest.

"Hush, hush, sweet baby," Kafutshi crooned. She rocked gently, all three children clinging to her.

Her voice muffled, Celestine said, "The bad men took us to the truck and left us there, so we ran away."

"You were very brave," Kafutshi said. "But you must tell me, where did this happen?"

Valerie could barely hear her response.

"Where the two roads meet."

The old grandmother seemed to grow even older as she stroked and cooed to the girl to soothe her. Her wrinkles deepened, her back bowed beneath the weight, as she absorbed the news of her own daughter's death. Celestine's sobs grew until they filled the schoolroom, joined in ululating chorus by the women sitting in the sewing circle on the floor.

They had each suffered their own tragedy, their own loss, their own family wounded by death or worse, disappearance. They absorbed the grief of Celestine and Kafutshi, put it with theirs in the bottomless vessel that was their own despair, and sang the universal dirge of mother death and daughter death.

Valerie felt assaulted by the tragedy. She was outraged and had to strike back at it; that was her way. She looked around the room and saw that Alben had left sometime during the horrible story. Valerie motioned to Nancy and Bobby and went outside, leaving the others to their grief.

She found Alben standing next to his Land Rover talking on a walkie-talkie. She heard him say something about putting the sentries on alert.

"Are you sending soldiers after the men who killed that girl's mother?" she demanded.

Alben clicked off the radio. "Of course not," he said. "We don't have guards to spare for chasing through the bush after Xotha's gang."

"Was that who did it?" Valerie asked.

"Him or someone like him," Alben answered. "They're all the same. Murdering thieves, every one of them."

Valerie exchanged glances with Nancy. At the mention of Xotha's name, a simple plan was half-formed. "Do you have any idea where this happened?" she asked Alben.

"I assume along one of the back roads toward Tshikapa. It could have been anywhere. I don't know where the girl came from."

Alben's lack of concern for Kafutshi and the children was blatant. While he stood outside buttoning up security for his diamond mine, they were crying out for the kind of succor a minister normally delivers. He didn't offer it, however, nor did he give any indication he even thought of it as part of his job.

Valerie's plan coalesced. She thought about asking him if they could borrow his Land Rover, then changed her mind in favor of direct action. "We're going to use your vehicle for a few hours. We'll be back," she declared. Taking the cue, Nancy stepped past Alben and jumped behind the wheel while Bobby climbed into the back with his camera. Valerie barely made it into the passenger seat before Nancy sped away. The surprised Alben shouted something after them, but Valerie couldn't make out the words.

Nancy sped through the village, honking the truck's horn once to scatter a small flock of chickens scratching in the road. Valerie turned to see if they were being followed, but there wasn't anyone coming—yet.

"Where are we going?" Bobby shouted, leaning forward and cradling his camera on his lap.

"To look for Xotha," Valerie said.

"What are we going to do if we find him?" he asked.

"Interview him, I hope," Valerie answered. "Ask him what he gains by killing mothers in front of their children."

"What are we going to do if he finds us first?"

"Duck and run like hell," Nancy said.

She drove for a few minutes into the countryside, past the small clearings where the brush and trees had been burned away so cassava and vegetables could be grown near the huts, then past larger fields where corn struggled to grow in the crusty soil. Farther from the village, she slowed as the Land Rover neared a crossroads. The undergrowth and trees that filled the landscape gave way to tall tufts of grass coated with the red dust from the road and finally gave way to a wide patch of bare earth where traders sometimes parked their trucks and handcarts to swap goods before going to the village markets. As Nancy slowed,

Valerie pointed to a pair of tracks through the grass obviously left recently by heavy tires. Nancy stopped the truck. Looking more closely, Valerie could clearly see where a big vehicle had left the road and driven across the grass toward the trees.

"These look like truck tracks," she said. "Follow them over there."

The Land Rover bumped over the mounds of grass along the track left by the truck. Nancy stopped at a bare patch of ground near the forest. It wasn't necessary to be an expert tracker to read from the lug-soled boot prints in the dirt that a group of men had gathered there. The boot prints ran through the sparse scrub on an old footpath. Peering into the trees, Valerie spotted a swath of blue cloth on the ground a few yards up the path.

"What's that?" she said, pointing. Just then, a man in a dirty white shirt jumped up from the blue cloth and dashed away into the trees.

"That guy looks familiar," Nancy said.

"Did he have a gun?" Bobby asked.

"Let's take a look," Valerie said.

They walked slowly into the woods, eyes swiveling back and forth on the lookout for other eyes watching them. A ripe coppery odor wafted through the trees. It grew stronger as they got closer to the blue cloth. Even from a distance, Valerie knew what it was. She covered her nose and mouth with one hand while she stepped closer. The blue cloth, a dazzling pattern of peacock feathers on a cerulean field, was a *pagne* draped carefully over the body beneath. A dark brown stain spread the length of the cloth, marking the shape of the torso. The mock eyes of the peacock feathers gleamed white through the dried blood. A matching head scarf, unmarked by blood, had been placed lovingly over the face as if to keep the person beneath from seeing what had been done to her body.

"I can't stand this," Nancy said, turning her head. A twig snapped. She looked up to see the man in the dirty white shirt watching them from behind a tree. "Hey!" Nancy called. "Can we talk to you?" The man bolted.

"Get the truck!" Valerie ordered. "Maybe we can circle around and find him."

They ran back along the path and climbed in. Nancy jammed the Land Rover into gear and took off through the tall clumps of grass. Valerie had to hold onto the dash with both hands to keep from flying out. Bobby cradled his camera in his arms to protect it while he bounced around unmercifully in the back. Nancy turned hard left around the stand of trees. Valerie pointed ahead to where the man trotted along the edge of the forest. Nancy stepped on the gas. The man heard them coming and started to duck back into the trees, then stopped. He looked at something deep in the forest, then back at the onrushing vehicle, undecided.

Just then, their left front wheel slammed axle-deep into a hole and the Land Rover came to an abrupt halt. Valerie caromed off the windshield and flew out the open side. She never felt the impact as she bounced hard then rolled over, her face buried in a clump of brittle grass.

Chapter 8
Atlanta

Alben waited impatiently for the telephone connection to Atlanta to go through. The bitch reporter was back in the village, banged up pretty good from what he heard. The cunt had lost his Land Rover, though, which pissed off Alben even more every time he thought about it. The bigger problem, though, was the rebel force getting ever closer to the mine. Moshe Messime's army was too busy keeping Kinshasa under control to provide any protection beyond the small force already in Mai-Munene under Yoweri. If Peterson wanted to hold onto his mine, Alben thought, their friend in Washington was going to have to hold up his end of the bargain. Alben was anxious to get things moving, but he wasn't too worried about getting the support they needed. As he waited for the call to go through, he remembered with some satisfaction how his idea had made the deal possible in the first place.

He'd revealed his scheme during his first trip back to Atlanta from Mai-Munene. Within his first few weeks in Africa, Alben had not only sized up the mine, but had figured out a way to leverage its profits exponentially. By the time he flew to Atlanta to report, he was ready with an eye-popping surprise for the Reverend Gary Peterson. He sprang it on him near midnight in Peterson's office in Atlanta.

The darkness outside had turned the floor-to-ceiling glass walls in Peterson's aerie into mirrors that eerily reflected the richly oiled paneling on the other side of the room and the huge wooden cross that dominated one corner. Watching his own reflection in the darkened glass, Alben had flicked open a razor-sharp pocket knife and flourished it like a hunter about to eviscerate a rabbit. Peterson chuckled nervously in anticipation. Alben jabbed the point of the knife just below the neck of a small rag doll and drew the blade carefully toward the crotch. The thin cloth parted.

"What a sweet fucking dolly," the evangelist said.

"With a sweet fucking surprise inside," Alben said as he finished slicing the doll open and carefully emptied the grains of plastic filler onto a sheet of white paper. The missionary sawed off the head and each arm and leg, turning them inside out over the paper to be sure every grain of filler was on the table. He pushed the empty, limp carcass to one side with his knife.

Alben felt the evangelist watching greedily as he poured the plastic pellets into a tall glass of water. A few of them settled to the bottom while most floated on top. "This cream doesn't rise, it sinks," Alben joked. He gently stirred the pellets floating on the surface so that a few more drifted down to the bottom. When the water stilled, he spooned the floating pellets out of the glass and into a bag for disposal. Then he poured the water through a sieve to catch the heavier grains that had collected on the bottom.

"Now let's see what we have here," Alben said. "Stand back. This acid isn't strong, but it might splash a little bit. You don't want it on your suit."

He carefully shook the contents of the sieve into a glass bowl full of clear liquid, where the mixture bubbled briskly for a few seconds. A film of dissolved plastic formed on the surface as a foul odor rose from the bowl. Several dozen pebbles of various pale colors and sizes settled to the bottom. Alben skimmed the plastic scum, then emptied the bowl through the sieve, leaving the pebbles. He carefully rinsed them with clean water and poured them onto a piece of blotting paper.

"I'd like to do the counting, Tom, if you don't mind," Peterson said. He carried the pebbles to his desk, where he weighed them on a small, very precise scale. He counted them out onto a green baize cloth. "Very nice," he said. "sixty-eight carats in fifty-two stones." He deftly inserted a loupe and held first one stone and then another in front of his eye. "These are nice. Assuming they're all gem quality as you say, that makes this little dolly's insides worth almost fifty thousand dollars, wholesale."

"We can ship a dozen dolls a week," Alben said.

Peterson took the loupe away and his eyes shone. "That's over two million dollars a month," he said.

"And your partner will never be the wiser," Alben added.

"Are you sure? How do you get the stones away from the mine without Messime finding out?"

The big missionary chuckled. "That wasn't hard. I reached an understanding with the captain of the troops Messime sent with me. His cut is pretty small in the grand scheme of things. The mine manager, de Santos, might be a problem sometime in the future, but he's not going to rock the boat until he's sure who's at the helm. Besides, he can't rat us out to anyone because we control all the communications. There is only one phone line, which is down half the time, and the captain took over that office as soon as he got there anyway. We rely on the army radio, mostly. And de Santos knows the captain would cut off his arm if he touched that."

"That's good. But won't Messime notice a drop in output if you start siphoning off this much every month?"

"We'll just step up production overall. De Santos says the place has been under-producing for a long time, especially gem-grade stones. As soon as I get back, I'm going to send the army out to recruit more workers. We're going to get some real work out of the simple bastards for a change too." He relished the motivational techniques he could use while he operated beyond the reach of civilization. He suspected that Yoweri, the F.I.C. captain, would have some ideas of his own along those lines. During the brief time he'd known him, Alben had come to appreciate the man's brutal sensibilities. "With a little pressure on the workforce, I can crank up the output and the skim will never be missed." Peterson nodded approvingly. "By the way," Alben continued, "U.S. customs sniffed around the doll for dope and explosives, but that was about it. They wouldn't see anything but plastic pebbles if they opened it up anyway."

"Excellent!" Peterson smiled. "I knew you were the right man for this job. This has all turned out even better than I expected." He leaned back in his over-sized leather chair.

Brother Tom had first connected with Peterson as the bank officer handling his accounts several years before. When he saw how much money Peterson legally raised for the church and then semi-legally siphoned off for his personal accounts, Alben developed a sudden religious calling. He asked for a job with the church. Peterson was impressed by Alben's facility with funds and his flexible morality, so he arranged for his ordination, made him an assistant pastor with responsibility for church finances, and used him for several transactions where discretion was paramount. He became Peterson's chief fixer.

In his own cynical way, Alben admired the evangelist. The Reverend Gary Peterson, corporate and spiritual leader of the Church of the

Angels, had taken over a two-bit revival-tent ministry and built it into a worldwide institution larger than half the corporations listed on the New York Stock Exchange. His daily TV programs had an audience numbering in the millions in the United States and were translated into six languages for broadcast around the world. The Holy Angels University had several thousand tuition-paying students and he had plans for building another campus in California. Contributions from believers rolled into his headquarters in Atlanta, pulled in by his cleverly presented broadcast appeals and a sophisticated ongoing direct mail campaign that would make a political fund raiser blush. And it was all tax-free, which made it quite lucrative to fund for-profit businesses with "loans" from the church treasury. Which is how Peterson got into diamonds.

Alben had joined the staff of the entrepreneurial evangelist about the time Peterson got his first taste of the riches in the Congo, when Ingaway Seto was still in power. The diamond mines were in the portfolio just long enough to give Peterson a taste for African wealth before Moshe Messime deposed Seto, nationalized everything, and gave Peterson's mine in Mai-Munene to the Namibians in return for their support. Peterson, denied his place at the Congo trough, had to bide his time until he could find a way back. Just before his buddy, President Billy Baker, started to campaign for re-election, Peterson took his Angel Crusade to Kinshasa, where he brought thousands of souls to Christ in a massive revival meeting. The next day, he and Alben met privately with Moshe Messime at his compound outside the capital for talks about more earthly concerns. Messime was not impressed by Peterson's frequent conversations with the Holy Ghost, but he had a deep appreciation for the preacher's direct line to the Oval Office. A deal was struck.

It wasn't long before Alben had visited the mine, sized up the potential profits and the dangers, and returned to Atlanta to show Peterson the doll filled with diamonds. After demonstrating the elegant simplicity of the scheme that night, he told Peterson that the biggest danger was the rebels.

"Messime can't handle them?" asked Peterson.

"Not without help. He's counting on it from Washington."

"Then he's one fucked monkey," Peterson said. "And so are we if Messime can't take care of them. When I asked Baker to send some troops after we cut the deal for the mine, he just laughed at me."

"Messime doesn't know that, I assume," Alben said.

"Of course not. We wouldn't have the mine if he did. I can string him along for a while."

"I don't know how much time you have. The country is falling apart around us."

Peterson scowled. "Goddamn, I hate the thought of losing that mine again. That's one of the sweetest fucking deals I ever got into."

"Maybe we need to share the wealth a little," Alben suggested.

"With Baker? He won't take a bribe. He's a practical man, but he's not stupid. He won't risk the presidency for money. Besides, his family could buy and sell the Congo and never notice the loss." President Billy Baker hadn't risen from a log cabin to the White House; his family's wealth dated back to one Captain Baker, who parlayed a single slave ship into a fleet of whaling vessels that eventually became a conglomerate that owned vast swaths of New England real estate, major defense contractors, and oil concessions in several Middle Eastern kingdoms. Billy Baker won the gene-pool lottery; the Oval Office legitimized him.

"What about his staff?" Alben asked. "There are a couple of guys who have his ear, aren't there?"

"I've got just the man," Peterson said. "Charles Hook."

The day after Alben's demonstration with the doll, he made a quick trip to Washington bearing a pouch of uncut diamonds as a gesture of Peterson's sincerity. The president's advisor gave him a scant quarter hour in his townhouse in Alexandria, Alben remembered, but that was long enough.

The phone clicked, bringing Alben back to the present and the growing danger in Mai-Munene. When Peterson came on the line, Alben didn't waste time with pleasantries. "The next shipment of dolls needs to go to Alexandria, not Atlanta," he said. "Tell your friend we need his help."

"How bad is it?" asked Peterson.

"There was an incident within a few miles of here today. I've been hearing rumors about Xotha moving this direction. We don't have a lot of time."

"I'll call in the chips. Any message for our friend?"

"Tell him the *minkisi* are *jaja*," Alben answered. "That means the dolls are dancing. It's time to send the cavalry."

"Very clever. Anything else?"

"Just a heads-up for you," Alben answered offhandedly. "There was a reporter here. Valerie Grey. You might know her from television." Alben sensed Peterson's alertness on the other end of the line. "Don't worry about it. The bitch stole my Land Rover, but she won't be telling any tales."

Chapter 9

Mai-Munene

Valerie's mother lay dying on a dirty Congo street surrounded by piles of burnt and blasted bodies of dead children. She needed a pillow, her mother whimpered; why wouldn't somebody give her a pillow? Valerie ran searching for one through the debris as an ancient smoke-belching earth mover crunched toward her mother, threatening to crush her under its cleated steel treads. She tried to turn away from the sour stench of the rotting children and run back to her mother to save her from the bulldozer, but she couldn't move.

Valerie awoke with a start. It wasn't a dream, at least not all of it. She really couldn't move; wide straps across her chest and legs held her fast. Another strap bound her head to the hard board beneath her. Her head throbbed. She closed her eyes and the stench came again. Someone was holding a bottle beneath her nostrils, forcing her to breath the gagging fumes. She choked and her eyes flew open.

She found Jamie Talon leaning over her. His expression was professional, but Valerie thought she detected some additional concern in his eyes not quite hidden behind their penetrating blueness. She tried to sit up, but the bindings held her down. Her eyes widened in panic.

"What is this!?" she croaked. She struggled against the straps. "Let me up!"

"Shhhh, it's okay," Jaime said soothingly. "Don't struggle."

She stopped. The sudden movement had set off a clangor in her head. It settled to a sick throb as he put a calming hand on her shoulder and she grew still. "You're strapped to a splint to immobilize your head and neck."

"You whacked your noggin pretty good, boss," Nancy said. She stood on the other side of the bed where Valerie lay bound to the board. Thick rolls of cloth braced either side of her head so she could move only her eyes.

"What happened?" Valerie whispered coarsely, her throat so dry it felt like it was cracked. "Can I have some water?"

"Just a sip," Jaime said. He held a plastic straw to her lips. She drew a mouthful of water and swallowed gratefully. Tepid as it was, the water was sweeter than anything she had ever tasted. She wanted more, but Jaime took the straw away. "Let's make sure that stays down first," he said.

"Are you okay? What happened?" Valerie repeated, shifting her eyes to Nancy. It was the only part of her body she could move and she felt rebellious already. She tried to wriggle a finger on her right hand. Thank goodness it moved.

"I hit an aardvark hole. Can you believe that shit?" Nancy said. "The jeep stopped short and you went flying. You whacked your head on the windshield, then you plowed into the ground face-first. I swear, I thought you were dead. You're going to need a little extra makeup for a while." Nancy lovingly brushed a stray lock of hair away from Valerie's forehead.

Some of the details started coming back—the bumpy ride across the grassy clearing, holding tight to the windshield frame to keep from being thrown out of the jeep, and Bobby bouncing all over the back with both arms wrapped around his precious camera. "Where's Bobby?" she asked. "Is he all right?"

"He's fine," Jaime said. "He was thrown clear but he made a soft landing. He scratched his eye in the elephant grass. It's not serious."

"He's pissed because the rebels got his camera, though," Nancy added. "They got Alben's Land Rover, too, while we were hiding with you in the bushes."

Valerie licked her parched lips and Jaime gave her another sip of the blessed water. "You have to stay quiet until we can get you to an X-ray machine. I think it's just a concussion and some trauma to your neck, but I can't be sure."

"How long?"

"There's a helicopter on its way from Kinshasa," Nancy said. "Should be here tomorrow. Then the network chartered a medevac flight back to New York." She grinned. "You should have heard them scream."

"Kind of blew Wilson's budget, huh?" Valerie said.

"Screw him and the budget he rode in on," Nancy said. "He's lucky you're alive." Nancy's eyes narrowed to their usual don't-tread-on-me squint as if she relished the idea of a fistfight with the president of the network news division.

"How did I get here?" Valerie asked. She willed one of her toes to move. It was almost numb, but she felt it press against the inside of her boot.

"Do you remember that guy with the dirty shirt? The one we saw near the body?" Nancy answered. "He saved our asses. He hid us in the woods, then he came and got Jaime."

"That was Siankaba, the *nganga* from Mpala," Jaime said.

"*Nganga?* What's that?" Valerie asked.

"He's a traditional healer," Jaime answered. "Siankaba also happens to be the headman of Mpala. That's sort of like the mayor. He was taking some hair from Felicitée's body to use in *minkisi* for her children when you saw him."

"Those little dolls like the women were making?" asked Nancy.

"Probably not. A *nkisi* can be any kind of vessel that holds spiritual things. He said he was going to put some of their mother's hair in amulets the children can wear around their necks to keep her spirit near their hearts."

"That's so sad," Valerie said. Her own condition didn't seem so dire.

"You need to rest," Jaime said.

"Can you at least untie my hands?" Valerie asked. "My nose itches."

Jamie ran his finger from the bridge of her nose to the tip, back up the left side and then down the right, then gave it a playful scratch on the tip. It was far from erotic, but Valerie enjoyed the touch.

"How's that?" he said.

She smiled. "Much better. But I still want my hands free, if you don't mind."

"You have to promise you won't untie anything else," Jaime said seriously. "You've got to stay still until we get a look at an x-ray."

"I promise," Valerie said.

"Good. Now get some rest." Jaime untied the cloth strips immobilizing Valerie's hands. "I'll look in on you later."

Valerie lay quietly in the hours before dawn, moving only her eyes as she passed the time figuring out how many ribs were in the tin sheeting above her head. There were twenty-four ribs to each sheet and the room was eight sheets wide. She did the math in her head. Four times eight is thirty-two, carry the three. Two times eight is sixteen plus the three makes nineteen. Stick the two on the end and you have 192 ribs. Now, she told herself silently, count them one by one to see if you are right.

Valerie really hoped she could be right about something for a change. Lately, it seemed, everything she touched went wrong. She had spent the last three weeks in the Congo, a place that teemed with the drama of human conflict and man's inhumanity to man, a brutal civil war fought over diamond mines and gold deposits, warlords, gangsters, tribal medicine men, starving children, motherless orphans, yet all she had managed to file were a couple of lame stories that could have been done by any rookie reporter with a passport. One, the interview with Messime, was nothing more than a vehicle for him to rehash the tired bombast of his corrupt regime. The other, the follow-up to the shelling in Kinshasa, consisted of useless official comments, her own unsupported suppositions, and flat footage of a day-old disaster scene. After that memorable performance, she had spent days of precious location time chatting up taxi drivers trying to get a line on a chimera who had probably been hiding right under her supposedly expert nose all the time. In desperation, she now recognized, she had tried to put together an exposé of something that was already publicly known; that Gary Peterson owned a diamond mine in the Congo. She may not have known about it, but no one seemed to be hiding it, so what kind of story was that? Conditions in the mine were pretty bad, she thought, trying to cut herself a little slack, but she couldn't even get a story about that on the air because all the footage had disappeared with Bobby's camera while she lay unconscious with her face in the dirt. What a mess I've made of it all, she thought.

She tried to concentrate on the ribs in the sheeting overhead, but she lost count. Start over, she told herself firmly. Start over like you should do with a new career. The one you have now is at a dead end, she thought. The loss of the anchor job to Preston Henry was a sign. It was a sign that Valerie Grey was all she was ever going to be, regardless of what David said.

Speaking of David, I'll probably botch that, too, she thought. She didn't know what she was going to say when she saw him next. She knew what he was going to ask her, but she didn't have a clue as to what her answer would be. That's assuming, of course, that she wasn't strapped helplessly to a board for the rest of her life.

Funny, she thought, I'm not too worried about that. If it happens, it happens. There's no one to blame for it, not even myself. A messed-up assignment is my fault; a twisted spine is just a bad throw of the dice. I can deal with it because I have to, that's all. It wasn't something I brought on myself by doing a poor job. I didn't dig that aardvark burrow in the wrong spot. Valerie Grey, brought to an ignominious end by a carelessly placed aardvark hole! The thought struck her just right and she laughed.

"What's so funny?" Jaime's amused voice came from the doorway. She started, her hands jumped off the bed and her body tensed, but she was still pinned down. He was silhouetted against the pale dawn light filtering through the doorway. He came into the room. How long had he been standing there? "Sorry, I didn't mean to startle you," he said.

Valerie's heart slowly stopped thudding in her chest. "That's okay," she said. "I'm fine."

Jaime took her wrist and checked her pulse, his fingers warm and dry. She didn't want him to let go. "Actually, I think you are," he said. "I don't want to give you false hope, but I really don't think you're hurt too badly. I just don't want to take any chances."

"Thanks, I appreciate your help," she said, then she realized how lame she sounded, like she was thanking the bag boy at the supermarket. She blushed. I'm screwing this up, too, she thought. Wait a minute! Screwing what up? Valerie felt like a schoolgirl. She felt herself blush.

"You never answered my question," Jaime said.

"Question? What question?" Valerie asked.

"The one I scared you to death with when I came in. What were you laughing at?" he asked again. Valerie forced herself to calm down. Then, her thoughts focused, she remembered. She laughed again.

"The aardvark hole," she said. "I was laughing at the damn aardvark hole. It's like something that would happen to Wile E. Coyote." She laughed again and Jaime laughed along with her, although a little politely, she thought. "Sorry," she said. "Guess you had to be there."

"I'm just glad you can laugh about it," Jaime said. "Not everybody could do that."

Valerie didn't know what to say, but that was all right because Jaime didn't seem to expect an answer. Finally, to fill the silence, she said, "Will the helicopter be here soon?"

"That's why I came in, to see if you were awake. It should be here any time now." Just then the whumping roar of the chopper blades sounded in the distance. Valerie wasn't sure she wanted to go.

Chapter 10

Cape Charles

David and Valerie discovered Cape Charles not long after he moved to Washington. The first time they went, they found the quaint old railroad town perfect for quiet weekends on Virginia's eastern shore and adopted one of its intimate bed and breakfasts as their own. The place was casual and just a little shabby around the edges, like the tiny town itself. The colorful couple who owned it served delectable breakfasts and provided a creaky porch full of rocking chairs. The old house was filled with antiques but free of electronic appliances other than a clock radio in each bedroom and a single television set in the parlor. Only a short bike ride away from the well-kept public beach on Chesapeake Bay, it was the perfect place for two people who wanted to escape the ugly things happening in the rest of the world so they could concentrate on each other. It was also the perfect place for Valerie to take the collar brace from around her neck at last. She was healed from the accident in the Congo and ready to get back to work. But first, she owed David a weekend.

Saturday passed perfectly, beginning with a lavish breakfast of mango pancakes and turkey sausage prepared by the considerate hostess. They borrowed the inn's rusty bicycles for a ride around town in the cool morning air, picked up sandwiches at the ancient deli on Main Street, and ate them later in the splintery gazebo overlooking the beach and sun-speckled bay. They went back to the inn for an afternoon nap. They made leisurely love when they woke up, then talked the proprietor out of a bottle of Pinot-Grigio and a couple of glasses to take back to the beach where they could watch the sun set over Chesapeake Bay.

Their favorite restaurant, the Pelican House, was blessedly free of boaters and other tourists that night. They chose a quiet booth away from a few locals occupying the tables next to the windows. After the waitress took their order, David reached across the table to cover Valerie's hand with his own.

"Happy?" he asked.

"Yes, very," she answered.

"Good," he replied. Before he could say anything else, the waitress came back with their salads and asked Valerie if she wanted freshly ground pepper. The girl seemed a little unsure of herself. Valerie wondered if she was new. When Valerie nodded, the waitress lifted a wooden grinder over her plate and twisted it a couple of times. David asked for some, too, but she ignored him. Valerie realized the girl was staring at her.

"I think I seen you on TV," the waitress finally said.

"Yes, I work for MBS News," Valerie answered with a friendly smile. It didn't happen often, but when a fan approached her in public, she appreciated the recognition. She didn't let it go to her head, but she wouldn't be human if she didn't get just a little charge out of it.

"I never waited on nobody famous before," the girl said.

"Thank you, but I'm not exactly famous. I just report the news,"

Valerie answered modestly.

"You're more famous than me, that's for sure." The waitress giggled nervously.

David cleared his throat.

"Oh, I'm sorry!" the girl exclaimed. "Did you want some pepper, hon?" Before he could answer, she swept the big pepper mill in his direction. It clipped the edge of Valerie's glass. Suddenly the tabletop was flooded with water. Valerie jumped out of her chair but wasn't quite quick enough to avoid the splash. "Oh damn! I'm so sorry," the waitress wailed. She pawed at the front of Valerie's skirt with her hands, trying to brush the water away.

"That's okay," Valerie laughed. "It's only water. No harm done." She gently took the girl's wrists and stilled her flailing hands. "Why don't you get a towel for me and we'll just move over there. Okay?" She smiled and held the flustered girl's eyes with her own until she settled down then let her go. "It's all right, really," she assured her. The waitress rushed away toward the kitchen, her head ducked in embarrassment. David shook his head and moved to the other table. Valerie shook her skirt before she sat down with him.

"I guess that's the price I pay for fame?" she asked.

"Something like that," David replied. The waitress came to the new table with fresh salads and retreated meekly. After a moment, David reached across the table and took her hand again. "Valerie, there was something I was about to ask you before all the …"

"I know," she interrupted. "Let's talk about it tomorrow, okay?" David withdrew his hand from hers.

"Sure," he answered, more than a touch of diappointment in his voice."

"Let's take a hike in the nature preserve tomorrow," Valerie said, changing the subject. They talked about nothing in particular the rest of the evening.

After dinner, lying in bed with David breathing softly by her side, Valerie puzzled over her feelings. She knew what he wanted to ask her but she was in such turmoil she didn't trust herself to make a decision. Her devotion to David wasn't in question; he was, in many ways, her idol. She admired his long career of superior reporting, much of it done in places where he got the story even though his life was in danger. He was a wonderful man with whom she shared a life just like the one she had escaped to in her dreams as a girl. He was a considerate, energetic lover, good looking in a mature way; they shared a love of the outdoors, fine food, and quiet evenings spent with a good book. Above all, she cherished his calm self-assurance. It made him a rock she could brace herself against. Valerie treasured David, but did she love him? She was haunted by fear that their professional relationship clouded her view of their personal one. She valued him as a mentor; she relished his companionship; she enjoyed his physical passion. But was that enough for love? She hated nights like this one when her mind refused to let her sleep.

The next day, David didn't give Valerie a chance to avoid the subject. They hiked the short Baywoods trail at Kiptopeke State Park, watching for deer and spring birds and puzzling over footprints left by a fox that seemed to have disappeared into thin air just after he crossed the path. They turned off the trail at the farthest boardwalk leading over the dunes onto the beach, deserted in the cool spring air. As soon as they spread their blanket on the sand, David said preemptively, "Let's get married."

Valerie didn't answer. She started to speak, then stopped, then turned instead to look at the cold blue water. She sat on the blanket and pulled her long legs up so that her chin rested on her knees. She didn't know what to say because she didn't know what she wanted. She loved David; but she wasn't sure she loved him enough to marry him. She wasn't ready.

"Someday," she said, unhappy with herself. She stared at the water so she didn't have to face the look of disappointment in David's eyes.

"That's a lousy way to say no," David said.

"It's not 'no,' David," Valerie tried to explain. "I love you. You know I do. I'm just not sure getting married is the best thing for me right now."

"We've been together for what, four years? How much time do you need?"

"I don't know," Valerie answered, getting a little defensive. "I also don't know why you're in such a hurry all of a sudden. I seem to recall a speech you made when you moved to DC. You said you were glad we were two people who didn't need a house in the suburbs or a marriage license." She caught herself before she said anything else.

"Touché," he replied. It was his turn to look at the water while he framed his response. "I'm not in any particular hurry; I just think getting married would deepen our relationship. I know that's a cliché and I'm not even sure what it means, but it's the only way I can say it. We're good together now—very good—but I think we could be even better. I guess that sounds like a line from a soap opera, but I don't know how else to express it. That's all I have to say. Think about it. That's all I ask."

"I will. I'm sorry, David," Valerie said.

"Me too."

They sat for a few more minutes in silence, each deep in their own thoughts. The sun rose high enough to take the chill off the air and David stood up. "We better head back," he said. "It's a long drive."

The TV was on in the parlor when they went back to the bed and breakfast to check out. As David settled the bill in the next room, Valerie idly watched President Billy Baker address the congregation in the Church of the Angels, the huge evangelical institution in Atlanta founded by Reverend Gary Peterson. The president, a born-again Christian who never missed a chance to tell the world about his miraculous conversion, stood behind a massive marble pulpit with Peterson posted two steps behind him. Framing Peterson and Baker was the largest stained-glass window in America, depicting Jesus Christ bottle-feeding a lamb with one hand while he lofted an American flag with the other. It was the same place the preacher stood during much of the preceding year's election campaign when Baker won re-election handily over a New England liberal candidate whose hopes of unseating the incumbent died the day after he was nominated. That was when Baker's campaign staff planted a rumor that the man had been accused of a homosexual incident during college. There wasn't a shred of truth to it, but the rumor knocked the legs out from under the candidacy within days.

Valerie was only half-tuned to the broadcast. She was steeped in guilt over David and angry with herself for being so uncharacteristically wishy-washy, but Baker said something that caught her ear. "David," she called into the other room, "come here a minute. You should hear this." He stepped into the room just as Baker raised his hand to quiet a round of thunderous applause. The president spoke:

"Yes, it is time, my fellow Americans, for us to stand before God and do the right thing. Not because there are American interests at stake, although there are, and not because our enemies are hard at work in this region, although they certainly are, but because it is only right that the mightiest nation on earth step in to protect one of the weakest. The Democratic Republic of the Congo has struggled for decades to get on its feet and realize its full potential as one of the great nations of the world, taking one step forward only to be pushed two steps back by thieving factions backed by greedy foreign powers. During that time, millions of people have been killed and millions more pushed into horrific living conditions, their only crime being the desire to live a simple, terror-free life. We cannot allow this injustice to continue. It is our duty, relayed to us through the Reverend Gary Peterson from the Master Of Justice himself, to step in and bring peace to this war-torn land."

Shouts and applause broke out in the congregation, led with gusto by the preacher standing behind the president.

"What is he talking about?" Valerie asked. "Is he sending troops to Africa?"

"God knows," David answered, reaching over to turn up the volume. Baker resumed as the applause died down.

"I am today sending American peacekeeping advisors to the Congo to help President Moshe Messime's armed forces hold the line against the evildoers who threaten to destroy that country. I also call on our allies around the world to join us in this holy war to stop the rape of this great African nation. To that end, I have instructed our ambassador to the United Nations to introduce a resolution in the Security Council endorsing our actions in the interests of world peace and am asking Congress for legislation authorizing the expenditure of sufficient funds to finance this holy endeavor.

"As Reverend Peterson has reminded us many times, it is our Christian duty to help the less fortunate. In the past, shamefully, the world stood by while nearly a million innocent people were slaughtered in Rwanda, while hundreds of thousands more were starved in Nigeria and untold numbers were murdered and driven from their ancestral lands in the Sudan. As long as we turn our gaze from these horrendous acts, they will continue. The peoples of Africa will never achieve their rightful place among the civilized nations of the world.

"I call for your support today, my fellow Americans, in standing up and saying, 'Look out, evildoers, America is coming!' Let us be heard loud and clear by those who would spread a cloak of violence over the world."

With a roar of approval, the congregation rose to its feet applauding madly while a massive choir blared out "Onward Christian Soldiers" and the Reverend Gary Peterson alternately pumped the president's hand and hugged him triumphantly.

"Where did all that crap come from?" Valerie asked. "American troops haven't set foot in Africa since Mogadishu! And Baker swore they never would!"

"I don't know. Something's not kosher," David answered. "We better get back. Do you mind driving so I can make some phone calls in the car?"

It didn't take long for them to load David's Saab and get on the road to Washington. While Valerie drove, David called the DC bureau to mobilize his staff around the breaking story. The assistant bureau chief had already arranged reaction interviews with various Congressional leaders and assorted self-anointed experts. David told him to call in every available reporter and producer so they could expand their coverage at the State Department and the Pentagon, check with the CIA to find out what kind of "advisors" had been put in motion, and track down spokesmen for as many of Messime's opponents as they could identify. Listening to him, Valerie admired his instant grasp of the situation and ability to expand his vision to encompass every angle to the story. She also realized how much she loved the news business at times like this. Anchor job or no, Valerie was hooked on it.

"There's more to this than Gary Peterson relaying a message from God to Billy Baker," David said between phone calls as Valerie maneuvered through the Sunday evening traffic around Richmond. "And you can bet it won't be just 'military advisors.' Besides, something's not right about the whole mess. I know for a fact that Baker wouldn't even see Messime when he tried to arrange a state visit last year."

"It was an odd time and place for the president of the United States to announce he intends to send troops to a foreign country, don't you think? I mean, Sunday afternoon in a church in Atlanta? Come on," Valerie said, thinking out loud.

"Not if you want to play as far under the radar as you can without making it a top secret mission," David answered. "He knew there wouldn't be much press coverage there. The White House made a point of implying the trip was routine when they announced it last week, so I'm sure everybody sent their 'B' team on the trip. We did. There also was no chance for reporters to ask any questions while the congregation was singing and carrying on."

"Why make an announcement at all?" asked Valerie

"It could be a trial balloon. After all, he said he was sending advisors, not troops." David looked thoughtful. "Or, the time and place of the announcement could have been a message in itself," he said.

"To whom?"

"Somebody connected to Peterson, probably," David guessed.

"What is he, Peterson's puppet?"

"That's what it looks like, but it's probably the other way around. The whole thing between Baker and Peterson is an act anyway, just like the rest of Peterson's shtick. It's all about money. Peterson blesses the president and his faithful followers contribute to the campaign chest."

"Peterson's diamond mine is involved in this some way, don't you think?" Valerie said.

"Without a doubt. But there must be other US economic interests in the Congo. And plenty more corporations who want to be there. I doubt you can pin this intervention or whatever they call it on Peterson's diamonds."

Valerie thought for a minute. "I think that angle is worth pursuing, though."

"New York won't go for it. Carter Wilson didn't think much of your last diamond mine story."

"I want this story, David," Valerie declared. "I need it."

"Then make the pitch about covering the whole Congo intervention. You should have no problem getting that assignment. You were just there and you've got the contacts."

"Yes, but I want to dig into the connection between Atlanta and the White House."

"Good luck on that score. The first words out of their mouths in New York will be 'Washington Bureau.'"

"Will you back me up?"

"I shouldn't, because my guys will think I'm undercutting them. But I will. And not because you sleep with me, regardless of what everyone will think. This story needs somebody who can connect the dots between Washington, Atlanta, and the Congo. Also somebody with enough guts to ask the hard questions."

"Thank you," Valerie said, taking her eyes off the road briefly to make eye contact.

"Do you want me to call New York for you?" he asked.

"No. I'm a big girl. I'll do it."

Chapter 11

New York

As David predicted he would, Carter Wilson told Valerie to leave the Washington side of the Congo story to the network bureau there. He didn't hesitate to give her the lead role in the coverage from Africa, though. That assignment should be hers as the network's top international correspondent. When she persisted, he reluctantly said she could pursue the murky connection to the Church of the Angels, even though he didn't see much that was newsworthy about Peterson's blessing of the president's decision to send advisors to the Congo. But he firmly told her that Washington wasn't part of her beat; there was a bureau there to cover the Pentagon and the White House, as she well knew. Besides, if anyone was going to interview the president, it would be Preston Henry, the newly crowned anchor of the evening news. Valerie wanted to scream that it wouldn't occur to that simple-minded headline reader to ask a follow-on question unless somebody fed it to him on the teleprompter in bright red capital letters, but she knew she had lost that argument when they chose Henry for the job in the first place. Resigned but undeterred, Valerie decided to start in Atlanta and see if she could uncover a lead back to Washington that the network wouldn't be able to keep her from pursuing. She'd follow it on her own if she had to.

Her first stop was Nancy's office. When Valerie stuck her head in the door, her nose was assaulted by the acrid smell of cold coffee and old cigarettes. Nancy, as usual, was simultaneously talking on the phone, typing on her keyboard and flicking her eyes from screen to screen in the line of television monitors on the overloaded bookcases across from her desk. A neglected cigarette smoldered in an overflowing ashtray next to her phone. When Valerie appeared, Nancy stopped pecking at the keyboard and hurriedly stubbed out the cigarette while she waved Valerie into the room. She cut her phone call short as Valerie moved a pile of magazines and newspapers off a chair and sat down.

"Hi, boss," Nancy said cheerfully.

"You're breaking the laws of the city of New York by smoking in this office, in case you didn't know," Valerie smiled. She waved in mock indignation at a wispy string of lingering smoke. "Not to mention endangering the health of every air-breathing creature on this floor."

"Sorry," Nancy answered with mock regret. "If I'd known you were coming—but anyway, it's not my fault," she added brightly. Impending deviltry made her eyes twinkle.

Valerie knew she was being set up, but didn't mind playing the goat for one of Nancy's routines. "How do you figure that?" she asked.

"Simple. You shouldn't be here," Nancy grinned. "I should be trotting down to your office instead of you coming to mine."

"That's a load of BS," Valerie bantered back.

"R–H–I–P like I've told you a hundred times," Nancy scolded with a smirk. "You've got the rank; you should use the privileges. You're supposed to summon me to your palace like the lackey that I am." She symbolically tugged her frizzy forelock and winked.

"You're pretty surly for a lackey, in case you haven't noticed," Valerie teased. "Besides, since when do we have time for protocol around here?"

She turned serious. "Do you feel up to a little road trip?"

"Back to Kinshasa?" Nancy guessed.

"Second stop. First one's Atlanta."

"Is our president invading Georgia too? Surely he doesn't think it's going to vote Democrat?"

Valerie laughed. "No, I want to interview Gary Peterson, our friendly neighborhood evangelist who just happens to own a diamond mine in the Democratic Republic of the Congo, in case you forgot."

"I know who he is," Nancy said disgustedly. She rolled her knobby shoulders like a bantamweight boxer getting ready for a bout. "Chief homophobe of the Church of the Holy Assholes." Nancy was un-stridently lesbian, but she was sensitive to the hypocritical politics that many headline hunters played with sexual orientation. "What's our excuse for going to see him?"

"There's a connection between the military action and his diamond mine someplace," Valerie answered. "Why else would Baker announce the military action from behind Peterson's pulpit?"

"Don't over-complicate it. You know Baker, anything for a contributor," said Nancy.

"He wouldn't go that far. A ride on Air Force One and a night in the Lincoln bedroom, no problem. A little creative rewrite of the tax code, consider it done. But sending troops to the Congo just because Gary Peterson asked him to? That's over the top even for Baker. There's something else going on here. Let's get started on the research. Get me an interview with Peterson. And start making the travel arrangements for the Congo."

"How soon do you want to go to Atlanta?"

"I've got a command performance at some charity function the network is sponsoring tonight. David flew in from Washington for it too. But Peterson won't be available on such short notice anyway. And we need a day or so for research. Let's shoot for the day after tomorrow in Atlanta. We can leave for Africa right after that."

"You got it, boss."

Jaime Talon didn't want to be in New York even though the clinic desperately needed the money he hoped to raise there. He admitted to himself he was enjoying the break from the numbing flood of festering wounds and debilitating disease that poured through Mai-Munene, but he still didn't want to be in New York, where the sharp optimism of his young career had been dulled on the hard stone of corporate medicine. It was also the place where he had walked away from his shallow marriage a few years before. New York was where all of his old demons lived. But he was there anyway, because that's where the money was.

Jaime's budget didn't allow for a room at any of the finer New York hotels. He wouldn't have been comfortable in one even if he had the funds. He stayed instead at a mission house near Gramercy Park made available to aid workers from all over the world by the Manhattan Mennonite Fellowship. It was cheap and clean and the people there understood his work. Jaime had seen the Mennonites in action in Africa. He admired their simple purposefulness. They were missionaries, but the ones he knew spent as much time helping people in this life as they did proselytizing about the next one.

The first call he made after he got settled in the city was to Dr. Michael Morone, who had been in residency along with Jaime at Bellevue. They may have started side by side, but Morone's career track couldn't have gone in a more opposite direction. He devoted himself to bigger and better corporate jobs in the medical industry, always keeping an ear open for career opportunity and seldom missing the sound when it came knocking. Today he was CEO of Medcare International, a conglomerate with large interests in pharmaceuticals, medical equipment and health care supply chain management. Of greater interest to Jaime, the company also sponsored a charitable foundation that funded public health initiatives in developing countries. Morone was a self-importantly busy man, but he took Jaime's call and agreed to make a place for him on his calendar that afternoon for old time's sake—or perhaps just to amuse himself by seeing how well his life had turned out in comparison to Jaime's. They met across a massive mahogany desk in Morone's Park Avenue office.

"You're welcome to apply for a grant from the foundation, of course, but I don't think it will be approved," Morone said after exchanging pleasantries and listening to Jaime describe the desperate state of Mai-Munene. "Your clinic, as commendable as it is, isn't in a region where the foundation is focused."

What he meant, Jaime knew, was that the Congo River Basin didn't hold the right kind of promise as an incipient market for Medcare products. Aid money from the foundation went to developing markets for well-publicized inoculation programs and dissemination of dietary supplements, all prominently labeled with Medcare's red and green logo. The money did a lot of good for a lot of needy people—as well as Medcare's shareholders. The programs softened up the countries for subsequent, more profitable endeavors. Recipient countries were chosen carefully on the basis of how close their economies were to having the ability to buy Medcare's profit-making products. Most of Sub-Saharan Africa failed that test because the local economies were near-wrecks that wouldn't become viable markets for Western products for decades, if ever.

"In other words, Mai-Menune is too poor to qualify for aid?" Jaime asked, unable to suppress the sarcasm in his voice.

"Don't be superior, Jaime," Morone answered sharply. "We can't be everywhere in the Third World. There's simply too much need and not enough money. I'm just trying to tell you that equatorial Africa is not one of our priorities right now, so you can save your breath." Morone stood up, signaling that the discussion was over. He ushered Jaime to the door but apparently relented on the way. "Look, I'm going to a fundraiser for AIDS relief tonight. There will be a lot of fat checkbooks in the crowd. Why don't you come along and I'll introduce you to some of them?"

"Thanks, but I put my tux in mothballs along with all my other corporate crap when I left for Africa," Jaime answered.

"Nonsense. That's why they invented rentals. I'll see you tonight at the Waldorf." Morone closed the door behind him.

Putting the arm on over-dressed people at a society fund-raiser was the last thing Jaime wanted to do but, since finding money was why he had come to New York in the first place, he might as well make the effort.

Later, as he fumbled with the bow tie of his rented tuxedo, Jaime thought of his ex-wife Katherine, who would have prepared for an evening like this like a soprano getting into costume to sing at the Met. It was the kind of affair that justified years of financial struggle in medical school and the poverty of hospital residency. As Katherine frequently reminded him, she had postponed the good things in life so Jaime could complete his education. She counted the days until he became a socially successful doctor like her father, whose stately white-haired visage regularly graced the magazine photo pages devoted to charity balls and the social scene around Philadelphia. She not-so-secretly assumed Jaime would join her father's practice some day. Jaime knew that was never going to happen, but he didn't talk about it much.

Those weren't exactly good times. His professional life was fine, although he worked so hard caring for the enormous number of patients drawn to Bellevue that he had little time or energy to do anything else. Jaime relished the work and gratefully lost himself in it. He saw Katherine for what seemed like only minutes every day, but that was all right too, because it spared him from listening to her crab about the endless sacrifices she made. Jaime would come home, often after being on duty for twenty-four hours, drop exhausted into bed, and go through the motions of asking about her day. He was usually breathing deeply—if not snoring softly—before she had uttered three or four sentences.

Katherine never understood why Jaime couldn't adjust to a more conventional lifestyle after he finished his residency at Bellevue and landed a position at New York Presbyterian, but she really blew up three years later when he announced he was turning down a promotion to Assistant Chief Internist in order to study tropical medicine at St. Barnabas in London. She flatly refused to give up her cozy Upper East Side apartment, her health club and charity teas, her dreams of a summer home in Southampton, just to follow him across the Atlantic and live again like a couple of poor students.

Jaime still wasn't sure why he had to do it either; he just knew he had to. All he knew was, every time he slipped out of his white lab coat and into a dinner jacket for the evening, he felt like he had been treating patients all day just to earn enough money to live the vacuous lifestyle cherished by his wife. The existence he and Katherine shared was somehow vaguely wrong-directed. The means were good, but the end was empty. Tired of fighting the internal dissonance, he finally walked away from it, leaving Katherine behind. He wasn't proud of ending his marriage, but in the end, it had been surprisingly easy.

The memories were depressing. Jaime finished tying his tie and looked at himself in the bright bathroom mirror. "Get over it," he ordered his reflection. "You've got work to do."

Valerie didn't really want to be at the Waldorf, but the network brass insisted. She had tried to explain that she had research to do on a complex, important story, not to mention getting ready for a trip to a war zone in Africa, but all they were concerned about was boosting the glitter factor at the fundraiser that night by increasing the number of news and entertainment personalities sprinkled through the crowd. Appearances at such affairs were part of her job description, they pointedly reminded her, a fact that didn't improve her disposition. But she put on her best meet-and-greet face and went to the Waldorf with David.

As soon as they entered the hotel's aptly named Peacock Alley, Valerie surveyed the scene to calculate how long it would take to make an acceptable circuit, fulfill her smiling duties, and make an unobtrusive exit. She spotted Michael Morone, whom she recognized as an advertiser from other network functions she'd attended, working his way through the crowd with a tall, sunburned man in an ill-fitting tuxedo. Valerie's breath caught when she realized he was with Jaime Talon. As they came closer, she saw Jaime's lips pressed together in a thin, grim line. When he saw her, they relaxed into a soft smile.

Valerie grinned her widest smile and reached both arms toward him before catching herself and turning the near-embrace into a warm handshake.

"I guess you two know each other," Morone said.

"We've met," said Jaime.

"Then if you'll excuse me ..." Morone turned and practically ran back into the crowd.

"What was that all about?" asked Valerie. His hand was gentle but solid in her grasp, and Valerie realized she hadn't let it go. She released her grip.

The muscles in Jaime's jaw clenched. "He's been parading me in front of all his phoney friends and I've been embarrassing them by asking for money. Although why he should object I don't know since that's why he made me come here tonight."

"You were looking for money the first time I met you," Valerie said.

"And the last time I saw you, you were strapped to a board. You look much better tonight."

Valerie suddenly became aware of the way her simple black dress clung to her body. She self-consciously touched the string of pearls at her throat and felt a flush beginning beneath them.

"Uh, excuse me," interjected David as he extended his arm between the two to shake Jaime's hand. "I'm David Powell."

Valerie blushed full crimson. "Oh, David, I'm sorry," she said. "This is Dr. Jaime Talon. He's the man who saved my life in Mai-Munene."

"Then I owe you a great debt of gratitude," David added.

As they shook hands, Valerie thought she saw Jaime's eyebrow flicker. She noticed the touch of gray at David's temples—something she normally didn't even think about—and wondered if Jaime was curious about their age difference.

"You don't owe me a thing," Jaime said. "All I did was shoot her full of antibiotics and ship her home."

"Regardless, I'm sure glad you did." As David spoke, he slipped his arm around Valerie's waist. She flinched a bit, and David must have felt it because he gave her a little squeeze and dropped his arm.

Small talk, she thought, we need small talk.

"Where are you staying?" she asked Jaime.

"I'm at the Mennonite Mission House in Grammercy Park," he answered. He suggested they get a drink and find a quiet corner to talk.

"How long have you been in the Congo?" David asked as they made their way through the crowd toward one of the bars set up around the room.

"I got to the country just before Seto got kicked out. I was at Kikwit when the coup took place."

"For the Ebola outbreak?" asked Valerie as she took a glass of wine.

"You remember that?" Jaime said. "Most people forgot about it after it dropped off the front page."

"I remember it very well," Valerie said. "That must have been a frightening experience."

"It was. I was scared as hell the whole time. We all were," Jaime answered. "The only good thing about it was that none of the soldiers on either side would come anywhere near us. They were scared to death too."

It was scary stuff, Valerie thought. Treating patients with a hyper-contagious disease that made you bleed through your eyeballs before it killed you had to be terrifying. Valerie didn't think he was playing down the brave side of his reaction to the danger, either, just as David never claimed to be a hero when he told of his front-line experiences as a war reporter. She caught herself comparing the two men and blushed again. I've got to make more small talk, she thought.

"How is your fund-raising going?" she asked.

"Not well," Jaime said. "I explain what we're doing and why, but nobody seems to really care. I feel like even if they gave us some funding, it would just be so they could list it on their resume or something. It's all so phoney." A grim scowl came back over his eyes. "I can't stand those people."

Just then Valerie saw Preston Henry making his way through the crowd toward them. The man was absolutely in his element, shaking hands, patting backs, leaving a wake of appreciative guests behind him. One of the things Valerie and many of the other journalists in the division particularly resented about the new anchor was his eagerness to perform. It was rumored he had a gag writer on retainer to provide material for corporate functions like this. "Speaking of phonies," Valerie muttered.

"Be nice," David said as Henry stepped up to them, smiling and nodding as if they had all been just standing around waiting for him to appear.

"Good evening, I'm Preston Henry," he announced, extending his hand to Jaime.

"This is Dr. Jaime Talon, Preston. He operates a clinic in the Congo," David said.

"No kidding," Henry said, his voice going flat. "I guess you're not an advertiser, then." But then he brightened. "So are you going to show Valerie all the best night spots when she comes to visit your war?"

Valerie's jaw almost dropped at the sheer vapidity of the comment— then she felt herself blushing at the implications. My God, I'm flashing off and on like a traffic light, she thought.

Before Jaime could answer, Henry turned to her. "When are you leaving for the dark continent?"

"I have to make a stop in Atlanta first," she said, trying to control her breathing. "Then I'm heading for the Congo."

"Well, I'm sure you'll file some exciting stories," he said in the tone of voice an adult would use to a four-year-old. "You always do."

Valerie gave up trying to control her temper. "And I'm sure you'll read the introductions like a real pro. I'll try not to use too many big words."

"Now, now, let's make nice for the network," David cut in, stepping between them.

"Excuse me, folks, but I've had enough corporate fun and games for one day," Jaime said. "I've got a seven AM date at Columbus Circle for a run in Central Park and lots of meetings tomorrow. It was nice meeting you, David. It was good to see you too, Valerie."

Valerie reached out to take his arm as he placed his drink on a passing waiter's tray and turned to walk away. He stopped for a moment, but she couldn't find any words to make him stay. She dropped her hand and he disappeared into the crowd.

Valerie didn't have much to say during the cab ride home after the party. As soon as they walked into the apartment, though, she said, "I need to talk to Jaime Talon about conditions on the ground now. I'm going to meet him at Central Park in the morning."

"Do you want me to come along?" David asked, his voice carefully neutral.

The question beneath the question startled Valerie. She realized how David must have seen the evening and a wave of guilt swept over her. "Of course, David," she answered.

His shoulders squared a little. "Good. You probably better call him tonight, though. Just to make sure he can still stand us."

"Good idea."

Valerie got the Mennonite House number from information and dialed it. The night clerk told her Jaime hadn't returned, but he would be glad to give him a message. "Please tell him Valerie and David are going to run with him in the morning," Valerie said.

As she ended the call, she wondered if he would show up.

Chapter 12

New York

The next morning, Valerie and David arrived at Central Park well before seven. They had started at a jog from their apartment at Eighty-First and Amsterdam with plenty of time to spare, but Valerie kept increasing the pace until they were practically sprinting by the time they got to Columbus Circle. When they stopped, David, normally the stronger runner of the pair, leaned over with his hands on his knees to catch his breath. Valerie paced, puffing around the Maine Monument looking for Jaime.

"For God's sake, Valerie," David gasped. "We're fifteen minutes early. Relax, would you?"

She came to stand beside him. "Sorry. I didn't want to miss him in case he didn't get my message last night."

"Right," David said. He took a gulp from the water bottle he carried strapped to his waist just as Jaime trotted around the corner from Central Park South.

Jaime spotted them and ran over. "Glad you could make it," he said. "I came early so I wouldn't miss you."

"Us too," Valerie smiled. "I wasn't sure you'd ever want to see us again after last night,"

"Oh, no," Jaime answered. "As long as you didn't bring that other asshole with you. Who was that jerk?"

"Nobody," David said. "Just a thorn in Valerie's side."

"In my butt, you mean," she interjected. She pointed through the stone pillars into the park. "This way? Let's go!"

They struck off at a moderate pace on the walkway leading diagonally into the park and away from the traffic already building around Columbus Circle. It was a fresh April day, slightly cool for the season, but perfect for a good run. They ran up Center Drive past the Carousel, silent and still in the morning, then skirted the dewy Sheep Meadow. When they got to the Olmstead Flower Bed, they turned onto the Literary Walk, where dozens of other early morning runners celebrated the fresh quiet of New York before rush hour by jogging under the towering elms that were just coming into bud. They turned west at the Bethesda Fountain to loop around the Lake to the Shakespeare Garden where they slowed to a walk to cool down. Traffic was picking up on Central Park West and the Seventy-Ninth Street Transverse.

"That was good," Valerie said as she walked between the two men. The air around her was filled with the un-perfumed musk of the two lean, strong men striding beside her.

"It felt great," Jaime agreed.

"Glad you met us," David said. "I don't suppose you jog much where you're at."

"You're right. The villagers would think I'd lost my mind if they saw me trotting up the road through Mai-Munene. Or they'd look to see if a hyena was chasing me." Jaime laughed.

"I'm starved," Valerie announced. "There's a coffee shop near the Museum of Natural History that David and I like. It has a few tables outside."

They settled into a table under an umbrella on the broad sidewalk and ordered breakfast. Jaime asked for a bagel with a schmear of cream cheese.

"There are two things I can't get in the Congo," he explained as the waiter walked away, "decent bagels and Twinkies."

"There's a message for America in there somewhere," observed David. "So tell me, what does your clinic do?"

"There are basically three kinds of medicine in the Congo: slim, next to none, and none. Slim is what you can find in Kinshasa and Kisangani and a few other major cities. Next to none is what we provide at Mai-Munene. It's mostly emergency care, although we do our best to provide some simple preventive medicine. Basic vaccines, pre-natal care, that kind of thing when we can afford the supplies. That's the kind of health care most of the population in the countryside gets by on. There are also many places where there are no medical services at all, mostly in the hinterlands and in the rebel-controlled areas on the borders."

"That's a pretty grim picture," Valerie said.

"Sorry, I didn't mean to dampen your spirits," Jaime said.

"No need to apologize. I didn't come to be entertained this morning. I came to see you."

As what she just said soaked in, she flushed. "I'm sorry. I didn't mean that the way it came out. For a reporter, sometimes I don't have a very good way with words."

"Something tells me you usually say exactly what you mean," Jaime answered.

"Uh, excuse me," David interjected. "If you two would like me to leave …"

"Oh, David," Valerie teased. She placed her hand over his on the glass tabletop.

"Sorry," Jaime apologized. "Guess that sounded like a cheap come-on, didn't it?"

"Don't worry about it," David finally laughed. "I'm used to guys making passes at Valerie right in front of me. Most of them assume I'm her grandfather."

"So what can you tell me about Peterson's mine?" Valerie asked. Despite the polite chitchat and apologies, Valerie sensed the tension between David and Jaime growing by the minute. Better change the subject, she thought. "Anything new there?"

"Not much, really," Jaime answered. "They put up taller fences and brought in more soldiers. I think they're pretty nervous about Xotha."

"Do you see much of Alben?" Valerie asked.

"No. He was supposedly going to start a school, but he didn't," Jaime said. "He never struck me as the kindly Mr. Chips type, anyway, if you know what I mean. He acts more like a front man for something."

"How do you mean?" Valerie said.

"Like he had something going on the side. He's pretty thick with the army. I suspect the missionary act is just an excuse to be there. Alben stays to himself pretty much, which is fine with me. One thing is a little peculiar, though. He has the village women working in shifts making *minkisi*."

"That's weird," Valerie said.

"What's that?" David asked.

"*Minkisi* is plural for *nkisi*," Valerie explained. "They're little rag dolls. You would think he'd have better things to do with his time."

"That's what I thought," Jaime answered. "But at least he's not abusing the women. It's honest work, I suppose, and he pays them for it from what I can gather."

"Very odd," Valerie agreed.

Before she could continue, a slouching man wearing too many

clothes—all very dirty—and a knit watch cap much too warm for the weather came across the street and approached their table. He looked furtively around for the waiter then whipped off his cap. He asked them in a low voice, eyes cast downward, "Can you spare a dollar? I ain't had nothing to eat since Wednesday." Valerie carefully ignored him and stared into her coffee, waiting for him to go away. David shook his head.

Jaime took half his bagel off his plate, wrapped it in a paper napkin and handed it to him. The man quietly thanked him. Just then the waiter came outside and started toward their table. The man saw him coming. He walked quickly back toward the park. The waiter came to their table and apologized for the intrusion. When he left, David said, "Conventional wisdom says we're not supposed to feed them."

"I remember that line of reasoning from when I lived here," Jaime answered. "I believed it then. Now I don't care what the bureaucrats say. Besides, I wasn't giving him a handout, I was sharing my meal with him. The man needed food and I had more than enough, so I gave it to him. There's a difference."

"The problem is," David persisted, "handouts from us keep them from going to the agencies where they can get proper assistance. Counseling and medical care and things like that."

"Yes, starvation is a great motivator," Jaime answered bitterly.

There was an uncomfortable silence at the table. He looked across the street at the panhandler, who sat on the curb with his feet in the gutter, eating the bagel and watching the traffic on Central Park West. "What matters is that right now—today—that man over there is hungry," he said. "Somebody needs to do something about that, not just ignore it and hope the holy and all-powerful market economy will provide a solution." The strawberries Valerie had eaten turned acidic in her stomach as Jaime went on. "That's the way people survive at the village level. They take care of each other as a matter of course, no questions asked. It's no big deal to them. If someone is hungry, you share your meal with them. If they need help, you help them. It's simple."

"You make it sound like Utopia," David scoffed.

"It's far from that. It's mostly a matter of survival. The more healthy people you have in the village, the better off everyone is. There's more labor for working the crops, hunting and fishing, taking care of the children, and so on. What matters isn't what you own, it's how many of you know where your next meal is coming from."

David raised up his palm to stop Jaime. "With all due respect," he said, "I don't think African village society is quite so altruistic. They have capitalist urges to better themselves just like the rest of us." He tapped his forefinger on the table for emphasis. "And they can dog-eat-dog with the best of them."

"Of course," Jaime snapped. "I'm not naïve."

"I didn't say you were," David shot back. "All I'm saying is the poor people of the Congo want to get ahead just like the rest of us. We just do it differently here."

"You're right," Jaime answered. He pointed to the panhandler across the street, who was now looking through a trash basket on the sidewalk. "Which is one reason I don't live here anymore."

Valerie fiddled with her coffee cup, unintentionally rattling it in the saucer.

Jaime looked at the sky as if trying to judge the time by the height of the sun. "I don't fit here in a lot of different ways," he said. "Listen, I hope I haven't offended anybody, but I have to get going."

"No, please. Wait," Valerie pleaded, surprising herself with the outburst. She searched for an excuse to keep Jaime from leaving. "I need to hear more about the mine. What's going on there?"

"Sorry, I told you what I know," Jaime answered. "If you want more, you'll have to see for yourself." He stood to go.

"I hope I'll get there," Valerie said. She tried to ignore the flash of hurt in David's eyes.

"That would be great," Jaime answered.

There was another awkward silence, broken finally by the blare of a taxi horn on West Park Drive. Jaime repeated, "I've got to go. Good luck on your story." He stepped to the curb and flagged a cab.

Valerie and David sat in silence, David intently studying the spoon for his coffee and Valerie staring vacantly at the traffic. After a moment, David said, "I'm sorry you didn't get to ask him the rest of your questions. I didn't mean to get in an argument with him."

"That's all right, David," Valerie said, pulling herself back to business. "I don't think he had much else to tell me." She took a final sip of orange juice and touched the napkin to her lips before laying it on the table. "Let's go," she said. "I need to pack." She pushed her chair back but David didn't move.

"Valerie," he said, "I need to ask you something."

From his sober tone, Valerie didn't think she wanted to hear his question.

"Are you in love with him?"

She took a deep breath before answering.

"No, David. I'm in love with you." She wished she felt as confident as she sounded.

Later that morning, David leaned against the bedroom doorway, watching Valerie pack. "Do you know what I admire about you?" he asked. He would be leaving their New York apartment for the airport himself in a little while to catch the shuttle back to Washington.

"I'm never sure if it's my lofty intellect or my boobs, to tell you the truth," Valerie answered while she carefully folded a wash-and-wear navy blazer in a plastic dry cleaner's bag.

"Oh, I greatly admire your boobs," David smiled. "But also, you really know how to pack for travel. That's an invaluable skill."

If there was one thing Valerie had learned as an international reporter, it was how to travel light. She had gear spread all over the floor in preparation for the trip to Atlanta and Kinshasa. Laid out that way, it looked like more than it really was. Considering that she was going into a war zone for an unknown period of time, though, it was remarkable how little she planned to carry. She had only one outfit for dress occasions—the navy blazer with matching skirt, a pair of slacks, a simple white blouse (everything no-iron wash-and-wear), a couple of colorful scarves and low-heeled pumps. For the rest of the time, she carried simple, functional tropic-weight khaki pants, shorts and shirts. Aside from her sturdy hiking boots, the most expensive clothing she packed was underwear made from non-chafing micro-fiber that wicked body moisture away from the skin. It could also be rinsed out and air-dried in minutes. She didn't use many personal cosmetics and only the simplest of costume jewelry for on-camera work, so everything fit into a durable travel duffle and the backpack she preferred for carry-on.

"Well, thank goodness," Valerie smiled back at him. "From the way you dragged me into bed this morning after we came back from the park, I thought all you cared about was my body." She recalled the hour they spent in bed after their morning run and breakfast with Jaime Talon. For some reason, maybe because she was leaving for Africa the next day, maybe because of the way the run had ended, David had been a particularly eager, energetic lover, taking more than his usual care to pleasure her.

David said, "I just didn't want you to forget about me when you get to Africa."

Over the next few days, Jaime made the rounds of the New York philanthropies who supported global health causes. He talked about the endless stream of injuries and infections he and Pieter treated in Mai-Munene, about the antibiotics needed to ameliorate dysentery and dengue fever, about the potential success of childhood inoculations against smallpox, tetanus, rubella, and hepatitis B—if he could only pay for a supply of vaccines. Depending on whether his listeners were supported by a fundamentalist church or not, he talked about distributing condoms in an effort to fight the spread of HIV/AIDS. At his first two meetings, he told the tale of misappropriated funds from the World Health Organization, but he stopped when he realized that was exactly the wrong thing to say to most of his prospects, who had no desire to see their own organization's funds go into the same private bank accounts.

His audience was unfailingly sympathetic but not very helpful. Many confessed they were overwhelmed with pleas for aid to Africa, which had an endless supply of victims created by ceaseless wars, rebellions and famines. Others said flatly that they wouldn't be funding anything in the DRC until they saw how the US military involvement panned out. If it proved successful and the situation stabilized, they were ready to pour resources into the country. If it made matters worse by increasing the instability in the region, as had happened in other recent interventions, they weren't going to put their already-strained budgets at risk. In either case, nothing would be done until the picture clarified itself. They all urged Jaime to file application after application and fill out form after form so they could consider regular aid to Mai-Munene during their annual budgeting process later in the year. Patients who needed treatment in the meantime would just have to wait for the bureaucracy to move. The mindset was maddening.

After a long day of mostly fruitless begging, Jaime trudged down First Avenue from the UN building toward the Mennonite hostel near Gramercy Park. He could have taken the subway, but the walk would help him clear his head of the bureaucratic nonsense he'd been hearing all day. As Jaime neared Thirtieth Street, Bellevue Hospital's twenty-five-story bulk loomed before him. The growling gears of a Medcare International delivery truck coming from the VA Medical Center down the street was a pointed reminder of what an utter failure his trip had been so far. He was sure the truck carried enough supplies to operate the clinic at Mai-Munene for a year, while he would be going home with his pockets empty. By the time Jaime started up the steps to the Mennonite hostel, he was walking under a black cloud, ready to give it all up and head back to Africa.

"Welcome home, friend," chirped a bright-eyed young man who came out of the Peace Library on the first floor of the hostel just as Jaime came through the door from Nineteenth Street. Jaime had met the man when he first arrived from Africa. He was one of several volunteers who lived at the hostel doing mission work among the homeless.

"New York is many things, but home isn't one of them," Jaime scowled.

"Wherever you are right with God, there is home," the young man offered. A bearded older man came out of the library behind him.

"Dr. Talon," the young man said, "I'd like you to meet my father, John Lerner."

Jaime shook the man's hard-calloused hand. "Sorry I snapped at your son," Jaime said. "It's been a rough day." He felt the older man calmly sizing him up.

"We all have them," Lerner said. "Martin tells me you run a clinic in the Congo. Is that right?"

"Yes I do," Jaime answered.

"I did mission work in Africa many years ago, mostly in the east. Tanzania and Kenya. Martin's older sister was actually born there."

"Are you still a missionary?" Jaime asked out of politeness.

"Oh no. I did my duty and brought my family home to Ohio. I'm in the hardware business. Got a little store in Gaitland. Martin tells me your clinic is in need of funds."

"That's why I'm here, actually," Jaime said. "Trying to raise enough money to keep it operating."

"Not having much luck, from the look on your face when you came through the door."

"My little clinic is a gnat on an elephant's backside as far as the big foundations are concerned," Jaime said. He was getting tired of hearing himself complain about the situation. "I've just about exhausted the possibilities here, so I'm getting ready to go back."

"Empty handed?" Lerner asked.

"Not entirely. I got a couple of small emergency donations this week, about enough to fill the supply cabinet one more time. After that's gone, I don't know …"

Martin spoke up. "See, Dad, I told you it was a serious situation."

"How many patients do you treat in a year's time?" Lerner asked.

"We see two or three hundred people a month," Jaime replied then added, "Why do you want to know?" Lerner ignored his question.

"So that's about three thousand people a year?"

"Give or take," Jaime answered, wondering where the conversation was going.

"How far would one hundred dollars per patient go?"

Jaime did the math in his head and answered, "That would be about six months operating expenses for us at that patient load. Assuming there aren't any disasters." Lerner nodded. Jaime began to wonder if his day was going to turn out all right after all.

"Dad?" the man's son asked hopefully. Lerner turned away without saying anything, took something out of his pocket, then leaned over a table in the hallway and started writing. He straightened up and handed Jaime a check.

"Martin says you're a good man doing good work. There aren't enough of those in the world. I hope this will help."

Jaime looked at the five-figure check, speechless for a moment, then he said, "Thank you! It will help quite a lot. But I thought—"

"You thought we Anabaptists were all horse-and-buggy farmers? Some of us are, mostly our Amish brothers. But none of us turn our noses up at making an honest dollar or two. Especially as long as the Lord's work gets its share."

"Dad's hardware store went on the Internet a few years ago. Now he ships goods all over the world," Martin said with more than a trace of pride.

"That's enough, son," Lerner said. "The Lord's been good to us; let's try to live up to his expectations. Now, let's go and let Dr. Talon get some rest." He stuck out his hand and Jaime shook it, speechless.

"Good luck to you, Doctor," Lerner said. "I know Africa, and I know you'll need it."

Chapter 13

Atlanta

Valerie dozed off and on against the drone of the engines during the flight to Atlanta. In her half-sleep, she contemplated David's proposal. She felt better about turning him down now than she had on the beach in Cape Charles, but she wasn't completely sure she would be against the idea forever. But Jaime Talon was in the picture too. Or was he? If so, how did he fit in? She needed to figure that out.

On the other hand, she didn't want to lose David. He was the first man in her life to treat her like a fully formed human being. Until she met him, she'd experienced two kinds of men. One was her father, who treated her the same way he treated all women—like dirt. The other kind was the men she dated after college. All of them longed to sleep with her and some of them worshipped her in a superficial way, but most of them wanted to parade her around town, a beautiful prize to be displayed like a Rolex with breasts.

Nancy gently shook her awake. "Hey, boss," she said, "I hate to bother you, but you said you wanted to look at the stuff on Gary Peterson."

"Thanks, Nancy," Valerie answered gratefully, blinking hard to push the sleep out of her eyes and the ugly memories out of her mind. She asked the flight attendant for a cup of coffee, then lost herself in the thick folder of clippings and notes from Nancy's research.

The Reverend Gary Peterson's connection to the Congo was a remarkably straightforward story, as near as Valerie could see. When General Moshe Messime shot his way into power, one of his first acts was to nationalize all of his country's natural resources, including, painfully, the timber concessions and diamond mines owned by Gary Peterson.

"I remember this," Valerie said, pointing to the page she was reading. "You and I got there not long after Messime nationalized everything, didn't we?"

"Yeah. There was a mob of investment bankers trying to get out of the country when we got to the airport. Most of them looked like they'd been bent over a barrel and fucked in their wallets," Nancy observed. Valerie smiled appreciatively. She'd always disliked the Wall Street crowd because of their single-minded fixation on money. No matter how much they had, they couldn't get enough of it. The money itself wasn't important, they always said; it's just how they kept score. Whenever Valerie heard that, she always wondered what game they were playing. She really couldn't comprehend that kind of greed, which was no different from Seto's and Messime's. The only real difference was that Wall Street was restrained—somewhat—by a few regulations.

The whole affair between Peterson and Messime should have triggered at least some interest from the news media, Valerie thought, but it hadn't. There were several reasons for this, she knew. For one thing, the story wasn't about Americans in emotional distress; there weren't any weeping mothers to interview or sheet-covered bodies to put on the screen, which was the favorite subject of most media. For another, this was also, at least on the surface, a story about business, which besides being inherently boring to viewers and readers, was a subject most reporters simply didn't understand. The biggest reason the story of the evangelist and his diamond mines stayed under the radar, though, was that it took place in Africa, a place so removed from the public consciousness that the deaths of millions of people from famine, drought and even genocide didn't warrant more than passing mention in the press. America didn't have any particular self-interest in the continent, so even mass death wasn't newsworthy, much less obscure investments in places no one had ever heard of.

"What happened to Peterson's holdings?" Valerie asked.

"Messime used official whiteout on the documents and Peterson's name disappeared along with his church's money."

"So how did he get the diamond mines back?" Valerie asked.

"He only got the one we saw at Mai-Munene—but it's a good one. Messime's army pushed the Angolans back out of the region a little over a year ago. There's been a lot of fighting in the area, but they seem to be holding it pretty well. Actually, the threat right now is Xotha and the Lunda Libre. They want to break away to form a country called Lundaland or something. They're fighting the Congolese government and maybe the Angolans. They could also be allied with the Angolans. It's hard to say."

"What about Peterson? How did he end up with the mine?"

"All I could find out was basically what Alben told us. Peterson took one of his Angel Crusades to Kinshasa last year and bingo, he turned up as a happy new mine owner a little while later."

"He must have delivered one hell of a sermon," Valerie said.

"From what I read, Messime gave him the head-of-state red-carpet treatment, private audience and all."

"You did some good work here," Valerie said, thumbing through the pages Nancy gave her. "Let's see what I can get Peterson to tell me about that meeting with Messime." Valerie jotted some questions on a legal pad for her interview with Peterson. After a few minutes, she asked, "I don't suppose you found any connection between President Baker and the Peterson deal?"

"Nada," Nancy answered. "You know about his relationship with Peterson. They're asshole buddies in Christ. As far as the Congo goes, Baker's always been dead set against doing anything for Africa. No place, no time, no way. Messime made a big deal out of asking for US help pushing back the Angolans, remember?"

"Sure. Baker was running for reelection at the time. His slogan was 'America First And Only.'"

"In other words, go pound sand. He's not the only one that feels that way," Nancy added cynically. "If the Congo were a major oil producer, or if the fifty million people there could pay for American-made cars or toilet paper, it would be a different story."

"Which makes Baker's about-face that much harder to understand," Valerie said. "The *Times* said this morning that thirty thousand troops were mobilizing for the first wave. That's more than just a few 'advisors' especially if there are more to come." She made a few more notes on her pad. "Let's see if Peterson can shed any light on the presidential thinking."

"There's something else you should ask," Nancy said with a mischievous lilt in her voice.

"What's that?"

"I'm sure the public would like to know if their Lord and Savior Jesus Christ weighed in on the decision to send troops to Africa," Nancy smirked.

"Let's not offend any more viewers than we have to, okay?"

"Aw, boss, you got no guts."

The world headquarters of the Reverend Gary Peterson rose like a crystal monolith over the rolling hills of the Atlanta suburb of Buckhead. Valerie and Nancy met Bobby, their videographer, in the visitors' lobby. He was dressed the same as when Valerie last saw him in Africa: Yankees cap, ragged blue jeans, photographer's vest over a Grateful Dead tee shirt, and the best pair of Danner hiking boots money can buy. Bobby was waiting for them with a lighting tech Valerie didn't know and a soundman she'd worked with before but whose name she could never remember. After making them wait a few minutes while security checked their identification, the receptionist sent them through a metal detector to the elevators.

A second receptionist showed them into an immense office, an aerie perched on the top floor of the crystal building. They entered the room through imposing double doors set into a wall paneled with well-oiled pecan and walnut. Nancy whispered to Valerie, "I've seen this style before. It's called Star Wars Gothic." The other three walls were floor-to-ceiling glass with views to the south of Atlanta's muscular skyline, to the east across the plains to Stone Mountain, and to the west to the meandering Chattahoochee River. The shimmering stream reminded Valerie of the tea-colored Kasai River that flowed through Mai-Munene. In one corner of the office was a casual seating area with three ultra-modern Eames chairs and an incongruous Louis XIV settee drawn up around a glass conference table. In the opposite corner were two leather arm chairs carefully arranged to face a heavy oak cross that stood in the junction of the two walls, rising from floor to ceiling and stretching its heavy arms across the glass. Valerie realized that if you were seated in the chairs, the cross would seem to float against a backdrop of Georgia sky. A good place for the Reverend Gary Peterson to contemplate the mysteries, she supposed, and to impress on visitors that he had a powerful ally. Dominating the other end of the room was a massive smoked glass desktop. It seemed to hover unsupported in the air, although Valerie saw the nearly invisible struts when she looked more closely beneath it. There wasn't much on top of its polished expanse except a telephone, a notepad flanked by a line of perfectly sharpened pencils, and a crystal vase full of freshly cut white lilies. Her eye was drawn to a threadbare rag doll leaning against the vase. The shabby plaything was totally out of place in the highly polished room. The doll was stitched together roughly, Valerie noticed, like it had been taken apart and sewn back together again by someone who didn't care. She looked a little more closely.

"Look," she said quietly to Nancy. "Isn't that a *nkisi?*"

Nancy stopped giving directions to the crew for a minute and glanced at the doll. "You're right. Must be a souvenir from good old Brother Tom." Something nagged at her, but Bobby broke her train of thought with a question about the seating. Nancy told him to rearrange the conference area so Valerie could use one of the Eames chairs while Peterson sat on the Louis XIV settee facing her with the conference table to the side. Just as they finished, a small door opened in the oiled-pecan paneling. The Reverend Gary Peterson himself strode into the room, followed by a small retinue of bodyguards and assistants. He looked much more like a banker than a minister, with razor-cut gray hair, three-button pin-stripe suit, and gleaming cap toe shoes. Peterson wasn't much taller than medium height and tended toward portly, but the extra heft just added to his air of capitalist prosperity.

"Miss Grey! How nice to see you," Peterson drawled, extending a well-manicured hand.

"Thank you for giving us some of your valuable time, Reverend," Valerie answered. The crew shuffled cameras, lights, microphones and a plethora of wires and cables around the improvised interview set behind her. Peterson looked at the seating arrangements with a professional eye and turned to one of his people.

"George, why don't you see if we can find a better setup here." He turned back to Valerie, giving her a deprecating one-pro-to-another smile. "You don't mind, do you?" he asked. "My folks are always giving me what-for about showing my good side to the camera, as if I had one." Before Peterson finished the explanation, George had stepped over to Nancy and pointed toward the opposite corner of the room where the giant wooden cross hung in the window.

"I leave those kinds of decisions up to my producer," Valerie replied. She preferred not to get into a power struggle with the evangelist—yet. She saw Nancy gesturing toward the cross and saying something that made Peterson's man shake his head vigorously. Finally, Nancy threw her arms up in resignation and the crew started moving gear across the room.

"It looks like everything got settled," Peterson said with satisfaction. "Now, I understand you want to ask me about our missions in the Congo. Is that correct?"

"Basically, yes," she said.

"Good, good. Anything else?" he probed.

"I'm primarily interested in Africa at this time, Reverend," Valerie answered. She didn't want to give him any warning about her questions before the camera could capture his response.

"That's a big area to cover, young lady," Peterson chuckled. "Are we going to talk about the entire continent?"

Valerie gave him a thin smile. "I'm just looking for a little background before we go over there to cover the US military intervention."

Nancy signaled that the equipment was set up for the interview, so Valerie and Peterson took their places in the leather armchairs. Peterson's own makeup person touched up his face and hair while Valerie attended briefly to her own. The microphones were clipped in place and tested. Valerie checked her notes and gave Peterson what she hoped was a disarming smile. He smiled back reassuringly, a TV pro all the way. No matter how Bobby framed the shot, some part of the huge wooden cross would be in the background behind Peterson.

Valerie did a simple intro into the camera, then Bobby zoomed out for an establishing shot of both her and Peterson. While Valerie asked her first question, Bobby locked in the shot and went to a second camera, trained over Valerie's shoulder on Peterson. It was a two-camera shoot, allowing the nimble videographer to keep one camera fixed while he moved the other so they'd always have two views of Peterson and Valerie to choose from in the editing booth. Valerie's "reactions" to Peterson's answers would actually be shot afterward and edited in.

After a couple of softball warm-up questions about the Church of the Angels and its missions in the Congo, Valerie got down to business. "Some people might say that it is unseemly for a man of God to own a prosperous diamond mine in one of the poorest countries on earth. What would you say to them?" she asked. Peterson didn't blink.

"I would say they should pay attention to the deeper meaning of prosperity," he intoned smoothly. "Apparently, the Lord has seen fit to bless me with worldly riches. I've never hidden the fact that even though I started as a poor minister of the Word, I've been very fortunate to prosper over the years. I can only assume that these rewards for my work are part of God's plan."

"What does God's plan say about the impoverished people of the

Congo, where the average person doesn't earn enough in a year to buy a pair of shoes like yours?" Valerie asked. Peterson still wasn't flustered.

"It says those people need help. And that is just what we're doing there—helping. Our mine gives jobs to several hundred men so they can feed their families."

Valerie cut in. "But from what we saw, Reverend, those men aren't allowed to live with their families. The workers are locked inside the mine compound. They live in dank, dark barracks like prisoners. And what about the working conditions? There is no safety equipment, no medical care, inadequate sanitary facilities. How is your mine different from one of King Leopold's?"

"That's simplistic nonsense, Miss Grey. We've modernized that operation considerably since we took over. Thousands of dollars in new equipment, new facilities, even new management. I don't know where you got your information, but I'd like to see evidence of the conditions you describe."

Valerie silently cursed the loss of Bobby's camera and its footage. Alben must have told Peterson about their visit. He knew she didn't have any video from the mine.

"Our investment in this mine is a humanitarian effort," Peterson continued. "When it becomes profitable, we intend to reinvest the profits for the people of the region. And don't forget, the mine generates tax revenues so the government of President Messime can provide essential services to the entire country. I feel blessed to be able to play some small part in making the Democratic Republic of the Congo a better place."

"Speaking of President Messime," Valerie interjected, "what does he get out of your deal?"

Peterson didn't rise to the bait. "I promised President Messime we would do God's work by establishing schools and medical facilities and churches where his people can hear the glorious words of our Lord."

"Perhaps my question wasn't clear," Valerie said, pressing a little harder. "His predecessor, Ingaway Seto, diverted billions of dollars to secret bank accounts—money that came from natural resource concessions nominally owned by the country as a whole. Does President Messime have an economic interest in your mine? Is he your silent partner?"

Peterson's eyes blazed with well-practiced righteous indignation. He straightened in his chair and clamped both hands on the arms to punctuate his rhetoric. "Absolutely not! I am a man of the cloth. I would not be a party to any such arrangement. Let me tell you unequivocally that my ownership of the mine in Mai-Munene was acquired in a completely transparent, above-board transaction through the Bureau of Mines of the Democratic Republic of the Congo with the full knowledge and approval of all appropriate authorities. You are welcome to inspect the documentation at any time."

Valerie kept her expression perfectly neutral in the face of Peterson's bombast. "Thank you, Reverend, I intend to. Let me ask you about something else. Did your investment in the diamond mine at Mai-Munene influence President Baker's decision to send American military advisors to the Congo?"

Peterson's bluster gave way to a flicker of surprise, but the moment was so brief Valerie wasn't sure the cameras caught it.

"That's ridiculous," he said icily, completely under control again. "What would ever give you any such idea?"

"The timing, for one thing," Valerie answered. "During his reelection campaign, President Baker pledged never to entangle American troops in any African conflicts. It seems to me that the only thing that's changed in the Congo since he made that promise has been your acquisition of a diamond mine." Valerie realized she had violated one of her personal rules as a reporter; she had stated her own conclusion on camera rather than let the viewer draw their own from the statements of the person she was interviewing. Peterson's smug, sanctimonious attitude irritated her, though, and she lost her journalistic objectivity. She also realized she'd violated another basic interviewing rule: she hadn't asked a question. "How do you explain that?" she added.

Peterson's demeanor remained calm but his rhetoric rolled out with great power. He spoke slowly, carefully enunciating each word for emphasis. "Your innuendo is so ludicrous I won't dignify it with a response. As President Baker said just a few days ago, the Democratic Republic of the Congo is a nation in distress. It is the Christian duty of the United States of America as the leader of all the nations of the world to render what aid it can to stabilize that situation. I wholeheartedly endorse that decision and praise President Baker for having the courage to make it."

Valerie was determined to crack his facade. "In his address, President Baker said, and I quote, 'It is our duty, relayed to us through the Reverend Gary Peterson from the Master Of Justice himself, to step in and bring peace to this war-torn land.' Did Jesus Christ give you a message for President Baker?"

"My conversations with God are not for me to reveal to you, Miss Grey. In fact, I find it impertinent that you would even ask such a question. If you are going to mock my beliefs—and those of President Baker—I think that's the end of our little interview." He looked steadily into the camera over Valerie's shoulder, his lips set firmly and his head held high. He played the role of press victim to the hilt. Valerie knew he would come across as the righteous martyr on camera, and she would be seen as the godless bitch reporter. Having lost the test of wills already, she took a blind stab.

"Thank you, Reverend," Valerie smiled sweetly. "Just one more question. I'm curious. Does President Baker have a financial interest in your diamond mine?"

"That's out of line, Miss Grey. Now we are finished." The evangelist looked sternly into the camera while he unclipped his microphone. He waited until the red light went out, indicating the camera was off, then motioned for his assistant. He whispered something in his ear, then walked stiff-backed out of the room with the rest of his retinue through the private entrance. The assistant told Valerie he wanted to review the tape.

"You'll see it when it airs," Nancy jumped in, "Just like the rest of the world."

"But that wasn't part of our agreement to grant you this interview," he protested.

"We did *not* give you advance approval of this story. We never do," Valerie said. She knew that short of assaulting Bobby to get the tape, there wasn't much George could do.

"So you can forget it," Nancy added bluntly, turning her back on the man. "Come on, we've got a plane to catch," she said to Valerie. Bobby handed Nancy the tapes and Valerie thanked the crew for their help as Nancy stowed the interview in her oversized bag.

"Are you going to Africa with us?" Valerie asked the cameraman.

"The assignment came through this morning," he said.

"Great!" Valerie said. "Need a ride to the airport?"

"No, thanks. I'll meet you there after I get these guys squared away."

While the camera crew packed their gear, Valerie and Nancy got in the elevator. Nancy pushed the button for the parking lot. "I thought you were going to leave Jesus out of this?" she teased.

Valerie was still mad at herself for losing control during the interview. "I couldn't help it," she said. "He's either calling the shots or He's the ultimate fall guy."

As they drove to the airport, Nancy said, "Say, when we saw the doll workshop in Mai-Munene, didn't Alben say they were shipping the *minkisi* to Atlanta?" she asked.

"Yes, I think so," said Valerie.

"Then why was that box full of them addressed to Alexandria, Virginia? You remember, the one the captain who wanted to shoot us outside the mine was carrying like the crown jewels?"

"Good question," Valerie said.

As soon as they got to Hartsfield Atlanta Airport, Nancy found a wireless connection for her laptop and called up an online reverse directory. The address in Alexandria she had written in her ever-present notebook when she saw it on the box under Yoweri's arm was listed as belonging to Charles Hook.

"That name is familiar. Isn't he on the White House staff?" Valerie asked.

Nancy did a quick online search. "Yes he is," she said, reading from the screen. "Special Assistant for National Security. Doesn't sound like somebody with a passion for rag dolls."

Valerie smiled and said, "Let's go ask him."

"It's *Sixty Minutes* time," Valerie said under her breath when a car pulled up in front of the Alexandria townhouse where she and Nancy had been waiting with Bobby for nearly an hour. No one was home when they arrived, but it was the end of the day so they had decided to wait for Hook to come home from work. The driver came around to open the door for the passenger, a tall, skinny man with a sharp hawk's beak of a nose.

"Excuse me," Valerie said, stepping up to him as the man got out of the car. "Are you Charles Hook?"

The man's eyes narrowed. "What can I do for you?" he said.

"I'm Valerie Grey with MBS TV News. Can you tell me how Reverend Gary Peterson's diamond mine influenced President Baker's decision to send American military advisors to the Congo?"

"That's not my area of responsibility," the man answered curtly. "I suggest you contact the White House Press Secretary with your question. I don't know anything about diamond mines in the Congo."

"Didn't you recently receive a shipment from that mine?" Valerie asked. "A box of dolls?"

"Dolls? I don't know what you're talking about."

"They're called *nkisi*," Valerie persisted. "They are made by women in the village near Reverend Peterson's mine. A box of them was sent to you a few weeks ago."

"You must be mistaken," Hook said. He stepped around Valerie and through his front door. "I have no interest in dolls. Now, if you'll excuse me." He closed the door firmly in Valerie's face.

Valerie looked at Nancy, who shrugged. "I guess now we know," she said.

Valerie answered, "Yeah, he's hiding something."

The telephone in Peterson's private inner office rang a few minutes later.

"I just ran off a television reporter outside my house asking pointed questions about dolls from the Congo," Hook said as soon as Peterson picked up the receiver.

"What!" Peterson said.

"Yeah. It looks like your brilliant scheme isn't so secret anymore."

"It must have been that bitch Valerie Grey," Peterson said.

"How do you know who it was?" Hook demanded.

"She was just here for an interview," Peterson answered. "She was in Mai-Munene a few weeks ago. But she doesn't know anything!"

"She sure as hell knew about those dolls."

"She's just fishing," Peterson said. "She'll forget all about it by the time she gets back to Africa."

"Africa! What's she going there for?"

"Covering the military intervention, I assume."

"What if she pokes around in the wrong places?" Hook asked.

"There's nothing for her to find. I'll make sure my man gives her the cold shoulder if she shows up at the mine."

"He better do more than that, Reverend." Hook twisted Peterson's title in his mouth with disgust.

"Don't worry, he'll handle it," Peterson answered.

"He better," Hook warned. "One more thing. Keep in mind that this was all your idea. If there is ever a leak, I'll assume it was you."

"Now, you know you don't have to worry about me. We've known each other too long for that."

"I do know you, Gary, that's why I said it."

The phone went dead in Peterson's hand. It was the middle of the night in the Congo, but Peterson called another private telephone number, waking Moshe Messime to tell him to keep Grey in the capitol if she showed up there. Then he called Thomas Alben and warned him to be on the lookout for her too, just in case.

In the meantime, Hook made another phone call of his own.

Chapter 14

Mai-Munene

Jaime hitched a ride from the airfield in Tshikapa to Mai-Munene in an overloaded pickup truck. As the driver rounded the last turn to Mai-Munene, he had to slam on his brakes to avoid running down a little girl fighting with another child in the middle of the road. Jaime jumped out to pull them apart, although neither one would loosen her grip on a fire-blackened can they had found in the village dump.

"Stop that!" he commanded, holding them apart at arm's length.

"Mine!" one screeched.

"Mine first!" the other yelled back.

"Stop it!" Jaime shouted. He didn't recognize either one of them, which was odd. Mai-Munene was so small he knew everybody in the village and most of the surrounding countryside, except the mine workers and soldiers, who came and went and kept to the barracks while they were there. These little girls were strangers. One was about seven years old, the other one maybe nine. They were both skinny and filthy from rooting about in the rubbish heap by the side of the road. Jaime looked from one to the other, then pulled the can out of their hands and held it above his head to end the dispute. The nine-year-old made a half-hearted leap to grab it out of his hand, then they both gave up so they could race back to the dump to join the other children picking through the trash. As Jaime watched, a little boy barely old enough to walk picked up something from the dirt. He put it in his mouth. His distended belly and sparse orange hair indicated advanced malnutrition. Jaime started toward him, but the boy ran to the other side of the pile. Jaime realized he was still holding the can. He didn't know how to keep the children from fighting over it, so he tossed it back onto the pile. Shaking his head, he walked back to the pickup.

At the clinic, children were everywhere. They milled around the dusty village square and sat in clusters in the shade of the huts near it. Some of the older ones tended smoky fires. A baby cried plaintively somewhere in the village. A gaggle of dirty youngsters surrounded the pickup when it pulled up to the clinic. Pieter met him at the door cradling a baby in one arm. A toddler clung to the hem of his shorts.

"Welcome home!" he said. "Want a kiddie?"

"What's all this?" Jaime asked. He paid the driver for the ride then pulled his bag out of the pile of unidentified cartons Jaime assumed the man was intending to smuggle across the border into Angola.

"Seems we've become an unofficial orphanage," Pieter said. "They started showing up last week while you were jetting about the world, dining in fine restaurants and dating Hollywood starlets and such not." The crowd of children parted as Jaime walked through them to the clinic doorway where Pieter stood. A few others straggled toward them from across the square.

Jaime acknowledged Pieter's jibe with a smile. "I'm gone a few days and you turn the place into a kindergarten," he said. "Where'd they come from?"

"I don't know," Pieter answered. "But I think this fellow had something to do with it." He stood aside as Christophe came out from the breezeway behind him. The boy smiled shyly at Jaime. "One of the little ones told me about a boy with a mark on his face who was going around the countryside telling them to come here, like some kind of infernal pied piper. Then this bloke showed up yesterday. I take it you know him?"

"*Bonjour*, Christophe," Jaime said. "How is your eye?" He crouched to get a better look at the boy's face. It was badly scarred, but it looked like the wound left by the branding under his eye was nearly healed.

"*Très bien, dakta*," he said. He looked at Jaime steadily and proudly.

"And where are your friends with the rifles?"

"Fighting the F.I.C. somewhere," he shrugged.

"So you escaped?"

"Yes, *dakta*," he smiled. "While they were busy attending to their bloody shits, I sneaked away."

"Good for you," Jaime smiled back. "What about these others?" He pointed at the gang of children gathered around them.

"I found someone like me, a boy hiding in the woods. He was very scared so I told him the *dakta* at Mai-Munene would protect him. He must have told someone else."

Jaime stood and surveyed the hopeful faces. "I guess the word spread," he said. "How many are there?" he asked Pieter.

"I counted two dozen this morning, but I think a couple more straggled in since," he answered.

"What are we going to do with them?"

"Take care of them," Pieter said. "What else?"

"Did our missionary friend volunteer any help?" Jaime asked, knowing the answer.

"All he did was double the guard on the old school. Wouldn't want any children getting in there now, would we? Then he left for Tshikapa with another one of his precious cartons of *minkisi*. I'm surprised you didn't run into him at the airfield."

"It looks like we're on our own, doesn't it?" said Jaime.

"As usual," Pieter shrugged. The baby squirmed and he shifted it to his other arm. "I don't suppose you came back from America with a bag full of money?"

"As a matter of fact, I replenished our bank account quite nicely, thanks to the generosity of a Mennonite millionaire I ran into," Jaime answered. "I stopped in Kinshasa and ordered a plane full of medical supplies to be flown to Tshikapa. We'll go meet it in a few days. There's enough left in the account so we can get some food too. Looks like we're going to need it."

Jaime threw his bags into his room and got to work. Pieter had been feeding the crowd from the clinic's supplies, but they were just about depleted, so Jaime dipped into the scant cash he had left over from his trip. He bought corn and rice from the mine store to supplement the nutrient-poor cassava on which most of the children had been subsisting. Along with beans and yams from local farmers and fruit gleaned from the surrounding forests, the grains would stave off starvation for a while. Jaime put some of the older children to work minding the younger ones and preparing the daily meal, which wasn't difficult since they had been doing so already. By the time he stretched out for the night, Jaime felt like he'd never been gone.

The next morning, he discovered that several more little ones had wandered into camp during the night. He told Pieter to round all the children up so he could give each one a quick physical before the morning meal was distributed. The results were discouraging but not unexpected: most of them were malnourished, there were a few cases of nutrition-based anemia and what he suspected was cyanide poisoning caused by eating poorly prepared cassava. A handful of the children suffered from yaws, which Jaime treated with his dwindling supply of ampicillin. He was sure there were HIV infections and probably some Hepatitis B, but there wasn't much he could do about those until he got the supplies he had ordered.

Nearly every child suffered from a wound of some sort. Not just scrapes on the elbows from tripping over roots in the forest or ragged punctures in the feet from stepping on a thorn on the trail, but also long, straight slashes from near misses by machetes and neat round holes made by 7.62 mm bullets, standard ammunition for AK-47s. One sloe-eyed girl had only a stump where her left arm should be. The mental wounds were even deeper. Many of the children slipped often into a vacant, distant stare, stopping what they were doing for no apparent reason and reliving the horrors they had seen. Jaime couldn't treat those wounds, but Christophe seemed to have a knack for bringing the sufferers back to reality and calming them.

Kafutshi and the other village women helped too, although she told Jaime they had to work in shifts because they were very busy making dolls for Brother Tom. Jaime wondered about that briefly, but soon forgot about it in the press of caring for the children.

Pieter seemed to be everywhere at once; handing out food, tending to dressings, sparking laughter wherever he went because he was usually followed around the camp by Kafutshi's twin grandsons, Kenda and Juvenal. The eight-year-old mimics rolled up their ragged shorts so their skinny legs stuck out in a good imitation of Pieter's long shanks. They trailed after him with exaggerated strides like half-pint marabou storks high-stepping their way along the riverbank. They tucked their hands into their armpits and flapped their elbows like wings. They craned their necks and bobbed their heads while they strutted along, evoking gales of laughter from the other children. Pieter pretended to shoo them away by waving his long arms in mock anger, which added to the merriment by making him look even more like a big blond bird.

The next day, Yoweri led a squad of soldiers through the camp, ostensibly guarding the village, but actually, Jaime suspected, simply asserting his position as strongman. The children melted away to the forest or into their makeshift homes when they saw the soldiers' uniforms and the carnivorous look in Yoweri's eye. Christophe was helping Jaime and Pieter tend to the children in the ward's three beds when the soldiers sauntered by. He went to the door and stood alertly in the breezeway as if he were protecting the occupants.

"Lunda Libre!" shouted one of Yoweri's men, pointing at Christophe's scarred face. The F.I.C. soldiers moved menacingly toward the clinic. Christophe stood his ground defiantly until Jaime stepped in front of him and pushed him gently back to the ward doorway. Pieter came to the door. He laid a calming hand on the boy's shoulder.

"This boy isn't Lunda Libre. He was a captive," Jaime said, holding up his hand to stop the soldiers.

"He is a terrorist," Yoweri glowered, "he must be questioned."

"He works for me now," Jaime answered without raising his voice. "I vouch for him."

Just then, a Land Rover escorted by another truck full of F.I.C. soldiers roared into the village. The last of the curious children disappeared completely. Tom Alben had returned from Tshikapa. Seeing a crowd of soldiers in front of the clinic, he skipped the turn into the mine compound and pulled to a stop behind them.

"Greetings, Doctor Talon!" he called out cheerfully. "Need some help here?"

"You can call off your army," Jaime replied. "They defeated the unarmed children." He didn't break eye contact with the glowering Yoweri.

"He hides a terrorist," Yoweri growled, taking a menacing step closer to the clinic. Jaime's right fist clenched reflexively at his side, but he stayed outwardly unshaken by the big captain's threat.

"I'm sure that's not the case, Captain," Alben said. "Is it, Dr. Talon?"

"Of course not. He's a Chokwe boy who was captured by the Lunda Libre and branded. The captain knows that," Jaime added.

"Then I think you'd best stand down, Captain," Alben said calmly. Yoweri glared at Jaime with eyes out of a nightmare. He barked a command to his men and they followed him back toward the mine. As he passed the truck full of soldiers escorting Alben, Yoweri snapped something to their driver, who turned the truck around to follow him up the hill. "Ugly brute, isn't he?" Alben said when they were out of earshot.

A brute who does your bidding, Jaime thought to himself.

"I guess you've been gathering pupils for my school when it opens," Alben said. He surveyed the now-abandoned cooking fires and makeshift shelters. A few children tentatively edged back across the square. Others watched from the shadows.

"There are plenty of children for your school, but our problem right now is feeding them," Jaime answered. "Can you give us some help with that?"

"I'll see what I can do," Alben answered. From the flatness of his tone, Jaime knew he had no intention of helping in any way. "Be sure to keep the little darlings away from the mine—for their own safety, of course," Alben added unnecessarily. He climbed back into his Land

Rover and wheeled it around to head back up the road without any further pleasantries.

Later in the day, Pieter cupped one hand under a patient's ear while he gingerly bathed the shallow wound above it with betadine solution. The orange fluid ran down the side of the patient's head and trickled into a small puddle in the palm of Pieter's cupped hand.

"If you used a kidney tray to catch the excess, you wouldn't have to walk around the rest of the day looking like you stuck your hand in a paint can," Jaime said with a grin as he looked up from the boy's eye he was irrigating to see what Pieter was doing.

"I would use the kidney tray if I could find the bleeding thing," Pieter replied. "Haven't seen it, have you?" Jaime gave the breezeway a quick scan.

"No, afraid not," he answered. He lifted the boy down from the examination table they had improvised out of two steel barrels and some rough planks. He motioned for the next person in line, an old woman cradling her left elbow in her right hand. Jaime knew her well; she came to see him for relief from her arthritic elbow nearly every day. "*Bonjour,* Kabisenga," he said briskly. "Does your arm still ache?" When the old woman gravely nodded, Jaime went into the dispensary and came back with two ibuprofen tablets, which he gave her solemnly and with a bit of ceremony. "Take one now and one before you go to sleep tonight," he said. It was the same prescription he gave her every morning. She thanked him and went away. Jaime didn't know whether she actually took the medicine or traded it for food, but either way it was a help to her.

Pieter finished treating the man with the head wound, then went into the dispensary to look for the white enameled kidney tray again. He had to make his way through the small gallery of children who had gathered to watch them deal with the patients. Empty-handed, the tall, long-boned South African came back outside and eyed the little ones suspiciously. "Any of you little stinkers seen my kidney tray?" he demanded with mock gruffness.

"What does it look like?" somberly asked Celestine. The way she jumped forward reminded Jaime of a little girl who wants desperately to be the teacher's pet.

"It looks like a blooming kidney about this big," Pieter said. He held his hands a few inches apart. "It's a bowl curved like this." He drew a short arc in the air with his index finger.

A light of recognition flickered in Celestine's eyes. Without a word, she ran away around the building. Two other girls followed her, keen to be part of the excitement, whatever it was. They ran the quarter mile to the river bank, where Celestine's younger brothers, Kenda and Juvenal, were assiduously building a pyramid of beautifully-styled mud bricks, each one molded into a perfect kidney shape in Pieter's tray.

"You bad boys!" Celestine scolded. "That belongs to the marabou *dakta*." Kenda looked at Juvenal and shrugged. Ignoring their sister, the two boys packed mud into the tray to make another brick. When it was full, Juvenal used a stick to even off the top before Kenda carefully turned it over and tapped on the bottom. A perfect kidney-shaped brick came out. "The marabou *dakta* needs this," Celestine declared. She snatched the tray out of Kenda's hands and ran back toward the village. The other two girls ran behind her.

"Ay!" Juvenal yelled. The two boys jumped up and ran after the girls, but their older sister's legs were longer so she easily outdistanced them. Celestine was proudly handing the muddy tray to Pieter when her brothers skittered to a stop behind her. Pieter looked from the mud-smeared faces of the boys to the matching residue in the tray and scowled at them ferociously.

"You're a couple of magpies, you two!" he scolded. "Stealing anything that isn't nailed down."

"They are very bad boys, *dakta*," Celestine chimed in, scowling at them ferociously herself. "I think you should beat them with a stick." Kenda stuck out his tongue at his sister while Juvenal eyed Pieter curiously to see if he was going to follow Celestine's instructions. Pieter couldn't hold his fierce pose any longer and laughed heartily.

"Maybe later, lovey," he said. "They're too dirty to beat now. Besides, I have to wash the mud off my tray." Before he knew what was happening, Celestine grabbed it out of his hands.

"I will wash it," she said, running back toward the river. By the time she came back, her brothers had disappeared and Pieter was busy wrapping another patient's leg with a bandage. Celestine proudly handed him the clean bowl.

"Aren't you little Miss Helpful!" Pieter smiled. "Thank you." Celestine beamed, a look of adoration in her eyes.

"It looks like you have a new aide," Jaime said.

"I could use one," said Pieter. "Would you like to be my assistant?" he asked the girl. She nodded vigorously. "What about your granmama? Doesn't she need your help with the *minkisi*?" he asked.

"Brother Tom made all the children leave," Celestine answered. "He said we make the ladies work too slow."

"In that case, you're hired," Pieter said.

"You'd rather work for the marabou *dakta* anyway, wouldn't you?" Jaime gently teased. Celestine nodded vigorously, a wide smile on her face.

Chapter 15
Kinshasa

Valerie's first report when she returned to the Congo was once again supposed to be an interview with President Moshe Messime. This one, however, was more difficult to arrange than the last one. When Nancy tried to set it up, Messime's staff insisted the president was too busy directing the arrival of the American military advisors to give her any time. Valerie and Nancy knew that was nonsense, of course, since the Americans had just begun to mobilize for the intervention and only a handful of advance troops were in the country at this point. There were many, many more to come, according to news reports, but this first contingent were engineers and quartermaster corps doing prep work. Nancy finally bullied her way through the paper pushers at the American Embassy and got them to twist arms in the presidential palace.

The interview this time was held in Messime's sprawling office inside the presidential palace. Messime sat in front of an array of colorful flags, one for each country on the continent, meant, Valerie assumed, to represent his ambitions for a Pan-Equatorial African Union. The new flag of the Democratic Republic of the Congo, which Messime had designed himself, stood at the center of the array next to the Stars and Stripes. It sent the unmistakable, if delusional, message that Moshe

Messime was the messiah of Sub-Saharan Africa.

Messime answered Valerie's first question about the role of American military advisors with a pre-packaged set piece about the "Alliance Against Evil" President Baker had begged him to join. Instead of expressing his gratitude in a paean to America, he expounded on the great favor he was doing for the United States by committing the F.I.C. forces to the battle against the godless dictators, gangsters, and pirates who were trying to dominate the world. By the time Valerie politely cut him off, he had made it sound as if the Democratic Republic of Congo was stepping forward just in time to save the United States of America from the ravages of evil. It was an interesting take on the situation, but definitely destined for the cutting room floor.

Valerie let him rant and rave about the good guys and bad guys a few minutes longer to gain his confidence then she homed in on the questions she really wanted to ask. "President Baker said there are American business interests at stake in the Congo," she began. "Yet you nationalized all of your country's resources when you took office. What American interests is President Baker trying to protect?"

"Perhaps you should ask him, Miss Grey. I can tell you, however, that in recent years we have quietly and selectively welcomed investment from the United States in several ventures in order to strengthen our economy and our ties to America."

"Investments like the one the Reverend Gary Peterson made?" Valerie asked as innocuously as she could. Messime's eyes became wary.

"Yes, although that is just one of many enterprises that have drawn American capital to the Congo. They are part of the larger sphere of commonality we share." Valerie knew he was about to slip away from the subject, so she interrupted before he could start another tirade.

"Do you have a personal business interest in the diamond mine at Mai-Munene—the one owned by Gary Peterson?" she asked point-blank.

Messime answered calmly, which surprised her. "I fought a hard, bloody war to liberate my country from corrupt leaders who stole the treasures of our land for their personal gain," he intoned. Judging by his steadiness, Valerie wondered if he had rehearsed the answer in case she probed the mine situation. "I won that war with the support of the people of the Congo, who know that I am a great father who could never steal from his own children. The Reverend Gary Peterson acquired the mine at Mai-Munene in a completely transparent, above-board transaction through the Bureau of Mines of the Democratic Republic of the Congo. It was completed with the full knowledge and approval of all appropriate authorities. You are welcome to inspect the documentation at any time, Miss Grey."

"Funny, that's almost exactly what Reverend Peterson said," Valerie observed.

"Then it must be true," Messime smiled benignly. Valerie knew she wasn't going to get any more out of him, so she brought the interview to a close.

When the camera was off, Messime asked where she intended to go next. She was about to say Mai-Munene, then thought better of it and said Mbuji-Mayi, a town over five hundred miles away where the country's Bureau of Mines was located. The dictator scowled. "That would not be a good idea," he said. "The Lunda Libre is operating throughout the south. That would not be a safe journey."

"I need to examine the documents authorizing transfer of ownership of the mine at Mai-Munene," Valerie said.

"If you insist on pursuing that fruitless line of inquiry, I will have them brought here to you," Messime shrugged. "That will be much easier and safer."

"Are any of your troops headed that way? How about American advisors? Can't I accompany them?" she asked.

"That is not possible," he said. "I must deny you permission to travel outside of the capital, Miss Grey. It is for your own safety."

Valerie didn't say anything as Messime, trailed by a crowd of staffers, left the veranda. She had no intention of sitting comfortably in the capital while the country crumbled around the borders. As soon as Messime was inside, Nancy moved her into position for a stand-up with the presidential palace as a backdrop. Looking steadily into the camera, Valerie ended the segment by saying, "As thousands of American troops embark for the Democratic Republic of the Congo, President Messime has made clear that this war is not about justice, peace, or human rights. It's not a religious feud, nor is it the outgrowth of so-called tribal strife. This war is about diamonds."

A black Humvee with a 50-caliber machine gun mounted above the windscreen pulled up to the presidential palace not long after Valerie and the crew left. Two men in well-worn bush jackets got out. Both were lean and hard, tall, with short-cropped hair. One of them had a long, thin scar along his jawline as if someone had tried to slash his throat but missed high. He went into the palace. The other stayed by the truck, leaning casually but alertly against it while he surveyed the landscaped grounds, neatly groomed paths, and the circular driveway snaking in from the guardhouse at the road. It was impossible to tell if he ever blinked behind his wrap-around sunglasses.

Inside, the man with the scar, Steve Scavino, silently flashed his National Security Agency identification to the corporal manning the reception desk, who immediately picked up the phone and spoke urgently to whoever answered deep within the palace. Moments later, an F.I.C. captain appeared, checked Scavino's papers, then ushered him into a corridor leading through a high-security station to the presidential quarters.

Ten minutes later, Scavino came back outside. He motioned to his partner to get into the Humvee. "We missed her," he said. "She's staying at the Hotel Intercontinental. Let's go."

Valerie and Nancy edited the story then sent it back to New York from the Reuters satellite communications center on the Avenue des Aviateurs. As soon as the transmission was confirmed, they piled into the blue Toyota van with a distinctive yellow top Nancy had rented when they arrived. Valerie told Bobby, who doubled as driver, to go east toward the ferry road instead of south toward their hotel near the French embassy.

"And lose our escort," she added, referring to the jeep with the two minders Messime had assigned to accompany them everywhere they went in the capital.

Bobby turned in his seat and grinned at Nancy sitting in the back. "Valerie's taking us on another little adventure!" He put the small van in gear. Turning back to Valerie in the front seat beside him, he asked cheerfully, "Are we going anywhere in particular?"

"Mai-Munene," she answered.

"Oh, good!" he exclaimed dryly. "Do you want me to stop at the roadblocks, or just crash through?"

"Don't do anything stupid, Bobby," she answered with a grin. "Unless you have to."

Bobby led the minders three blocks east toward the American embassy, slowing there as if to turn left into the compound, then suddenly gunned it the opposite way around the corner into the crowded street that ran past the big Belgian embassy compound. At the next corner, he leaned on the horn and whipped left, cutting off a lumbering delivery truck and sending pedestrians and bicyclists scattering to the sides. He grinned when he glanced in his mirror; the minders were mired in the melee at the corner behind them. He raced down the bumpy street that passed between the railroad station and the ferry road. The congestion in front of the railroad station slowed them down, but he pushed the van through the crowd until it popped out onto the river road. Just past the turnoff for the ferry, they ran into the first roadblock.

Cars, carts, motor scooters, bicycles and a mob of pedestrians stood on both sides of the barricade waiting in numb resignation for the F.I.C. soldiers to examine their papers and let them through. Those without official papers simply folded some currency into a piece of scrap paper and handed it over; those with no money hoped for some leniency from their fellow countrymen—and many got it—but it all took time. Officials in government cars were moved through immediately while foreigners like Valerie and her crew were waved forward and given extra attention.

"Papers, madame," an F.I.C. corporal demanded brusquely through the van window when they reached the head of the line. Another soldier stuck his head through the back window to look around while two others opened the rear door and rummaged among the camera gear and supplies. Nancy watched them carefully while Bobby kept his eyes glued to the rearview mirror looking for the minders. Valerie gave the corporal her press pass.

"This means nothing," the corporal stated flatly. "You must have a national security document to travel outside the capital. I must see your passport as well."

"President Messime personally authorized this trip," Valerie answered boldly. She put a twenty-dollar bill in her passport before she handed it to him. She wasn't sure what the right amount would be, but she knew most F.I.C. soldiers were paid less than fifty dollars a month when they were paid at all, so this was a substantial sum. Offering too much could backfire by making her seem too eager to get through the roadblock. Valerie must have been right because he turned his back to the truck, slipped out the bill, and turned back with a smile to return her press pass and passport.

"Very well, madame. Enjoy the beautiful countryside," he said without a trace of sarcasm as he waved them through. Bobby slipped the van into gear with a sigh of relief.

The road paralleled the Congo River until it reached Kimpoko, then turned southeastward toward Kikwit, about two hundred and fifty miles from the capital. For the first few miles outside Kinshasa, it was packed with travelers to and from the capital, traders with carts full of goods, farmers riding or pushing bicycles loaded with bundles of manioc leaves and other produce, and occasional overloaded trucks whose drivers always had room for one more passenger. The bicycles pushed the pedestrians off the road, cars elbowed the bicycles aside, and the trucks trumped them all. It was the main highway in the country and, except for the river, it was the principal route for supplies into Kinshasa from the interior, so it had been paved and even maintained fairly regularly at one time. Like the rest of the infrastructure in the country, though, it had suffered from total neglect. What pavement remained held up for the first forty miles, but the deterioration was so severe the roadway was basically reduced to one lane, causing slowdowns every time another vehicle came from the opposite direction. After the pavement ran out, the roadway became a bumpy track, dusty in high places and muddy in low spots, that forced the van to a maddeningly slow pace. Valerie alternated between looking nervously back for pursuers and forward to spot roadblocks as Bobby pushed the vehicle as fast he dared on the bone-jarring surface.

Between the roadblocks and the road conditions, it took several hours to crawl the hundred miles to Takundi even though the traffic had eventually thinned to mostly locals traveling from village to village. Fortunately, there had been no sign of the minders since they lost them in Kinshasa. They decided to pull off the road for the night rather than try to push on toward Kikwit in the dark.

Bobby maneuvered the van into a dry patch under some small iroko trees near the side of the road. They would leave at first light, hoping to stay ahead of Messime's men. After quick bathroom trips into the bush, they settled restlessly into the van seats to get some sleep. The darkness closed in around them rapidly as the lullaby of the Congo evening arose. Valerie heard a small creature padding around outside the truck, then caught the distinctive scent of a civet marking his territory, something she'd smelled the last time she was in the country. Not long afterward, she heard a faint chuffing sound and wondered if that was the civet as well or some larger animal hunting it. She slept restlessly among the sounds of the African night.

Scavino underestimated Valerie. He assumed she would want a cool bath and a leisurely afternoon after her interview with Moshe Messime. After he found she wasn't in her room, he waited for her outside the hotel where he thought it would be easier to complete the mission and escape into the crowded streets unimpeded. But Valerie didn't appear. He and his partner waited longer than they should have, so by the time they heard from Messime's security chief that she had escaped her minders in the traffic, it was too late to try to follow her. Darkness was falling on Kinshasa and not even these men would travel into the Congo countryside at night. They decided to wait until morning to pick up her trail along the main highway. The reporter's blue van with its bright yellow top shouldn't be hard to spot and, if they missed her along the way, they could just jump ahead and wait for her in Kikwit. Assuming she was headed for Mbuji-Mayi as Messime reported, she would have to pass through there on the way.

Scavino didn't know why he was chasing Valerie Grey; he only knew what he had been explicitly commanded to do when he found her. It wasn't an unusual assignment for him, nor was it out of the ordinary for the unexplained orders to come from within the White House. He had successfully executed several similar missions in the past. Scavino was confident he would find Valerie Grey and deal with her as he had been ordered.

Chapter 16
Kikwit

The next day, sporadic traffic moved across the concrete and steel bridge over the Wamba River at Kenge even though the rusty structure looked like it could collapse at any time from lack of maintenance. Bobby brought the blue and yellow van to a stop in front of a line of boards studded with tire-mangling nails strung together and dragged across the road by F.I.C. guards on the approach to the bridge. Aside from a man pushing a bicycle laden with a bundle of rags back toward Kinshasa, no one else was on the road. Another handful of soldiers guarded the other end of the bridge and Valerie wondered if she would have to pay off both of them. She slipped a twenty into her passport in preparation for the first one as a scowling sergeant ordered them out of the van.

"I don't like facing these guys without witnesses," Nancy said under her breath as the three of them gathered in front of the van.

"Just stay calm," Valerie said. "It's all routine."

"Papers!" the sergeant demanded, holding his hand out to Bobby. The cameraman gestured toward Valerie, who handed over her press credentials and passport. The sergeant glanced at the documents, put the money in his pocket, then motioned for two soldiers standing nearby to search the van anyway. They opened the back door and started throwing gear onto the road.

"Hey! Careful with that!" Nancy shouted. She hurried to the back of the van just in time to snatch the aluminum case holding their satellite telephone out of the hands of one of the soldiers. Bobby was right behind her, trying to pull his video camera case away from the other one. The soldier shoved him roughly away, flipped the catches, and opened the case.

"A camera!" he shouted to the sergeant in front of the van where he stood with Valerie, who didn't want to let their papers out of her sight.

"We're journalists," Valerie explained, pointing to the press pass in the man's hand.

"You cannot be journalists," the sergeant answered without hesitation. "Journalists are not allowed outside the capital, so you must be spies." He pulled a pistol out of his belt and pointed it at Valerie's chest. She carefully took a step back to lower the tension level. "Bring the other spies here!" he shouted to the men with Nancy and Bobby at the back of the van. One man un-slung his rifle and shoved Bobby toward the front. The other yanked the telephone case out of Nancy's hands.

"Give me that!" she snapped, trying to wrest it away from him. The first solider whipped his rifle around toward Nancy. Valerie heard the safety click.

"Stop!" Valerie demanded. Bobby pulled the fuming Nancy away.

"Bring that here!" ordered the sergeant. When the soldier handed him the aluminum case with the distinctive MBS-TV logo, he laid it down on the ground and popped it open. He unfolded the small satellite dish so it stood above the panel that filled the bottom of the case. "What is this!?" he said triumphantly. "The only people who use devices like this one are bloodsucking spies for the colonialists."

"We're journalists!" Valerie protested. "Look at my press pass. It's signed by President Messime himself!"

"I told you, you cannot be journalists," snarled the sergeant, standing up and facing them. "How do I know you have not forged the president's signature on this worthless paper?" Valerie thought the man might be angling for another bribe but she couldn't be sure. She had another idea.

"Bobby, put the tape with the Messime interview in the camera," she said quickly. When he turned to go to the back of the van and get the tape, the guard stepped in front of him and blocked his way with his rifle.

"We want to show you a message from President Messime," Valerie insisted to the sergeant, who finally nodded to let Bobby go. Bobby ran to the back of the van, found the raw footage of Valerie's interview, and slipped it into the video camera. He came back to the sergeant and opened the LCD viewer so the man could view the tape. The establishing shot of Valerie and the president came up, but there was no sound. Uncertainty passed over the sergeant's face.

"What does he say?" he demanded. Nancy scrambled through the equipment until she came up with a headset and quickly plugged it in. Valerie gave it to the sergeant, who held it hesitantly to his ear. He listened to Messime's answer to one of Valerie's questions, then handed the headset back to her.

"You see, we are journalists working with President Messime's permission," Valerie said, hoping she sounded more confident than she felt. The sergeant looked at her impassively. Valerie prayed he was considering that President Messime would not have sat in his office and conferred politely with her if she were a spy, so she was probably telling the truth about being a journalist. Of course, he could also be deciding which jail to stick them in or simply how much to charge them for the privilege of passing over his bridge.

"In this district, journalists are required to purchase a special permit to use cameras," he finally announced.

Relieved, Valerie said, "Would one hundred American dollars cover that permit?"

"Yes, that is the exact fee," the sergeant nodded grandly. "However, you should also give a *cadeau* to my men for their help in loading your vehicle." He looked expectantly at Valerie.

"Of course," she answered, ignoring the irony of the comment about loading the vehicle as she looked at the pile of equipment the men had left on the road behind the van. "Get that stuff back in the truck and let's get going," she said. Bobby and Nancy hurriedly packed the gear and stuffed it into the back of the van while Valerie handed the sergeant a handful of bills. "I have also included a *cadeau* for the men on the other side of the river. Are they under your command?" she asked.

The sergeant puffed up importantly. "Yes, those are my men also." He counted the money. "This will be sufficient," he said. He shouted across the bridge and waved the fistful of bills over his head. One of the soldiers on the other side waved back in acknowledgement. Valerie climbed back into the van as the sergeant told one of the soldiers to pull the makeshift tire-shredders out of the way. Bobby drove over the bridge toward Kikwit.

Valerie wanted to urge him to drive faster but knew he couldn't. She hoped there wouldn't be many more roadblocks; each one slowed them down and one of them, she assumed, would soon have the word to stop the three Americans fleeing the capital.

Valerie Grey had nearly a half-day's lead, but Scavino wasn't particularly concerned as he and his partner drove out of Kinshasa. Their black Humvee would make better time on the rough road than the reporter's van and, if need be, the 50-caliber M-9 machine gun mounted above the windscreen would insure a road clear of traffic. The only time he expected to stop was at checkpoints to question the guards at the roadblocks. As incompetent as he knew the F.I.C. forces to be, he thought even they would remember a blue van with a bright yellow top and a beautiful white woman in it. The black Humvee bullied its way to the front of the long line at the bustling checkpoint on the outskirts of Kishanga, where Scavino grilled the captain in charge about whether he had seen Valerie or her vehicle. The captain then made a big show of describing them to his men, but reported they had seen nothing. The next checkpoint was just a few miles further east at Kimpoko, where Scavino heard the same denials, although he didn't fully believe them. He suspected the guards weren't willing to admit they had let someone without the proper papers through their checkpoint because it would get them in trouble. At Takundi, Scavino got fed up with the know-nothing attitude and shoved his Glock 9mm into the face of the corporal in charge, who then admitted the blue and yellow van had passed through the day before. It was late in the day, he said, nearly dark. They would have stopped somewhere nearby for the night, Scavino figured.

At Kenge, the bridge over the Wamba River was full of women with bundles on their heads and men pushing carts across in both directions. It must be market day somewhere nearby, Scavino thought. He sent his partner to question the smaller contingent of soldiers on the eastern side while he strode purposefully up to the sergeant who looked to be in charge of the western end of the bridge. The F.I.C. sergeant was obviously impressed by Scavino's heavily armed vehicle, but he turned blankly cold when he heard the description of the van and Valerie Grey.

"We have seen no vehicles or persons like that," he bluffed haughtily. "If we do, we will take them into custody and notify headquarters immediately." The sergeant's manner didn't ring true and Scavino's already-thin patience had been worn away by the intransigence he'd been dealing with all day.

"We know she came this way. Assemble your men," Scavino ordered. "I will question them myself."

The sergeant hesitated just long enough to raise Scavino's suspicions another notch. "Do it now, sergeant," Scavino said with a deadly undertone. Just as the sergeant turned to call his men together, the other agent came trotting across the bridge.

"They went through here this morning," he said.

"Those men are mistaken," the sergeant said urgently. "I allowed no such persons to pass my checkpoint, so how could they have gone through theirs?"

Scavino suddenly grabbed the sergeant by the collar and slammed him backwards against the guardhouse wall, using a gym-hardened forearm across the throat to hold him there. "When did she pass here?" he snarled, his face nearly touching the sergeant's. The scar along Scavino's jawline shined white against his angry red face. The sergeant raised his arms to push back but Scavino grasped his wrist. He squeezed and twisted it sharply. Something in the sergeant's wrist cracked audibly. He screamed as Scavino leaned in and drove him to his knees.

"How long ago?" he demanded. The troops in the garrison uneasily fingered their weapons, but Scavino's companion stared them down over the barrel of an Uzi pistol that had appeared from nowhere.

"I do not know! This morning. Many hours ago. I forget!" the sergeant answered incoherently between clenched teeth.

Scavino savagely twisted the sergeant's wrist to grind the bones against each other. He glared into the grimacing face before him. The sergeant whimpered. Scavino decided there was no more information to be gained. He gave the corporal's wrist a final yank, then dropped it in disgust. He turned to his companion and jerked his head toward the Humvee.

"Let's go. If she passed through here this morning, she's halfway to Kikwit by now. If we keep moving, we can catch her before dark."

Bobby made good time on the highway between Kikongo and Masi-Manimba. The people in the two villages had taken it upon themselves to painstakingly repair the crumbled roadbed as best they could after the last rainy season, so he was able to move along at a faster pace. After the turnoff for Putumba, the road fell back into general disrepair and he slowed again to a bone-jarring crawl. As the afternoon began and Bobby navigated a particularly rough stretch of broken pavement, something in the van's suspension system broke with a resounding crack. He crept along carefully for a hundred yards, then pulled to a stop in the shade of a grove of malolo trees. A man squatted in the fragrant shade of the thick leaves surrounded by an array of jugs and bottles full of gasoline. The man arose and walked toward the van with a friendly mercantile smile.

"This could be a good sign. We need gas too," Bobby said as they got out of the truck to greet the smiling man. After an exchange of greetings and some explanation, Bobby and the gasoline vendor crawled under the van and conferred for a moment, then slid back out. "A rear suspension strut snapped," Bobby said.

"That sounds serious," Nancy said.

"This guy says his brother can weld it," Bobby shrugged. "It will make it to the garage if I keep it slow."

"Then let's go," Valerie said. "It's not like we have many choices."

"Not so fast," Nancy interrupted. "Where is this garage?"

The gasoline man pointed down a path through the malolo trees. It looked just barely wide enough to accommodate the small van. "Not far," he said helpfully. "I would take you, but I must stay here to tend my merchandise." He waved his hand over the collection of gasoline-filled glassware.

"How do we know it's safe?" Nancy asked doubtfully.

"If somebody wanted to mug us, they'd just do it right here," Valerie said confidently. "Let's get moving." Bobby helped the man pour gas into the van, filtering it through a funnel fitted with a piece of cloth that caught most of the foreign objects. They climbed back into the van and Bobby steered it carefully down the path. When they got past the malolo grove, the undergrowth closed in behind them and scraped the sides of the van, but the distinct path was easy to follow. It was probably a road abandoned when the main highway was cut through the region, Valerie guessed.

"Do you think Joseph Conrad made it this far?" Nancy cracked nervously.

Her words were almost drowned out by the sudden rumble of a heavy vehicle passing the malolo grove on the main road behind them. Valerie couldn't see it through the heavy foliage, but it sounded like it had come from the direction of Kinshasa. It slowed, but didn't stop, as if the driver were looking for something, didn't see it, and drove on. The gasoline vendor must have disappeared into the brush when he heard the heavy vehicle coming.

Bobby kept the van creeping forward. In a few minutes, the path widened. They came to a grease-stained patch of bare ground surrounded by a few mud-brick huts with thatch roofs in general disrepair. Oddly, all the little houses looked like they had been abandoned years before. Several of them appeared to have burned. A colonial-era Citroen sat tiredly on blocks on one side of the clearing. Next to it was a hut in slightly better repair than the others with a gently smoking fire pit in front of it. A small pile of old car parts lay rusting into the ground nearby. A block and tackle hung from a convenient tree branch. A man came out of the house and stepped forward to greet them. It was obvious from the shape of his wide smile that he was the brother of the gasoline man.

"*Bonjour*! I am Mbaya," he said, extending his hand. "May I be of service?"

Bobby shook the man's hand and gestured to the back of the van. "The man by the road said you could weld a strut," he said, looking around doubtfully.

"Certainly," the mechanic said. "Let me see." He scooted under the van, rattled something for a moment, then called out, "My brother is correct. I can fix this easily. It will be a temporary repair, but it should hold if you are careful." He slid back out and stood up. "If you will let me use your jack, it will go faster," he said to Bobby. "Please make yourselves comfortable out of the sun," he told Valerie and Nancy, pointing to his house.

While Bobby dug around in the back of the van looking for the jack, Valerie and Nancy stepped into the house, stopping just inside the doorway to let their eyes adjust to the darkness. A tarp covered something standing on wheels next to the door to their right. On the other side of the single room, two metal cots sat with their legs in cans of old motor oil to keep crawling insects off the bedding. A small wooden table stood in one corner. It held three Polaroid photographs in plastic frames propped against a box. Valerie stepped closer to look at the faded pictures. One was of a woman standing in front of the house flanked by two happy children. There was also one of the woman by herself. In the third picture, an elderly man in a chauffeur's cap stood stiffly next to the Citroen at a time when it still had tires. A single short candle burned in front of the pictures like a shrine. The mechanic came into the house wiping his hands on a rag.

"Your family?" Valerie asked, gesturing toward the table.

"Yes," he answered simply.

"They are beautiful," she said.

"Yes, thank you." He paused before adding quietly, "They are gone now." He pulled the tarp off the object standing next to the door. It was an old acetylene welding rig, with two tanks and a carefully-coiled pair of hoses joined by a brass nozzle on the end. A pair of welding glasses hung from the valve on one of the tanks.

"I am sorry," Valerie said softly.

"Thank you. They are still in my heart," Mbaya answered. Valerie sensed he wanted to talk about them.

"How old were your children when this picture was taken?" she asked.

"My son, Innocente, was six and his sister was five. This was my good wife, Khelendende. This fine strong man was my father. He taught me to repair automobiles." He stopped for a moment and regarded the picture of his father. "The doctor said he brought it back from Kikwit when he delivered a truck to a customer there."

"Brought what?" Valerie asked gently.

"The Ebola. It was not his fault. He did not know that the disease could jump on you so easily, even from a dead person. The man who owned the truck died and my father helped to bury him before he came home. A few days later, my father got very sick. Then my children got sick and they all died. Khelendende tried to care for them, but the disease jumped to her, too. My brother and I were working in Lusanga. When we returned home, we found only the pit where they had been buried with the others. Everyone else in the village had fled. At first, the doctor would not let us enter our house, but later he did. I never saw my beautiful family again." He looked at the pictures. "They are why I cannot leave. This is how I remember them. Beautiful."

"Yes, they were," Valerie said quietly. Mbaya wheeled the welding rig out of the house. Now Valerie understood what had happened to the village. When Ebola struck, the residents who were able to escape ran away. The authorities quarantined the site while Mbaya and his brother were gone, then kept them out while they sanitized the area. It looked like Mbaya and his brother were the only people willing to return and live there.

"This place is creepy," Nancy said when the mechanic was out of earshot. "We should get out of here before we catch something."

"That was a long time ago," Valerie said as they walked out into the clearing to watch Mbaya weld the piece from the van back together.

"I don't care. Ebola's nothing to mess with," Nancy answered, lighting a cigarette nervously. Bobby and Mbaya finished and walked over to them. "We ready to go?" Nancy asked.

"What's your big hurry?" Bobby asked. Nancy glanced nervously at Mbaya.

"You need not fear catching the Ebola from me. Dr. Talon told us it is safe here now."

Valerie's pulse quickened slightly. "Dr. Talon?" she said. "Was Jaime Talon here?"

"Oh yes," Mbaya's eyes glowed as he remembered the doctor. "Dr. Talon was here when I returned. At first I hated him because he would not let me die with my family. Then he helped me understand that I must live to keep their memory. Dr. Talon could not heal them, but he healed me. He is a very great doctor."

Valerie felt a twinge of the confused emotions she experienced when she met Jaime in New York. "We hope to see him soon," she said. "I will tell him what you said."

Mbaya grabbed her hand and shook it vigorously. "Oh yes, please give him my very best regards," he exclaimed.

"If we don't get moving, we're never going to get there," Nancy interjected.

"We're never going to get through all these roadblocks anyway," Bobby added. "Somebody's going to stop us sooner or later.

Mbaya said, "Excuse me, but you wish to evade the authorities to see Dr. Talon?" Valerie nodded and he grinned. "I will take you on the old road. Follow me."

They got back in the van. Bobby carefully drove through a narrow opening Mbaya created by pulling back the vegetation on the other side of the clearing from where they had entered it. It was the remnants of the old road they had been on before. Mbaya led them on the nearly-invisible path through the forest by walking ahead and chopping back vegetation that threatened to choke the road off completely. After a half hour or so, he held up his hand and stopped. Peering through the windshield, Valerie thought she saw the glint of water behind a screen of leaves. Mbaya came to her window.

"Wait here. I will retrieve the ferryman. You will pay him ten dollars.

Okay?" he said. When Valerie nodded and handed him the money, he disappeared through the undergrowth. Branches and leaves pressed against the van windows giving Valerie a feeling of being trapped within a gigantic inside-out terrarium. Something dropped onto the top of the van with a soft thud, then slithered off and disappeared.

"I'll never complain about the booths at Tavern on the Green being claustrophobic again," Nancy said.

Valerie forced her door open and got out of the van. She pushed the curtain of leaves out of the way until she could see the river about a car's length away from where she stood. It was less than a hundred yards wide. She assumed from the direction they had taken that the river was the Kasilu, which meant that Kikwit was somewhere downstream, probably not very far if Mbaya could summon a ferry from here.

A colony of black and gold weaver birds flitted about their intricately built nests in a tree hanging over the water. The river rolled by quietly beneath them, lapping at the shallow muddy bank. The busy male birds wove their complicated nests to attract females; the sight reminded Valerie of David and his unanswered proposal. She stood quietly watching the complex domestic scene. Did she want a partner for the rest of her life? If so, David would be perfect in every way; giving her room to grow, to run off to Africa or someplace else if need be, even to chuck her career and try something new. But did she want a partner at all? She wished she knew. The thoughts chased around in her head like the weaver birds flitting nervously among the branches of the tree.

She was about to go back to the van when she heard a chugging engine on the river. A few minutes later, a small pontoon ferry appeared around the bend with Mbaya on the deck. He waved vigorously. Valerie signaled to Bobby, who started the truck and eased ahead until she could get back in. Mbaya jumped off the ferry holding a rope that he quickly tied to a small tree. The ferryman threw him another rope. After it was tied off, they slid two thick planks off the ferry deck until the ends rested on the riverbank. The planks weren't much wider than the van's tires, but Mbaya confidently guided Bobby across. By the time the van was all the way on the ferry, the deck was nearly awash in sluggish red-brown water. The ferryman reversed the engine and the craft plowed slowly across the narrow stream to a barely perceptible path on the opposite bank. When the boat neared the bank, Mbaya hopped off with a heavy rope that he ran twice around a stout tree trunk as the ferryman gunned the engine to push the craft up closer to the shallow bank. Mbaya tied off another rope, pulled the two planks forward onto the shore, then signaled for Bobby to drive forward. Bobby put the van into gear and drove it onto land. Valerie exhaled with an audible whoosh. She realized she must have been holding her breath all the way across. Mbaya ran up to the van window.

"I must leave now and help this man return his ferry to its proper station," he said. "Follow the old road until you come to the big highway. You will be on the other side of Kikwit." He smiled. "Please give my greetings to Dr. Talon."

Valerie thanked him again and Bobby drove forward into the thinning forest.

After he finished with the morning patients, Jaime walked to the mine compound to once again press Alben for help to feed the orphans. More children had filtered into the camp overnight and, between the young refugees and the village kids, it seemed like there were children everywhere. Their crude shelters and smoky fires filled the usually empty square. Most of the refugees were malnourished. They had survived by begging manioc roots and corn flour from women in the countryside to make fou-fou, a starchy paste that helped cut their hunger pangs but gave their thin bodies very few nutrients. Nsima, made with corn meal, was a little more nutritious, but not much. Jaime could supplement their diet with bananas, peanuts, oranges, and other produce his patients brought to barter for clinic services, but he knew he could never keep up with the demand, especially if more children showed up. What he really needed more than anything were nutritional supplements that provided protein, like fortified powdered milk. He explained the situation to Alben as soon as he walked into the missionary's office in the concrete-block mine headquarters.

"If you can't spare us any food, it would be helpful if you could loan us a truck for a day or two," Jaime told him. "I need to send Pieter to Tshikapa to meet the plane bringing in my medical supplies and he could bring back extra food if he had one of your trucks."

"I'll see if Joao can spare one," Alben answered, pretending that the mine manager had some authority. "How many little mouths are you feeding now?"

"There are fifty-two so far. If we get any more, we're going to have to figure out a way to get them to the refugee camp at Bukedi. We don't have the facilities."

"At least then they'd be out of your hair," Alben said.

Jaime ignored the pointed hint. "I'd also like to use the school as a temporary barracks for the kids," he said. "The shelters in the square won't hold up when the rains come. The school is the only empty building in the village."

Alben frowned. "That won't be possible, I'm afraid. As you know, we're using the building as a factory of sorts. It's full of materials and tools."

"Why can't the women make their dolls at home like they did before?" Jaime demanded, starting to lose the battle to stay calm.

"We've modernized the operation," the missionary answered like a plant manager explaining his operation to a visiting minor shareholder. "It's much more efficient making them on a little assembly line. And the more dolls the women make, the more money they earn. You wouldn't want to deprive them of the chance to better themselves, would you?"

"How much profit does your church make from this little factory?" Jaime snapped.

"Not a dime, Dr. Talon! And I'm offended by that remark!"

Jaime backed off, remembering that he still needed something from the man. "Fine. Sorry. Can we use a truck?"

"Yes, I suppose so," Alben answered, dropping his charade about the mine manager.

"Thanks," Jaime said brusquely. He left to tell Pieter.

Jaime waved as Pieter climbed into the broken-down Mercedes 4 X 4 that Joao de Santos loaned him to drive to Tshikapa. Pieter waved back, then threw a silly kiss to Celestine, who stood frozen at Jaime's side. As Pieter drove away, she snuffled softly. When the truck rounded the bend toward Mpala and disappeared, she lifted her head to the sky and wailed. Jaime quickly crouched and put his arms around her.

He lived with hysteria like hers all the time. People in the outside world saw pictures of sad-faced children who were hungry, diseased, perhaps even grievously wounded, but they were almost always caught by the camera in moments of anguished elegance. Photographers shot pictures of dignified poignancy because that's what editors bought. The reality, Jaime knew, was that these children were wonderfully resilient but they weren't automatons; they were humans who suffered random moments of despair and often broke down into ugly, snot-running, twisted-face, sobbing spells at the slightest—or even without any—provocation.

Tears streamed down Celestine's contorted cheeks as Jaime knelt beside her. He tried to soothe her by telling her that Pieter would be back in a couple of days, but she was inconsolable. The girl had lost most of the important people in her short life and she was sure another one had just disappeared. Celestine's wails became louder and louder so Jaime picked her up and held her tightly. She quieted somewhat in his embrace, but kept sobbing wetly against his shirt as he carried her into the dispensary.

Inside, he saw the *nkisi* Kafutshi had given him when he treated the girl for a pricked thumb. He handed it to her, but she would not be comforted. Jaime stroked Celestine's back soothingly. The *nkisi* helped quiet her sobs, but she refused to let go of his neck. He carried her awkwardly to the school to find Kafutshi.

The school, built of handmade cement blocks at the other end of the village, had two big windows to let light through each wall, with wooden grates across them to keep out intruders. Entry was through a second open-air classroom covered by the same tin roof but where the block walls rose only waist high. Yoweri sat at a rough table with two other F.I.C. soldiers in the open room. The women chattered as they worked behind them inside the enclosed classroom. None of the soldiers got up when Jaime came in, but the scar-faced captain held up his hand.

"No one is allowed to interrupt the women while they are working," he said gruffly. Celestine clamped her arms even tighter around Jaime and hid her face in his neck when Yoweri growled.

"Nonsense," Jaime said. He walked past the table toward the inner room. One of the soldiers jumped ahead of him to block the door. "Get out of my way," Jaime snapped. The soldier's eyes didn't flicker as he stolidly crossed his arms across his chest and widened his stance defiantly.

"You have no business here, *dakta*," said Yoweri.

"I'm going to see Kafutshi. This girl needs her grandmother. Now get out of my way," Jaime ordered. The soldier puffed out his chest and didn't move, apparently enjoying the confrontation with the white doctor.

Yoweri smirked, "Go away and leave the girl. We will take care of her until her grandmother is finished." One of the other men chuckled wetly. Celestine flinched and whimpered, trying to push her face under Jaime's collar. The *nkisi*, which had been squeezed between them, worked loose and fell to the ground.

"Where did you get that!" Yoweri demanded sharply, rising to his feet and pointing at the doll. The third solider grabbed his rifle as Yoweri jumped up.

"It's just a doll," Jaime responded angrily. He leaned over awkwardly to pick up the *nkisi* with Celestine clinging to his neck.

"It is stolen!" Yoweri barked. He pushed Jaime out of the way and snatched the doll up off the ground.

Celestine howled with fright at the shove. Her cries brought several women running out of the enclosed classroom. Kafutshi squeezed past the guards to take Celestine out of Jaime's arms and clucked softly into the girl's ear to quiet her. Celestine fixed her big, wet eyes on Jaime and sniffed.

Jaime reached for the *nkisi* in Yoweri's hand, but the captain stuck his pistol in Jaime's face.

"Are you going to shoot me for a doll?" Jaime asked, astounded at the threat but un-cowed by the gun. Turning to Kafutshi he said, "You better take her home." Kafutshi looked confused for a moment.

"It is Celestine's," she said to Yoweri. "It is an old *nkisi*. Look inside. It does not have the new American filling Brother Tom gives us for our new ones."

Yoweri ripped a leg off the little rag doll and chunks of corncob poured out of the hole. He threw the doll at Jaime's chest and abruptly turned to the women. "Back to work!" he shouted fiercely. "This shipment must go out tomorrow!"

Chapter 17

Bukedi

The refugee camp in Bukedi was the last hope of six hundred desperate people, mainly women and children, the women raped and battered, the children malnourished and diseased. Many crowded around the news crew's blue and yellow van as it entered the camp, following it hopefully to see if it brought supplies or people to help them. A collection of ragged shelters tacked together from plastic sheeting and scrap lumber stretched along either side of the road. As they drove through the camp, Valerie realized it was the only place on the highway where they had not encountered a roadblock. Bobby carefully threaded his way through the crowd until he came to a low concrete-block building with a UN flag hanging limply from a pole on the front. The crowd parted politely as Valerie, Nancy and Bobby got out of the van. A serious-looking woman came out of the building to see what was going on. She wore khaki shorts and a white tee shirt under a dust-colored vest. Her dark brown hair was pulled back in an efficient ponytail. She looked at them with lively eyes that shone through steel-rimmed glasses.

"Hi. Who are you?" she asked, friendly but cautious.

"We're from MBS TV News," Valerie answered, holding out her hand. "I'm Valerie Gray and this is Nancy Justine and Bobby Blaine.

Who are you?" She smiled to soften the blunt question.

"Franziska Starnhart, pleased to meet you," the woman smiled back as she shook Valerie's hand. "Just call me Frannie. I'm the camp director. That's not as important as it sounds. It really just means I'm the one who gets to listen to everybody's problems and distribute the beans and rice before the army can steal them." Valerie immediately liked her. From the way she talked, Frannie's feet were on the ground and her eyes were wide open. She also sounded like she wasn't overly impressed by her own saintliness.

A woman wearing a yellow and green *pagne* and matching scarf wrapped around her head pointed furtively toward Valerie and Frannie. She said something to her neighbor, chuckling behind her hand. Their whispering titter erupted into soft laughter as her words spread to the rest of the crowd. Valerie's smile widened although she didn't see the joke. She looked quizzically at Frannie, who smiled and shrugged. Nancy spoke up.

"I don't know the language, but I think she said you two must be twins who were separated at birth," she explained with a smile.

Valerie and Frannie looked at each other and laughed along with the small crowd. Valerie's hair was slightly darker and her gray eyes were a shade lighter, but she and Frannie were almost exactly the same height and had the same leggy build. Their slim faces, firm jaws, and slightly-too-wide smiles could have been mirror images except for Frannie's glasses. The women in the crowd were enjoying the sight immensely.

"Come on in out of the sun, sis. You can tell me what's going on in the world," Frannie said. She turned and led them into the low building. As they walked into the room that apparently served as the camp's office, a radio crackled in the corner. She picked up the microphone.

"Come ahead, Bukedi camp here. Over," she said.

"Frannie! It's Pieter. Want to meet me in the bush and fool around?"

"Pieter! Behave yourself! I have guests in the room. Where are you calling from? Over."

"I'm at the airfield in Tshikapa. Jaime was wondering if you could spare some protex. We have a herd of children who seem to have adopted us."

"How many do you have?"

"There were about four dozen when I left, but who knows how many are there now."

"What is their condition? Over." Frannie was all business now. Her eyebrows met in a deep furrow of concern.

"The usual. Been living on fou-fou and filling up on manioc leaves. No protein, so their immune systems are wrecked. Most of them are sick with one thing or another. You know the story. I'm here to pick up a load of medical supplies and some food, but we don't have any protein supplement. Can you help?"

"Yes, of course. It's getting late, though. I can meet you with it tomorrow if you want."

Valerie interrupted as Pieter was answering. "Is that Pieter Jakobsen from Mai-Munene?" she asked. When Frannie nodded, she added, "That's where we're headed. We can take the supplies with us and save you the trip, if you want."

"That would be great," Frannie said. The radio squawked again. She keyed the microphone. "What were you saying, Pieter? Over."

"I said you're a doll. As a reward, I'll take you out for a quick roll in the bush."

"Not this trip, you over-sexed bastard. There are some journalists here who seem to know you, poor things. They're coming your way.

They just offered to carry the protex with them. Can you meet them tomorrow in Tshikapa? Over."

"Can do. I'll hang out at the market until they get here."

"I'll put them on the road first thing in the morning. Out." She put the microphone down and turned to Valerie with a smile. "Pieter has this delusion that I'm going to sleep with him, but other than that he's a great guy. Those two do real good work in Mai-Munene."

"That's what we saw," Valerie said. "We were there a few weeks ago and then I saw Jaime Talon again recently. We had a little difference of opinion in New York."

Frannie smiled and nodded knowingly. "Jaime doesn't fit into civilization very well, does he? That's good for us. He's much too valuable in this corner of Africa to lose him to the bright lights of the big city."

An aid worker came into the office to tell Frannie about a problem with the water supply. She made a suggestion that was technically incomprehensible to Valerie, but it satisfied the man, who left.

"What makes him so valuable here?" Valerie asked.

"Jaime is dedicated. There are many people here you can say that about, but there's something about him that's unique. He does the right thing without wrapping himself in ideological bullshit. He's no saint, but he's a lot more interested in solving people's problems than with spouting dogma."

Valerie remembered how Jaime dealt with the panhandler outside the restaurant near Central Park. "So what drives him?" she asked.

"I don't know for sure, but I think it's simply that he can't stand to see people suffer. It's like he's compelled to help. There's something else about him too; nothing bores him more than bureaucrats who talk socio-economic theory while people are hurting. He just plugs up his ears against the blather and does what needs to be done."

"Sounds like he picks a lot of fights."

"No. Just the opposite. He simply ignores whoever stands between him and what he wants to accomplish. The only time he fights is when somebody doesn't get out of the way. Then he's a bull." Frannie chuckled as she thought of something. "Let me tell you a story," she said.

"It happened after the Ebola outbreak. Jaime had gone back to America on leave for a while. He wasn't in the States long before he decided he couldn't take civilization, so he returned and re-opened the clinic at Mai-Munene. It had been shut down by the fighting over the mine. That wasn't the safest place in the world, you know, but Jaime saw nothing there but a whole bunch of people with no medical care for miles and miles, so he did it. One night right after he got there, a gang of rogue soldiers—Angolans, I think—kidnapped a bunch of village women. For some reason, they thought they were the girl friends or the wives of the mine managers, so they demanded a ransom of diamonds to release them. Of course, the guys who ran the mine couldn't have cared less about those women. They may have been screwing them on the side, but their real families were in Kinshasa or Mbuji-Mayi or someplace. So Jaime went to the rebels and explained that he was an American doctor who was a lot more valuable to the mine operators than those women. He asked the soldiers to let the women go and take him as a hostage instead. And they did!

"As soon as the women were home safe, Jaime started coughing and carrying on in front of the Angolans. He pissed his pants and fell down like a rag doll and started gasping for air." Frannie laughed. "Then he let slip that he had just come from Kikwit and maybe, just maybe, he caught Ebola there. So, would they mind taking him back to the clinic so he could get some medicine? He told them he wouldn't be much good as a hostage if he died. They ran like hell, of course, and left him there to die. He just walked back to the village and went back to work. Typical Jaime."

"That's a great story," Valerie said, shaking her head in appreciation. Somehow, she didn't have any trouble imagining Jaime Talon pulling off a stunt like that. Frannie was a great storyteller, too, which gave Valerie a story idea of her own. "I'd like to tape an interview with you," she said. "Would you mind?"

"About what?"

"It will be about the people on the ground who give real help. Like you and Jaime. Who you are, where you come from, why you're here. That sort of thing. You can start by telling me the story of how you came here."

"I'm boring," Frannie answered. "I'm just a girl who wandered away from Madison, Wisconsin, and ended up working for the World Hunger Program. You should do a story about something that matters," she urged. "Do one about these people and what they've been through."

"If you'll tell it to the camera, I'd love to," Valerie said, seizing the opportunity to get the woman on tape. Without waiting for Frannie's answer, she nodded to Nancy and Bobby, who went out to the van to set up the equipment. Valerie led Frannie to a cluster of palm trees where Nancy placed two chairs so that tents from the camp would be in the background. A small crowd of refugees gathered to watch. Nancy settled Valerie and Frannie into the chairs and clipped on their mics while Bobby shot footage of the tired but open faces of the refugees. He lingered on one solemn-eyed woman wearing a pink scarf with green and yellow stripes. When she realized the camera was on her, she ducked her head and turned, disappearing into the crowd.

"That is Ogastine," Frannie explained quietly. "She was raped by seven men in front of her husband and children. One of them used

202 ■ DAVE DONELSON

a plantain to humiliate her even more." Bobby turned the camera on Frannie, who ignored it and kept talking. "She had to take her children and go live in the hills when her husband kicked her out."

"Why did he do that?" Valerie asked.

"He was sure she had contracted a disease from the men who raped her, so he didn't want anything to do with her anymore. Her children all died in the bush. There were three of them."

As Frannie told Ogastine's story, Valerie felt the anguish draw around her like a dark curtain. She mentally pushed it back so she could focus on Frannie and the story. "How did her children die?" she asked gently.

"I don't know for sure, but probably from what you and I would consider a minor disease. It could have been just a simple infection. Like most of these kids, they were probably under-fed to start with. Weak. That means just about any medical problem becomes life threatening. The massacres and battles get press coverage, but nobody ever reports on how many people die from the real effects of civil war. Disruption of the food supply and lack of medical care kill a lot more people than bullets. More than five million have died in the Congo since 1998. The shame is, almost all of them die from treatable diseases like malaria and diarrhea, aggravated by living in a permanent war zone."

As her outrage and despair mounted, Valerie fought them off by concentrating on getting the story. "Why can't they get treatment?" she asked.

"They're too busy running for their lives. The rebels drive whole villages away from their fields and homes. Sometimes the army does too. The few hospitals that exist are looted and the nurses and doctors run off along with everyone else. Fields aren't cultivated for a season or two, livestock dies; the whole family support system breaks down because people get separated. The few that make it to camps like ours are depressed and traumatized."

"Like Ogastine?"

"Yes, exactly like Ogasinte," Frannie answered.

"What will happen to her?" Valerie asked.

"Honestly? I just don't know." Frannie's voice faltered. She dropped her head. Valerie signaled for Bobby to stop taping and leaned over to put her hand on Frannie's. There was nothing more to say.

After a quiet moment to compose herself, Frannie walked back toward the camp office. Valerie pulled herself together too. She added an intro and some closing commentary to the interview on the tape, standing in front of one of the food lines where a couple of Frannie's staffers passed out the day's ration of food. When she finished, Bobby hooked up the camera to the satellite phone to transmit the report to New York for editing while Nancy dialed for a connection. Nothing happened. Cursing softly, Nancy told Bobby to move to another spot. She fiddled with the temperamental folding dish antenna and tried to establish a signal. Again, nothing. Bobby checked all the connections, the batteries, everything else he could think of. Finally, he dismantled the top panel of the satellite phone case and found the problem: a corner of the motherboard had a crack, probably from rough handling by the guards at the Kenge roadblock.

"Can't you repair it?" Nancy demanded.

"I can't fix a broken circuit board, even in the shop. Too many tiny connections. It has to be replaced."

"I don't suppose you have a spare?" Valerie asked hopefully.

"No, not for the motherboard," he answered. Without the satellite phone, there was no way for Valerie to file reports from anywhere in the country except the capital. It looked like they would have to turn back. "I could maybe find a replacement in Kinshasa," Bobby said. "The Reuters guys probably have a supplier."

Valerie knew if they went back to the capital they'd never get back to the countryside again. They'd be lucky if Messime let them leave their hotel rooms. Then she remembered the airfield in Tshikapa. She decided that Bobby would fly from there to Kinshasa, repair the phone, and catch up with her and Nancy later. They would press on. The story of human suffering caused by war over the riches of the Congo was too important to lose because of a piece of cracked plastic.

The next morning before dawn, they loaded several cases of protex into the blue and yellow van. Frannie explained that the protein supplement was a wonder food that could be mixed with water to make a rich porridge, stirred into the ubiquitous fou-fou to give it more nutritional value, or even mixed with corn meal and a little water and fried in palm oil to make a passable fritter. The overloaded van made it as far as the side of the headquarters building before it dipped into a small pothole. Valerie's spirits sank as she heard the recently welded strut snap. The sun was just rising above the trees and the day's heat was beginning to build.

Frannie came to the rescue. "Take my jeep and leave it at the airfield," she offered. "I'll get your van fixed and swap them out in a couple of days. You can go to Mai-Munene with Pieter, and Bobby can pick up your van when he flies back."

"Are you sure that won't leave you stranded in the meantime?" Valerie asked.

"I'll be fine. Nothing ever happens around here except the food line getting longer. You guys get moving; Jaime needs that protex." They put the protein supplement into Frannie's jeep, but that left little room for their baggage. Bobby managed to squeeze in the camera and broken satellite phone as Valerie and Nancy winnowed their already slim luggage down to the bare minimum. Frannie said they should reach Tshikapa by noon.

That morning, the heavily armed black Humvee followed the rough highway southeast from Kikwit, detouring at each crossroad to check the side roads for a few hundred yards and slowing as it passed every place in the road where the van could be hiding. Scavino was determined Valerie Grey would not elude him again today.

By noon, the black Humvee crept through Bukedi. The 5-caliber machine gun mounted on the windshield and the two hard-faced men in the truck signaled that this vehicle brought death, not supplies. People shrank away from the road, some of them slipping into the bush outside camp to hide. Mothers gathered their children and disappeared into their shelters.

Scavino spotted the blue and yellow van just as a white woman with dark hair came out of the building next to it and grasped the rear door handle. A tight grim smile creased his face. "Bingo!" he said.

"Where are the others?" his companion asked.

"Fuck them. She's the one we want," Scavino answered. He stood up behind the 50-caliber machine gun, unsnapped the restraining strap, and swung the heavy barrel around toward the van. As he locked the bolt down to engage the ammunition belt in the chamber and enable automatic fire, the woman seemed to notice the Humvee for the first time. She stopped pulling on the door handle to squint toward the approaching menace, her glasses flashing in the sun just as Scavino fired a burst at practically point-blank range. Her slim body slammed against the van. She rebounded and collapsed into the dirt. A handful of shocked refugees ran toward her where she lay next to the van.

"Let's make sure," Scavino said. His thumb pressed the trigger again sending a hail of 50-caliber slugs slamming into Frannie's limp body. Then he turned the gun on the van, shattering the windows and riddling the body. One of the tires exploded. Scavino's partner said they needed more casualties for effect. Scavino fired four short bursts into the scattering refugees. He nodded a command, and his partner swung the black Humvee toward Kinshasa.

They pulled over as soon as they were out of sight of Bukedi. Scavino took a hand-held satellite phone out of his pack, dialed a number, listened to the call connect and then click off; then he waited. It was before dawn in Alexandria, Virginia, but the phone beeped with the returning call a few minutes later.

"Mission accomplished," he said without waiting for the caller to identify himself.

"Are you sure?" asked the man on the other end.

"Visual confirmation at close range," Scavino answered.

"Good. Tell the government to report she was killed in a rebel attack."

"Right." The phone went dead. Scavino dialed the presidential palace in Kinshasa.

Chapter 18

Tshikapa

Tshikapa is a large rural village, not a city. Its mud-and-tin houses and a few two-story concrete-block buildings gather languidly along informal streets where the Kasai and Tshikapa Rivers come together, fly apart, then finally join again like the legs of a loose woman. Open ditches run down the sides of the unpaved streets carrying sewage to the rivers. Along the crumbling, pothole-riddled highway from Kinshasa, a few struggling merchants endeavor to earn a living out of the front part of their simple homes. Women squat by the side of the road with vats of millet beer and jugs of palm wine.

The open-air market on the riverfront is the true beating heart of the town. There, rough plank tables form a dense maze packed with shoppers, merchants, beggars, children and people from the countryside simply gathering to visit with each other. Ragged umbrellas and weathered tarps provide some relief from the sun while smoke from dozens of cooking fires wafts through the market like acrid fog. Soukous rises from radios everywhere. The smooth guitar and snappy brass jazz mixes with puttering motorbikes and clattering carts jostling for passage through the lanes. The market is a place of commerce, though, so the din of bargainers happily haranguing the vendors rises above it all.

Amid the tumult, the women in brightly patterned dresses and creatively tied headscarves, the hustling merchants and their piles of gray-market sundries, second-hand clothes, and fresh produce from the countryside, Valerie spotted the lanky, freckled man loading a truck near the river. She smiled as she remembered Frannie calling the amiable South African a "long-legged horny bastard." He waved cheerily as they drove up.

"Hallo! If it isn't our favorite journalists!" he called.

"How are you, Pieter?" Valerie smiled back. Bobby shut off Frannie's jeep and they climbed out. After hugs and handshakes all around, Bobby helped Pieter finish loading the truck with a few remaining bags of rice.

"You folks hungry?" Pieter asked when they were finished.

"Famished," Valerie answered.

"Then this is the place to be," he said. "Let's see if we can find something that suits your fancy." He gave a boy a few coins to watch the truck and jeep while they were gone, then led them into an aroma-filled lane lined with makeshift booths. The plank tables were filled with plantains, sweet potatoes, sugar cane, squash, bananas, peanuts, manioc leaves and mangoes. There were pots of steaming rice and the maize porridge, nsima, as well as thick, smooth fou-fou made from pounded cassava tubers. They passed vendors with baskets of dried minnows, racks of smoked fish, and tubs where freshly caught perch finned about in murky water. Skinny chickens fussed nervously in cages next to their recently plucked kin. Ducks squawked. Shy young girls offered trays of fat white grubs, smoked caterpillars, and peppery fried grasshoppers. Pieter stopped before an exceptionally smoky booth and invited Nancy to make a selection from the fire-blackened twists of meat hanging above the brazier.

"I don't eat anything I can't identify," she said firmly.

"Then allow me to identify it for you," Pieter said. A mischievous smile tugged at the corners of his mouth. He leaned forward to inspect one of the hanging pieces for effect. "This bushmeat looks like haunch of monkey. I guess he moved too slowly for his own good. Care for a bite?"

"No thank you," she said emphatically, rolling her eyes while Valerie and Bobby laughed along with Pieter. A thin man standing near the booth watched the exchange and smiled broadly. He held out a piece of greasy newspaper, giggling as Nancy examined the roasted rat it contained. She shuddered when the man put the rat's head in his mouth and crunched it between his teeth, her reaction making his eyes dance with delight.

"You Americans will probably find this a little more to your liking," Pieter said, leading them to the next table, where a pot steamed fragrantly next to a large bowl of fou-fou. He asked the woman behind the table for four bowls and handed her a few coins. The woman rolled balls of fou-fou in her hands, then put one into each bowl along with a heaping spoonful of stew. Nancy looked closely at her portion before giving Pieter a sharp glance.

"This is moambé," he said reassuringly. "It's stew made with peanuts, palm oil, and perfectly harmless chicken. It's a little spicy, though." He deftly pinched off some of the fou-fou and used it to scoop up a mouthful of the stew. "Delicious," he said, winking at Nancy. Valerie gamely did the same. She echoed Pieter's pronouncement, so Nancy tentatively dipped some fou-fou into the stew and nibbled at it.

"Julia Child it ain't, but it will do," she said, dipping into the bowl for another bite.

The effervescent soukous blaring from a nearby radio cut off in mid-song as an announcer interrupted the broadcast. Valerie missed the first few words of the story, but she almost dropped her bowl when the announcer said, "American television reporter Valerie Grey was killed in the attack on the camp." Everything around her jumped into extra sharp focus as the bizarre announcement sank in.

"Can you turn that up, please?" Valerie implored the radio's owner, a plump woman selling yams and manioc leaves. The woman cheerfully twisted the dial, but all they heard before the music started again was the announcer's excited bulletin that President Messime promised swift punishment for the rebels who conducted the raid. Valerie turned to Pieter, whose face was somber. "Something happened at Bukedi," she said. "Where can we radio Frannie?"

"The airfield. Let's go," he answered. They dashed through the crowd to the vehicles. Bobby followed Pieter's truck to the edge of town where a squat building sat next to the short dirt airstrip. A well-used Cessna Caravan was parked on the runway. Pieter ran into the building and Valerie, Nancy, and Bobby crowded through the door after him.

"Joseph, did you hear any news from Bukedi?" Pieter asked the airfield manager, who sat behind a worn civil service desk playing cards with the plane's pilot. Without waiting for an answer to his first question, Pieter added, "Can I use your radio to check on Frannie?"

"Certainly. What has happened?" the airfield manager asked, moving aside so Pieter could get to the radio behind him.

"Bukedi Camp! Bukedi Camp! Come in please," Pieter said into the microphone. While he waited for an answering call, he told the airport manager that there had been some kind of attack on the refugee camp.

"This is Bukedi Camp. Who is calling? Over," a strained voice came through the radio speaker.

"Pieter Jackobsen. Who is this and where is Frannie? Over."

"This is Etienne, Pieter. Something terrible happened. We were attacked this morning. Frannie has been killed. Many others too. People are fleeing the camp."

"Attacked!?" Pieter exclaimed. "What happened?"

"It was very bad. They drove in and started firing for no reason. Many people were hurt. Over."

Pieter didn't reply. Valerie asked him for the microphone and he numbly handed it to her.

"Etienne, this is Valerie Grey. We were with Frannie this morning. Can you tell me who attacked you? Over."

"No. I think it must have been the F.I.C., but there were no markings on the vehicle. Kinshasa radioed us after the attack to say they were defending us against a Lunda Libre attack. But we saw no attackers! Just the black truck. It fired a machine gun. Then it drove away. It was all very fast, very confusing."

"And Frannie Starnhart was definitely killed?" Valerie closed her eyes, hoping for another answer.

"Yes." Static filled the air for a moment. "Another woman and two children are dead also." Etienne's voice broke. "Six more wounded. All refugees. Over."

Another momentary wave of unreality swept over Valerie as she imagined Frannie Starnhart dead, her young body ripped by machine gun fire, her vital, generous heart ravaged. The woman had devoted her life to taking care of others; she was certainly no threat to anyone. It takes a certain type of monster to kill the caregivers. Anger brought Valerie back to the present. She took a deep breath to bring it under control. She thought for a moment, then turned to Bobby with a determined look. "Something's not right here. Set up the camera, would you? I want to do a new intro to the story on Bukedi before we send it to New York." She went outside while Bobby pulled the camera out of the jeep. She stood in front of the concrete block building with the forlorn air strip in the background. As soon as the red light came on, she started talking.

"Franziska Starnhart, an American aid worker trying to help refugees in the Democratic Republic of the Congo, was killed this morning in what the authorities say was an attack by rebels on Bukedi Camp, about three hundred miles southeast of the capital city of Kinshasa. Another woman and two children were killed as well, and six more people were wounded. All were unarmed civilian refugees trying to escape the senseless violence that wracks this country. President Moshe Messime's government reported that Lunda Libre rebels attacked the camp, but eyewitness sources say the deaths were from friendly fire. They report that an unmarked government vehicle fired repeatedly on the refugee camp even though no rebels were in sight. It was possibly a tragic mistake, but it's not known at this time why the attackers fired on the refugees.

"Franziska Starnhart preferred to be called 'Frannie.' She was a selfless woman from Madison, Wisconsin, who devoted her life to comforting the countless victims of this civil war. She healed their broken bodies with non-stop care and eased their troubled hearts with kindness. I interviewed Frannie Starnhart the day before the attack." Valerie paused, gave instructions for the editor to cut to the interview, then added, "In a strange footnote to this tragic story, DRC radio erroneously reported that I was killed in the incident. My crew and I had left Bukedi Camp just a few hours before the attack." Valerie started to give her standard location-specific sign-off, then instinctively altered it instead. "From Kasai Occidental Province on the way to Mbuji-Mayi, this is Valerie Grey for MBS News."

Bobby stopped the recording, then played back the tape to check it. As he finished, the pilot came out of the building. He nodded as he walked briskly past them toward his plane.

"Excuse me," Valerie called to him. He stopped and turned and she said, "Are you going to Kinshasa by any chance?"

"Yes."

"Can you take some passengers?"

"Yes, but I'm not leaving until day after tomorrow. I'm waiting for a shipment from the mine."

"Think you can entertain yourself for a couple of days?" Nancy asked Bobby. "We need to go to Mai-Munene with the supplies."

"I want you to go with him," Valerie told Nancy. "You can send the story to New York while Bobby gets the sat phone fixed."

"Not on your life, boss," Nancy responded without a beat. "I'm not leaving you here alone in the middle of this mess." Valerie started to argue, then realized it would do no good.

"I'm not crazy about leaving either of you guys here," Bobby interjected.

"We'll be fine, Bobby," Valerie said. "Mai-Munene is probably the most heavily-guarded place in the country right now because of the mine. Go on, get that story on the bird. We need the sat phone, so catch up with us as soon as you can."

Bobby grabbed the satellite phone case and the tapes and walked after the pilot. "We'll leave the jeep here for you!" Valerie shouted after him. Then she thought of something else. "Wait!" she called and ran across the dirt landing strip after him. "Call David Powell when you get to Kinshasa, would you? Here's his home number in case he's not in the studio in Washington." She wrote the number on a scrap of paper and Bobby stuffed it in his pocket. "Let him know I'm okay." As Bobby started back to follow the pilot she added, "Watch what you say on the phone, though. You never know who's listening. I don't want Messime's goons to know where we are."

"No problem," Bobby answered. "You tell Nancy to be careful with my camera, okay?"

David Powell sat numbly at his desk in Washington staring at the wire service copy reporting Valerie's death. "I'm so sorry, David," said the assistant who handed it to him. She waited only a moment for a reply, then stepped quietly from the room to give her boss privacy.

David didn't hear her go. He read the short text twice more, looking for some hope among the words on the page. The edges of his world closed in slowly as a hazy scrim obscured the page before his eyes. He blinked hard, then looked out at the newsroom. A small knot of staffers turned away guiltily and tried to look busy when he gazed at them, but it didn't matter. He was looking in their direction but he didn't see them. He was too busy staring into the void that yawned before him.

David and Valerie were apart more often than they were together, especially since they worked in different cities. But David kept her by his side in other ways. They talked on the phone almost every day, sometimes for an hour, sometimes for just minutes, sometimes about the big events of world history unfolding before them, sometimes just to complain about how much trouble they had getting a cab after work. Even when he wasn't talking to her, David often sensed Valerie just beneath his thoughts. When he walked from his apartment to the network's studios, he sometimes tried to see the Washington sidewalks they way she would. When he grabbed a quick bite at the hibachi restaurant around the corner from his apartment, he remembered how she wouldn't eat there because she said the food was tasteless. Even when they were apart, he felt close to her in spirit. He felt they were going through life hand in hand. Now David was alone.

He turned back to his work to stave off the black despair coming on. He knew he would have to deal with it later, but now he had a job to do. He picked up the phone to call his White House correspondent. "See if the president has any comment on Valerie's death, would you?" he asked in a strained voice. Then he called his Pentagon reporter. "Let's get some details on what happened. What units were involved, how many bad guys, was this part of a larger action? You know the routine." Neither call was necessary; both men were already working on the story, but it gave him something to do. Then he took a call from Carter Wilson, the news division president in New York.

"David, I'm very, very sorry about what happened," Wilson said. "We were all shocked when the story came in. I know you and Valerie had a special relationship. This must be a terrible loss for you."

"Thank you, Carter." David felt a muscle in his neck start to cramp. "There's no mention in the AP story about Nancy Justine or their cameraman, what's his name? Bobby? Any word on them?"

"Not yet. We've made inquiries through the embassy, of course, but the only confirmed death we have is Valerie. I thought you'd like to know, Preston is putting together a tribute piece for tonight's evening news." The cramped muscle in David's neck clenched sharply.

"Tell that asshole to keep his ego out of the story," he snapped.

"I'm going to ignore that, David," Wilson said, unruffled. "Do you want to take a few days off?" David gripped the side of his neck to ease the spasm and wished Valerie were there to massage it for him. He wanted the call to end.

"No," he said. "I'll be all right. I'm going out to take a walk and collect myself. Everybody here is on the story already. We'll have some updates and official reaction clips for tonight."

"Good. Take care of yourself, David."

"Right." David put down the phone and walked out of the office. The numbness was going away, the despair beginning.

Chapter 19
Mai-Munene

When Valerie got out of the truck in front of the clinic at Mai-Munene, Celestine almost knocked her off her feet trying to get to Pieter. He scooped the girl up into his arms and hid his face in her hair. His shoulders shook as the girl nuzzled into his neck. Valerie realized she was crying and Pieter might be too.

"Celestine!" the gangly man whispered hoarsely, "What is this?"

"She missed you, you simple dolt," came the cheerfully teasing answer from someone in the small crowd behind Valerie. She turned to see Jaime Talon walking through the villagers.

"And I missed her," Pieter replied. He gave her a squeeze and closed his eyes as he found a moment of peace in the girl's embrace. Valerie saw the tension drain out of his shoulders as he held his little friend, but his face looked stricken.

"Are you all right?" Jaime asked him with concern.

"Frannie was killed," Pieter said. "Gunned down by an F.I.C. truck at the camp."

"Oh, no. When?" Jaime asked.

"This morning. It was on the radio."

"What happened?" The muscles in Jaime's jaw tightened as Pieter told him what little they knew about the attack. Valerie could see they both cared a great deal for the spunky camp director. "Bastards," he said when Pieter finished. He took a deep breath and looked around at the villagers gathered at the truck. He seemed to notice Valerie for the first time. "Sorry. I didn't mean to ignore you. Hello and welcome." He held out his hand formally and managed a small smile. "It's good to see you again," he said.

"I'm sorry about your friend's death," Valerie answered. "She seemed like a wonderful person." He nodded an acknowledgement. When he didn't release her hand right away, Valerie thought she felt something more than a polite handshake in his touch. He could be unconsciously seeking solace, she thought, or it could be something else. From the look in his eyes at the contact, he felt it too. Confused, she dropped his hand.

Whatever Valerie saw in his eyes, it was soon gone, replaced by the needs of the here and now. He gestured toward the small crowd around the truck. "We've got people to feed," he said. "Let's get this stuff unloaded."

The villagers and some of the refugee children quickly formed a line that passed the bags and boxes from hand to hand into the clinic. It didn't take long to unload the truck and store the sacks of rice and containers of protex. As Valerie carried a box of sterile dressings into the dispensary, she noticed a fringe of children around the truck. They were too small to help but they stayed close, their wide, dark eyes following the food as it passed along the line of helping hands.

When the truck was empty, Jaime and Pieter set a plank across two drums to use as a serving table in the road. The children formed a line without prompting as Jaime gave each of them some rice, a little palm oil, and a measure of the protein supplement. He didn't have to tell them what to do with it.

"I'm sorry I ran out so fast on you in New York," he said as Valerie helped him open another can of palm oil.

"That was in a different place," she said. Valerie was glad he made the effort to apologize.

After everyone in the food line was gone, they sat down for a quick supper of their own. Pieter had gradually brightened during the day as he let the concerns of the living smooth away the pain of Frannie's death. He was almost his normal, cheery self as he did the cooking. It turned out Pieter had a talent for making edible somethings out of practically nothing. He made even the protex fritters almost tasty, although the fou-fou reminded Valerie of the library paste pre-schoolers use—the kind in plastic jars that is eaten on a dare as often as it's used for construction paper projects. Pieter passed a jar of bright red relish to Nancy after ladling a heaping spoonful onto his own plate. Jaime started to say something, but Pieter silenced him with an impish wink.

"Why do I think you're trying to poison me?" she asked suspiciously.

"I wouldn't dream of such a thing!" Pieter protested with a huge grin. "This is just, umm, a local version of your American ketchup."

Nancy lifted the jar cautiously to her nose to take a short sniff. Her eyes teared up. She gasped and quickly set the jar down. "What is that stuff?" she asked. "It smells like it would burn the skin off your tongue."

Jaime laughed. "It's *pili-pili*," he said. "A chili sauce. You're right too. It will do some damage if you're not careful."

Nancy gave Pieter a mock scowl.

"I wouldn't have let you hurt yourself, love," he assured her.

"Tell her about the Korean engineer," Jaime urged with a chuckle. Pieter guffawed.

"That was a good one, that was!" he exclaimed. "He came last year to look at the mine or something. Joao de Santos tried to warn him to take it easy on the *pili-pili* at dinner the first night he got here. The next morning, de Santos brought him to us to fix him up. He said the fool declared he grew up on *kimchee* so this *pili-pili* stuff was for babies. He grabbed the jar and gobbled it by the spoonful just as fast as he could scoop it up. Going to prove what a man he was, I guess. He couldn't get out of the loo all night!" Pieter laughed so hard he had to push his chair back from the table and bend over to catch his breath. When he came back up, his eyes were wet from laughter. He gasped for air and added, "Wanted me to treat him for burns on his arsehole!"

Valerie and Nancy were practically in tears too. Laughing, Nancy slid the jar of fiery relish to Valerie. "Here, boss," she said. "Put a little spice in your life."

Flushed from laughing, Valerie answered, "I'm hot enough already."

"I'd agree with that, wouldn't you?" Pieter said to Jaime.

Jaime turned red too, then coughed and briefly ducked his head. Valerie blushed a deeper red. After an awkward moment, Jaime cleared his throat and said, "Did you make some dessert, you troublemaker?" Still laughing, Pieter got up from the table and came back with sliced bananas, papaya and a plate of lime wedges.

Valerie decided it would be a good idea to talk about something besides how hot she was.

"So," she said, "how has the mine changed since the last time I saw you?"

Jaime thought for moment before he answered. "I don't know for sure, but I know they're stepping up production. They've recruited a lot more miners from the countryside. I almost never see the workers, though. They keep them working all hours. F.I.C. soldiers have the place locked up tight. The only workers I see are the men who get mangled in the machinery. I don't have much time to go poking around up there, though. I've got my hands full right here." Jaime nodded toward the village square where the children were gathered around their cooking fires.

"How about you," he asked. "Have you found your story yet?"

His eyes stayed on her while she answered and Valerie discovered she enjoyed having him look at her.

"I've seen worthwhile stories everywhere we've been," she said. "Most of them are about how hard warfare is on ordinary human beings. I could fill a two-hour special with just the women at Bukedi." She turned toward the clearing across the road where the children huddled around their fires and simple dinners. "And probably another one about these kids." She turned back to Jaime and found him still attentive, his knowing eyes still on her face. He was easy to talk to. She also became even more aware of his physical presence. She made herself think about the story she came for. "I still want to know what's going on with this mine, though. At the heart of it, the fighting is really over wealth like that, isn't it?"

"Yes it is," Jaime said seriously. "The rest is pure rhetoric trying to cover up the fact that plenty of Africans want to be rich too. Your significant other was right in that regard."

"Who?" Valerie said.

"Uh, I think he means David?" chided Nancy.

"Yes, I'm sorry, his name had slipped my mind," Jaime said.

David had slipped Valerie's mind too, which suddenly distressed her. She was attracted to Jaime, but David was still the partner who stirred her—at least when she thought of him. She felt a strong pang of guilt.

"That's okay," Valerie hurried to say. "I got thrown a little when you called him my 'significant other.'"

"Sorry," Jaime said. "Maybe I misunderstood your relationship—which is none of my business either." He was reddening again.

"Really, that's all right," insisted Valerie. "David and I have been together for several years and he's sort of my fiancé ... or something." She decided to shut up before she stuck the other foot in her mouth.

Jaime said, "Oh, I see ... I guess."

Nancy smirked at Pieter, who rolled his eyes and shook his head.

"I think it's time to call it a day," Valerie said.

On that note, they went to bed, with Pieter moving into Jaime's room at the other end of the clinic so Valerie and Nancy could have his for the night. Nancy insisted that Valerie take Pieter's bed while she made do with a foldout cot. She draped a mosquito net over two chairs, tucked it under the edges of her pallet and crawled inside, swearing that she was perfectly comfortable and completely safe from creepy crawly things on the floor. "I'm curious about something, though," she said once Valerie had climbed into her bed and arranged the netting around it.

"What's that?" Valerie asked sleepily.

"Did you have the hots for Jaime Talon in Brazzaville when we met him, or is this a new development?" Nancy asked with a note of knowing mischief in her voice.

"What are you talking about?" Valerie said. She sat up. She couldn't see the expression on Nancy's face through two layers of mosquito netting, but she knew her normally protuberant eyes were crinkled with merriment.

"You've been making goo-goo eyes at him ever since we got here,"

Nancy replied. "Don't try to deny it. My bullshit detector is turned on high, you know."

"I have not been making goo-goo eyes at the man!" Valerie protested. "That's ridiculous." She lay back down with a snort.

"Admit it, boss! And he was making eyes at you too." Nancy suppressed a girlish giggle.

"That's nonsense. I'm not going to dignify it by talking about it any more. Good night!"

Nancy snickered softly. "Good night, boss."

Valerie closed her eyes and listened to the village as it settled in for the night. Someone had a persistent cough, but they were far away, as were the hippos bellowing and splashing in the river. Somewhere, a baby fussed and a young voice crooned to it. Alone with her thoughts for the first time all day, Valerie began to wonder how much of her attraction to Jaime Nancy had actually seen. She might deny it to Nancy, but she couldn't lie to herself about what she felt. The real question was what kind of attraction it was. Part of it was certainly sexual; Valerie was a vibrant woman who found herself physically attracted to good-looking men all the time, so that part didn't surprise her. But this was stronger than that. Maybe her sensibilities were simply heightened by the rigorous road trip through the Congo looking over her shoulder for Messime's men or by the shock she'd had when the radio news announced she had been killed. That was pretty farfetched, she thought. Besides, despite what she told Nancy, she had been drawn to Jaime in Brazzaville and then in New York before any of those things happened. Even during the conversation after their run through Central Park, she'd felt more than just a spark of something when she looked at the man across the table.

She visualized Jaime in her apartment in New York, but hurriedly dismissed the thought. After watching him work with the villagers, she realized he would never be in his element anyplace but here. He was at home here, secure among his people doing work that gave meaning to his life. He might be capable of functioning in New York, she thought, but he would never be happy there.

Face it, she said to herself, you're probably just falling for his James Dean aura. He may be the first man you've ever met who is completely his own person, free of ambitions and unconcerned about conventional success. That makes him intriguing—and probably a challenge to tame. God, what crap, she thought. But there was a kernel of truth in it. She felt like a kitten crouched next to a rushing stream; she didn't want to fall in, but she was tempted to touch the ripples with her paw.

But just because there was an attraction didn't mean anything had to happen, did it? You have a man in your life already—a good, strong man, she told herself. Valerie believed in old-fashioned monogamy—at least she thought she did. And the fact that she found Jaime attractive didn't mean she didn't love David. Maybe it did, though. Unlike Jaime Talon, David was successful in the corporate world, even if he was first and foremost a journalist. Was that it? She had always thought she admired David's ability to advance his career while maintaining his integrity as a journalist. But perhaps she unconsciously mistrusted his corporate persona. When you got right down to it, what did she feel for David, anyway?

The night thoughts chased themselves incessantly around the maze of her mind. She owed it to David to make a decision about his proposal. Maybe she owed it to herself too. And once she decided, what was she going to do about Jaime Talon?

Chapter 20
Mai-Munene

The next morning, Valerie and Nancy sorted supplies in the dispensary while Pieter and Jaime tended to the patients who filled the ward on the other side of the breezeway. None of them paid much attention to Kafutshi's grandson Kenda, who stood idly at the corner at the other end of the clinic building. He was a lookout, and from where he was stationed, he could see the front of the dispensary as well as the path that would serve as an escape route into the woods. He also had a view of the door to Pieter's room, where his brother was busy nosing around the contents of the visiting women's backpacks. Juvenal was having a hard time deciding whether to steal Valerie's simple makeup kit with its shiny mirror and little pads of colored powders or the funny-feeling underwear he found in her bag. He had already slipped a package of Nancy's cigarettes and her lighter into the pocket of his shorts. He knew what they were for from watching the soldiers standing around smoking. He eyed the aluminum camera case with the bright MBS logo enviously, but decided it was too big to carry away undetected. For eight-year-olds, the twins were becoming quite adept at sneak thievery.

Kenda soon became bored as a lookout. He was distracted by a scab on his knee that was just about ready to be picked off. He was so engrossed in flicking it with his finger that he didn't see Christophe emerge from the forest on the path behind him. The older boy, seeing only one of the twins hanging around the open doorway to Pieter's room, immediately sized up the situation. He grabbed Kenda by the back of his shirt.

"Run!" Kenda cried to his brother. Juvenal dropped Valerie's underwear and raced out the open door only to be snagged by Christophe's free hand.

"*Dakta! Dakta!*" Christophe shouted. He held tight as Jaime rushed out of the ward followed by the others. Pieter laughed when he saw the culprits squirming frantically in Christophe's grip. "They are thieves, *dakta*," Christophe said. "I caught them stealing from your room. Do you want me to shoot them for you?"

"No, that won't be necessary—this time," Jaime answered, trying to keep a straight face.

"These blokes have the stickiest little fingers I've ever seen," Pieter said.

The twins froze when Christophe threatened to kill them. Kenda hung his head and scuffed the dust with his toe while Juvenal tried his best to look contrite. He couldn't resist slipping his hand into his pocket to check his loot, though, which drew attention to the bulge in his pants.

"What do you have in there?" Jaime asked, looking stern. Juvenal pulled out the cigarettes and lighter and gave them to him without a word.

"I'll take those," Nancy said.

"We ought to make them smoke until they turn green," Pieter said with a smile. "That's what my da did the first time he caught me filching fags. I puked for an hour."

Valerie couldn't help but be charmed by the two little criminals. Their poorly played remorse struck her as adorable. "I'll tell you what," she said impulsively. "Release them into my custody and I'll keep an eye on them."

"You'll need both eyes, I imagine," Jaime said. He was interrupted by the growl of a truck coming down the road from the mine, getting louder as it approached the clinic in a cloud of dust. Yoweri drove and a squad of soldiers rode in the back. Tom Alben jumped out of the cab.

"Welcome back to Mai-Munene," he said jovially to Valerie. "I'm delighted to see you. Especially considering the radio reports I heard that said you'd been killed." He took her hand in his sweaty palm, releasing it only after a moist squeeze. It was all Valerie could do to keep from wiping her hand on her shorts. "Here to finish your story about the fine work Dr. Talon does, I assume?" he asked.

"Actually, I'm more interested in the mine," Valerie answered truthfully.

"Really?"

"Yes, we never got to air the story we shot originally, as you may recall."

Alben chuckled. "I certainly do recall. Your camera disappeared, didn't it? Right along with my Land Rover."

"That was unfortunate, wasn't it?" Valerie said. She supposed he expected her to apologize for taking the vehicle, but somehow she didn't feel compelled to. "We came back to re-shoot the video," she said to change the subject. "How soon can we get another tour of the mine?"

"Oh, we can't have any more photographs taken," Alben answered quickly. "The situation is much too tense. Quite frankly, when your last video fell into the hands of the guerillas, we had to make a lot of changes in security."

Valerie wasn't surprised at his refusal, but she wasn't going to give up. "What about the school?" she asked. "Surely there aren't any big security concerns there." The question caught Alben off guard and he hesitated. "You haven't turned it into a sweatshop have you?" Valerie chided.

Alben answered "Of course not! We can go right now if you'd like."

"Great! Let's do it," Valerie said. She nodded to Nancy, who went to get the camera from their room. When she came back, Valerie took Juvenal's and Kenda's hands and said cheerfully, "I hope it's okay with you, but these boys are in my custody, so they'll have to come along."

"You can turn your prisoners over to their grandmother," Jaime called after them as they walked toward the other end of the village. "Her name is Kafutshi. You met her before at the workshop."

As they walked past the truck full of soldiers, Valerie got a good look at the terrifyingly scarred face of Yoweri, who sat behind the wheel glowering at them.

"You can ride with us," Alben offered.

The boys shrank against Valerie's legs.

"No thanks. We'll walk," she said.

Alben shrugged. "Suit yourself," he said as he got back into the truck.

The twins walked on either side of Valerie on the road up the hill through the village, each holding one of her hands. As they passed through the village, the other children stared. One little girl, a year or so younger than the twins, followed shyly behind for a few steps. When she worked up the nerve to get close enough to touch Valerie, Kenda stuck out his tongue fiercely to scare her off.

"That wasn't very nice," Valerie said gently as the little girl ran away. Kenda shrugged and tightened his grip on her fingers, making Valerie laugh. She couldn't remember ever feeling this way; she was needed, she was trusted, she was making these two little boys feel special. It must be the way a new mother feels the first time she takes her baby for a walk in the park.

Alben was waiting for them at the school. With a stiff smile on his face, he ushered them impatiently past the guards and into the workshop.

Kafutshi stood when she saw the twins come through the door with Valerie. "What have you bad boys done?" she demanded.

Valerie smiled reassuringly. "Nothing serious," she said. "They were just poking their fingers into other people's luggage. No harm done." She nudged them toward their grandmother. They went reluctantly. "How have you been, Kafutshi?" Valerie said to defuse the tension.

"I am well, madame," the old woman said. She grabbed an ear on each twin and twisted it a bit to get their attention. "I will teach you later to keep your fingers where they belong," she said sternly. Valerie struggled to keep from grinning at the sight of the two boys squirming in their grandmother's grip. When Kafutshi let go of their ears with a sharp pinch, the twins scuttled quickly out of her reach. She turned to Valerie and reached for her head; Valerie recoiled a bit, thinking Kafutshi was going to give her ear a twist too. "How is your head, madame?" the old woman asked, concern in her voice. "Do you want me to send for the *nganga*?" She gently brushed Valerie's hair back from the side of her face as she stood on tiptoe to examine her scalp. Valerie relaxed and smiled.

"I am fine, thank you," she said. "Dr. Talon took good care of me."

"Yes, the *dakta* is a good man," Kafutshi said. "He needs a good woman too," she said. Valerie blushed and Nancy burst out laughing.

"I, uh, we need to, uh ..." Valerie stammered.

"What's the matter, boss? Is there something you want to say?" Nancy teased.

"We need to shoot some more video," Valerie said, composing herself. She scowled at Nancy.

Kafutshi laughed like a wicked imp, then let Valerie off the hook by asking, "Do you want us to show you how to make the *nkisi* again?"

"Yes, please," Valerie answered.

"Let's start with a shot of the women working," Valerie said. Kafutshi sat down in the circle of women on the hard-packed dirt floor. She picked up the *nkisi* she had been working on and held it up for Valerie to see.

Just then, Juvenal jumped in front of the camera waving his arms and dancing around shouting, "Me! Me! Take a picture of me, madame!"

"Stop that! You bad boy!" Kafutshi scolded while Valerie laughed and everyone watched the boy bound insanely around the room. While their attention was drawn to his brother, Kenda snatched a *nkisi* from the row of finished dolls on the table with the pellets and slipped it under his shirt. He stepped back next to Valerie just as Kafutshi grabbed Juvenal by the arm to stop his wild gyrations with a quick shake.

"Did you get that on tape?" Valerie asked Nancy between laughs.

"In all its frenetic glory," Nancy chuckled.

Kafutshi finished the *nkisi* then took it to the table to be filled with pellets. She handed it to the solider, who put it in the row with the others. Then the soldier turned to the blackboard to make a mark next to Kafutshi's name. The soldier with the clipboard made a mark as well.

"That's to make sure she gets paid for her work," Alben pointed out. As he spoke, Yoweri strode purposefully through the door. "What are you doing here?" Alben said. Yoweri whispered something in his ear.

Hatred suddenly filled the missionary's face. "Showtime is over," he snapped. "I have to deal with a situation."

"Tell me again—what is a *nganga?*" Valerie asked Jaime when she got back to the clinic. He was in the dispensary inventorying the medications they had brought from Tshikapa the day before.

"A *nganga* is someone who communicates with the spirits of your dead ancestors," he replied. "Sort of what we would call a shaman. Why do you ask?"

"Kafutshi asked me if I needed one for my head," she said. "I remember now from before. She told me the *nganga* used to put bones from the ancestors in the little dolls, the *minkisi.*"

"That's so you can have your ancestors near you when you need them. They believe the spirits can help you," he explained. "The *nganga* talks to them. They tell him if a witch has put a spell on you. And how to get rid of it. Things like that." Jaime made a note on a clipboard and laid it on his desk. "You remember the guy that hid you in the woods the last time you were here? Siankaba, the *nganga* from Mpala? We could probably find him if you want. Did you happen to bring any of your ancestors' bones with you?"

Valerie smiled at his gentle humor. "I carry around plenty of baggage from my ancestors, but it's all up here." She pointed to her head and laughed ruefully.

"Don't we all," Jaime said. "Are your parents living?"

"Only my father. I haven't heard from him since I finished college." Jaime didn't interrupt as Valerie continued.

"My mother passed the year before I graduated," she said. Unexpectedly, the memory of her mother's death flooded over her.

She fought to shut it off, but Jaime's simple, unmeasured acceptance made that impossible. Talking to someone like him, someone without any agenda except to understand you, was a foreign experience for her. Valerie had survived her youth by hiding her feelings deep inside. She saw how her father picked at every hint of emotion in her mother, digging at it and gouging it until he could get both hands inside it and rip the woman apart. Even though he tried hard, Valerie never let him do that to her. She protected herself with a carapace that eventually covered all her feelings. Now, for some reason, she felt compelled to tell Jaime about her mother's death, and the burden she still carried from it. "It was sad. I think she was glad to go."

"That must have been sad," Jaime said. "Did she have a difficult illness?"

"No, not particularly. I mean, she was glad to escape from my father. He was a bastard." Her voice took on a faraway timbre as she let go her confession. "I felt so guilty when she died. I had lost so much respect for her because she let him treat her the way he did. I never told her that, but I felt it. I loved her, but I didn't respect her. If she knew, she never let on. I still hate myself for feeling that way." She looked at Jaime, her eyes pleading. "Does guilt last forever?"

"I think so," he answered gently. "But if you can accept it, you can live with it."

Valerie wanted him to hold her in his arms and stroke her hair. His body leaned toward her, an invitation, she thought. She took a tentative step toward him, anticipating the smooth muscles of his chest against her cheek. A rap on the doorframe stopped her.

It was Celestine. "*Dakta* Jaime," she said. "*Dakta* Pieter asks you to come, please. He says, will you help him with a sick woman?"

Jaime looked into Valerie's eyes for a long moment, then left.

Chapter 21

Mai-Munene

Later, at the other end of the village in the mine office, sweat stung Joao de Santos' eyes as he sat across the desk from Thomas Alben. He couldn't wipe it away because his hands were lashed to the arms of his chair. His ankles were bound to the chair legs. All four limbs trembled uncontrollably. He closed his eyes against the stinging sweat but Yoweri grabbed his hair and slammed his head back against the chair.

"He smuggled a diamond out of the sorting room," Yoweri growled.

"How?" Alben asked, his eyes narrowing.

"He hid it under his tongue."

"Idiot. Why would you do something so obvious?" Alben asked disgustedly.

"It was just one small stone," de Santos pleaded. "I will never do it again."

"I am certain of that, Joao," Alben said.

Mine security had always been tight, but Alben had clamped down even harder. Since he arrived, the workers were forced to live inside the mine compound, sleeping in barracks that the soldiers searched frequently. The perimeter of the mine was surrounded by a pair of chain-link fences topped with razor wire so nothing could be passed by hand to the outside. There was only one way in and out of the compound, past the guardhouse where everyone was subject to a final search before being allowed to pass. At the end of every shift, the workers stripped to be hosed down while soldiers shook out their clothing. Random body cavity searches became commonplace. The first time Yoweri caught a worker trying to steal a diamond, Alben had the man publicly beaten. He was ostensibly taken to jail in Kananga, the provincial capital, as a warning to the other workers. Everyone knew that the man would never make it there alive, but the announcement made everything look official. Until now, it had only been necessary to deal with that one thief. If the mine manager himself felt bold enough to steal, however, Alben decided it was time to repeat the lesson—more emphatically.

"Where are the other stones you took?" Alben demanded calmly.

"There are no others. I swear! This was the first."

"I'm sorry I can't believe you, Joao, but any man who will steal from his employer will also lie about it. Where do you hide them?"

"I have no more. You must believe me!" de Santos pleaded.

"He is lying, Captain," Alben said to Yoweri. "Persuade him to be truthful."

Without warning, Yoweri shoved de Santos' chair over backwards. The mine manager's head thumped hard against the concrete floor. Yoweri quickly ripped off de Santos' shoes then stripped off his thin socks to expose the pale soles of his feet.

"No! Please! I have no more stones!" de Santos whimpered from the floor.

Yoweri picked up a piece of rebar as long as his arm and looked at Alben, who nodded intently. Yoweri cocked the ribbed iron rod like a baseball bat. He swung it heavily into the bare arch of de Santos' right foot. His first scream was cut off by a blow to the sole of his other foot.

It took a half-second for that shock to register, then he howled. Yoweri paused and de Santos whimpered.

"Where are they?" Alben demanded. Speechless, de Santos pleaded for mercy with his eyes. When Alben nodded again, Yoweri smashed the heavy iron bar into de Santos' right heel, driving it up toward his ankle. The blow ripped the tender skin of the man's foot and smashed the small bones inside while driving a jolting shock into his knees and up his legs into his spine. The next strike crushed the ball of his left foot and hinged it back to the shin, snapping the ankle. At every blow, De Santos' cries echoed through the mining camp and into the village. Alben's eyes glowed as he gestured for the blood-spattered Yoweri to hit the man again and again. A final swing of the bloody bar landed across both soles, leaving de Santos' feet masses of crumpled tissue where blood oozed through the crushed flesh. The manager was unconscious, his breathing shallow.

"Drag him to the barracks and wake him up. Then finish him. Colorfully. I want the workers to see what happens when they steal from me."

"What about the journalist?" Yoweri asked.

"I'll deal with her later," Alben replied. "She won't report anything."

De Santos' screams were faint in the distance, but still harrowing enough to silence the line of children gathered outside the clinic to receive their rations for the evening meal. Their eyes widened in fright. They looked to Jaime to see whether they should run for the woods.

"What the hell was that?" Nancy asked nervously as the sound faded away.

"There must have been an accident at the mine," Jaime said, purposefully loud enough for the frightened children in line to hear him. He looked steadily at them, keeping a calm demeanor so they wouldn't panic. "Valerie, you and Nancy stay here and make sure everyone gets a ration. Pieter, get the dispensary ready. I'll go see if they need help." Without giving anyone a chance to argue, he took off at a fast walk for the mine compound while Valerie grabbed the spoon to fill the waiting bowls with rice.

Once he was out of sight of the children, Jaime ran all the way through the village to the mine compound. Before he could duck under the barricade at the entrance, two guards stepped out to stop him

"No one in or out. Captain's orders!" one of the soldiers shouted.

"Go away, *dakta*," the other one added, exercising his own tiny authority.

"Let me through," Jaime ordered. "Someone's been hurt!"

"No one in or out," the first soldier repeated emphatically.

"How bad was the injury? How did it happen?" Jaime demanded. The soldiers looked at each other and didn't answer. "I want to see Alben immediately," Jaime said impatiently. "Call him right now." He pointed at the gatehouse, where he knew there was an intercom to the mine headquarters building. "Now!" he barked.

The first soldier strutted arrogantly into the gatehouse and picked up the handset. Jaime couldn't hear what was said, but a pleased look came across the man's face. He swaggered confidently back to Jaime. Grinning, he put a hand on Jaime's chest and pushed him away from the barricade. "Captain Yoweri orders you to go away." The soldier un-slung his AK-47. "Go now. Captain's orders." The second soldier flipped off his weapon's safety.

Stymied, Jaime turned to walk back to the clinic. Then it occurred to him that there was no one else visible in the mine compound except the two guards. It was evening, but usually there were off-shift workers and a handful of other soldiers lazing around. "Where is everybody?" he asked brusquely.

The soldier smiled. "It is lesson time," he said. Just then a piercing scream rose from somewhere inside the compound. It was cut off with a gurgle. An ominous silence fell. "That man has learned his lesson," the soldier said menacingly. "Now go away or I will teach you something too." He raised his rifle to his shoulder and aimed it at Jaime's face. Jaime glared at him then backed slowly away.

Guilty consciences didn't normally bother Juvenal and Kenda, but fear of punishment did sometimes give them pause. When the horrible screams echoed through the village while they were eating their dinner with Kafutshi and Celestine, they immediately assumed there was trouble headed their way. Juvenal caught Kenda's eye. He twitched his head toward the sleeping hut. They waited for Kafutshi to go into the other hut, where she did the cooking during the rainy season, then put the bowls with their half-eaten dinner on the ground and hurried away from the fire. They stopped at the door of the sleeping hut, whispered together briefly, then Kenda slipped inside while Juvenal looked back to see if his grandmother was watching. She was still out of sight, so he waved an "all clear." Kenda ran out of the hut with the stolen *nkisi* stuffed under his shirt. The two boys ran through the village in the twilight, trotting past the clinic to the riverbank.

Christophe was finishing his meal at the clinic when he saw the two little troublemakers run by. Suspicious, he followed them at a distance as they hurried down the path to the river, then turned onto a barely discernible game trail. He hung back to avoid being seen and ducked behind a bush when the twins stopped at a big red mahogany tree on the riverbank. Juvenal made a sling with his hands and boosted Kenda to where he could reach the first branch of the tree. He scrambled up to a big fork where there was a hammerkop nest made from hardened mud and sticks. It was larger than the boy and, for a minute, Christophe thought Kenda was going to try to climb over it. Instead, he leaned far out over the river and reached up to push something into the nest through the opening on the bottom. Then he scampered down and the two boys ran back up the path toward Christophe. He stayed behind the bush as they passed. They were in too much of a hurry to see him in the gathering darkness.

As soon as they were out of sight, Christophe shimmied up the mahogany tree trunk to the hammerkop nest. It made him nervous to be so close to the nest, since legend had it that if a hammerkop followed you home and landed on your hut, someone within would die. Christophe didn't hear the shrill, piping whistle of the bird, though, so he stretched out over the river to put his hand inside the nest. Just then, something heavy snapped a twig on the path to the river at the end of the game trail. Startled, he almost lost his grip and fell into the water, but he caught his balance at the last minute. He looked carefully around the nest through the thick leaves. Yoweri led two soldiers. They dragged a bloody body. As Christophe watched from his perch, the soldiers flung the limp form out over the water. It splashed loudly, then floated back to the surface and drifted slowly downstream. The body turned over in the water and Christophe saw that it was a white man.

He thought it was the short greasy man who worked in the office at the mine, but he wasn't sure. As Yoweri and the soldiers disappeared back up the path toward the camp, Christophe heard a soft splash from the opposite riverbank, then saw the water undulate as a crocodile snaked across the river toward the body. He hoped the white man was as dead as he looked.

Quietly, Christophe reached under the hammerkop nest to find the opening. He stuck his hand inside and groped among the dried mud and twigs, then his fingers touched something made of cloth. Carefully, he pulled it from the nest. It was a *nkisi*. It looked like something the twins' sister Celestine would play with, he thought. He figured they probably stole it to torment her.

Beneath his perch on the tree branch there was a flurry of splashing in the river. In the moonlight, he saw the carcass of the white man in the center of a writhing knot of crocodiles. They ripped the body to pieces and repeatedly dragged it under the surface. It took only a few moments for the body to disappear completely then the water stopped churning. Christophe climbed down the tree with the *nkisi*. He knew the doctor would want to know what he had witnessed.

Alben spent a few minutes relishing the slow death of Joao de Santos. When his heart finally slowed, he called Atlanta.

"I thought you should know we have a couple of situations here," he said when Peterson got on the phone. "I caught the mine manager stealing."

"I assume you dealt with him appropriately," Peterson said.

"Oh yes," Alben answered. There was a hint of pleasure in his voice.

"But the main reason I called was to let you know that the reporter, Valerie Grey, came back."

"What! I thought she was dead," Peterson exclaimed.

"I guess you can't believe the media these days," Alben said.

"That bitch is nothing but trouble," Peterson said. "Deal with her."

Alben said, "You can count on it."

Chapter 22

Kinshasa

That same day in the capital, Bobby hurried across the tarmac from the beat-up Cessna Caravan that had brought him from Tshikapa to Kinshasa. Two tall men in well-worn bush jackets and dark glasses passed him as they walked toward an unmarked private jet parked by itself.

Bobby stopped to set the aluminum satellite phone case with the prominent red and blue MBS logo on the pavement so he could shift the canvas bag full of tapes from one shoulder to the other. As he picked up the phone case and went on, he heard one of the two men say something to his partner. One of them caught up with Bobby just inside the terminal.

"Excuse me," he said, tapping Bobby on the shoulder. "Are you with MBS? Is Valerie Grey here?"

"No, Valerie's not here," Bobby answered, caught off guard by the man's question. Then he realized it was weird that the man acted like Valerie was alive when the news reports had pronounced her dead two days ago. He looked more closely at him but couldn't read his eyes, which were hidden behind his dark glasses. There was a long, thin scar along his jaw. "Who are you?" Bobby asked suspiciously.

"I'm a big fan of hers. Where is she? I'd like to get her autograph."

Bobby didn't know whether to lie to the man and tell him Valerie was dead or try to make up some other story. He stepped instinctively away. "I don't know. Look, I've got to go." He turned to walk away, but the second man in dark glasses stepped out of nowhere into his path.

Before Bobby could react, the man with the scar gripped his arm from behind and jabbed something hard into his ribs. "Shut up and walk," he ordered. The second man grabbed his other arm. Bobby was no weakling; he'd lugged cameras around before they became miniature digital wonders and had the wiry muscles to show for it. He was no match for these two guys, though. They hustled him past a squad of unseeing F.I.C. soldiers and down a short corridor where they shoved him through an unmarked door into a windowless room.

"What is this?" Bobby protested as the first man spun him around so he could see the Glock 18 in his hand. He roughly jerked the bag of tapes off Bobby's shoulder.

"Were you with Grey when she got killed?" the man asked coolly as he opened the bag and looked inside.

"Who the hell are you?" Bobby demanded. "Give me that! It's network property." He tried to snatch the bag back but the second man seized his arm and wrenched it behind his back. Bobby gasped at the sharp pain.

"Were you in Bukedi during the attack?" the first man asked, unruffled. The second man twisted Bobby's hand higher between his shoulder blades. Bobby rose to his tiptoes trying to relieve the pressure on his shoulder socket.

"No," he grunted.

"Where were you?"

"We were in … I was in Tshikapa," Bobby stammered.

"You said 'we.' We who?" the first man said sharply. The second man tightened his grip on Bobby's arm.

"Me and Nancy. Valerie's producer. We went for supplies," he sputtered, hoping he had covered his tracks.

"You're lying, but that's okay. You'll tell the truth pretty soon. What's this?" the man with the scar asked, holding up the tape with Valerie's report from the Tshikapa airfield. Her initials and the date of the attack were written on the label.

"That's uh, that's one of Valerie's tapes. It was her last report," Bobby improvised.

"What's it say?"

"It's about the refugees. The camp. She interviewed the director."

"That's all?"

"Uh, yeah, I think so," Bobby said, sounding unconvincing even to himself. He knew he wasn't a very good liar.

"Let's just make sure," the man said. "We can use the equipment on the plane. If you come along quietly, you won't get hurt." Bobby nodded and the second man released his arm and nudged him toward the door.

"Wait!" Bobby said, reaching for the satellite phone case on the floor where he had dropped it when they first came into the room.

"You won't need that anymore," the second man said. He pushed Bobby into the corridor, walking close behind him. No one stopped them as they walked rapidly to the unmarked Gulfstream IV sitting by itself on the runway. The equatorial heat rose palpably off the concrete as they strode across the tarmac. Bobby didn't want to climb the steps to the jet. He wasn't sure he would come out of it alive.

Inside the luxurious plane, the man with the scar slipped the tape into a video player behind a panel under a TV screen built into a bulkhead. The other man pushed Bobby down into one of the oversized leather seats as Valerie's face appeared on the screen. Her voice filled the plane's cabin with her report on the attack on the refugee camp. She ended with the observation that the reports of her own death were wrong.

"She doesn't look very dead to me," the second man said.

"No she doesn't, does she?" the first man answered, his face hard. "Where are her glasses?" he asked Bobby.

"Glasses? Valerie doesn't wear glasses," Bobby answered, puzzled.

The man with the scar shook his head and said, "I hate fucking mistakes." He turned his attention back to the screen.

When Valerie ended her report by saying she was on the road to Mbuji-Mayi, the man turned to Bobby. "I thought you said you didn't know where she is," he said.

"I don't! I shot the video and left. I don't know where she is now." Bobby didn't feel as confident as he was trying to sound.

"Look, camera-boy, I don't like smart alecks," the man said, not raising his voice but biting off every word in a terrifying way. "How is she getting around?"

"We borrowed a jeep from the camp," Bobby answered, his eyes wide.

"She could have flown, too," the second man said.

"Radio Tshikapa and find out what flights went out of there in the last couple of days," the man with the scar ordered. He must be the boss, Bobby thought. The second agent went forward into the cabin. Bobby heard him talking to the plane's crew as the cabin door closed. Alone with the hard-faced man with the scar, Bobby's resolve weakened further.

"What are you going to do with me?" he asked falteringly.

"That depends on how truthful you are from here on out. You lied to me twice so far. A third strike and you're absolutely out." He paused as if to make sure the message had registered with Bobby, which it had. "Is she really going to Mbuji-Mayi?" He took off his dark glasses and glowered.

Bobby couldn't seem to get enough breath to answer. He didn't know what to do. Finally, summoning strength from somewhere and hoping to buy some time, he said weakly, "That's where the mine company records are." He swallowed hard.

"Good point," the man said thoughtfully. He put his sunglasses back on as the second man came back from the cabin. He reported that no flights besides Bobby's had left Tshikapa airfield for the last two days.

"At least, if you believe the black bastard that answered the radio call," he added.

"Go round up a chopper and a pilot," the boss ordered.

"Do we still need him?" the second man asked, jerking his head toward Bobby.

"Maybe," the boss answered. "Bring him along and we'll find out if he's telling the truth."

It didn't take the second man long to commandeer a Blackhawk helicopter and pilot from Messime's army. They made a brief stop in Kananga, where the man with the scar left in a government car that met them at the airport. While Bobby sat in the back of the sweltering chopper with his hands shackled to his seat, the second man kept watch, obviously bored but still alert. He relaxed only when his boss came back and the craft took off.

"He's lying, you know. We should just toss him out now and get it over with," the second man said when they were airborne.

"I know he's lying, but we may need him later," the boss said. "We can cover Mbuji-Mayi in less than a day. If she's investigating a mine transaction, she'll want to see the records and that's where they are. She should be there by now if that's where she's really going."

Bobby kept his eyes fixed on the passing landscape for the rest of the flight. He was scared he would inadvertently give something away if he looked either man in the face. He didn't know what he was going to do when they found out he was lying. He just hoped he could find a way to escape before they did. The scrubby red savannah beneath him was broken by green river banks and occasional small fields laboriously watered by hand. As they neared the mining capital, the scant greenery gave way to harsh slashes in the earth and piles of grimy tailings from the mines. From time to time, Bobby spotted deep individual holes about the size of cars dug seemingly at random in the middle of nowhere. The holes were always surrounded by brush and patches of small trees left undisturbed to screen them from view at ground level. As the helicopter started to descend, he saw a man crawl from one of the holes and run toward the sheltering brush. The holes were illicit diamond pit mines, he realized, and the man was running to escape what he thought was death from the air.

A car and driver met them at the airport and took them to Les Bureaux des Gecamines in the city's crumbling business district. The boss left Bobby in the car with his companion while he went inside to see if Valerie had been there. After he left, a thin man wearing a ragged Detroit Pistons jersey tapped on the window next to Bobby's head. The man motioned for him to roll down the window. When Bobby shook his head, he shouted through the glass, "You buy diamonds?" holding up a small plastic bag with a scant dozen stones in it. Bobby's guard motioned for the man to go away but he knocked on the window again, shaking his bag invitingly. The guard pulled a pistol from behind his back and gestured menacingly with it. The man scurried backwards away from the car and into a knot of men standing in the shade of the mines building. He said something to them, glancing back over his shoulder at the car. The men dispersed into the scattered clots of pedestrians milling slowly through the district.

The boss came out of the building and got into the front seat with the driver. "They don't know anything about any American reporter," he said. "We'll check the hotels tonight, then backtrack on the highway tomorrow." He reached across the seat back and grabbed Bobby's chin, jerking his head around so he could see into his eyes. "You got anything more to say before we find out the hard way if you're telling me the truth?" he asked.

"All I know is this is where we were going. She said she had to check the mine ownership records. That's all I know," Bobby said, his speech garbled by the steely fingers gripping his jaw.

"She going anywhere else besides Mbuji-Mayi?" the man demanded. He squeezed hard for emphasis, then loosened so Bobby could talk.

"I don't know, I swear. I'm just a peon. All she tells me is where to set up the camera and when to turn it on."

The man with the scar dropped Bobby's chin. "You're going to be a very sorry peon if we don't find that bitch." He turned to the driver. "Start at the Cape Sierra Hotel."

Chapter 23
Mai-Munene

Thomas Alben's dinner, a piece of fish washed down with a cold beer, turned sour in his stomach as he counted the *minkisi* in the shipping carton one more time. There was undeniably one missing. As the acid burbled upward in his esophagus, he glared at the two soldiers standing nervously before him. One of them looked again at the clipboard in his hand as if staring at it would make the marks change.

"Did the dolls ever leave your sight?" Alben barked.

"No sir," the soldier with the clipboard answered immediately.

"Both tallies show four dozen—forty-eight?"

"Yes sir," the other man mumbled.

"Then why are there only forty-seven dolls?" Alben roared.

The first soldier opened his mouth to speak then shut it abruptly. He didn't have an answer for Alben's question.

"Which one of you took it?" Alben asked menacingly.

The two men looked uneasily at each other, then back at Alben. The soldier with the clipboard dropped his eyes to the floor under the intensity of Alben's stare.

"Captain!" Alben snarled. "Take this man into the other room and find out where he hid the doll. I will deal with his partner."

Yoweri pulled the soldier with the clipboard into the radio room and slammed the door. Alben looked hard at the other solider. "Tell me where he hid the doll, and you will be spared," he said firmly.

"I don't know, sir," the soldier shook his head miserably.

"But you were supposed to watch him, weren't you? And he was assigned to watch you. Is that not correct?"

"Yes sir."

"Then you must be derelict in your duty!"

A dull slap came from the next room, followed by a groan. The soldier's eyes widened. Alben stared back at him and started to speak, but a dull snap and a scream from the other room cut him off. The soldier in front of him gasped.

"He is going to tell the captain that you have it, you know," Alben said. "You'd better tell me where it is."

The terrified soldier shook his head speechlessly. Alben snatched a ballpoint pen from his desk and drove it into the man's eye. The soldier howled and crumpled to the floor, the pen stuck in his face and blood streaming through his fingers. Alben took two fast steps and kicked him heavily in the ribs. As the man fell over onto his side, Yoweri came through the door dragging the other soldier by the collar behind him. One of the man's legs was bent sideways at the knee. He was unconscious.

"He knows nothing," Yoweri said.

"This one either," Alben answered. "Search the village. Find everyone who was in the schoolhouse today. The women, those two boys, and the reporter and her dyke friend. One of them has the doll. I want them alive."

Valerie had just crawled into bed when Christophe urgently stage-whispered, "*Dakta! Dakta!*" outside Jaime's window. She heard Jaime open the door where Christophe stood in the moonless darkness.

"What is it?" he asked in a low voice.

"I saw the F.I.C. captain and some soldiers throw a man into the river," Christophe said. "Then the crocodiles ate him!"

"Who was it?" Jaime asked.

"I think it was the *muzungu* from the mine. The little man with the greasy hair."

"Joao de Santos?"

"I do not know his name. They threw him in the river, then they went away."

"What is it?" Pieter asked. He lit a lantern.

"Christophe says Yoweri fed Joao de Santos to the crocodiles," Jaime answered.

Valerie and Nancy came to the doorway, aroused by the talking.

"What the hell's going on?" Nancy asked as they came in.

"Christophe saw a body in the river. From the mine," Pieter said.

"Something very bad is going on at that mine," Valerie said. She saw the *nkisi* in Christophe's hand; it looked like it was made in Alben's workshop. "Where did you get that?" she asked. He handed it to her.

"Those bad boys hid it in a hammerkop nest," he said.

"Juvenal and Kenda?" Valerie asked.

"The little thieves," Nancy said. "Has anyone checked to see if the kitchen sink is still here?"

Valerie turned the *nkisi* over in her hand. She could feel the pellets inside through the cloth and she remembered Kafutshi calling it "special American filling." She also remembered the poorly-sewn *nkisi* sitting on Peterson's desk in Atlanta. She squeezed the doll; the pellets felt hard between her fingers. Curious, she asked Jaime for a knife. She carefully worked a seam open and shook a plastic pellet about the size of a pea into her palm. She pressed her thumbnail into it, expecting it to split or crumble but it didn't. The rubbery surface gave a little but her thumbnail stopped against something hard inside. She set the pellet on the table and tried to cut through it with the knife, but the blade bit into a hard core inside and the pellet squirted out of her fingers and onto the floor. Nancy picked it up and handed it back. Valerie braced the pellet on the table. She carefully scraped the plastic off the hard core, blew away some pieces of resin, and held it up to the light. "Is this a diamond?" she asked, holding it out to Jaime.

"That's what it is, all right," he said.

"Let's see if there are any more," Valerie said as she slid the knife into the seam and opened it further. She shook a few more pellets onto the table. When she sliced away the plastic resin, the cuts revealed rough diamonds in almost every pellet. She held one in her fingertips and looked at it thoughtfully.

"That explains the special American filling," she said.

"No wonder they're so popular in the Church of the Holy Angels gift shop," Nancy said.

"How much do you suppose Peterson knows about this?" mused Valerie.

"He's Alben's boss. He's got to be in on it," Nancy offered. "But why? He owns the damn mine, doesn't he?"

"It could just be a way to screw the Congo on the royalties," Jaime said. "The white man's been doing that for centuries."

"Or to skim some off the top and screw someone else—like a partner," Valerie added thoughtfully.

"Doesn't Peterson own the mine outright?" Nancy said.

"Don't forget, this is the Congo," Jaime answered. "It's a sure bet Messime's got at least one finger in the pie somewhere."

"There may be someone else too," Valerie pointed out.

"Like someone who lives in Alexandria, Virginia?" asked Nancy.

"Could be. Peterson has friends in high places. And those friends have friends—friends with whole armies at their disposal," Valerie answered.

Her speculation was cut off by distant cries and commotion from the other end of the village near the school.

Valerie remembered the soldiers marking tallies on the blackboard as the women turned in their completed dolls. "Christ! They're looking for this *nkisi*," Valerie exclaimed. "We've got to warn Kafutshi!" Nancy started for the door, but Jaime pulled her back.

"You and Christophe stay here and get a few supplies together," he instructed firmly. "If Alben comes, we may have to leave in a hurry."

He ran out with Pieter, who grabbed a heavy flashlight on the way. Valerie went after them.

The truck squealed to a stop outside Kafutshi's hut. The old woman awoke with a start just before Yoweri ripped aside the piece of old tarp that served as her door. He swept the interior with a powerful flashlight. Kafutshi pushed Celestine and the twins behind her while she peered around the thin white curtain that separated their pallets from the main room. Two more soldiers crowded into the tiny hut, followed closely by Alben.

"Where is the *nkisi*?" Yoweri demanded, shining the light into Kafutshi's face. Bewildered, she didn't answer. He motioned with his light, ordering the soldiers to take her outside. One of them ripped down the curtain. He roughly yanked Kafutshi up by one arm. As he dragged her out the door, the other soldier pointed his AK-47 at the three children and motioned for them to follow.

Yoweri ran his hand along the top of the mud wall beneath the thatch roof. Alben kicked over the wooden box that held Kafutshi's few possessions. Some scraps of cloth, a spool of thread, two knives, a large metal spoon, a pot with a broken handle, and a plastic box with a few buttons inside spilled onto the floor. He dumped her sack of cornmeal, emptied a partly full bag of beans and one of rice then kicked through the pallets where Kafutshi and the children had been sleeping a few minutes earlier.

Outside, Kafutshi and the children huddled in the headlights of the truck. She encircled the children with her skinny arms, shielding them as best she could from the soldiers. Other lights flashed through the scattered village as more soldiers searched the huts. There were cries of surprise and protest as other women were dragged from their huts and herded into the road.

Alben and Yoweri stormed out of her hut. "Where is the doll?" Alben demanded. Kafutshi blinked her eyes in confusion. "Put the brats in the truck," he said to the soldiers. One dragged the twins out of Kafutshi's arms while the other yanked Celestine to her feet. Her *nkisi* dropped to the ground. Thinking they'd been saved, Kafutshi snatched it up and held it out to Alben.

"Take this *nkisi*, Brother Tom," she said hopefully.

Alben grabbed the doll with a greedy grin, but his face clouded as he heard the corn shucks rustle inside it. He ripped off the head and poured out the worthless filling.

"Stupid cunt!" Yoweri bellowed. With one swift movement, he

seized a rifle and slammed the stock into Kafutshi's mouth. The old woman slumped to the ground and he smashed the wooden gun stock down on her head.

"Stop! Question her first!" Alben ordered.

Yoweri roughly turned her crumpled body over with his foot, but it was too late. Celestine screamed. Yoweri whirled on her, raising the rifle.

"No! Put them in the truck!" Alben commanded. "I will interrogate them later."

He ducked into the round cooking hut. He kicked aside Kafutshi's blackened pots and rummaged through the firewood stacked against the wall. Yoweri ordered the soldiers to guard the children and followed Alben into the cooking hut.

Celestine's scream reached them as Valerie, Jaime, and Pieter passed a hut not far down the road. Valerie saw Kafutshi lying on the ground in the lights of the army truck. She started to run to her, but Jaime grabbed her arm and held her back. "Wait!" he whispered. He pulled her behind a reed fence where they could watch the scene. "We need to know what we're jumping into." Valerie realized that the rules had changed. She saw Alben issue orders to the soldiers, then disappear into the cooking hut. His thin pretense of missionary goodness was gone, revealing the brute beneath the surface.

Pieter craned his long neck above the fence. They could hear Celestine sobbing in the back of the truck. "I only see one soldier," he whispered.

"There's another one behind the truck," Jaime said.

"Alben and somebody else are in the cooking hut," Valerie added.

A flashlight swept past the doorway.

"We've got to hurry," Pieter said urgently.

Valerie jumped up and whispered, "I'll distract them." She darted across the road before Jaime could stop her. Pieter and Jaime circled around the hut in a crouch, working their way quietly along the reed fence toward Kafutshi's hut. Valerie went behind a hut on the other side of the road. She found a rusted can. Creeping closer, she tossed it over Kafutshi's cooking hut. It clattered on the ground next to the truck. The soldier in front of the truck raised his rifle and walked cautiously toward the sound. The one behind the truck turned too, giving Pieter a chance to crack him in the head with his heavy flashlight. The first soldier turned back toward the sound of the blow. Pieter leapt toward him as Valerie dashed past the cooking hut. The man fired without aiming but the bullet caught Pieter in the side just below his belt, doubling him over. Jaime tackled the soldier from behind before he could fire again. Valerie snatched the gun out of his hands just as Yoweri came out of the hut. She had never fired a weapon at another human, but Yoweri didn't know that. She turned the AK-47 on him and he leapt backward through the low door, knocking Alben back inside behind him.

"Let's go!" Pieter shouted, dragging himself into the driver's seat of the truck. Valerie clambered into the back and told the children to lie down. She kept the rifle trained on the hut, hoping Yoweri wouldn't force her to fire it. Jaime jumped in next to her as Pieter started the engine with a roar. He floored it and the truck sped down the dark road through the village. Yoweri raced out of the hut firing his pistol into the cloud of dust the truck left behind.

Alben ducked through the low doorway behind him. "Get them!" he ordered. "But bring that bitch reporter back alive!"

Yoweri bellowed for the other searchers to give chase on foot then sent a man to the mine compound to get another truck.

Jaime jumped out as soon as the truck squealed to a stop in front of the clinic. Nancy and Christophe stood outside with a small pile of supplies. Nancy grabbed a bag of corn meal and started lifting it into the back of the truck. "No. We can't get away from them on the road," Jaime said, stopping her. "Get the children out of the truck, would you?" he said to Valerie. She handed down Juvenal from the back and reached for Kenda.

"How the hell are we going to get out of here? Sprout wings and fly?" Nancy asked.

"We'll go on the river," Jaime answered as he took Kenda from Valerie and put him on the ground next to his brother. "Hurry, we don't have much time," he said as Valerie tried to persuade the sobbing Celestine to get up from where she lay curled on the truck bed. Pieter came around from the driver's side. The moon hadn't yet risen, so no one saw the large dark stain on the front of his shorts and the sticky black blood trickling down his leg.

"Come here, love," he said softly, holding out his arms. The girl lifted her head. She crawled slowly across the truck bed to him. He lifted her out and Valerie jumped down.

"What about the other kids?" Valerie asked. They couldn't just leave the refugee children behind, she thought. God only knew what Alben and Yoweri would do to them.

"They're gone," Pieter answered. "They scattered when the first shots were fired."

"They're hiding in the hills by now," Jaime added.

Valerie was stricken by an urge to find the fleeing children and protect them, to give them shelter and reassurance and shield them from the hungry evil that haunted their lives. But they were gone and she had no time to find them now.

"Look!" Nancy exclaimed, pointing through the village where flashlight beams jogged down the road toward them.

Jaime turned to Christophe. "Did you see any mokoros on the riverbank when you were there?"

"Yes, *dakta*. There were two," the boy said. "Small ones left by the fishermen. There will not be room for everyone."

"We'll have to make room," Jaime said. "Come on, let's go!" He picked up Juvenal and started toward the path to the river. Nancy took Kenda's hand and followed.

"You'll have room. I'm staying," Pieter said. He handed Celestine to Valerie. "Here, you take good care of this one, all right?"

"That's nonsense!" Jaime said. He stopped on the path to confront Pieter. "We're not leaving anybody behind."

"Not to worry. I'll play the red herring," Pieter said confidently. "I'll lead them on a wild goose chase in the truck. Then I'll meet you down river at the Banin ford. You know, where the villagers bring their cattle across to the islands."

"No!" Jaime protested.

"Yes! You get out of here—now," Pieter said firmly. He pointed up the road, where truck lights were backlighting the soldiers on foot. They were almost within rifle range.

"At the Banin ford! You better be there!" Jaime ordered grimly.

"I'll see you, love," Pieter said tenderly, giving the girl in Valerie's arms a peck on the cheek. Then he jumped into the truck. The gears clashed noisily as he stood on the accelerator, speeding away from the river in a cloud of dust that followed him into the forest. There was only one road through Mai-Munene; Pieter would have to get back on it soon because the forest was too thick to navigate with the truck. His only chance was to circle back around Alben's men to get a head start on them going away from the river. If he got back on the road too far behind them, they might miss the bait and keep on after Jaime and the others.

"Let's go," Jaime said urgently. "Follow Christophe."

The boy led them to a shallow part of the riverbank where two dugout canoes, the mokoros Christophe had seen, rested on the bank. A small aluminum motorboat was pulled part way onto the bank and tethered to a tree stump to hold it against rising water.

"Hey, we've got speed!" Nancy said excitedly.

"Too noisy," Jaime said, shaking his head.

"They'll use this to come after us when they figure out we're not with Pieter," Valerie said. She climbed into the aluminum boat, found the plastic tube running between the gas tank and outboard engine, and yanked it until it came off at both ends. She threw it into the river. There were a pair of wires hanging from the engine, so she yanked them off too.

"Good idea," Jaime said as Valerie climbed out onto the bank. Jaime twisted the lid off the gas tank. "Get some sand," he said. Valerie poured a double handful of sandy mud from the riverbank into the tank. The two of them pushed the boat into the water, where it drifted into the stream. It floated into an eddy, coming to rest against the bank just a few yards away.

"At least it will slow them down," she said.

Christophe pushed a mokoro with Nancy and the twins away from the bank into the current. Jaime heaved the other canoe by one end across the mud to the water. "Get in and stay low," he said urgently.

Valerie helped Celestine into the small craft, then stepped tentatively over the side herself. The canoe immediately started to tip under her weight, but righted itself as she bent over and grasped the sides. Staying low, she carefully worked her way to the bow behind Celestine. Jaime pushed the craft the rest of the way into the river before stepping in cautiously himself. Standing uneasily, he pulled a long-handled paddle from the bottom of the boat and pushed them into the current.

A half-moon finally rose over the treetops but Valerie sensed rather than saw the trees and other vegetation along the riverbank they had just left. The other side of the wide river was lost in the darkness. The pale moonlight glinted on the water riffling around rocks and snags as Christophe deftly guided them into the center of the stream, allowing the current to propel them and steering with his long paddle. Jaime followed closely behind.

"Keep an eye out for hippos," he said quietly.

"Christ! That's all we need," Nancy said under her breath. Her head immediately swiveled from side to side. Valerie peered across the moonlit river, searching for obstacles in the black water while keeping an eye out for soldiers on the near bank. They glided silently downstream, the only sound an occasional drip from the paddles. Valerie heard a crocodile slip into the water behind them.

"This is where they threw the man into the river," Christophe whispered. Valerie looked around carefully, but there were no traces of anyone. Something else splashed stealthily nearby.

A burst of distant gunfire came from the direction of the village. Valerie involutarily dug her fingernails into the mokoro's wooden sides. She heard nothing else for a few moments then came another short burst. She thought she could see lights flickering far away from the river, but there were too many hills and trees between to see anything for certain.

"Did you hear that?" she asked Jaime quietly. She didn't want to alarm Celestine, who sat mutely in the bottom of the mokoro.

"Yes, it sounds like Pieter has circled around beyond the camp."

"I haven't seen anyone behind us, have you?"

Jaime turned his head to check. "No. It looks like Pieter's diversion worked."

In a few minutes, lights far in the distance rose above the treetops along the riverbank. At first, there was only one set of headlight beams climbing a hill on the far horizon. Then two more pairs came behind the first one.

"Look," Valerie said, pointing toward the lights, which now bobbed along the crest of the hill on the horizon. They looked like warning lights on planes flying low in the dark sky.

"That should be Pieter on the road going north," Jaime said. "It parallels the river once we get past the mine." He didn't need to point out that the second and third pair of lights were gaining on Pieter.

The bottom of the mokoro rumbled lightly as the canoe skimmed over a submerged boulder. Jaime's paddle scraped against the rock so he pushed them into a line through the water more directly behind Christophe's. The light from the moon helped, but the rocks and islets were scattered thickly across the river; there wasn't any one channel to follow. To Valerie, the water's surface was a constantly changing patchwork of glinting light and inky shadows. She didn't see how Christophe and Jaime could navigate through it.

The distant headlights drew her back.

"He's going up the hill toward Mpala," Jaime said, his voice tight.

"They're right behind him," Valerie observed softly.

"Yes," he answered.

Headlights flashed briefly in their direction, then turned away as one of the followers pulled off the road. They saw muzzle flashes and tracers before the chatter of gunfire reached the river. Just as Pieter's lights crested the hill, a thin trail of white raced up the hill toward him, followed by a brilliant explosion. The sound thundered in their ears a moment later as the fireball faded to an orange blaze on the top of the hill. The pursuing lights closed in and stopped.

"Damn," was all Jaime said.

Celestine wailed once, a forlorn cry of lost hope. Valerie pulled the girl closer. She cradled Celestine's head against her breast and stroked her cheek. As Valerie's heart welled up, she squeezed her more tightly. Everyone needs someone to comfort them, to see them through devastating loss, but who did Celestine have now? Valerie wondered how these children withstood the recurring tragedies in their lives. Kafutshi's grandchildren were complete orphans now, having lost first their father, then their mother, and finally their grandmother to brutal assault. Now, Celestine had lost even Pieter, who meant more to her than anyone in the world. Such blows repeated over and over again were like the slugs a boxer takes to the heart; they don't kill but they weaken.

As the mokoro slid slowly down the river, Valerie's thoughts turned to the future. If they escaped Alben's search parties, she would fly safely home to the US, but where would the children go? Who would feed them? How would they avoid being killed like their parents—or worse? She didn't have the answers to any of those questions.

It was midday in Washington, where David Powell's grief took on an angry edge as the stories about Valerie's death grew increasingly contradictory. No one could or would tell MBS's reporters exactly who had attacked the camp at Bukedi. Given other reports coming from the Congo, there didn't seem to be any Angolan troops near the camp nor was Lunda Libre active in the immediate area. Adding to the confusion, the State Department couldn't explain why Valerie's body wasn't on its way home despite President Messime's public assurances that the area around the refugee camp was now completely under the control of his troops. After days of mounting frustration, David decided to take matters into his own hands. He called New York.

"I'm going to the Congo," he said when Carter Wilson came on the line.

"I know you're upset, David, but I don't see how that is going to help anything," Wilson answered. "Besides, we sent Robert Fraser to replace Valerie. He's already filed his first report from Kinshasa."

"I'm not going there as a reporter, Carter," David explained firmly. "I'm going to retrieve Valerie's remains. Call it a personal leave if you want to, but I'm leaving tonight. I don't know when I'll be back."

"I really wish you'd reconsider, David. I'm sure the authorities can handle the details better than you can. It's what they do. Besides, with the war effort ramping up, we need you in Washington right now. I understand if you want to take a few days off, but I'd prefer that you stay within driving distance of the bureau. The sweeps are coming up, and you know the policy about vacation during the ratings period."

David was wordless for a moment then exploded at Wilson's crass remark.

"You are a sick son of a bitch if you think I'm going to let Valerie Grey's body rot in Africa for an extra rating point! I'm going to the Congo. If I still want a job here, I'll call you when I get back." He slammed down the phone.

Chapter 24

The Kasai River

Jaime told Christophe to head for a wide island in the middle of the river before the dawn sky brightened. He told Valerie he wanted to be fully hidden long before Alben's search party got on the river and started hunting them down. They paddled into an inlet on the island, jumped out, and pulled the heavy mokoros across the sandy mud into a stand of tall papyrus. Valerie, Nancy and the boys smoothed the sand behind them. The reeds where the boats had been dragged through were flattened down, so they wove a rough screen from broken stems and leaves and filled in the gap. When they were finished, the only way the mokoros could be seen was from the air.

Christophe led them deeper into the island along a rough hippo path. Valerie noticed he took care to keep a screen of vegetation between them and the riverbanks on either side while he listened closely to make sure they weren't about to meet a hippo coming the other way, heading back to the water after a night spent feeding on the island. The path led to a clearing under a huge sausage tree in the middle of the island. It was on a rise high enough to stay dry even during the rainy season when the river rose several feet and most of the island disappeared under water. The ground beneath the tree was bare and firm, trampled by hippos who came from the river to eat the sausage-shaped, pulpy fruit that dropped from the tree. There wasn't a single thick-skinned pod left on the ground after the night's feeding, but a few maroon flowers had fallen from the tree and been left behind among the hippo's scat. Valerie sat down with her back against the tree trunk. She gently pulled the sad-eyed Celestine down beside her. She gave the girl the *nkisi* filled with diamonds and Celestine curled up around it with her head on Valerie's lap.

"We'll hole up here today. With any luck, they'll eat up the daylight searching the islands we passed," Jaime said, sitting down beside her. "Tonight we can paddle a little further downstream in the dark, but we'll have to go ashore when we get to the Nnenne rapids. We can't handle them in the daylight, much less at night."

"How long do you think it will take them to find us?" Nancy asked. She sat with the twins on the other side of the tree.

"I think we'll be okay today. We passed maybe fifty islands last night and they'll have to search them all," Jaime answered.

"They have to check the other side of the river too," Valerie added.

"Good point," Nancy said with a yawn. "So I can get some sleep?"

"We all should," Jaime said. "Christophe will take the first watch."

Valerie stroked Celestine's head until the girl settled into a fitful sleep. Nancy comforted one of the twins, who sniffled softly. After a few minutes, Valerie nodded, exhausted by the night's events. As she gave herself up to sleep, her body slumped lightly against Jaime's.

A little over an hour after Valerie nodded off, Jaime jerked violently in his sleep. Awakened, Valerie eased away to give him some room. Celestine turned over restlessly but didn't awaken. Jaime twitched again, then opened his eyes.

"Sorry," she said quietly.

"No, my fault," Jaime said, rubbing his hand across his face.

"Bad dream?"

"No, just a muscle spasm."

"You had a tough night."

"Yeah. Paddling in the dark is hard on the back. It's still tense."

"Losing Pieter was hard too," Valerie ventured. Jaime took a long breath and looked into the distance.

"Pieter Jakobsen was a very good man. One of the best I ever knew. He did whatever needed to be done to help other people." Jaime's eyes fell. "He died too soon," he added.

Valerie thought he wanted to say something else but held back. She waited, trying not to pressure him. After a moment, he spoke slowly. "Look," he said, "I know you think I need to talk about this. But I don't. I have my own ways of coping with things like Pieter's death. Talking it out isn't one of them. I can't change it, so I try not to dwell on it. I don't like it, but I accept it and move on." Then he added, "Do you understand?"

"Yes, I think I do," Valerie answered. She laid her head on his shoulder—awake this time—and he leaned lightly into her.

"Good," Jaime said.

Valerie did understand. She realized she often dealt with sad events in her life the same way, by focusing on something else. Maybe it was simple denial, but she had learned that there was no use in rehashing tragedy. Jaime couldn't go back and alter the chain of events that led to Pieter's death any more than Valerie could relive her childhood and choose a different father. More often than not, hindsight leads to regret. Bad memories are like a centrifuge endlessly spinning faster and faster and becoming more and more forceful. To keep from slinging off into dark oblivion, you have to slow it down. Then, if you can shove sadness down inside where it hardens into a resolve, you will be stronger, better braced against the next tragedy that comes along. Valerie knew such pillars often have a core of unquiet anger, but they give you the guts to face absolutely anything.

An unseen bird in the reeds screeched like a rusty gate. Christophe stepped from behind a bush on the other side of the clearing carrying the rifle Valerie had snatched from the solider the night before. It struck her that it looked perfectly natural for him to have it, even though he was only fourteen years old. Jaime gently moved his shoulder against Valerie's cheek. He had to get up to relieve the boy's watch. She sat back against the tree. The bird screeched again and Jaime took the gun and crept into the undergrowth to watch the river. Christophe smiled encouragingly at Valerie before he curled up on the ground and closed his eyes. Valerie watched the boy slip into sleep in the morning sun. Christophe's scar gave a fierce cast to one side of his face while the other side was that of a smooth-cheeked adolescent ready to become a serious young man. The scar was hidden in the crook of his arm as he lay sleeping now, but she knew it would always be there. His life teetered on the edge of blackness; it would take little more than a breath to push him into a pit of mayhem where he could become a killer or a victim, or both.

Valerie struggled to push aside her thoughts about their bleak future. She couldn't afford to become dysfunctional right now. A clear head was crucial. She gently lifted Celestine's head off her lap so she could stand up. As the blood rushed back into her legs, she welcomed the pins and needles that signaled the need to move around and do something useful. She peeked around the tree trunk to check on Nancy and the twins, then found the trail where Jaime had disappeared into the brush. Right then, she wanted to be near him more than anything else in the world.

At Mai-Munene, Alben knew in his gut that Valerie Grey had the *nkisi*, whether she stole it or not. Why else would she have tried to shoot him at the old lady's hut, then run away with that bastard doctor?

Alben drove from the riverbank to pick up a squad of soldiers to search the near side of the river valley on foot. They had already ferried another squad to the opposite bank and Yoweri combed the islands in the small launch with three other soldiers. The sun was well up before they got started because of the time it took to repair the sabotaged boat, which they had found bumping against a snag in an eddy downstream just before dawn. Alben fumed and snarled at Yoweri to hurry up, but the sand in the gas got sucked into the engine and fouled it, adding to the delay. Alben knew they had to check every island large enough to hide their quarry. He was sure they had gone to ground at sunrise rather than risk being spotted on the open water. It would take time to search thoroughly, but not more than a day. In the meantime, the soldiers on either side of the river would make sure they hadn't come ashore someplace and struck off on foot across country.

As Alben drove by the clinic on his way to get the second squad, he ran through the trashed bedding and supply boxes his men had ripped apart the night before after they discovered that Grey and her accomplices weren't in the truck with Pieter Jakobsen. He enjoyed seeing the reporter's belongings scattered among the clinic's wrecked furnishings. As he passed the market square, he noticed with satisfaction that the snot-faced refugee children had all disappeared too. Their flimsy stick-and-cardboard shelters across from the clinic were abandoned. The ground was littered with blackened tins, half-burnt twigs from their cooking fires, and the other debris of panicked flight. No one worked in the fields beyond the scattered huts of the village. In fact, he didn't see a single soul along the dusty road. The villagers were either hiding in their mud-walled huts or had fled into the countryside when the soldiers swept through last night. He didn't care either way as long as he had workers for the mine. That was assuming he'd still have a mine to run, which wouldn't be the case should that bitch reporter get away to tell the tale of the *nkisi*.

He pulled into the mine compound and shouted at the squad waiting there to get in the truck. "Move! Move! Move! I want that bitch dead by sundown!"

Yoweri combed the river. He skipped the low islands that were too small to hide a mokoro, although he examined them closely as they went by. He concentrated on the ones with enough undergrowth to screen the fugitives. The boat's pilot let him and two soldiers off at the upstream end, then met them at the other end of the island after they had spread across it and tramped its length, poking into every pile of driftwood and stomping through every stand of reeds. They didn't bother to work quietly. Yoweri figured the fugitives would panic and bolt when they heard him coming like the crocodiles that slithered into the water ahead of their footfalls. He kept an eye on the surrounding islands too, watching for sudden disturbances among the birds that might signal his prey moving around. At first, he caught occasional glimpses of his squad on the far riverbank, but they moved faster than he did. They soon disappeared downstream. He didn't think they would find anything there, but it was necessary to close all possible escape routes.

Yoweri was a hunter who knew how to drive game to its death. You began with a line of beaters spread wide. They pushed relentlessly forward even when the game was unseen, either driving it to ground or trapping it somewhere with no escape. You had to drive, drive, drive the prey, shove it into a corner for the ultimate slaughter. An ancient blood lust roared through Yoweri as he thrust his machete into every brush pile, hoping each time to slash the flesh of Valerie Grey.

Chapter 25

Kinshasa

In Kinshasa, the first wave of American troops had arrived and another was on its way. The Americans added a jangle of opportunistic prosperity to the filthy hustle of everyday life. Smug businessmen from many nations strolled the teeming streets with strutting officers from both armies. Hopeful hustlers and brazen con men buttonholed them right on the sidewalks while hookers preyed on them in the hotel lobbies and crowded bars. Everyone practiced capitalism in its cannibal form, feeding on the raw extravagances of war.

David had seen it before, first as a young reporter in Saigon and later in Managua, but the overall effect still disgusted him. His odium increased as he went from office to office looking for someone with information about Valerie's death. He had started at the American embassy, where they smoothly told him they didn't know exactly where her body was at the moment but they hoped to hear something soon, whenever that was. He tried Messime next, but an aide brushed him off by sending him to the DRC minister of the interior, which was another dead end. He wasted a full day cajoling, haranguing, and threatening various bureaucrats in Kinshasa. He went from office to office using every contact he could muster from the other journalists in the capital, but the bureaucrats just gave him blank stares while they held out their hands for bribes. Most were so accustomed to automatic payoffs they didn't even bother to pretend they could give David any help.

Running out of options, David went to see Robert Fraser, the MBS reporter who replaced Valerie in the Congo. He was staying at the Intercontinental Hotel, where most of the news media were sequestered in relative comfort. In the urbane young reporter's hotel room, David got right to the point.

"I want to hitch a ride to the south with you. How soon do you plan to leave?" he asked.

"Now hold on a minute, David. I'm not sure that's a good idea."

"Why not? That's where the fighting is."

"I know." Fraser fiddled with a teacup on the room service tray he'd called for when David came. He seemed nervous, so David thought he should lighten the mood

"It's not like I'll be in the way. And I guarantee I won't try to steal your air time," David joked awkwardly. "I haven't been on that side of the camera in years. Besides, it's not like I'm here on official business."

"Official business. That's part of the problem," the reporter said, seizing on a ready excuse.

"Are you worried about New York? Look, I'm sure they told you I'm not here in an official capacity. But I'm still employed by the network. If Carter Wilson gives you any grief, just tell him I threw my title at you and made you do it. I'll take the heat."

Fraser looked even more uncomfortable. He wouldn't look at David now. David dropped his jocular tone. "If you think you have to nursemaid me, get that out of your head. I was reporting from hot zones when you were in kindergarten."

"I'm not worried about that," he answered. "The, uh, problem is that the southern part of the country really is dangerous right now." He looked out the window. "And Messime won't let anybody travel outside Kinshasa."

David saw through him immediately. "So you're going to report this war from your hotel room?"

"Of course not! Besides, how I do my job is my business," the reporter protested lamely.

"That's bullshit. You're chicken," David said with disgust. He slammed the door on his way out.

Later, he sat at the bar in the Hotel Memling, nursing a scotch while he weighed the likelihood of finding Valerie's body by himself in the countryside. He assumed her remains hadn't made it to Kinshasa or the American embassy would have known about it. That meant he needed to go to Bukedi and search there. It was possible her body was in transit, but he guessed it was still there someplace. He could hire a car and driver, bribe and bluff his way past the roadblocks out of the city, and hope the highway wasn't cut by rebel forces before he got to the refugee camp. Once there, surely someone would know where Valerie was buried.

As he pondered his dwindling options, an American army colonel walked into the bar with a group of junior officers trailing him like pilot fish. Even in the bar's murky light, David recognized him from military actions where their paths had crossed in the past. He was a career soldier David knew to be bright and non-political.

"Mike Masters!" he called out. The colonel peered through the cigarette haze and saw David waving a glass at him from the bar. He sent his men to find a table and worked his way through the crowd to shake David's hand.

"David Powell! What the hell are you doing here? Aren't you a little old to be playing hotshot war reporter?" he cracked.

"Guess I took a wrong turn on the way to the old folks' home," David answered. He held up his glass and motioned for the bartender to bring one for Masters. While they waited, he turned solemn. "I'm not here on business. I'm looking for someone."

"Who?"

"It's Valerie Grey, my fiancée. Actually, I'm looking for her remains," David said. "She was reported killed several days ago, but nobody seems to know where her body is. I came to find her."

"I'm sorry, David," Masters said, laying his hand on David's shoulder. "Is there anything I can do?"

"I need to get to the interior, but Messime's paper pushers won't let me travel outside the city."

"We might be able to help. Where do you want to go?"

"Bukedi. That's where she was killed."

"Just a minute," Masters said. He gestured to one of his officers. "Captain Inwood, this is David Powell. Ignore the fact that he's a reporter. He's one of the good guys. You've got a convoy heading for Kikwit tomorrow, don't you?"

"Yes, sir."

"Would it help if we got you that far?" Masters asked David.

"Yes it would," David answered gratefully. "When do we leave?"

"Are you staying here?" the captain asked. When David nodded, he said, "I'll send a jeep for you at 0400 hours."

"Mike, I owe you," David said.

"I'm sorry about your trouble, David," Masters said. "You deserve better."

The next day, after the convoy had carried him as far as Kikwit,

David made his way on to Bukedi by walking along with a man returning to the camp with a bicycle-load of aluminum tent poles. The man didn't ride the bike; the bundle of poles was strapped to it and he simply pushed it along. With David pushing too, he made better time over the bumpy road. The US Army captain who brought David to Kikwit tried to dissuade him from going into the guerilla-infested countryside by himself, but he insisted on pressing forward.

The refugee camp at Bukedi was one of the worst David had ever seen anywhere. Guerillas pushed northward to cut the main highway so they could isolate the mining region before American troops arrived. Once they owned the area, they would ask for a truce and negotiate to hold it behind existing boundaries. Their raids on villages along the way pushed the terrified population before them like a herd of frenetic impala, creating confusion and diverting the soft-hearted Americans' attention away from their military mission. The tiny village of Bukedi was directly in the path of the fleeing populace. There were nearly three thousand people there, he estimated, at least five times what it was capable of holding even under the best of circumstances. The hamlet had completely disappeared, subsumed by a squalid expanse of ragged tents and scrap-built lean-tos stretching along either side of the road into the fields beyond.

The wretched people squatting outside their shelters didn't bother to come see what David's companion had brought; they saw from a distance it wasn't food, so they didn't care. As David and the man passed through the camp with the overloaded bicycle, most of them didn't even lift their heads.

A long line of refugees stood in resignation outside a concrete building flying a tattered UN flag. David apologized as he pushed his way through the line to the doorway, but no one protested. Inside, he asked for the camp director. Someone pointed to a tired young man wearing a shirt with a UN patch over the left breast. He shook his head in sad helplessness as a thin woman softly pleaded with him for something for the motionless baby in a sling on her hip. Discouraged, the woman shifted the baby's slight weight and shuffled away when David approached the desk.

"I'm sorry to interrupt," he said. "My name is David Powell. Are you the director?"

"I am the temporary director. My name is Etienne," the man answered. He was obviously exhausted, but trying not to be brusque. "Can I help you?"

"I hope so. I am looking for Valerie Grey's body. I understand she was killed here."

The man looked at him blankly for a moment then asked, "Mademoiselle Grey was the journalist who came here?"

"Yes. There was a report of an attack on the camp and she was killed. Her remains were never sent to the United States, so I came to retrieve them. Do you know what happened to her body?"

"The reports were mistaken, Monsieur Powell. Many people were killed in that attack, including Frannie Starnhart, the real director of the camp, but Mademoiselle Grey was not one of them."

At first, David didn't comprehend what the man was saying. "What do you mean?"

"Mademoiselle Grey left camp before the truck came that day. She and her companions took our jeep with a load of protex to Tshikapa. They left before the attack."

David felt lightheaded. He leaned against the table Etienne was using as a desk. The young man jumped up and put his hand on David's arm. "Are you all right? Can I get you some water?" he asked.

276 ■ DAVE DONELSON

David shook his head. "Do you mean she is alive?" he whispered hoarsely.

"As far as I know," Etienne replied earnestly. "I spoke to her on the radio after the attack. She was at the airport in Tshikapa."

A small sob caught in David's throat. He didn't know what to think, what to do next. His eyes misted. He wiped them quickly with the back of his hand. Etienne handed him a tin cup of tepid water and he took a sip. "Thank you," he said. He shook his head to clear the fog of disbelief. "Why would they say she was killed?"

Etienne shrugged and shook his head. "I cannot answer that question. We have heard no news since the attack. They said on the radio that the government was sending troops to guard us but none came. There was nothing to guard against anyway. Not at that time."

"What do you mean?" David asked.

"The shots came from an army truck, not the Lunda Libre. The news reports were wrong."

"An F.I.C. truck?" David asked. "Are you sure?"

"The F.I.C. are the only ones with such vehicles."

"But why would the government attack a refugee camp?" David asked. "That's insane."

"This is the Congo, monsieur," Etienne answered.

David shoved that particular puzzle to the back of his mind to work on later. The reality that Valerie was alive somewhere was sinking in. "Do you know where Valerie Grey is now?"

"Sorry, no. We have been overwhelmed since Frannie was killed. The rebels are driving people from the south, many more than we can help."

"Yes, of course," David said. "I'm sorry. Did you say she was in Tshikapa when you spoke to her?

"Yes. At the airport." The young man paused, then thought of something. "The protex was for the clinic at Mai-Munene, but I don't know if she got that far." An old man in the line suddenly collapsed to the floor and Etienne hurried around the desk past David. "You must excuse me," he said.

David knelt next to the old man with him. He offered the tin cup of water he still held in his hand. "How far is Mai-Munene?" he asked.

"You cannot go there now," Etienne answered while he propped up the old man's head and dribbled water on his lips. "The Lunda Libre has surrounded Tshikapa and nothing can pass on the roads."

David helped him get the old man into a chair near the wall. As he did, he looked out the door at the line of people standing stoically waiting for help. He sensed their despair, but didn't share it. Instead, he felt elated with relief that Valerie was alive. Now all he had to do was find her.

David made his way from Bukedi to Tshikapa with surprising ease. A single-engine supply plane landed on the road in Bukedi with a load of sorely needed medical supplies for the refugee camp. The pilot was going back for another run and agreed to take David along. On the way, the pilot told him US forces were upgrading the airstrip in Tshikapa so their transports could use it. A handful of US Rangers had secured the Tshikapa airfield and was waiting for the main force, on its way from Kinshasa. As the pilot circled the town to line up his approach, David saw the road to the south completely clogged with refugees. The busy pilot just shook his head when David asked if there was any way to get to Mai-Munene.

Once in Tshikapa, David found out the pilot was right. He was truly stuck. Nothing moved south toward Mai-Munene; the Lunda Libre drove everyone north and massive numbers of refugees sought safety in the town. The Ranger commander told David that F.I.C. forces held the mine at Mai-Munene for the moment, but no one seriously expected them to stand up to a real assault when one came. Until US forces opened the road, there was no way to get there. David hoped Valerie was in the stream of refugees making their way to Tshikapa. He started searching for a vehicle he could hire—or steal—to take him to Mai-Munene.

Chapter 26

The Kasai River

"Any sign of them?" Valerie asked quietly as she sat down next to Jaime on a weathered log. She could see the full width of the river from behind the thin screen of reeds near the inlet where they had dragged the mokoros ashore in the early morning. The river flowed ceaselessly toward them, roiling languidly over unseen rocks, burbling around snaggly trees felled by the floods during the last rainy season, parting at the head of their island to snake past either side like an endless, watery caravan.

"No, it's quiet so far." He swept his gaze from bank to bank. "They're coming, though."

The day was still and humid, the heat ominous. Moment by moment the temperature climbed as the sun rose higher above the river. The wide sky overhead was featureless, colorless, without depth, offering no relief from the claustrophobic closeness of the sultry air around them. Sitting and waiting in the oppressive stillness made Valerie edgy. She saw a drag mark in the sand they had missed when they hid the mokoros that morning. She stood to wipe it out but Jaime took her wrist and drew her back down next to him.

"Keep out of sight," he said, keeping his voice low. "You can be seen from the riverbank."

"Right. Sorry."

They sat and waited in silence, Valerie's unease growing with each passing second.

"Look," Jaime said. He pointed upriver toward the tip of the sandbar that separated the inlet from the river. Valerie stared, her eyes widening in an anxious search for whatever he had seen in that direction. Then she caught a blur of motion in the air closer to them just a few feet above the water. Jaime pointed to a kingfisher that hovered like a giant hummingbird above an eddy where the water was smooth and unruffled by the current. The blue and white bird with its pointy beak and bristly feathered crest nervously jigged from side to side in midair, searching beneath the glare on the surface of the water. Suddenly it dove into the stream with a small splash. It bounced right back up into the air with a silver minnow wriggling in its beak. It landed briefly on a driftwood branch, gulped down its prey, then sprang back up into the air again to resume its frenetic hovering vigil. Valerie relaxed, grateful for the distraction. She watched the bird dance from side to side in the air.

"Does he ever stop?" she asked.

"I suppose he has to sometime."

"He must need every bit of energy from each fish just to catch the next one," Valerie said, marveling at the blurring speed of the wings that suspended the bird in the air.

Just then, a flock of black pelicans scattered from a rocky outcrop on the far riverbank. Moments later, an F.I.C. soldier stepped through the bushes, glanced left and right, then went down to the water's edge. He slowly scanned the river again. Valerie thought his eyes lingered on the spot where she and Jaime were hidden and she scrunched her head down into her shoulders. He didn't sound an alarm, and she relaxed a little when he casually unbuttoned his pants and took a leisurely piss into the water. When he disappeared back into the brush on the riverbank, she released the breath she had been holding. She peered back up the river.

"I don't think that was the last of them," Jaime said.

"If they're on that side of the river, they found the boat and got it running," Valerie said. "So they're searching the islands right now."

"I better make sure the others stay out of sight," said Jaime. "Can you stand watch for a while?"

"Sure."

Jaime left the AK-47 leaning against the log for her. He crept cautiously back through the reeds, staying bent almost double to keep his head beneath the vegetation as he followed the hippo path back toward the sausage tree. Valerie felt a brief moment of vulnerability when he disappeared around a bend in the path.

"Toughen up, girl," she said to herself, shaking it off.

She checked the bank where the soldier had peed, then examined the opposite one. Just as she looked back up the river, the chug of a motor came from upstream. Valerie watched with growing dread as a launch came into view. It stopped at a small sandbar covered by an acacia thicket. Even from a distance, Valerie could identify Yoweri in the bow of the boat. He got out and stomped through the brush with two other soldiers. As she watched them from behind her screen of reeds, a drop of sweat trickled between her shoulder blades. Yoweri climbed back into the waiting launch. Valerie laid the AK-47 at the ready across her lap as the launch pulled back into the main river channel. Yoweri pointed to another island closer to where Valerie sat hidden in the reeds. Her grip tightened on the stock of the automatic rifle. She wanted to stand up and shoot him, to gun him down like a rabid dog. She itched to do anything but crouch like a rabbit in a burrow watching the hunter creep closer and closer. Her scalp prickled with sweat and a drop crept past her temple and down in front of her ear. The launch headed for a larger island toward the far side of the river. He would be here soon. She wanted to jump up and run to warn the others, but any sudden movement would alert the soldiers in the boat. Besides, she thought, surely Jaime heard the motor. She pushed the safety on the AK-47 to single shot, then pulled it back to full automatic and aimed at the approaching launch.

The peen of the hammer had hit the precise spot on Bobby's face where Scavino knew it would cause the most pain. By deftly striking the peak of the zygomatic arch—the cheekbone just below the outside corner of Bobby's eye—he could hurt him severely without interfering with his ability to speak, a key requirement for getting the information they needed from him. Until the swelling closed it, he could even hold Bobby's eye open to force him to watch the impending blow, a technique that magnified the terror. The resulting fractures were irreparably deep, but that didn't matter. He could also repeat the procedure on the other side of Bobby's face if he needed to, but he didn't. The third crunching blow with the hammer made him talk.

As the helicopter rose above Mbuji-Mayi, Scavino's partner dragged Bobby toward the open door.

"Cuff him to a seat," Scavino ordered.

"I was going to get rid of him when we got over the countryside. He's got nothing else to tell us," the agent answered.

"Not yet. We might need him later."

Alben was on the hilltop at Mpala searching with his squad from hut to hut in the little village when he spotted the Blackhawk helicopter coming low over the horizon from the east. He watched the chopper zig and zag to throw off the aim of any rebels with shoulder-fired missiles possibly hidden in the forest, then it turned back on course for Mai-Munene. He radioed Yoweri and told him to get back to the mine, then called for the men searching the village to get back into the truck. The Blackhawk could only mean trouble. He raced back down the hill to the market square in Mai-Munene just in time to see the helicopter land in a cloud of gritty dust. As the rotors slowed, a man jumped down and walked rapidly toward the truck. Alben noticed he had no insignia on his well-worn fatigues. He hurried out of the truck to intercept him.

"Have you seen an American reporter named Valerie Grey?" the man said brusquely. He had a long thin scar along his jaw line.

"Who are you?" Alben snapped. He took note of another man in the helicopter who casually fingered the yoke of the 50-caliber machine gun mounted in the door. He thought there was someone else in the chopper, but he couldn't see all the way into the dark interior. The man with the scar flipped open an identification wallet and briefly flashed it in front of Alben's face.

"My name is Scavino. I'm here on official business. Where is she?"

Alben sized up the situation quickly. He looked at the armed helicopter, remembered the radio report of the attack that supposedly killed the reporter, and linked it all to Peterson's warning about her. Not sure how far he could trust the man, he decided on a version of the truth.

"We're looking for her ourselves," he said. "She stole some

diamonds—her and the two-bit doctor who ran the clinic here. They ran off last night."

"Where did she go?" Scavino said without emotion.

"Why are you looking for her?" Alben replied.

"My boss wants me to talk to her," the agent answered. "Where did she go?"

Alben had a good idea who the man's boss was, but he had learned long ago that volunteering everything you know often led to danger. Besides, he wanted to know why Hook had sent someone to look for Valerie Grey at Mai-Munene. No matter the reason, it couldn't be good. It could, in fact, mean that Hook intended to wipe out all traces of his connection to the mine. With so much at stake—including possibly his own life—the mental balancing act of bluffs, lies and half-truths made Alben sweat more than usual. That was the only sign he was anything less than totally in charge of the situation.

"They escaped on the river last night," Alben said. "I've had men searching the islands and riverbanks all day." Alben nodded toward the helicopter and raised his eyebrows in a question. "Your bird could speed the process considerably."

"Yes, it could," Scavino answered.

"Good. Let's go." Alben said eagerly. If he could get his hands on Valerie Grey before Scavino, he might be able to forestall a complete meltdown.

"You won't be coming with us," Scavino said.

"But I know the countryside," Alben countered.

"I said it won't be necessary." Scavino's voice firmed just enough to let Alben know he was now in charge.

Alben considered just shooting Scavino and taking the helicopter for himself, but he backed off when he glanced toward the bird and saw the man in the doorway now overtly aiming the 50-caliber machine gun at his stomach. From that range, the slugs would cut him in half.

"Of course," Alben replied. "But I'll follow you on the ground. Radio if you spot them and we'll move in."

"Just make sure your men don't get in my way," Scavino answered. "How many people are with Grey?"

"There are at least two others: the doctor and her assistant. Maybe some children."

"Children?"

"Refugees," Alben explained dismissively. "The little bastards follow them everywhere."

Scavino shrugged. "What are they traveling in?"

"They stole a couple of dugout canoes from the local fishermen."

"How long a lead do they have?"

"They left about five hours before dawn, so they can't have gone very far. The current is no more than three miles an hour and they couldn't go any faster than that because the water is low. It's full of snags. They probably made ten to twelve miles downstream before sunrise. I'm sure they got off the water somewhere when the sun came up."

"Where are they going?"

"My guess is Tshikapa. They can get a vehicle there." Alben had had enough of the interrogation. "It's getting dark. You better move. I'll radio my men on the river."

"Tell them to stay out of my way," Scavino warned again. He turned to climb into the helicopter. His partner moved aside, but didn't take the machine gun off Alben until the rotors whipped back to life and the chopper sprang into the air.

Valerie lowered the rifle as Yoweri and his men abruptly changed course and turned back up river. She watched in disbelief, afraid to even exhale until the boat disappeared around a bend. She tried not to move in case it was a ruse to draw them out. She waited another moment, then started to get up. Jaime's voice came from the bushes behind her.

"Keep down a minute longer, just in case," he said. She settled back down and looked back up the river, relieved that she was no longer facing the threat alone. When the boat didn't return, Jaime emerged from the trail with Nancy and the children. Christophe was behind them. "I think they're gone," Jaime said. "We better go while we have a chance. I don't want to travel in daylight, but we don't have any choice." They uncovered the mokoros and pushed them into the river.

Valerie looked nervously at the riverbank where the F.I.C. soldier had stopped to pee. The river was several hundred yards wide, but they would be within easy rifle range from either side. "Stay low," she warned quietly as she slid down as far as she could go in the dugout. Celestine lay between her knees.

"Can you say 'sitting duck' boys and girls?" Nancy cracked nervously as she scooted down in the other mokoro with Kenda and Juvenal.

They paddled hard down the stream and made better time than they had the night before. They stayed as close to the center of the river as the islands, snags, and sandbars would allow. The current was so sluggish it added little to their speed but it made the mokoros a little easier to maneuver. A small pod of hippos snorted a restless warning as the boats approached. Christophe paddled far to the right of them and Jaime followed. As they passed, two young males started a wet, noisy squabble. Intent on intimidating each other, they ignored the passing mokoros. Once the hippos were behind them, Valerie could hear nothing from the bottom of the mokoro but the tiny splash of

Jaime's paddle and the water sluicing by the hull. The end-of-the-day sun pounded on them in the exposed boats like a relentless hammer. Its blows came from everywhere, beating from above and glaring back up from the surface of the water. Valerie ripped the tail off her shirt and dipped it in the water. She tenderly wiped Celestine's face with the cool rag, wet it again and pressed it against the back of her own neck for a moment before dipping it in the stream once more and passing it to Jaime, who stood paddling in the stern. It gave them some relief from the heavy heat. A weak breeze brushed Valerie's skin as the sun finally slid behind the tops of the hills on the western bank. As soon as it disappeared, darkness fell quickly. She began to hope they could hide beneath it after all.

"*Dakta!*" Christophe called back urgently from the lead canoe. "Listen!"

Jaime stopped paddling. Valerie strained to hear something besides the light breeze in the treetops and the water lapping against the wooden canoe. She pushed herself up on her elbows to get her head further above the water line. Her foot thumped against the side of the boat as she shifted around.

"Shhh," Jaime said.

The breeze died. Valerie heard nothing for a moment. Then she heard a low drone. It was far upstream but coming their way.

"Come on!" Jaime called to Christophe. They struck out for shore as fast as they could paddle.

"Over there!" Valerie said urgently. She pointed to a fisherman's lean-to on the east bank. A large mokoro was pulled up onto the sand next to the low hut, but its owner was nowhere in sight. Jaime and Christophe cut across the slow current and the mokoros touched the bank just as Valerie realized the throbbing drone was a helicopter.

"Hurry! Get inside," Nancy urged.

"No! Not there. In the ditch," Jaime ordered, pointing beyond the hut to a dry streambed that fed the river during the rainy season. Valerie and Nancy scrambled out of the mokoros with the children. They hurried them into the gully while Jaime and Christophe pulled their two mokoros up next to the other one, hoping they would look like they belonged there. Jaime and Christophe slid down into the deep gully with Valerie just as the helicopter swept around a bend far up the river, barely visible in the gathering darkness. The Blackhawk darted back and forth from island to island, edging ever closer. The evening darkness rapidly deepened as the machine hovered over something. It flitted to a nearby islet, paused for a few seconds, then flew to the next one like a wasp searching for prey. Every zig and zag brought it nearer to where they crouched in the gully.

"How did Alben get a helicopter?" Jaime asked as they watched the Blackhawk methodically search the river.

In the few minutes it took the chopper to reach the island directly across from them, darkness had fallen completely. The beam of a spotlight suddenly shot out of the helicopter and swept across the river as the pilot worked his way toward them. The roar got louder. The spotlight's beam touched the mokoros outside the shelter, swept the bank of the dry stream bed where they were hidden, then fixed on the fisherman's hut.

"Stay down," Nancy hissed. Celestine hid her face in Valerie's side.

The glare brightened as the helicopter locked the spotlight's beam on the hut and angled closer. The roaring blades raised a cloud of water and sand that glowed eerily in the blinding light. The pilot made a tight circle around the area, staying above the tree line as the spotlight probed the scene. He feigned a move away then came back. A burst of machine gun fire ripped through the thatch roof of the hut. Celestine trembled in Valerie's arms but didn't cry out. The spotlight moved to the mokoros on the riverbank and another, longer burst splintered them. The helicopter pilot waited to see if the shots would flush any targets, then drifted slowly away. The spotlight turned back to the river, searching for another island. The helicopter's throbbing roar faded down the river. The dry steam bed was filled with darkness. They might be safe for the moment, but Valerie didn't relax.

Chapter 27

The Kasai River

"Is anybody hurt?" Jaime asked.

"The boys are okay, but I may have pissed my pants," Nancy answered grimly.

Valerie ran her hands gently over Celestine's trembling body and found no injuries.

"Christophe?" said Jaime.

"I am not hurt," the boy answered.

"How about you?" Valerie asked Jaime.

"A scratch, but it's nothing to worry about."

"Let me see," Valerie said.

"It's nothing, really," Jaime answered as she slid closer so she could see him in the dim starlight. There was a thin black line of blood from his temple, but the slight wound appeared to have stopped bleeding already. "It must have been a splinter," he said. "It just grazed me."

Nancy led the three children warily toward the hut. "What comes next, the tank attack?" she nervously joked.

"We need to keep moving," Valerie said. "Can we get to the road from here?"

"After the moon comes up," Jaime answered. "I think we'll be safe here until then."

"Is there an all-night diner in the neighborhood?" Nancy asked. "These kids haven't eaten since last night."

"Whoever built this hut must live around here someplace. Maybe we can get something to eat from them," Valerie ventured.

"Maybe. But we need to wait for moonlight to see the path. Try to get some rest in the meantime," Jaime said.

"You need it more than anyone," Valerie said. "I'll take first watch." While everyone settled down to try to sleep, she went outside to sit with her back against the wall facing the river. It was so dark she couldn't see the water, but she could hear it slapping lazily against the bank. Somewhere far downstream, a hippo snorted and splashed. A few minutes later, a hyena whooped, then another one answered on the far side of the river. The muscles in her calves twitched as Valerie became still on the soft sandy soil. She shifted her back against the rickety wall of the lean-to. The children whined and whimpered a little inside, but they eventually found a way to sleep on the ground inside the bullet-ridden hut. Soon, the only sound from inside the lean-to was the slow breathing of sleep. Lulled by the steady, lazy lap of the river against the bank, Valerie felt her eyelids droop as she relaxed into the soft night. She shook her head from side to side to stay awake.

"Who is there?" a stern voice suddenly demanded from the darkness beside her.

Valerie rolled over hard, scrambling on all fours to get away from the voice. She leapt to her feet as a tall, dark figure stepped from behind the hut. A machete gleamed in the sparse starlight. The man glanced quickly into the hut, then back at her. Before Valerie could call out, Jaime came through the doorway, fists cocked. The man raised his machete, then stopped it in midair and cried in disbelief, "*Dakta* Jaime! Is that you?"

Jaime pulled up short. "Who are you?" he asked. As the man dropped the machete to his side, Jaime looked more closely at him. "Is that you, Ngyke?" he asked, relief in his voice. Just then, Christophe came out of the hut with his rifle raised, but Valerie held him back.

"Yes, *dakta*, it is me, Ngyke. I came to see if my mokoro was damaged. Then I heard someone in my hut."

Valerie's heart slowed its frantic pounding. She put her hand on Christophe's shoulder and felt the adrenaline-fueled tremors in his body. Ngyke looked around in the dim starlight, then knelt to run his hands over one of the canoes. He felt the splintered wood and straightened up.

"It has many holes, but it can be patched," he said.

"I am sorry," Jaime explained. "They followed us here."

"It is not your fault, *dakta*. These bad people destroy everything." His simple declaration of the way things were disheartened Valerie. What a sad way to live, she thought; the man was always waiting for the next savage visit from his fellow man. "We should leave this place in case they return," Ngyke said. "Come with me." He turned to climb up the riverbank.

"But they will follow us," Valerie protested. "We don't want to put your family in danger."

"We are always in danger, madame," Ngyke answered solemnly. "Come." He smiled when Nancy came out of the lean-to with the three children. "You have little ones," he said. "Good, someone should always look after the children." They followed him up the riverbank, away from the water, through the bushes and scrub forest. The mopane trees had been chewed off just above head-height by elephants who foraged through the scrub every day. Above her head, Valerie saw a sky full of stars oblivious to the hurtful world below them. After a few minutes, they came to a cluster of three more huts not far from the water but high enough that they would not flood during the rainy season.

"Mother Kabisenga," Ngyke called softly as they approached. "I have brought *dakta* Jaime and some children."

A wizened old woman came out of a mud hut as everyone gathered around the smoking remains of a fire in the center of the clearing. Jaime recognized her from the clinic. "How is your arthritis, Kabisenga?" he asked.

"I ache always, *dakta*. It is worse today. I went to the village for my medicine, but you were gone," she chided gently.

"Hush, mother," Ngyke said. "*Dakta* Jaime doesn't need to hear your worries. Bring *nsima* for him and the children. They are hungry." The old woman went into another hut and came back with a pot of cold cornmeal mush. The children didn't need to be encouraged; they gathered around the pot and plunged their fingers into it eagerly when the old woman set it on the ground.

"You must have read my mind," Nancy said as she dipped her fingers into the pot.

Valerie knelt to take some herself. "We're going to bring trouble here," she said. "We can't stay long."

"She is right, Ngyke. They will follow us here," Jaime said to the fisherman. "We must go as soon as there is enough moonlight to see the path."

"No, *dakta*. The Lunda Libre are in the forest. I saw their fires before. You must stay here and be safe. Tomorrow I will take you to Mr. Sami. He can take you where you need to go in his truck."

"What do you think?" Valerie asked Jaime.

"The Lunda Libre is a problem," Jaime said. "We don't want to stumble into them in the dark. They're bound to be jumpy with all the activity up and down the river. Where can we stay for the night?" he asked Ngyke.

"The hut of my sons is empty. They were killed last year. The women and children can sleep there. You and the boy can stay in the cooking hut," he answered.

"Thank you," Valerie said.

"I will watch the trail in the forest," Ngyke said.

"Good," Jaime said. "Christophe, give me the rifle and I'll stand the first watch on the river."

Valerie wanted to go with him, but instead went into the smaller hut to help Nancy get the children settled. Their bellies full, they were nodding off already.

Valerie lay down and tried to sleep, but too many unanswered questions chased around her mind. The helicopter pursuit frightened her more than anything. She sensed it was tied to the attack on Bukedi somehow, which meant they were being chased long before she knew about the *nkisi*. Messime hadn't wanted her to leave the capital, but she couldn't imagine him devoting a precious helicopter to the pursuit of a simple disobedient reporter. It made even less sense for him to viciously attack the refugee camp at Bukedi and murder Frannie Starnhardt and a bunch of innocent refugees. Why would Messime do that? Or anyone else, for that matter? Someone had been searching for them since they shook off Messime's men and escaped from Kishanga. Whoever it was, they obviously wouldn't hesitate to kill Valerie and anyone else who got in their way.

What if she struck off on her own; would that draw the danger away from everyone else? Maybe, but she probably couldn't get away quickly enough, considering she didn't know the countryside at all. What if she just gave the *nkisi* back to Alben; could she prove her story without it? Would he even let her live to try? What if she sent Nancy and the children ahead with Jaime and the doll; could she keep Alben occupied long enough for them to get to safety? Or should she give up the *nkisi* to whoever was chasing them in the helicopter? No matter how she rearranged the players and their roles, there didn't appear to be any sure way to keep them all safe.

Beneath all the possible scenarios lurked a doubt that the news story was worth the price she was paying for it. A rich preacher was getting richer by screwing a crooked tin-pot dictator—who cared? Exposing his penny-ante scheme wasn't worth the lives of innocent people like Kafutshi and Pieter, not to mention Nancy and the children. Or Jaime.

But the White House was in the middle of it all, too, she thought, and American troops had their lives on the line. A war based on lies and half-truths raised the stakes. This wasn't a game of alley-alley-ox-in-free. They couldn't just stop playing. If they did, they would all die for sure.

Valerie twitched on her pallet for what seemed like hours. She was sure her squirming was going to wake up Nancy and the restless children. Finally, after she had tossed in the darkness as long as she could stand it, she got up quietly and crept outside to be alone with her thoughts. She sat down on a log in front of the hut. Valerie missed the cozy overstuffed chair she usually curled up in at home. There, when she woke up at three AM with the details of a story racing through her mind, she'd slip out of bed and go into the living room so as not to disturb David while she jotted down notes. Just getting her thoughts on paper often stopped their mad chase around her mind. More often than not, David would find her asleep in the comfy chair with a book in her lap when he got up the next morning.

Christophe came out of the cooking hut to relieve Jaime and saw her sitting alone on the log. He looked at her solemnly for a minute then came over and squatted in front of her. She forced a crooked smile. He took one of her hands in both of his.

"Do not be afraid," he said softly. Valerie nodded once and patted his hands; she didn't know how else to respond. For a quiet moment, the simple power of one human comforting another flowed between them. Then the boy stood and walked down the path to the river. As Valerie watched his slim figure disappear into the darkness, a thick blanket of despair fell over her. She put her face in her hands and leaned forward under its weight. She was responsible for dragging that brave boy and the others into danger. Her guilt wasn't rational, she knew, but it was very real nonetheless. She took a deep breath and straightened up, trying to shake it off, and found Jaime standing in front of her.

"You okay?" he asked quietly.

"Oh, yeah. I'm just great," Valerie answered.

A fussy moan came from inside the hut. After a moment, Nancy crooned a lullaby to Celestine to soothe her.

"Come on," Jaime whispered. He reached for her hand. Valerie allowed him to pull her up. She held onto him and followed him out of the moonlight into the cooking hut. It wasn't just dark inside the hut, it was sightless black. Blind in the void, Valerie's other senses sharpened. She smelled the freshly cut fire wood stacked against the round walls. The tang of last season's smoky cooking fires was in the thatch above them, unseen but tasted. Her foot brushed a pallet on the floor; the blanket whispered against the dirt.

Jaime's fingers loosened, but Valerie tightened her grip; she didn't want to let him go. He pulled her gently to him. She lifted her face slightly to his. She felt him looking at her in the darkness. He hesitated a brief moment before putting his lips on hers. She pressed her body against him as his hand found the small of her back to pull her closer. She kissed him once, quickly, tentatively, then again fiercely. When she pulled back a little, he sighed, but when her fingers started fumbling with the buttons on his shirt, he breathed a soft "yes" and helped her. They quickly undressed, pausing only to sightlessly run their fingers over bare skin. Jaime knelt to pull down Valerie's shorts, lifted each of her ankles in turn to slide them off then ran his hand slowly up the soft inside of her legs. She yielded as he reached the moist juncture of her thighs, but his hand slid through and up between her buttocks, first his forearm and then his firm, smooth bicep rubbing against her sex as his fingers spread against her back and he pulled her closer to bury his face in her smooth belly. Valerie pressed down against his arm and he held her there a long, long moment. Then he released her and leaned backward to lie on the pallet on the hard dirt floor. She straddled his chest and slid her body down until their mouths were together again. She touched her tongue to his sun-cracked lips. He groaned slightly as she reached down to guide him into her. Valerie lifted her head and arched her back, drawing him further inside. She rocked on her knees until their bellies were flat against each other. Jaime's hands found her hips. He pulled her hard onto him, then lifted her up, then pulled her down hard again as his body arched and thrust upward. Their rhythm grew faster. She leaned forward and he lifted his mouth to her nipple. They abandoned themselves to a world of sensation, unbound by time, grinding, thrusting, panting in the close sweaty blackness until Valerie stiffened and Jaime followed immediately after, lifting her on the arc of his powerful hips. She collapsed onto him, burying her face in his neck. The smell of the hard-packed earth beneath them filled her nostrils. The tension drained from her. Slowly, her heart stopped thudding against him. She felt Jaime's chest pounding too, their hearts keeping perfect time while the world around them paused for a brief moment.

Jaime stirred slightly beneath her. Valerie rolled off his chest and found a perfect spot in the crook of his arm. He turned on his side toward her.

"Feel better?" he asked.

"Oh, yes."

"Me too," he answered.

They slept until just before dawn. They didn't stir when the helicopter passed up the river on its way back to Mai-Munene in the night.

Chapter 28

Mai-Munene

The next morning, Alben had a growing feeling he was losing control of the situation and he didn't like it at all. The search the night before had been fruitless. He and Yoweri had tried to follow the helicopter down the river in the motor launch but had to turn back when darkness came. Despite the helicopter's lights, Scavino hadn't spotted the fugitives either, so he had called off the search shortly after midnight. When Scavino returned empty-handed, Alben called Peterson. The time difference made it late afternoon in Atlanta.

"Did you get rid of that reporter?" Peterson asked when he came on the line.

"No. That's why I'm calling," Alben answered. He plunged ahead bluntly. "I thought you should know she escaped and managed to steal one of the dolls from the last shipment."

"What?" the preacher exploded.

"I know. That makes her a serious threat." Alben tried to calm Peterson down. "We're searching for her now. It's only a matter of time."

"You better eliminate that threat, Tom." Peterson's voice lost its preacherly drawl and became menacingly sharp. "No excuses."

"We're on it. There's something else, though." Alben knew he was about to drop a bombshell. "A couple of bad-asses in a helicopter are looking for her too. Our friend sent them. They're here now. Right in the middle of it."

"Shit!" Peterson bellowed. "You get to that bitch first, you hear me? If we don't plug that leak ourselves, we're dead. Literally dead. These people don't fuck around, Tom."

"I know. I know. I'm on it. She won't get out of the country alive," he promised grimly.

With dawn breaking and Grey still on the loose, he looked outside only to see Scavino talking privately to Yoweri in the clearing where the helicopter squatted. The F.I.C. captain stood impassively with his arms folded across his chest, but Alben could tell from the slight tilt to his head that he was taking orders from the American agent. Scavino said something and the two men squatted in the dirt, where Yoweri scratched some lines with his finger. He pointed to a spot on the ground, Scavino nodded, and they stood up again. A decision had been made. Alben hurried out of his office. He had to get the operation back under his own control.

"What's going on?" he asked.

"I was just telling the captain we're going to fly along the road to Tshikapa as soon as the sun gets above the hills," the American agent explained brusquely. "He will follow the helicopter with his men."

"That's wrong. We should go back and pick up their trail on the river," argued Alben.

"The road goes by the river near the Nnenne rapids," Yoweri said. "The rapids will stop them from going farther in the mokoros. They must leave the river there. They will cut across country to the road." He pointed to the rough map drawn in the dirt at his feet.

Alben reluctantly agreed but added, "Spread the troops on foot in a line to sweep both sides of the road. She's smart. She'll double back or hole up in a village until we pass. We have to keep her from going to ground again."

"That will take too long," Scavino said. "If the trucks follow me, I'll draw her into the open. Then they can surround her."

"She'll just disappear into the bush again when she hears the chopper!" Alben insisted.

"Not today. She'll come out," the agent said.

"Why?"

"I have bait." He nodded toward the helicopter door, where Bobby sat numbly with his legs hanging over the edge and his arms tied to his sides.

When Valerie and Jaime came out of the cooking tent into the early morning light, Nancy raised an eyebrow and smirked. Celestine was solemnly showing her how to stir the pot of *nsima* that bubbled thickly on the fire before them. Nancy took the long wooden spoon from the girl's hand and pushed it through the stiffening mush.

"You look very domestic," Valerie said, kneeling next to her.

"Just call me Betty Crocker," Nancy answered. She glanced sidelong at Jaime then back at Valerie. "And I'll call you the cat who ate the canary." Valerie's eyes twinkled and a slight smile played across her lips. She felt at peace in the rosy glow of dawn infusing the ground fog with a soft radiance. Valerie's anxiety was gone, replaced by confidence that somehow, some way, they would get through this.

Kenda came out of his hut with Kabisenga, followed by Juvenal with Ngyke. Valerie sobered as she thought again how she had dragged the children into this mess. As if he read her mind, Jaime said he would like to talk to her and Nancy about something before they left. He asked Ngyke to come with them and led them away from the fire and the children.

"We're not doing these kids any good by dragging them around the country," he said when they were out of earshot. Valerie saw right away where he was going.

"Would they be safe here?" she asked.

"You mean would they be safer with people who don't get strafed by helicopters?" chimed in Nancy.

"It's up to Ngyke," Jaime said. He looked at the tall, calm man. "Can the children stay here?"

"I am glad you asked, *dakta*," the tall fisherman answered. "I thought about it last night while I watched the trail. I was going to suggest that to you this morning."

"What if the soldiers come looking for them?" Nancy asked.

"They will hide in the woods with my mother," he said calmly. "We have done so many times in the past."

"I don't think Alben is after them," Valerie said. "It's the *nkisi* he wants."

"And you," Nancy added.

"What about Christophe?" Valerie asked.

Jaime gestured for the boy to join them. "Let's ask him," he said. When he came, Jaime said, "We are going to Tshikapa, but Celestine and her brothers are staying here. Do you wish to stay also? It will be safer here."

"I will go with you, *dakta*," Christophe said without hesitation. He pointed to the scar on his cheek. "With this, I am not safe anywhere."

"Then that's settled," Jaime said. "Can you show us the way to the road?" he asked Ngyke.

"Yes. I will take you to Mr. Sami. He owns a truck. Perhaps he will take you in it to Tshikapa."

Valerie felt hope for the first time since they fled Mai-Munene.

"Let's go before Alben shows up again," she said. They went back to the fire, where Kenda and Juvenal were busy dipping their fingers into bowls of *nsima* while Celestine helped Kabisenga dish up the meager breakfast for everyone else. Jaime gently asked Celestine if she and her brothers would like to stay with Kabisenga. The girl nodded shyly with a look of relief in her eyes. Valerie realized there was something else to take care of.

"Celestine," she said, "I must bring the *nkisi* with me. Is that all right with you?"

The girl didn't hesitate. She ran into the hut and came back with the doll. "Take this *nkisi* far away," she said soberly. "I think it is evil."

"Yes, I think so too," Valerie answered. Celestine put her arms around Valerie's waist, burying her face in her stomach.

"We should go before the sun gets too high," Ngyke said. The wispy ground fog was already melting away even though the sun was still below the horizon.

Nancy suddenly bent to pull Kenda and Juvenal to her. "You guys behave yourselves," she said, her voice thick. "Keep your grubby little fingers off other people's stuff, you hear?" The twins nodded once. She patted Juvenal on the behind and stood up, wiping her eyes. "Let's go," she said.

Ngkye led them on a narrow track that wound through the sparse trees in the low hills above the river. Christophe brought up the rear with the AK-47. They walked rapidly but quietly. After several minutes, as they neared a copse of acacia bushes on a ridge, Ngkye held up his hand and signaled them to wait. He crouched, working his way slowly forward, keeping the thorny bushes between himself and the horizon. He carefully craned his neck until he could see around the bushes and down the other side of the hill. After a moment, he stepped out from behind the bushes. He took three tentative steps over the ridge, then waved to them to follow. As Valerie topped the ridge, she saw the remains of a large camp. The ashes of several fires still smoldered from the night before. "Lunda Libre?" she asked quietly. Ngkye nodded but didn't stop walking.

As soon as the sun rose above the hills to the east, the air became hot and hard to breathe. The trail meandered back and forth, but generally wound upward as the land rose into the hills away from the river. The brush thickened and trees grew more closely together where the terrain was too steep to be burnt off and cultivated. The sandy soil carried the overlapping footprints of impala and bushbuck, baboon and mongoose, as well as the splayed toes of barefoot people and the lugged soles of combat boots. As they neared the road, the trail widened and the animal tracks were completely obliterated by boot prints as if a herd of heavily shod soldiers had stomped over them just before dawn. At a bend in the trail, Ngkye held up his hand for them to stop. A slight breeze carried a fetid smell from somewhere up ahead.

"*Dakta*," Ngkye whispered.

Jaime stepped up beside him so he could see around the bend. He stared for a moment then shook his head. "Are they still here?" he asked. He kept his voice just above a whisper.

"I don't think so," Ngkye answered. He surveyed the area. "I think they left after they finished this bad job. But they are not gone long."

"Oh, my God," Valerie gasped as she stepped around the bend and saw the source of the putrescence filling the air. Nancy joined her. She clamped her hand to her mouth to cut off a gagging choke. Christophe came behind them, his eyes alert, his shoulders tensed.

Before them was a small clutch of thatch huts scattered beneath a huge mahogany tree beside the road like giant weaver bird nests fallen to the ground. The morning light would slant under the tree, but the thick leaves would block the hot midday sun. A vegetable garden protected by a sickle-bush fence lay nearby. In the shadows under the tree, the hard-packed earth between the huts was littered with shapeless, glistening lumps, the sprawled bodies of people who had been hacked to death. They had not been dead long, Valerie suspected, because red blood still gleamed on some of them. The fetor that filled the air was ripe with the blood and piss and shit of brutal death by machete. It was not yet the green-meat stench that would come after the bodies had decomposed in the sun for a few hours.

"Did those Lunda Libre assholes do this?" Nancy asked from behind the hand still clamped across her mouth.

"Lunda Libre, F.I.C., Angolans, someone else, it is all the same," Ngkye said.

Jaime walked among the bodies, looking closely at each one for any signs of life. Valerie followed him, treading carefully to avoid the pools of blood and scraps of flesh glistening on the ground. It was hard to tell how many people there had been because many of the bodies were strewn about in pieces as if the killers had chopped off hands and arms and limbs and flung them into the air. The blood was almost fresh, still sticky on the bodies and seeping into the dry soil. Flies covered everything, so fat and fixated on their feast they didn't bother to rise as Valerie walked through the horrible scene. She came to one of the huts, cheerfully decorated with ochre stripes painted diagonally around the bottom of the whitewashed mud wall. The decorations were stained by a brown splash of dried blood mixed with clumps of hair and bone. The body of a tiny boy lay crumpled next to the wall, his head like a crushed, pulpy papaya.

"This was the family of Mr. Sami," Ngyke said. His throat was tight. "He lived here with his mother and his sisters and their children. His brother lived over there with his family." He pointed to another brightly painted hut a few paces away from the tree. "They were businessmen, Mr. Sami and his brother." There was a single-room cement block building with a tin roof across the road. It was whitewashed too, with great lime green circles and a large sign painted on the front proclaiming it "Happy Store – Good People." Valerie remembered how proud Mr. Sami had been when he showed them his store the first time she came to Mai-Munene. She had promised then to come back to meet his family.

Ngkye stopped near a body sprawled next to the doorway of the largest hut. There were slashes all over the torso where the flesh curled back in obscene slices. One arm was missing, severed just below the shoulder. The body lay in a pool of fly-covered mud just outside the doorway. Valerie was glad they couldn't see the face.

"This was Mr. Sami," Ngyke said. He looked around then added, "They have taken his truck."

Jaime said he didn't care about the truck. He was still going from body to body to see if anyone was alive. His face was stern, his movements quick but gentle as he bent to touch each one to find a pulse.

"Can I help?" Valerie asked, kneeling next to him where he squatted beside a woman splayed against the giant roots of the mahogany tree, footless.

"There is no one left to help," he said bitterly.

"It is like my village," whispered Christophe. He stood helplessly with Nancy in the midst of the carnage.

"Why did they have to do all this? Why didn't they just take the goddamn truck?" Nancy asked in disgust.

"It creates terror," Jaime said, standing up and wiping his sticky hands on his shorts. Valerie stood with him and put her hand on his forearm.

"What the hell does that accomplish?" Nancy asked.

"Terror is its own purpose," replied Jaime.

Ngyke came back to them. "We must go warn Mother Kabisenga and the children. Come with me."

"We have to go on," Valerie said.

"But the truck is gone. It will not be safe for you to walk on the road," Ngyke pleaded.

"It won't be safe for us anywhere," answered Valerie. "You go back and take care of your mother and the children. You have done so much for us already."

"Please be careful," the fisherman said. He solemnly shook Valerie's hand, then Jaime's. The gesture was strangely appropriate. Then he walked rapidly back to the trail. As he disappeared around the bend, Valerie looked at the people lying butchered outside their homes beneath the mahogany tree. Last night while she slept, sated, in Jaime's arms, these innocent souls were awakened by war screams and machete-waving marauders. They were dragged from their beds and chased from their quiet homes, terrified and shouted at and chopped and hacked in a sudden vicious nightmare. Valerie looked around the clearing and imagined their panicked pleas for mercy echoing beneath the clouds of blood-crazed flies. She felt surrounded by frightened spirits. Jaime took her hand and they started toward the road.

Chapter 29
Mpala

Christophe waited for them by the road, watching warily in both directions with his rifle at the ready. Just as they reached him, the thrumming drone of the helicopter arose faintly in the distance. They heard it coming up from the south along the road.

"Not again," Nancy moaned.

"Come on!" Jaime ordered. "The store!"

They rushed past the blood-streaked body of a man lying in the middle of the road to the concrete-block building with its jaunty slogan painted on the front. The door had been kicked in and the meager merchandise racks overturned. Loose batteries, packages of laundry powder, candy, toothpaste, instant coffee and other merchandise had been ground into the floor under lug-soled boots. A can of motor oil leaked into the dirt in one corner. At least there were no bodies inside, Valerie thought with guilty relief. They huddled together against the wall.

The throb of the helicopter grew steadily louder. Valerie couldn't see anything through the open doorway except the twisted body lying in the road beneath a patch of faded blue sky that was rapidly becoming the glare of noon.

"I feel like a bug trapped in a jar," Nancy said, an edge of panic in her voice.

The helicopter came into view flying slowly just above the road. Something dangled on a cable beneath it.

"What is that?" Valerie said. She slipped to the wall beside the doorway to peek around the frame, keeping her face in shadow. The helicopter's growl got louder and louder as it came closer. It flew slowly, almost hovering. She realized with horror that the object hanging beneath it was a person, a man trussed like a piece of meat and swaying gently in the air. The face was blue-black and swollen, but as it came nearer she could make out the features.

"Oh my God! It's Bobby!" she cried. His eyes were squeezed tightly shut, his disfigured face contorted with fear. He looked like he was sobbing, but she couldn't hear him over the roar of the helicopter blades. The chopper slowed even more as it neared the site of the massacre. It hovered above the road right outside the low store building while Bobby twisted on the cable at roof height. From there, he would be clearly visible from everywhere around the clearing. They couldn't see her in the building, but Valerie knew they were dangling Bobby like a worm impaled on a fish hook just in case she was hiding nearby.

That was enough. More than enough. The story of Gary Peterson and his crooked diamond mine wasn't worth anyone else getting killed, Valerie decided. Too many innocent people had already died because of it. She hadn't been able to prevent their deaths, but this one was different. The choice was easy.

"I'm going to give them the doll," she said, stepping out of the doorway.

"Wait!" Jaime exclaimed. He darted toward her but she was out in the open before he could stop her. Nancy was right behind him.

Valerie dashed to the middle of the road waving the doll over her head. She pointed to Bobby and then to the *nkisi*, indicating she was willing to trade. The helicopter descended slightly, bringing Bobby's feet closer to the road. She walked hesitantly toward it, shielding her face with her arms from the blinding dust raised by the whirling blades.

Jaime was just a step behind her. As the helicopter swiveled in slow motion above the road, its interior gradually became illuminated by the sun. Valerie saw the silhouette of a man sitting on the floor with his knees raised well away from the door of the chopper. The man raised an automatic rifle to his shoulder and braced his elbows on his knees. He aimed at Valerie. "No!" Jaime shouted. He knocked her to the ground just as a burst of rifle fire blasted past their heads. Before they could scramble away, the man in the helicopter slipped behind the machine gun mounted in the doorway. The barrel swung toward them. Valerie's flesh crawled in anticipation of the 50-caliber bullets about to rip through it.

A sudden whoosh swept from the other side of the road. The helicopter tail rotor exploded in a ball of fire. The crippled bird swiftly twisted into the ground, crushing Bobby beneath it. Flames from the shattered tail section engulfed the wreckage.

"Bobby!" Valerie shouted. She struggled out from under Jaime. She tried to crawl to the burning helicopter to get to the cameraman. She didn't feel the scorching waves of super-heated air pouring off the fiery pile of twisted metal in front of her. She ignored the gunfire spewing from the other side of the road and the tracer rounds slicing down the road in response. A battle raged around her, but all she wanted was to reach Bobby and pull him out from under the blazing wreckage. Jaime grabbed her around the waist and pulled her back from the mounting flames. He lifted her upright and steered her forcibly away.

"He's gone!" he shouted, trying to be heard above the clamor of the guns and the roaring fire.

Valerie struggled in his grip, teetering on the brink of shock. He shook her gently then clasped her to his chest. She felt a moment of safety in his embrace despite the bullets splitting the air around them. Reluctantly she nodded acceptance.

Then she remembered Nancy. She pushed back from Jaime's arms and looked around frantically. Nancy lay motionless between the helicopter and the store building, her face covered with blood. "No!" Valerie cried in horror. They ran to her.

Jaime eased Valerie aside and knelt over Nancy's inert form. He quickly found a shallow wound in her scalp, which produced a lot of blood but didn't look serious. "I think she's okay," he said. As he pushed her hair back to see the wound, Nancy's eyes opened and tried to focus. "Probably a light concussion," Jaime said. "But we've got to move her anyway."

Valerie, sobbing with relief, grabbed Nancy's wrists to pull her to her feet. "Come on!" she shouted desperately over the clatter of the guns firing around them. Nancy looked at her blankly. Quickly, Jaime put his hands under her shoulders and lifted. "Move, woman!" Valerie shouted again, leaning back to pull her upright. Uncomprehending, Nancy stood up. "Now come on!" Valerie screamed. They led the dazed woman to the side of the store building, out of the lines of fire from two different directions.

"Run while they fight each other," Christophe called over the mounting gunfire.

"Let's go!" Valerie urged. They ran up the road away from the battle and the burning helicopter, dragging the numbed and stumbling Nancy with them.

Alben crouched behind a truck door trying to figure out what the hell had happened. Yoweri had ordered the men out of the trucks and waved them forward in a skirmish line as soon as Grey emerged from the store waving the *nkisi* over her head and running toward the helicopter. When a shoulder-fired missile sailed out of the woods and exploded against the chopper's tail, the soldiers froze then ran back to the trucks. A barrage of automatic weapon fire from the woods pinned them down. Alben lost track of Grey. Now the black oily smoke from the burning helicopter blocked his view of the reporter, who disappeared right after the chopper was blasted out of the air by the missile from nowhere.

When the chopper fell, Alben was too busy returning the relentless Lunda Libre fire to pay attention to the scorched man who leapt from the helicopter's wreckage and fell among the bodies under the mahogany tree by the road.

The guerilla attack was ferocious but disciplined. They directed their fire away from the trucks, which they apparently hoped to capture undamaged. Yoweri's squad was severely outnumbered and nervous, firing wildly, wasting ammunition. Alben saw a soldier crawling backward toward a ditch. The man's rifle lay behind him near a fallen tree trunk where he had left it. Yoweri shouted an order over the gunfire, then fired a warning shot. The soldier jumped to his feet, stumbled, then leapt for the ditch. As he scrambled up the other side, Yoweri shot him in the back. The only chance they had for survival was to keep the men from running away.

Jaime and Valerie didn't bother trying to stay out of sight in the chaos raging around them. They ran straight up the middle of the road alternately pulling and shoving the uncomprehending Nancy along while Christophe trotted ahead. The guerillas' attention was focused on the F.I.C. squad they had pinned down. The skirmish could end as quickly as it started, so they had to get as far away as possible while they had the chance. Valerie frantically pushed Nancy at a lumbering trot, which was as fast as she seemed capable of moving, while Jaime pulled her by the hand. Valerie knew they weren't moving fast enough; she barely held back tears of frustration. Nancy stumbled along, her eyes open but not seeing. "Move, Nancy! Please," Valerie sobbed. If Nancy went into complete physical shock she would collapse. They would never get her up again.

Suddenly, Christophe stopped dead still in the middle of the road. He stared straight ahead. Jaime halted. Nancy started to slump but Valerie propped her up. Then she saw why Christophe had stopped.

An old Toyota pickup pulled slowly onto the road from behind a thick stand of mopane saplings just a few yards ahead. It was rusty and the paint was sun-faded and there was no glass in any of the windows, but it was covered with brilliant lime green and white circles. Valerie recognized it as Mr. Sami's. Two men stood in the back and two more in front with the driver. The pickup turned and rattled over the rutted road toward them as if the driver had all the time in the world. As the truck bore down on them, the men standing in the back grinned like hyenas.

Chapter 30

Mpala

The thunder of Lunda Libre gunfire tapered off, but bullets ripped through the bushes around him every time Alben moved. The rebels were trying to avoid damaging the vehicles, so he stayed behind the truck door leaving the F.I.C. soldiers to bear the brunt of the attack. As the gunfire slackened, Yoweri shouted a warning. A line of guerillas on the other side of the road, using the smoke from the burning helicopter as a screen, moved to outflank them on the right. Alben looked to his left and saw another squad trotting between the road and the hills overlooking the river, working their way around through the sparse woods to come at them from behind. It was time to cut and run. Let the F.I.C. soldiers fend for themselves.

Alben scuttled on his belly under the truck to the driver's side. He reached up and yanked open the door, then pulled himself into the cab behind the steering wheel. Yoweri dashed toward the truck, firing at the guerillas as he went. The F.I.C. soldiers broke cover to rush toward the trucks too. The Lunda Libre mowed down the running soldiers with fire from three sides. Gunsmoke and dust filled the air; angry shouts of betrayal and confusion added to the chaos. Yoweri, screened by the turmoil, made it to the truck just as Alben got it started. He sprang inside as the truck began to roll.

Alben couldn't go forward; the truck had been parked with its nose to a ditch. The second truck was behind him. He slammed the gears into reverse and stomped on the gas pedal. He smashed into two soldiers trying to climb into the back, pinning them against the second truck. Oblivious to their screams, he kept the gas pedal on the floor and pushed the other truck out of the way. Then he jammed the lever into first gear and shot forward.

"Left, you fool!" Yoweri barked. Alben cranked the wheel and the truck rocketed toward the road.

Christophe pointed the rifle at Jaime's face.

"Get down," the boy pleaded as the pickup rolled closer.

Valerie fought the urge to scream. What was Christophe doing! He tapped the barrel of the AK-47 against Jaime's cheek then roughly pushed him sideways with the rifle stock until he dropped to his knees. Jaime turned to her and jerked his head, motioning for her to get down. Nancy groaned and slid through Valerie's arms toward the ground. Valerie thought she saw a glimmer of awareness in Nancy's face, but it slipped away as Christophe turned the gun on them.

"You too! Get down!" he ordered loudly.

Nancy's weight pulled Valerie down until both of them knelt in the dirt with Jaime. "What are you—?" she protested, then she caught the frantic plea in Christophe's eyes. She realized what he was up to just as Nancy rolled her head around on her shoulders like a boxer shaking off a punch. She tried to get up. Valerie locked her grip on her arm to hold her down. She jerked her around so she could look hard into her eyes just as the pickup stopped next to them with a metal-on-metal squeal of its worn brakes. "Stay still!" she hissed. She squeezed Nancy's arm harder, trying to force the message through her stupor.

"They are my prisoners!" Christophe exclaimed triumphantly when the guerillas jumped out of the pickup. The men fingered their guns as they cautiously gathered around the kneeling figures in the road. "I caught them! They are my prisoners," Christophe declared again. He kept the gun trained ostentatiously on Jaime and pointed away from the rebels.

"What do you have there, little brother?" the driver demanded. One of the other men laughed. The driver looked back down the road as the sound of the battle in the distance intensified then died back.

"These are my prisoners. I take them to Commander Xotha," Christophe said boldly. At the mention of the Lunda Libre leader, the driver looked at him closely. He saw the scar beneath the boy's eye.

"Who are you?" the driver said. "I have never seen you in camp."

Christophe ignored the question. "I captured them running like dogs from the battle," he bragged. "Take me to Commander Xotha in your truck. I order you on his authority."

The driver snorted at his boldness and the other men laughed. "I will make a bargain with you," the driver said. "Give us the women and we will let you take the other one to Commander Xotha." He cupped Nancy's chin in his hand, turning her face toward him. He smiled, revealing blackened stumps where his lower front teeth should have been. One of the other rebels took an eager step closer to Nancy.

Valerie sensed that the ruse wasn't working. "Leave her alone!" she cried. She grabbed his wrist and tried to yank his hand away from Nancy's face, but he slapped her with the flat side of his rifle stock. Valerie went sprawling into the dirt.

Nancy's eyes widened as her blank gaze followed Valerie's body to the ground. She suddenly came to life. As the man turned back toward her, she swung her fist upward with all her strength into his crotch. "Bastard!" she grunted. Shocked, he clutched his groin and doubled over, dropping his rifle. The other men laughed in surprise.

Without thinking, Valerie snatched the AK-47 out of the dirt and swung it around. She fired a short burst from the hip. Two of the men collapsed like wet paper dolls. Another turned to run and she fired again, holding the trigger longer this time. The force of the slugs spun the rebel all the way around before he collapsed face down. The last man scurried around the pickup and escaped into the woods on the other side of the road. Valerie squeezed the trigger once more, emptying the clip in a long, loud, angry blast, but he was gone. In the sudden silence, Valerie looked at the bodies lying in the road. I just killed three men, she thought. She was surprised she felt no remorse.

Just then, the driver scrambled to his feet. He lurched at her but Jaime leapt between them, driving his shoulder into the rebel's stomach like a linebacker. As the pair hit the ground, Christophe smashed his rifle stock into the man's temple.

"Get in the truck!" yelled Jaime. He turned the old pickup around and they took off for Tshikapa.

The guerillas were quickly closing in on the F.I.C. truck bouncing through the underbrush toward the road when the Lunda Libre commander heard ragged shots behind him. They came from his rearguard somewhere back up the road. He whistled a signal to halt his charging men while he tried to determine if they were being attacked from behind. When the firing from that direction intensified, he decided to pull back. They had had a successful day already and there was no sense getting caught in a crossfire. The F.I.C. trucks would be left for another time. He signaled again with two sharp whistles and his men melted into the forest.

At first, Alben didn't comprehend what was happening. A final shot whizzed past his window, then the guns went silent. He steered the truck onto the road just as the last of the rebels disappeared. He started to turn south, then stopped when he realized his attackers were gone.

"What are you waiting for?" Yoweri demanded. "Get out of here!"

"No. Look! They're gone," Alben replied. He peered north up the road. "The bitch can't be far." He turned the wheel the other way and drove to the ruined store next to the burning helicopter. "Good riddance, you meddlesome prick," he snarled toward the chopper as he got out of the truck. "You check the store," he ordered.

Alben got out to give the huts on the other side of the road a cursory look while Yoweri went into the store to make sure Valerie wasn't hiding inside. Alben walked among the bodies but kept his attention focused on the woods around the hut, watchful in case the Lunda Libre came back as quickly as they had disappeared. Out of the corner of his eye he thought he saw one of the bloody bodies move just as Yoweri called out that the store was clear. He ignored the movement; it wasn't the woman anyway.

Alben ordered Yoweri to drive. Not far up the road, they found some fresh Lunda Libre bodies and Yoweri slowed to go around them. "Don't stop. She can't be far ahead," Alben said. They sped north as fast as the rough road would allow, raising a trail of dust into the midday air.

The helicopter smoldered in the road. The wreckage hissed and popped as the twisted metal slowly cooled in the drifting smoke. A wounded soldier moaned somewhere in the underbrush. Steve Scavino rose slowly from the pile of bodies where he'd fallen after leaping from the helicopter just after it crashed. He had passed out when he fell, but awakened as someone searched through the bodies nearby. He stayed down until they left.

Scavino was dazed but mostly unhurt except for his left knee. It was swollen to twice its normal size and throbbing. Standing up dizzily, he tested his weight on it. Sharp pain stabbed through the leg, but he could stand. He had gritted it out through worse. He wobbled carefully through the bodies to the road. He was alone. It was quiet, but he knew he had to get away before the Lunda Libre came back. A desperate cry from a wounded soldier drew his attention down the road. An F.I.C. truck sat in the weeds on the other side of a ditch. Painfully, he made his way toward it, dragging his injured leg behind him. If he could drive to Tshikapa, he thought, he could get out of this godforsaken country. With luck, he might even find Valerie Grey on the way and finish the mission.

Chapter 31
Tshikapa

Alben smelled his prey in the dust cloud hanging over the road ahead of them. "Step on it," he urged. Yoweri pressed the truck to its limits, bucking and rattling over the rough road. Alben braced himself with one hand on the dash and the other on the window frame. The road wound through the hills, descending gradually toward the river. Tshikapa was only a few miles away. The twists and turns in the road kept the vehicle they were chasing out of sight, but the dust it raised lay in the thick, still air to mark a perfect trail. Alben wasn't sure it was Valerie Grey they were speeding after, but his gut said so. It was inflamed with the thought of catching her.

Valerie looked back through the glassless window in the pickup to check on Christophe, who sat in the pickup bed facing backward with the rifle. Jaime drove and Valerie was in the passenger seat with Nancy jammed between them. As Valerie offered Christophe an encouraging smile, she caught sight of another heavy dust trail rising behind theirs on the road winding down through the hills. She watched for a moment as it inexorably closed the gap between them. She didn't know who it was, but she knew it couldn't be good; the only people with vehicles in this part of the world were trying to kill them. Christophe pointed to the plume of dust with his rifle to make sure she saw it. Valerie reached through the opening to put her hand reassuringly on his shoulder. She turned back inside to Jaime. "Someone's chasing us," she said. "How much further to Tshikapa?"

"Just a couple of miles," Jaime answered as he wrestled the steering wheel from side to side in a fruitless effort to avoid the biggest ruts and potholes. The battered pickup jolted over the choppy surface. Even with the gas pedal on the floor, they moved with excruciating, if bone-jarring, slowness. When Valerie looked back again, she saw a heavy F.I.C. troop carrier round a bend behind them. It was obscured by the dust the pickup raised, but it moved so fast she knew it would catch them in minutes.

"There they are!" she warned. Jaime glanced back over his shoulder then snapped his eyes forward again as the pickup bounced over a deep rut that almost pulled the wheel out of his hands. They passed a cart with a broken axle abandoned by the side of the road. Valerie realized there was a pall of dust in the air from something moving on the road ahead of them. She turned to look behind them again. The troop truck was so near she could see Alben's eager face through the windshield. Yoweri was behind the wheel. "It's Alben!" she cried.

"That bastard," snarled Nancy.

Christophe kneeled and raised his rifle to his shoulder, but the pickup slammed into a pothole and he almost went flying over the side. Just as he aimed the rifle again, Yoweri gunned the truck. The heavy troop carrier rammed the pickup forward like a twig before a tidal wave. Valerie's body slammed back against the seat and Christophe fell on his face in the bed.

"Stay down!" Valerie shouted through the window.

The road bent around a hill thick with acacia bushes. Jaime jerked the pickup through a sharp blind turn. Yoweri slowed down to keep from overturning the top-heavy truck as he rounded the bend right behind them. Jaime came out of the turn and stepped on the gas, then immediately stomped on the brakes. The pickup lurched to a stop, throwing Valerie and Nancy against the dash. An old man and a woman struggled with a barrow piled high with their belongings in the middle of the road in front of them. The road was thick with refugees heading for the bridge straddling the river to Tshikapa in the distance. Yoweri's truck barreled around the turn and rammed the stalled pickup again, shoving it brutally forward. Christophe was struggling to his feet when the impact sent him flying over the side. He landed in the road face down with the rifle beneath him. He didn't move. The old man and woman darted out of the way just as the pickup plowed into their barrow.

Alben sprang out of the truck. He raced to the pickup just as Valerie shoved her door open. He grabbed her arm, jerked her out of the truck and threw her down onto the road. As Jaime scrambled out on the other side, Yoweri shoved him to the ground. He tried to get up but Yoweri stunned him with a kick to the temple. Jaime fell again, his arms curled over his head. Yoweri dashed around the pickup as Alben dragged Nancy out, throwing her down next to Valerie.

"Where is the doll!" he snarled. Valerie fumbled in her shirt to get it, but Nancy sprang defiantly to her feet.

"It's gone!" Nancy snapped. Yoweri grabbed her by the hair and yanked her head back. Alben jammed his pistol under her jaw.

He glared at Valerie. "Where is it!" he barked. Nancy screwed her eyes closed. Blood streamed down her face from the re-opened scalp wound. The sound of Alben cocking the pistol brought Valerie to her feet with the *nkisi* in her hand. Yoweri flung Nancy away with a clout to the head. Alben turned his pistol on Valerie.

"Who did you tell about this?" he demanded.

"Everybody," Valerie declared. "I filed a report the day I found it."

"You're a liar!" Alben snapped. He snatched the *nkisi* out of Valerie's hand and raised the pistol to her face. "I've had enough of your crap," he growled.

"No!" roared Jaime, rising painfully on the other side of the pickup. Alben wheeled and shot him in the chest. Valerie desperately grabbed his arm as he fired again and the bullet slammed into the ground. He shoved Valerie back, pointing the gun at her again just as Jaime crawled around the front of the pickup and pulled himself up on the fender. Without taking his eyes off Valerie, Alben swung the pistol back to Jaime and fired again, then again. Jaime slumped over the pickup's fender. He clung to it for a moment then slid to the ground leaving a bright red smear over the gay green and white circles.

"Oh God, no!" Valerie whimpered.

"Kill that bitch," Yoweri growled as Alben turned the gun once again toward Valerie.

Rifle fire cracked the air. Alben screamed. His back bowed and his chest blossomed red before he toppled forward. Yoweri whirled toward the shots. The rifle stuttered again, slamming a volley into his stomach. He doubled over then dropped onto his knees. He struggled to rise again, but toppled onto his face and lay still. Christophe ran around from behind the pickup, the AK-47 still held to his shoulder. His face was twisted with blind fury. The scar under his eye had been ripped open when he was thrown from the pickup and blood flowed down his cheek. Alben groaned and rolled over at Valerie's feet. Christophe furiously fired point-blank into his fleshy face. The missionary's blood splattered across Valerie's shirt.

The world was suddenly silent. Christophe stood with the rifle at his shoulder, aiming at Alben's bloody carcass. Nancy crouched in the road. Acrid gun smoke hung in the air. Wordlessly, Valerie stepped over Alben's body to kneel by Jaime. Christophe slowly lowered his rifle. Nancy stood and took the blood-drenched *nkisi* from Alben's hand. She waited helplessly in the road as Valerie put her hand to Jaime's throat looking for a pulse.

"He's alive!" Valerie finally whispered, her face shining with desperate hope. The old man and woman crept closer. A handful of other refugees appeared. Valerie laid her ear next to Jaime's mouth. She barely heard his thin breath. "We need a doctor!" she exclaimed, filled with frantic purpose. None of the hesitant refugees stepped forward, but the old woman mumbled that there was a hospital in Tshikapa. Valerie tried to lift Jaime but couldn't. "Help me get him in the truck," she pleaded. Nancy and Christophe knelt and, with the old man lifting too, they gently tumbled Jaime into the troop truck, leaving a trail of blood across the back.

"I'll drive," Nancy said. She helped Valerie into the back of the truck with Jaime. Valerie carefully lifted his head onto her lap and wiped the dust off his face with the soft back of her hand.

"Hurry," she pleaded.

Nancy ran around to the driver's seat while Christophe picked up his rifle and climbed into the cab. Nancy cranked the engine but the truck wouldn't start. She cursed and tried it again. This time the engine fired. The gears screeched as she roughly shifted into first. The fan clattered against something, probably the radiator where it had been pushed in when Alben rammed the pickup, but the truck crept forward, Nancy feathering first the clutch and then the gas to keep it moving. As she eased it around the stalled pickup in the middle of the road, a woman trotted up behind and lifted her child into the back then jumped onto the bumper. A young man came out of the woods beside the road. He jumped up with her, hanging onto the rear panel and reaching back to boost a friend up onto the bumper. By the time Nancy maneuvered the truck back onto the road, there were refugees hanging from every handhold.

They hadn't gone more than a quarter mile, easing ahead through the ever-thickening crowd of refugees, when a horn blared behind them. Another F.I.C. truck bulled its way past on their left, sending people diving into the ditch beside the road to keep from being crushed.

Nancy sped up to follow in the other truck's wake.

Valerie couldn't take her eyes away from Jaime's face. She tried to cradle his body against the worst of the bumps. She didn't know what to do about his wounds; there were black-rimmed holes in his shoulder and stomach as well as his chest. She tried to stanch the bleeding with her hands but that was fruitless. The woman hanging from the bumper unwrapped the orange and green scarf from around her head and handed it to her silently. Valerie pressed it against the hole in Jaime's chest, which seemed to make his breathing easier. After a few minutes, the other wounds stopped bleeding as heavily, though there was still a trickle from the one in his stomach. She hoped this was a good sign. He groaned once, feebly, and her heart jumped. "Please don't die. Please don't die," she pleaded softly. The child the woman had lifted into the back of the truck sat against the side near Jaime's feet, watching with wide, serious eyes.

The truck hit a bump and Jaime's eyelids flickered open. Valerie leaned closer to him. His throat moved as if he were trying to swallow. His lips parted almost imperceptibly. "Be strong," he whispered.

"Strong?" Valerie asked, but his eyes closed before he could explain.

She felt the life go out of his body. She had lost him.

By the time Nancy reached the approach to the bridge and saw the other F.I.C. truck being waved through the army roadblock, a solid mass of people jostling to get across the river into safety brought her to a complete stop. She honked and eased forward. The refugees clinging to the sides of the truck shouted, "We have wounded. Let us go to the hospital!" The crowd reluctantly parted as Nancy made her way to the roadblock. F.I.C. soldiers held back the refugees long enough to shake down promising individuals before allowing them to cross the bridge. When they saw the truck, the soldiers stepped into the road to block it. An F.I.C. captain signaled her to halt. As Nancy slowed, the captain yanked a man off the side of the truck so he could jump onto the running board himself. He stuck his head through the window.

"Back off, asshole!" Nancy shouted in his face.

The captain reached in to grab the wheel but Christophe jabbed the rifle barrel in his face. The captain recoiled in surprise. He saw the mark on Christophe's cheek as he fell away from the truck. "Lunda Libre!" he shouted, fumbling to get his pistol out of its holster. The soldiers surrounding the truck raised their weapons uncertainly as the riders jumped off, scrambling to get away. Nancy rammed the truck forward. F.I.C. soldiers scattered like dry leaves as she raced toward the bridge. The captain fired once, but the shot was wild. The truck was over the bridge and into the crowded streets of Tshikapa before he could fire again.

Nancy turned away from the bridge toward the market as soon as she was across. She told Christophe to keep his face out of the window then stopped the truck to ask Valerie if she was all right. She sat in the back with Jaime's head on her lap. There was no answer.

"Boss, are you okay?" Nancy asked. Slowly, Valerie raised her head to look at her.

"He's dead," she said almost wonderingly then turned to the back of the truck. Her eyes were open, but she didn't see the ramshackle market stands empty of merchandise or the milling crowd in the street. She looked back down at Jaime's torn face, but she didn't see the crusted wound on his temple left by Yoweri's boot or the trickle of dried blood at the corner of his lips. What she saw was Jaime in an ill-fitting tuxedo in the glittering ballroom of the Waldorf Astoria shifting uncomfortably from one foot to the other. She saw his smoothly muscled legs pumping easily through Central Park the next morning. She saw his steady fingers stitching a deep gash in a dirty child's skinny ankle. She saw him smiling in the breezeway at the clinic with Celestine in his arms. She saw the outline of his body against the stars just last night, reaching out to lift her up from where she slumped despondent outside Ngyke's hut. The darkness she felt then was as nothing compared to this black emptiness in her soul.

The truck door slammed open. Christophe ran around to the back. He climbed quickly over the tailgate into the back with Valerie. He knelt by Jaime's body. "*Dakta?*" he said, his young voice hushed with reverence. He touched Jaime's cold, lifeless hand. He bowed his head. Then he looked up into Valerie's face as a tear ran down over the blood-crusted scar on his cheek. "I go," he said. The simple statement brought Valerie back to the present, but before she could answer, he climbed out of the truck and ran down the street. She called after him, but he disappeared into the crowd in the market

"Boss?" Nancy interrupted softly. "Let's go find some help, okay?"

Valerie replied with resignation, "Yes."

Chapter 32
Kinshasa

"Excuse me, sir," a muscular young Ranger said from the entrance to the mess tent where David sat by himself staring into a cup of cold coffee. He raised his head. "The captain says a couple of reporters just came in from across the river. He thought you'd want to see them. They're at the field hospital by the airstrip."

"Reporters? Women?" David asked as he pushed his cup away and stood.

"I don't know, sir," the Ranger answered. He stepped aside as David dashed out of the mess tent.

"Thanks," David called back over his shoulder. He trotted through the bustling camp, dodging equipment crates and Rangers tending their gear. As he ran up to the hospital tent, medics lifted a body out of the back of an F.I.C. army troop carrier. He recognized Nancy, who stood with her back to him watching them handle the limp form. He got to the truck just as Valerie climbed down from the back after the body. Her clothes were torn and blood-spattered, her skin thick with road dust, she was bruised and disheveled and filthy; David thought she had never looked so wonderful.

"Valerie!" he cried.

Nancy turned at the sound of his voice. Her battered face split into a joyous grin as she exclaimed, "David Powell, how the hell did you get here?"

Valerie froze, startled by David's sudden appearance on the scene. She gaped at him in disbelief, then looked back at the body on the ground next to her. She stared at it for a long, long moment, then tore her eyes away and stepped gratefully into David's arms.

"I am so glad you are alive," David whispered fiercely into her hair as he crushed her to him.

As Valerie melted against David's chest, relief washed over her. She felt safe for the first time in days. It was finally over. She was back in civilization and nothing bad could happen to her now. Her spirits sank again, though, at the sound of a large zipper. She opened her eyes as the medics closed the body bag over Jaime's face. She turned back to David and laid her cheek against his chest.

"He's dead," she said so sadly David caught his breath.

"Jaime Talon?" he asked.

"Yes. I …" Valerie stopped, not knowing what she was about to say. She wanted to tell David about Jaime, about his warm breath and his knowing eyes and his steadfast devotion to his patients. She wanted to tell him about everything that had happened, the *nkisi* filled with diamonds, the frantic flight down the river and all the horrible, needless slaughter, the brutal blows and the killings, Bobby's barbaric execution, but she couldn't. It was all there, but her mind was filled with a thick-misted cloud of Jaime; the cold brume of his abrupt death froze the words in her mouth. She couldn't talk about it now, even though she felt it all welling within her. There was too much of Jaime in the way.

"Everything will be all right," David said gently. He stroked her hair. All he could utter was worn reassurance. "It will be okay."

She didn't answer. She looked once more at the body bag. She watched the Rangers carry the bag into the hospital. She wanted to lie down in the road where she stood and curl up and close her eyes. It seemed like the only thing to do.

"Valerie?" he said firmly. At the moment he gripped her arms to shake her, a child's high-pitched giggle rose above the murmur of the people milling around outside the camp. The gleeful cry cut like a beam of light through Valerie's dark miasma. She remembered why it had all happened in the first place. She shoved her despair back into the black hole where it could stay, alive but under tense control.

"I've got to get my story on the air," she said. She stepped out of David's embrace. She pulled the *nkisi* out of her shirt and held it out to him, her eyes focused with fierce intensity on the rag doll.

"Peterson was smuggling diamonds out of the country in these," she explained. "I don't know if Messime is his silent partner in the mine or not, but I'm sure he didn't know Peterson was skimming off the top. Either way, the Congo was getting screwed and Messime will not be happy when he finds out. I wouldn't be surprised if he nationalizes the mine."

"If he can," David said, all business now. He told her the Lunda Libre was closing in on Mai-Munene. "US forces are on the way. That's how I got here."

"But if Messime nationalizes the mine, there won't be any American assets to protect," Nancy pointed out. "I wonder if Baker will put US troops under fire then?"

"Good question," David answered.

"All the more reason I've got to get this on the air," Valerie said. "Can we get to Kinshasa? I can use the Reuters uplink."

"Let's see if we can get a ride at the airfield," David said.

Valerie took a last look at the hospital tent where Jaime's body had disappeared, then turned and strode decisively away.

"You're in luck," the Ranger captain said. "I've got a VIP who just jammed his White House credentials down my throat to commandeer one of my choppers for a special trip to Kinshasa. If you don't mind flying with a grade-A prick, there's room in the bird for you."

"How soon is it leaving?" Valerie asked.

"Right now. That's it over there." The captain pointed to an open-sided Sikorsky Eagle warming up on the tarmac. He picked up a handset and called the pilot. "You have three more passengers on the way," he told him. They couldn't hear the pilot's answer, but the captain clicked off and turned to David. "Better hurry," he said.

They ran across the field to the helicopter and climbed in. The rotors whirled as the big machine trembled, eager to get airborne. The lone passenger sat facing the open doorway on a fold-down seat behind the pilot. He wore clean combat fatigues with no insignia. His left leg extended stiffly into the center of the cabin and he put out his arm to protect it as Nancy folded a seat down next to him. He grunted in response to Nancy's greeting when she sat down. Valerie took a seat across from him, careful not to bump the wounded limb. His eyes narrowed when she sat down. He had a thin scar along his jaw. As soon as David was on board, the man tapped the pilot's shoulder and pointed emphatically skyward.

Valerie wondered briefly who he was and what kind of pull he had to commandeer a military helicopter in the middle of a war zone, but she pushed the question aside to concentrate on how she was going to tell the story of Peterson's diamond smuggling scheme. If she didn't focus on that, her thoughts would turn to Jaime. She didn't want to think about him now; she would save him for later. She mentally ticked off what she knew about the mine. Messime, for no apparent reason, practically gave it to Gary Peterson. Not long afterwards, President Baker reversed a well-established doctrine of non-intervention in African affairs and sent US troops to the Congo. His decision had a veneer of noble purpose on it, but was also predicated on the always-useful catchall need to protect American interests in the region. As far as Valerie knew, the only American interest in the Congo was Peterson's diamond mine. The buildup of US troops heading for the mine confirmed that connection. So Messime gave the mine to Peterson as the price of making the US his ally in the battle against the Lunda Libre.

But what did President Billy Baker get out of the deal? Valerie had been around the corridors of power too long to put any credence in the humanitarian mumbo jumbo Baker used to justify the action. He was not a statesman; he was a professional politician, so every position he took had to pay off in one of three ways: votes, power or money. He was in his second term, so he had no need for votes and, by most estimations, the office he held already made him the most powerful man on earth. That left money. Could Billy Baker be a silent partner in the mine at Mai-Munene? It sounded preposterous that the president of the United States would prostitute himself for what had to be relative chump change, but Valerie knew of those who had done it for less. She also knew that Baker had so much money he couldn't possibly want more.

He did have advisors, though. Men who had his ear. Men like Charles Hook who wouldn't be above accepting a handful—or a doll-full—of diamonds. Besides, it was the only conclusion that made sense, even though she knew she couldn't prove it with the information she had.

What she could prove was that Peterson was smuggling diamonds out of the Congo in adorable little angel dolls, the *minkisi*. Valerie knew that exposing the scheme would force Baker to repudiate his relationship with Peterson—at least publicly—and quite possibly shake loose the cover over the president's real interest in protecting the mine. Putting the *nkisi* and its diamonds on the TV screens of America could cause a tremble or two in Washington. And sometimes those trembles grew into earthquakes.

Valerie glanced out the open doorway as the thick green jungle canopy passed beneath them. They must be getting closer to Kinshasa. She leaned closer to David so she could be heard over the roar of the helicopter. "I was so glad to see you, I forgot to ask. What are you doing here?" she shouted. A more important question still lay unanswered between them. Valerie knew she owed David a straight, definitive answer. As soon as this is over, I'll give him one, she promised herself.

"I came to bring you home," David shouted back.

"Thank you," she said. She felt herself smile for the first time in many days.

Just then, the man in the fatigues yelled over the rotor noise, "Excuse me. Are you Valerie Grey?"

"Yes I am," Valerie answered, turning to face him across the small cabin. She wasn't surprised at being recognized; it happened to her all the time. Her earlier question about his presidential credentials popped back into her head. "Who are you?" she asked.

"I've been looking for you," the man answered. He reached down to a holster hidden on his ankle and pulled out a Beretta.

"What?" Valerie shouted.

The man raised his arm and aimed the gun at her point-blank. The end of the small-caliber barrel looked like a cannon just inches from Valerie's face. As his finger tightened on the trigger, Nancy lunged out of her seat next to him to grab his wrist. David jumped between them. The gun went off with an almost delicate pop. David cried out and fell heavily across Valerie's lap.

"No!" Valerie screamed.

Despite Nancy's grip on his wrist, the man fired again, but Nancy threw her weight on his arm and the slug went through the chopper's floor. The pilot turned, shouting something over his shoulder. The helicopter lurched in the air. He turned back to get it under control, but it bucked and bounced like a mechanical bull. The man swung at Nancy's head with his left fist but he couldn't get any leverage into the punch across his own body. She shook off the weak blow and sank her teeth into his wrist.

The Beretta slipped from his fingers, skittering away while Valerie struggled to get out from under David, who was groaning in her lap. She eased him to the floor as the man managed to stand up in the bouncing helicopter. He shook Nancy loose with a rock-hard fist to the side of the head. He dove over her slumping body toward the gun sliding toward the back of the cabin. Valerie lunged after it too, but he got to it first, grabbing the pistol before it went out the open door. Behind him, the jungle canopy raced far beneath them. As the man raised the gun to shoot her, the chopper lurched sideways. His bad knee collapsed under the sudden strain. He toppled sideways out the open door but caught the bottom frame with his free hand. He dangled from the chopper while his legs churned in the air desperately trying to find a hold. Instinctively, Valerie flopped onto the floor and reached out to save him. Her fingers scrabbled for a grip on his shirt but, before she could grab it, he lost his hold on the doorway. The man plunged screaming toward the jungle far below.

Someone grasped Valerie's ankles and pulled her away from the open door. It was Nancy.

"Damn, boss," she said as Valerie sat up unsteadily. "Is there anybody else after you?"

David groaned. He rolled over on the floor between the seats. Valerie crawled to him just as he tried to sit up.

"No! Don't move!" she ordered. "How badly are you hurt?" She frantically tore his blood-soaked shirt away from the wound. The bullet had made a small hole in his shoulder just below the collar bone.

David shook his head and took a deep breath before he said, "I'll be okay, I think."

At the Reuters communications center, David called Carter Wilson just minutes before air time for the evening news in New York.

"You've got to make a slot for a live report by Valerie," he insisted. When Wilson protested that Robert Fraser was already slotted for one, David exploded. "Are you going to run another report from that chicken-shit's hotel room?" The wound in his shoulder screamed at the sudden tension in his muscles. He took a deep breath and got himself under control. "Look, Carter, Valerie Grey has been shot at by both sides and damn near got thrown out of a US Army helicopter on the way here. The White House sent a spook to keep her from telling this story, so you can bet she's onto something that needs to be on the air. Right now!" He took another deep breath against the pain in his shoulder. "If you don't put her on the air, I'll find a network that will."

"How much of her story is verified?" Wilson asked.

"She's literally got the proof in her hands," David answered firmly.

"All right," Wilson said rustling a piece of paper. "She's on in four minutes. This better be good, David."

During the few moments Valerie stood in front of a camera waiting for her cue to start a report, she always tried to wipe her mind clean of everything except the story at hand. At that point, she didn't think in words, she thought in pictures, scenes of the story she was about to tell. In the studio in Kinshasa, the pictures in her mind were portraits of the dead and mutilated people, black, brown and white, African and American, who had been killed for the Congo's diamonds. Her anger built as she saw their torn and bloodied bodies in her mind. Jaime Talon's head on her lap in the back of the speeding troop truck melded into the sad haunting eyes of the little girl sitting on the floor beside him. Valerie's emotions were seething when the floor director finally pointed to her and the red light flashed.

"American troops are putting their lives on the line for a lie in the Congo," she said, fury just beneath her voice. "They were sent here ostensibly to protect the nation against violent insurgents backed by neighboring countries. But that's not what they are doing. There are no American troops, or Congolese troops for that matter, guarding the villages and refugee camps in the path of the rebel armies. While the people of the Congo are driven from their homes and slaughtered by the thousands, US troops are racing to defend not them, but a diamond mine in the southern part of the country. It's a diamond mine owned by American evangelist Gary Peterson.

"Peterson is well-known as the principal spiritual advisor to

President Billy Baker. In fact, the president announced his intentions to send US troops to the Congo from the pulpit of Peterson's Atlanta church not long after Peterson was given the mine by Congolese President Moshe Messime. We may never know if there were any quid pro quos among the three powerful men, but the sequence of events is suspicious."

Off-camera in New York, Preston Henry snapped his eyes toward the control booth. He shouted at Carter Wilson, "What does she think she's doing? You better cut her off!" He could see the producer arguing with Wilson in the booth.

Wilson turned and leaned into the microphone. "Valerie staked her life on this. We're going to run with it," he said. Henry shook his head in resignation, careful not to disturb his perfectly-coiffed hair.

"But even the diamond mine operates under false pretenses," Valerie said. "We've learned that the Reverend Gary Peterson has been skimming off a large share of the mine's output almost from the beginning. He's been smuggling diamonds into the United States inside these innocent-looking dolls." She held the ragged cloth figure up for the camera. "This is a *nkisi*. It's the handiwork of Congolese women who were duped into filling them not with corn husks, as they did traditionally when they made them for their children, but with these pellets." Valerie turned the *nkisi* around and carefully opened the seam. She shook a few pebbles into her palm and held them out for a closeup. "Each of these is a gem-grade diamond, hidden beneath a plastic coating to fool US customs inspectors. There are several hundred stones in this one doll. And Peterson has been sending boxes of diamond-filled *minkisi* to presidential advisor Charles Hook's home in Alexandria, Virginia."

Valerie picked the largest pebble out of her palm. She handed the doll and the other diamonds to the floor director off camera. Then she scraped the plastic off the diamond with her thumbnail and held it up so it caught the light. The uncut stone glinted dully. "This is why the United States went to war in the Congo," she said. "I'm Valerie Grey, reporting from Kinshasa."

On the flight to New York, Valerie did her best to make David comfortable with the skinny pillows and thin airline blankets, but his heavily bandaged shoulder and the sling on his arm made it impossible for him to get much rest. He dozed off and on, helped by the painkillers the army doctor gave him to tide him over until he could get to the States for further treatment. During most of the flight, Valerie sensed him watching her from beneath his drug-heavy eyelids. She knew he was wondering what their future held. Nancy snored lightly in the seat behind them, but Valerie could only pretend to sleep. She wondered about the future too.

Dawn caught up with them as they started the descent into New York. She would check David into the hospital and then go home, alone.

About the author

Dave Donelson's world-roving career
as a broadcaster and journalist is reflected in
writing assignments for *Disney's FamilyFun,*
Westchester Magazine, Las Vegas Magazine
and *The Christian Science Monitor. Heart of
Diamonds,* his first novel, is an adventure-
thriller set in Congo and Washington DC.
He is also the author of *Creative Selling* and
Hunting Elf.

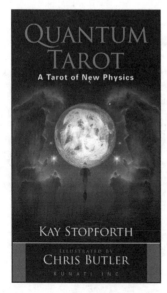

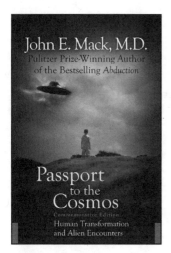

Passport to the Cosmos

Commemorative Edition: Human Transformation and Alien Encounters

■ John E. Mack M.D.

In this edition, with photos and new forewords, Pulitzer Prize–winner John E. Mack M.D. powerfully demonstrates how the alien abduction phenomenon calls for a revolutionary new way of examining the nature of reality and our place in the cosmos. "Fascinating foray into an exotic world. From Harvard psychiatry professor and Pulitzer Prize-winning author … based on accounts of abductions." —*Publishers Weekly*

US$ 14.95 | Pages 368 | Trade Paper 6x9"
ISBN 9781601641618

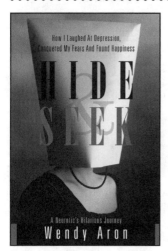

Hide & Seek

How I Laughed At Depression, Conquered My Fears and Found Happiness

■ Wendy Aron

Hide & Seek shows how to tackle important issues such as letting go of blame and resentment and battling negative thinking. Instructive without being preachy, it is filled with humor and pathos, and a healthy dose of eye-opening insight for the millions who suffer from depression and low self-esteem. "Learning how to cope with hopelessness has never been so fun." —*ForeWord*

US$ 14.95 | Pages 256 | Trade Paper 6x9"
ISBN 9781601641588

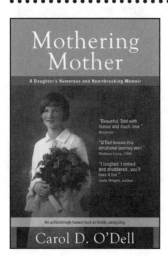

Mothering Mother

An unflinchingly honest look at family caregiving

■ Carol D. O'Dell

Mothering Mother is an authentic, "in-the-room" view of a daughter's struggle to care for a dying parent. It will touch you and never leave you.

"O'Dell portrays the experience of looking after a mother suffering from Alzheimer's and Parkinson's with brutal honesty and refreshing grace."—*Booklist*

US$ 12.95 | Pages 208 | Trade Paper 6x9"
ISBN 9781601640468

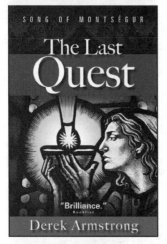

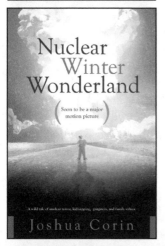
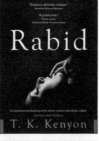
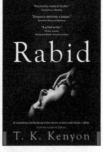
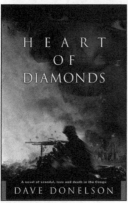

KÜNATI

MADicine
■ Derek Armstrong

What happens when an engineered virus, meant to virally lobotomize psychopathic patients, is let loose on the world? Only Bane and his new partner, Doctor Ada Kenner, can stop this virus of rage.

■ "Like Ian Fleming, he somehow combines over-the-top satire with genuinely suspenseful action ... Celebrate the upcoming centenary of Ian Fleming's birth by reading this book." —STARRED REVIEW *Booklist*

■ "Tongue-in-cheek thriller." *The Game* —*Library Journal*

US$ 24.95 | Pages 352, cloth hardcover
ISBN 978-1-60164-017-8 | EAN: 9781601640178

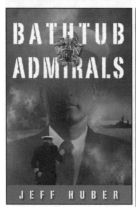

Bathtub Admirals
■ Jeff Huber

Are the armed forces of the world's only superpower really run by self-serving "Bathtub Admirals"? Based on a true story of military incompetence.

■ "Witty, wacky, wildly outrageous...A remarkably accomplished book, striking just the right balance between ridicule and insight." —*Booklist*

US$ 24.95
Pages 320, cloth hardcover
ISBN 978-1-60164-019-2
EAN 9781601640192

Belly of the Whale
■ Linda Merlino

Terrorized by a gunman, a woman with cancer vows to survive and regains her hope and the will to live.

■ *"A riveting story, both powerful and poignant in its telling. Merlino's immense talent shines on every page."*
—Howard Roughan,
Bestselling Author

US$ 19.95
Pages 208, cloth hardcover
ISBN 978-1-60164-018-5
EAN 9781601640185

Hunting the King
■ Peter Clenott

An intellectual thriller about the most coveted archeological find of all time: the tomb of Jesus.

■ *"Fans of intellectual thrillers and historical fiction will find a worthy new voice in Clenott... Given such an auspicious start, the sequel can't come too soon."*
—ForeWord

US$ 24.95
Pages 384, cloth hardcover
ISBN 978-1-60164-148-9
EAN 9781601641489

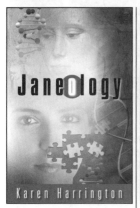

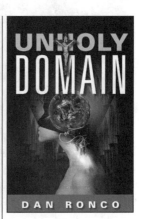

KÜNATI

Provocative. Bold. Controversial.

Kunati Book Titles

Available at your favorite bookseller

www.kunati.com

• •

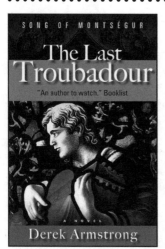

The Last Troubadour
Historical fiction by Derek Armstrong

Against the flames of a rising medieval Inquisition, a heretic, an atheist and a pagan are the last hope to save the holiest Christian relic from a sainted king and crusading pope. Based on true events.

■ "... brilliance in which Armstrong blends comedy, parody, and adventure in genuinely innovative ways." —*Booklist*

US$ 24.95 | Pages 384, cloth hardcover
ISBN-13: 978-1-60164-010-9
ISBN-10: 1-60164-010-2
EAN: 9781601640109

• •

Recycling Jimmy
A cheeky, outrageous novel by Andy Tilley

Two Manchester lads mine a local hospital ward for "clients" as they launch Quitters, their suicide-for-profit venture in this off-the-wall look at death and modern life.

■ "Energetic, imaginative, relentlessly and unabashedly vulgar." —*Booklist*
■ "Darkly comic story unwinds with plenty of surprises." —*ForeWord*

US$ 24.95 | Pages 256, cloth hardcover
ISBN-13: 978-1-60164-013-0
ISBN-10: 1-60164-013-7
EAN 9781601640130

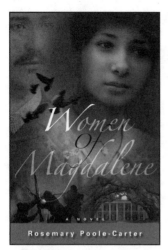

Women Of Magdalene
A hauntingly tragic tale of the old South by Rosemary Poole-Carter

An idealistic young doctor in the post-Civil War South exposes the greed and cruelty at the heart of the Magdalene Ladies' Asylum in this elegant, richly detailed and moving story of love and sacrifice.

■ "A fine mix of thriller, historical fiction, and Southern Gothic." —*Booklist*

■ "A brilliant example of the best historical fiction can do." —*ForeWord*

US$ 24.95 | Pages 288, cloth hardcover
ISBN-13: 978-1-60164-014-7
ISBN-10: 1-60164-014-5 | EAN: 9781601640147

On Ice
A road story like no other, by Red Evans

The sudden death of a sad old fiddle player brings new happiness and hope to those who loved him in this charming, earthy, hilarious coming-of-age tale.

■ "Evans' humor is broad but infectious ... Evans uses offbeat humor to both entertain and move his readers." —*Booklist*

US$ 19.95 | Pages 208, cloth hardcover
ISBN-13: 978-1-60164-015-4
ISBN-10: 1-60164-015-3
EAN: 9781601640154

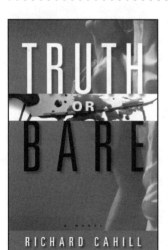

Truth Or Bare
Offbeat, stylish crime novel by Richard Cahill

The characters throb with vitality, the prose sizzles in this darkly comic page-turner set in the sleazy world of murderous sex workers, the justice system, and the rich who will stop at nothing to get what they want.

■ "Cahill has introduced an enticing character ... Let's hope this debut novel isn't the last we hear from him." —*Booklist*

US$ 24.95 | Pages 304, cloth hardcover
ISBN-13: 978-1-60164-016-1
ISBN-10: 1-60164-016-1
EAN: 9781601640161

Provocative. Bold. Controversial.

The Game
A thriller by Derek Armstrong

Reality television becomes too real when a killer stalks the cast on America's number one live-broadcast reality show.
■ "A series to watch ... Armstrong injects the trope with new vigor." —*Booklist*
US$ 24.95 | Pages 352, cloth hardcover
ISBN 978-1-60164-001-7 | EAN: 9781601640017
LCCN 2006930183

• •

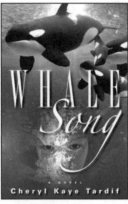

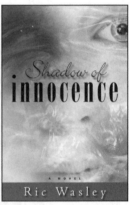

bang BANG
A novel by Lynn Hoffman

In Lynn Hoffman's wickedly funny *bang-BANG*, a waitress crime victim takes on America's obsession with guns and transforms herself in the process. Read along as Paula becomes national hero and villain, enforcer and outlaw, lover and leader. Don't miss Paula Sherman's one-woman quest to change America.
■ "Brilliant"
—STARRED REVIEW, *Booklist*
US$ 19.95
Pages 176, cloth hardcover
ISBN 978-1-60164-000-0
EAN 9781601640000
LCCN 2006930182

Whale Song
A novel by Cheryl Kaye Tardif

Whale Song is a haunting tale of change and choice. Cheryl Kaye Tardif's beloved novel—a "wonderful novel that will make a wonderful movie" according to *Writer's Digest*—asks the difficult question, which is the higher morality, love or law?
■ "Crowd-pleasing ... a big hit."
—*Booklist*
US$ 12.95
Pages 208, UNA trade paper
ISBN 978-1-60164-007-9
EAN 9781601640079
LCCN 2006930188

Shadow of Innocence
A mystery by Ric Wasley

The Thin Man meets *Pulp Fiction* in a unique mystery set amid the drugs-and-music scene of the sixties that touches on all our societal taboos. *Shadow of Innocence* has it all: adventure, sleuthing, drugs, sex, music and a perverse shadowy secret that threatens to tear apart a posh New England town.
US$ 24.95
Pages 304, cloth hardcover
ISBN 978-1-60164-006-2
EAN 9781601640062
LCCN 2006930187

The Secret Ever Keeps

A novel by Art Tirrell

An aging Godfather-like billionaire tycoon regrets a decades-long life of "shady dealings" and seeks reconciliation with a granddaughter who doesn't even know he exists. A sweeping adventure across decades—from Prohibition to today—exploring themes of guilt, greed and forgiveness.

■ "Riveting ... Rhapsodic ... Accomplished." —*ForeWord*

US$ 24.95
Pages 352, cloth hardcover
ISBN 978-1-60164-004-8
EAN 9781601640048
LCCN 2006930185

Toonamint of Champions

A wickedly allegorical comedy by Todd Sentell

Todd Sentell pulls out all the stops in his hilarious spoof of the manners and mores of America's most prestigious golf club. A cast of unforgettable characters, speaking a language only a true son of the South could pull off, reveal that behind the gates of fancy private golf clubs lurk some mighty influential freaks.

■ "Bubbly imagination and wacky humor." —*ForeWord*

US$ 19.95
Pages 192, cloth hardcover
ISBN 978-1-60164-005-5
EAN 9781601640055
LCCN 2006930186

Mothering Mother

A daughter's humorous and heartbreaking memoir.
Carol D. O'Dell

Mothering Mother is an authentic, "in-the-room" view of a daughter's struggle to care for a dying parent. It will touch you and never leave you.

■ "Beautiful, told with humor... and much love." —*Booklist*
■ "I not only loved it, I lived it. I laughed, I smiled and shuddered reading this book." —Judith H. Wright, author of over 20 books.

US$ 19.95
Pages 208, cloth hardcover
ISBN 978-1-60164-003-1
EAN 9781601640031
LCCN 2006930184

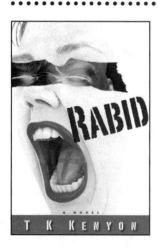

Rabid

A novel by T K Kenyon

A sexy, savvy, darkly funny tale of ambition, scandal, forbidden love and murder. Nothing is sacred. The graduate student, her professor, his wife, her priest: four brilliantly realized characters spin out of control in a world where science and religion are in constant conflict.

■ "Kenyon is definitely a keeper." —STARRED REVIEW, *Booklist*

US$ 26.95 I Pages 480, cloth hardcover
ISBN 978-1-60164-002-4 I EAN: 9781601640024
LCCN 2006930189